THE FAITHFUL

Rachel Reuben

Rachel Reuben/BTTW
www.rachelreubenauthor.com

Publisher's Note: This is a work of fiction. Names, characters, places, and incidents are a product of the author's imagination. Locales and public names are sometimes used for atmospheric purposes. Any resemblance to actual people, living or dead, or to businesses, companies, events, institutions, or locales is completely coincidental.

The Faithful/Rachel Reuben
ISBN 978-0-9885989-6-6

For my mother, Trudy, my first inspiration, my first reader.

In memory of my friend, Robin Shulman

CHAPTER ONE

The plan was to get drunk in the girls' bathroom before lunch and see what happened.

The book bag at Rachel's feet bulged with something more intoxicating than literature and lessons. The night before, after everyone was asleep, she'd snuck into the basement, shivering in her nightgown, bare feet picking up fine dust from the cold cement floor, and taken a bottle of wine from the well-stocked rack. She'd tiptoed back up the dark stairs and wrapped the bottle and a corkscrew in the sweater that was balled up at the bottom of her backpack—the one that was always there at her mother's insistence, "in case you should get cold."

That part of the scheme complete, Rachel would now have to get the wine out of her house, into school and safely hidden in her locker. Then, later in morning, she would meet her best friend, Lark Shulman, in the lavatory to drink the whole thing before the noon bell. There was no other particular strategy beyond that. The whole adventure was her idea, though if they got caught, it was certain to be blamed on Lark who was the "experimental" student at school.

Unlike Rachel and the rest of the students who attended the all-girls, ultraorthodox institution, Lark was not from a traditional Chasidic family with long roots in the neighborhood and the *shtetls* of Eastern

Europe before that. She was part of a family of *bali teshuva* who had moved to the community nearly four summers ago, just before freshman year. *Teshuva* was the word for repentance, but meant literally "to return." These "returnees" were non-religious, secular Jews who adopted the Chasidic, strictly observant way of life with a vengeance.

Born-again.

Rachel had a hard time with the concept of the *"bali choovas."* It was one thing to be born in to this life. What else did you know? But to volunteer, to choose to go from a secular life with no boundaries or limitations to the Chasidic life, rife with so many, made her scratch her head. Of course, this line of thinking was entirely private. The girls she went to school with—anyone she knew for that matter—didn't long for anything outside of what was known, specified or allowed. If they did, they didn't talk about it. Even Rachel never talked about it until she met Lark, whose inclusion in her parents' spiritual odyssey was strictly involuntary. Her rebellious friend attended the yeshiva with her heels dug in, disrupting lessons with questions that made the air in the classroom heavy, the teachers furious.

"What's the point of eating kosher?"

Because God wants us to.

"But where does it say it, specifically? Like, where does it mention 'no cheeseburgers'?"

The rabbis interpret a number of different passages in the Torah to indicate that we should eat according to certain guidelines.

"Oh, the rabbis! And they are what? The psychic hotline to God?"

At first, Rachel's parents were nervous about their daughter's attraction to this new girl, this outsider with experiences in the secular world they strove so faithfully to shelter their children and themselves from. They worried because Rachel was unlike her older sisters.

"You ask too many questions for your own good, Roh-chella," her father would often tease her, pronouncing her name as everyone did, with the hard Hebrew "ch" that gargled from the back of the throat.

Rachel grew frustrated when he said such things, realizing early on that it was his way of changing the subject and avoiding her inquiries.

Her sisters had not asked such questions. Rachel knew her parents were disappointed to have had three girls in a row, and not a single boy to continue the family business or to honor them with his scholarly achievements. But, at least they could find comfort in the temperate, obedient natures of their two eldest girls.

"My Rachel is another story altogether," Miriam Fine, Rachel's mother, could be heard moaning about her daughter to anyone listening. She was less than thrilled about her third and last child being, as people often commented, "as deep as a well."

"So deep! Feh!" She'd dismiss the vague compliment, seeing it for the chastisement that it was.

It was bad enough God had decided that after giving birth to three girls, Miriam could have no other children. Just like that. This curse, in a community where families, spurred on by their Rebbe, routinely had families of eight to twelve children in order to help replace all the Jewish souls lost under the Nazis, and thereby hasten the coming of the Messiah. With all this, Miriam had enough to mourn over. The last thing she needed was a "deep" daughter.

"A girl could drown with so much thinking," she'd mutter under her breath, but not so far under that you couldn't hear it.

Most of the yeshiva girls' parents had discouraged their daughters from forming a friendship with Lark, who had joined the community at nearly fourteen. She'd seen too much already. They'd heard the stories of how she openly questioned the rabbis at school, mocking teachings and beliefs that ruled their world. She was a bad seed who could lead their girls to make bad decisions or entertain doubts. To Rachel, Lark had been sent as a gift, delivered into her life so that she could hear out loud her own long-standing doubts and get answers to her questions for the first time.

"Are you sure it's not a big mistake to let her spend time with this girl?" Rachel heard her mother say quietly to her father one evening. Rachel had just met Lark and asked if she could invite her new friend to *Shabbes* dinner.

"There are no mistakes, only messages," Dovid Fine had said, peering over his reading glasses and the top of the Yiddish newspaper he tried to read through each evening.

Rachel's father had a noble streak. He'd wanted to be a rabbi, to spend his days in study, but as the last of four boys who had already answered the call to scholarship, he got relegated to the family business.

"This girl is coming to us because *Hashem* has something to reveal to her—the beauty of a *frum Chasidish* home–and He is asking us to be the shining example for her."

Thus, according to her father, the Fine family would extend their influence like a warm blanket over Lark, and she would be drawn in by the perfection of a life devoted to God in the Chasidic way. Her father had spoken on the subject, so that's how it would be, despite her mother's fear that just the opposite would happen.

"I know my Rachel," her mother said, addressing the ceiling and God. Her "deep" daughter might be more likely to fall to the bottom of that murky well for all her curiosity about secular life than help someone out and up toward the light.

Rachel had outwardly adopted her father's mission concerning Lark, but inwardly she was thrilled to have this new confidante, someone she could explore the possibilities that had bounced around inside her head for so long.

* * *

"I think you should become a lawyer."

Lark surprised Rachel with this out-of-the-blue career counseling one day as they worked together on some *Perkei Avos* homework in the library. These "ethics of our fathers" were the backbone of Jewish law.

"You've got this stuff down. Besides, you're a Libra. They're all about justice. I'm Scorpio, the crabby one. I'd make a better actress or something incredibly dramatic like that."

Though they were forbidden to study or believe in astrology—it was considered "pagan"—Rachel was fascinated when Lark told her that her Zodiac sign's symbol was the scales of justice, and that her life's work was to seek balance, to weigh the evidence. Lark pulled an encyclopedia from the shelf and showed Rachel a picture of "lady justice." She wondered why the woman holding the scales was blindfolded.

"Shouldn't she have her eyes wide open, to make the best judgment?"

"No. The point is that she can't be influenced by anything around her. She has to find the truth by looking inside herself," and emphasized this point by poking Rachel in the chest.

The idea of going to college and becoming a lawyer excited Rachel. Why did her parents insist that the only truly honorable use for her life was to manage a home, cook endless amounts of food for ever-repeating rounds of holidays and Sabbaths, have endless children, and "serve" a long list of the needy that began with her future husband and ended with the entire Jewish population?

Her own needs, her own name, would not be on the list. The women she was meant to model herself after prided themselves on knowing their priorities. Those priorities had little or nothing to do with personal gratification, fulfillment, or growth that led beyond the parameters of the life prescribed by the Torah, and the divinely inspired interpretations of the Torah scholars. Lark opened the door to a broader world, one in which there seemed to be hope for Rachel's own desires.

"You're daydreaming, Rachel. Do you see the time? Eat your cereal. I don't want you buying junk later from that school store because you had no breakfast."

Her mother's voice and the clicking of her slippers against the floor as she passed through the kitchen snapped Rachel back to reality. It was easy to daydream at breakfast these days, now that she sat at the well-worn table alone most mornings. She was hardly used to the silence. Her sister Sara's wedding was almost a year before, but Rachel still caught herself expecting the stunning girl to be monopolizing the bathroom with her beauty rituals or snoring lightly in her room down the hall. Her other sister, the bookish Ahuva, was married only weeks ago to a young rabbi who, through good family ties and more than generous pledges of financial support from her father, was assigned by the Rebbe to an out-reach position in Berlin. There they started a *shul* and were working to bring Jewish education and observance to Eastern Bloc Jews who had never been able to freely practice their religion.

Rachel played with the Cream of Wheat in front of her, making stiff swirls amid the clumps. She was just waiting for the right time to make her move, feeling rather like a cunning spy and a cornered animal all at the same time.

Her father was not home, the remnants of his breakfast still on the table, so he was not going to be a problem. Rachel rarely saw her father in the morning, he left early to join other men for morning prayers at the shul, after which he went on to "The Store," a kind of Judaic Wal-Mart on Empire Boulevard.

When her grandfather, a German immigrant, had the store long before Rachel was born, it was a small bookshop specializing in scholarly, rare and out-of-print Judaic books. Her parents took it over after the old man died within weeks of his wife of 50 years. Rachel's father had worked in the shop since he was ten years old—sitting amongst the stacks, doing his homework, stocking new arrivals, shifting old books around, trying to create more shelf space where there was none. When he became the shop's owner, he had to face the fact that, as prestigious as the tiny place was, the book trade had its limitations—his growing family's needs seemed not to.

Miriam Fine had a head for business from the start. "How many times a month is someone going to buy a rare book? We need repeat customers! Let's move some of these books to the back and get some items in here that people can use up and come back again for every week."

They started adding things here and there—holiday and seasonal items like handmade menorahs and Chanukah candles, or some gold-leaf-rimmed Seder plates imported from Israel. On the sidewalk they'd spread card tables with plastic tablecloths and sell scarves, hats, and gloves in winter, umbrellas in the rain, fake-designer sunglasses in summer. Within a few years, as business boomed, they knocked down walls and took over the store next door and the one next to that. Now, alongside the yellowing prayer books and the oversized Talmuds, there were buckets of kosher bubblegum, racks of greeting cards for any Jewish occasion (always a little pocket to slip in a check), and bolts of kosher fabric (no linen and wool mixed!). You name it, in English or Yiddish; they had it somewhere in the overflowing emporium. Things were "Fine at Fine's" —Miriam's made-up slogan plastered all over the store and on their awning. They were blessed with a more than handsome living, even if they hadn't been blessed with sons.

Rachel looked at the kitchen clock. She had to get going, and though her father was gone, getting past her mother this morning could be tricky. Miriam was extremely "hands-on": touching, prodding, pinching, checking, organizing, and managing. Rachel and her sisters had privately called her "Inspector General": peering into your ears, assessing the condition of one's underwear, the legibility of homework assignments, the relative pinkness of one's gums, the length and cleanliness of fingernails and toenails, the quality of a bowel movement.

"Don't flush, I have to see," she'd announce while knocking at the bathroom door, telegraphing to the entire world the details of a mortified young girl's private bodily functions.

What would save Rachel today was that it was Friday, and on Friday, from the minute her mother left her bed to the moment she lit the candles at sundown, like every other mother in the neighborhood, she was consumed with the preparations for the Sabbath. Like any Jewish holy day, Shabbes actually began the night before and lasted for a full 24 hours. Friday was the only day, besides Shabbes, that Miriam didn't put in hours at the store. The Fines had guests almost every Friday night for dinner after services, so Rachel didn't understand why her mother seemed particularly wound up today. She heard from the next room, her voice already filled with impatience.

"Maria, I don't want you should hurt yourself, but perhaps today you could actually lift up the sofa cushions and finally vacuum under there—and I'm scared from what could be growing on top of the hutch. If you can't reach up there to dust, they invented something called a 'stepstool,' you might be interested to know." She raised her voice the way people do when talking to immigrants, as though inadequate volume was the barrier to complete understanding. "Step. Stool. I even have one in the back hallway closet, the one you probably have never opened to clean."

Rachel suspected that Maria, a compact Dominican woman who was their full-time housekeeper and cook, conveniently pretended not to understand much English whenever her mother began to give her detailed instructions. Maria listened politely then proceeded at her own island pace, regardless.

Her mother might have told her who tonight's guests were, but Rachel couldn't remember. One thing was certain; Miriam seemed even more relentlessly focused on perfection than usual. She was busy yelling into the back hallway closet for the step stool to reveal itself to her, when Rachel slipped on her backpack with its illicit treasure and slipped out of the house without a sound. Just to make sure she was out of Inspector General's range quickly, she ran two full blocks before slowing down and walking the rest of the way to school.

When she got there, she went directly to the makeshift chapel—really just a room behind the principal's office better suited to storing supplies than inspiring the girls to commune with God. The daily morning *davening*, the prayers, were something these girls were taught to memorize bits and pieces of even before they could read. As an 18-year-old senior in high school, Rachel could, with head bowed, body swaying, knees dipping, and lips murmuring, efficiently speed-read the 20 minutes of prayers that heralded the morning without a hitch.

In Hebrew, the prayers expressed gratitude to God for allowing one to survive the night, among many other blessings—in the case of boys, for making them men and not women. The girls omitted that passage in their prayers, but there was not another one substituted that thanked The Almighty for making them women, as though it were not something worth expressing gratitude for.

Many times throughout the years of mornings spent in this room, Rachel lifted her eyes during the davening and tried to find in the faces of her schoolmates, in their posture or attitude, something holy—something that would reveal that a connection to God was being made. It had become rote for her and nothing transcendent seemed to take place within her during these memorized moments. The rabbis who taught at the school said that the *mitzvah*, roughly translated as good deed, came not from what you felt or didn't feel while davening, but in simply doing it each day as was commanded of you. Still, Rachel always held on to the idea that more must be available, that some people could access it, and if she saw it or felt it happening, she would recognize it. And indeed, she recognized a glimmer of that something, some connection she hadn't seen before, in the strange new girl who'd entered their world nearly four years ago.

These days, Lark didn't bother showing up for davening, but back then—her first week of high school in Crown Heights—Lark stood at the only window in the "chapel," a tiny one overlooking an alley that ran behind the school. She was a tall girl—Rachel's guess put her at 5'10", at least four inches taller than Rachel. A thick bushel of curly red-auburn hair was temporarily restrained behind her head in a plastic clip that looked ready to burst. Holding a *siddur* open in front of her, Lark wasn't looking at it. A thin, dusty shaft of light passed through the grimy window and illuminated this new girl's pale, lightly freckled face. Her eyes, peering over round-rimmed glasses, seemed intently focused on something—something other than her immediate surroundings—something deeply inward and more vastly outward.

Lark turned and looked directly at Rachel, whose intent staring had more than likely raised the hairs on the back of Lark's neck by then. Rachel wanted to turn away, embarrassed, but held her gaze. Lark flashed Rachel the first of her signature "smart-ass" smiles, winked, and then turned back to the window. Rachel walked toward her, both encouraged and confused by the toothy grin and wink, trying to capture for herself what this decidedly different girl saw through the glass. It was just an alley, the weak sun peeking over some gray buildings at the other side.

"What are you looking at?"

"Nothing. Just praying. That's what we are here for isn't it?" Lark looked around the shabby room, her nose wrinkled as though she'd just had a whiff of something foul.

"I didn't see you—well, I mean, you weren't even looking at the *siddur...*" Rachel regretted the accusation, but Lark just laughed.

"What this?" She slammed shut the prayer book. "I can't keep up with this. I can barely read Hebrew. I just talk to God in my head. It's 1987. I'm pretty sure God understands English by now. What d'you think?"

"Well, yeah. I guess. But what do you say...when you're, uh...talking to Him?" Rachel wanted to know.

"Whatever." Lark shrugged her narrow shoulders.

"Whatever?" Rachel wanted it to be more.

"Well, I might say something like, 'Why are you doing this to me?' or 'Why am I here in this place?' or like, 'What is the purpose of this endless suffering? Can you please give me a sign, send me a message?' Stuff like that."

"Oh, I see," Rachel said. Then asked quickly, before the odd girl could turn away, "Do you get an answer?"

"Not always," Lark said, then looked at Rachel for a long moment, taking her in. Her second "smart-ass" smile appeared. "But today, I think I did."

That was forever ago. In two months they'd be graduating. Lark had exposed Rachel to much more than her "conversations" with God, over time. Today's little adventure would be Rachel's way of proving to Lark that she had the guts to tear off the "Torah-scroll blinders" her friend insisted all the girls at school had strapped to their heads.

At her locker, Rachel was about to transfer the paper bag containing the wine when Lark came up behind her. "Put it in my locker, just in case."

Rachel knew she meant to take the blame if anything went wrong. "It's okay, I can keep it," Rachel said.

"No, I don't think so. Anyway, I'm looking for a good excuse to get kicked out of this place."

They both laughed and Rachel handed Lark the bag to stash. They went over the plan to get out of their respective classes and meet in the ladies' room at 11:45.

The morning routine at their school went largely unchanged over the years. They had Judaic studies until lunch, studying religious texts, laws, the sages, the commentaries—all geared toward their becoming Chasidic homemaking wives. "Secular" studies took place after lunch in their *Reader's Digest* versions, as Lark so coined them.

"What's Reader's Digest?" Rachel had to ask.

Lark tried to remember that her new friend was a complete blank when it came to popular culture. Rachel's life was so tightly controlled that although she was in her teens when Lark met her, she'd never seen a movie, a TV show, thumbed through a fashion or gossip magazine, or read a best seller.

"Reader's Digest? They do everything short and sweet—kind of the opposite of in-depth. Like our science teacher...why bother with all the science out there when you have Genesis to explain how the planet and mankind got here."

"Oh, I get it!" Rachel gave her a late and slightly forced laugh at the joke, sensing another of Lark's "rants" coming and hoping to cut it short. No chance.

"Why get into algebra, trigonometry, geometry, calculus, when all we need around here is a little bookkeeping to earn a living if, God forbid, we are not married by the time we're twenty, or to help earn a living if our husbands turn out to be losers? Don't get into any American or world history; it'll just distract you from Jewish history! Or who cares if we cover any great English literature or grammar or world geography when we can just stay here in Crown Heights our whole lives and speak Yiddish to each other, and the most complicated thing we'll read once we're married is a recipe, anyway!"

There was a perfunctory health class, required by the state, but no sex education—the Chasidic version of that came later, taught by women especially versed in the laws of "family purity," and only to girls who were engaged to be married. No fine art, other than crafty projects undertaken by the girls to decorate the school during various holidays. No dramatic arts, except for the all-girl "plays" they put on each year, for all-girl audiences, with their homespun scripts and heavy-handed moral outcomes. Women were not allowed to perform in front of men, and it was a sin for men to watch women perform. No other electives were offered in the curriculum. Rachel felt like her whole life was about no electives, no choices. What for? Whatever the world at large had to offer, whether it was great literature or sitcoms or blockbuster movies, the Chasid had no use for it, even feared it.

Rachel checked the clock again for the millionth time that morning. By 11:40 the waiting was becoming physically painful—her right calf muscle began to cramp after hours of bouncing her leg at a frenetic pace below her desk. Her neck ached from trying to appear as though she were paying attention to the earnest young teacher at the front of the room while watching the clock over the doorway on the left. Rebitzen Rothstein, only a few years older than they, wore the title of rebitzen—the wife of a rabbi—like a crown. She came in once a week to instruct the senior girls in some of the finer points of making a Chasidic home.

Many of the girls in the room were already "matched," betrothed to young men from the neighborhood or from around the world, and would likely have summer or early fall weddings. The Chasidic world, the world of their particular sect of Chasidism, was a small one. Eligible boys and girls from good families seamlessly became part of a global matrimony roundup. That Rachel was a line item in this unwritten catalog was something she avoided thinking about. Her sisters had raced toward matrimony, embracing it as the ultimate destination. She wanted only to think of now. *Right now. This minute I am Rachel; I belong to me.* And now she had to get out of that classroom to meet Lark.

Rachel was grateful that she wouldn't have to ask permission to go to the ladies' room. Once girls in the school were "mature" or past premenstrual age, they were allowed to excuse themselves from class without announcing it or asking first. This was done out of *tsnius*, the guiding tenant of modest behavior and dress for these religious women, precluding, among many things, public or casual discussion of private and unclean bodily functions. But all that didn't stop a handful of girls from giggling when Rachel stood more abruptly than she'd have liked, and walked to the door at exactly 11:44 a.m.

"Rachel," Rebitzen Rothstein interrupted her lecture to stop her, "we are going to lunch in fifteen minutes. Can't you wait?"

Rachel froze momentarily, and then relaxed as the perfect answer sprang to her lips. She lowered her eyes and spoke softly, "For the sake of modesty, I don't think so." The giggling intensified. Rachel turned her back and walked from the room before she could appreciate the rising blush on the face of the temporarily speechless instructor.

She ran to the ladies' room at the end of the long hall lined with gray lockers and little in the way of decoration. Pushing her shoulder into the heavy door, it swung open, banging against the wall. The chemical smell of disinfectant hit her nostrils and made her already-nervous stomach take half a turn.

"Would you care for a cocktail?" a voice offered. Rachel pulled open the metal door of one of the two stalls, and there was Lark perched on the toilet lid, squatting like a peasant, her skirt lifted over her knees and bunched up in her lap, the open wine dangling between her legs with a flash of lime-green panties as its backdrop.

"Nice underwear."

"You should see my bra." Lark handed her the bottle. "Your turn. I couldn't wait. I was a nervous wreck waiting for you, so I started."

Rachel brought the bottle to her lips and smelled the sour-sweet aroma of the wine. She hesitated.

"What's the matter?" Lark asked, raising an eyebrow.

"Well..."

"Well, what?"

"Well, shouldn't we say a *bracha*?" Rachel had never tasted a sip of wine that wasn't a part of a religious ritual, that wasn't preceded by the saying of bracha, a prayer of thanks to God.

Lark was patient with her. "Look, we aren't exactly at Shabbes dinner here, Rocky." Rachel laughed. She loved Lark's nickname for her.

"Anyway, you're damned if you do and damned if you don't because, first, you are not supposed to say God's name in the bathroom—am I right? And you are not even supposed to bring food or drink in here, correct—too unclean? Body fluids and all that, right?

Rachel nodded, but still couldn't drink.

"We don't have all day here, Rock. In about six minutes we'll be surrounded by the skirts." She characterized the other girls in school by the long shapeless skirts that modesty required them all to wear—well below the knee, opaque stockings or heavy woolen socks, blouses that covered the collarbone and elbows.

"*Okay, okay...*" thought Lark. "Bracha...bracha...let's make one up, okay? Go ahead. Make one up."

"Make what up?"

"A prayer...for the wine—without mentioning You-Know-Who. Go ahead."

"Just make one up?"

"Yeah."

"Like what?"

Lark grabbed the bottle back from her and took a long swig, stood up on the toilet, and declared, "I feel so incredibly grateful for wine. What a cool world! Amen." She handed the bottle down to her dubious friend.

"I feel so incredibly grateful for wine, what a cool world?"

"Amen," finished Lark, smiling stupidly.

"Amen," repeated Rachel. She drank deeply, swallowing two or three times. She pulled the bottle from her mouth, took a deep breath, and let out a long, froggy burp.

They quickly passed the bottle back and forth until it was empty. Lark stuffed it back into the crumpled paper sack along with the cork, which had rolled back behind the toilet. Rachel put the corkscrew in her purse. The two girls bumped each other struggling to get out of the narrow stall, trying not to laugh through tight teeth and shushing lips, sending a shower of spit on each other in the process.

"What should we do with the bottle?" Rachel asked.

Lark looked around, and then used half a roll of paper towel to wrap it up until it looked like the mummy of a large cat. She then pushed it to the bottom of the long trash can, already half-filled with discarded, damp towels." I don't want it in my locker, just in case," she said.

"I thought you wanted to get kicked out?"

"Maybe next week, when it's boring again."

The girls laughed as though it was the funniest thing Lark had ever said. On the way to the door they paused to look in the mirror over the sink. Lark threw her arm around Rachel's shoulders and they stood, framed for a moment, as if posing for a snapshot.

"Well, you are drunk, I think," said Lark.

"And what about you?" giggled Rachel.

"I'm drunk, too. And hungry." A bell sounded and they could hear the hall outside filling with girls. "To lunch!" Lark announced like a battle cry and pushed Rachel to the door.

They nearly collided with a line of girls heading for the bathroom. The ordinary scene in the hall, one she'd been an ordinary part of for years, suddenly seemed incredibly chaotic to Rachel. She grabbed for Lark's waistband and held on, trying to steady herself against the feeling of the lockers leaning toward her and the floor slanting away.

They retrieved their brown-bag lunches, made their way down the noisy steel stairwells and ended up in the large room on the ground floor that served as a lunchroom, assembly room, and gym. The early May day was the first truly warm one to come along, so the back doors were propped open to the alley behind the school, to let the girls enjoy it. They sat around on molded plastic stacking chairs—there were no tables. Some dragged chairs outside to eat and talk in the still alley air. High windows let in the sun. A line of girls waited by an open sink to perform the ritual washing of the hands before eating bread. Rachel automatically drifted toward the line, pulling Lark with her. But Lark pulled away and headed outside, singing a bit too loudly, "Let the sunshine, let the sun shine in!"

Once she reached the sink, Rachel put her bulky bag down on the floor by her feet. She wanted to put her whole head under the tap, she felt sweaty and hot all of a sudden. Instead, she took the washing cup, a twenty-four-ounce plastic container with a handle on each side, and began to fill it with water. She turned the water on too high, so the cup filled fast and slipped from her hands, plopping hard on the bottom of the shallow sink and sending a spray of water up toward her blouse, neck, and face. She heard giggles behind her. "Rachel, come on, I'm starving!" "Rachel, just the hands, please, not a bath!"

Rachel quickly turned the water pressure down and carefully filled the cup again, grasping the right handle tightly so that her knuckles bulged. Spilling the water once, twice, three times over the left hand, then switching her grip to the other handle and spilling three times over the right. A sudden feeling of panic came over her as she thought, *Am I doing this right?* Her head swimming, she tried to focus. *Is it the right hand first, then the left?* She began to recite the simple one-line blessing and felt the panic growing. *Is that the right bracha?* Rachel turned to walk away from the sink but forgot her lunch lying at her feet. Stumbling over the bag, she lost her already tenuous hold on the floor and landed hard and flat on her chest, her chin jamming into the floor, teeth clamping down on her tongue. As Rachel tasted blood in her mouth, she had a loud and clear thought: *God is punishing me!*

A mob of classmates surrounded Rachel, who was curled up on the floor, sobbing, clutching her banged-up chest with one hand, and smearing the blood from her mouth with the other. In the crowd she briefly saw Lark's worried face. The sea of girls parted suddenly and there appeared Rabbi Mintz, the school's principal, with his round and red-cheeked face brimming over his dense black beard, hanging over her.

"What is going on here?" he demanded, then stopped dead in his tracks when he saw Rachel on the ground, her mouth filled with blood and crying out again and again for everyone, including God, to hear, *"I'm sorry! I'm so sorry!"*

CHAPTER TWO

Baruch Hashem," Yakov muttered, as he entered the small room—his sanctuary at the top of the sprawling building that housed his family's home, his grandfather's office, and the community's shul. He smiled as he noticed his habit of thanking God, or more literally, blessing God, each time he reached the threshold of the room. Out of breath, he wasn't saying it because he had finally reached the end of all those stairs—four long, narrow flights from the ground floor—but because the room was there up under the eaves and it was his alone. He blessed the exquisite isolation of it, the very privilege of entering it and closing the door behind him and feeling out of the world's line of vision for a change.

He did what he always did upon entering the room. He turned the small lock under the worn glass doorknob and walked to the window, a sliver of light that gave him a vantage point of the street and a view of the less-than-robust city treetops that lined it. For a few minutes he watched the people, mostly men, far below, the many black hats floating and bobbing in the turbulent flow of life on this street, around this house. Though Yakov lived there all of his life, he never felt quite like it belonged to him, unless he was in this room. How could something belong to him if, like his grandfather, known to all as The Rebbe, it be-

longed first to the community and then to Judaism and then to God before he could claim any piece of it for himself?

It wasn't always his room. It had been a private study and library for
his grandfather, holding his valuable collection of antique holy books
and interpretive tomes, but after the Rebbe's stroke, they moved everything he wanted at his disposal to the street-level parlor, including the
motorized hospital bed that had been donated for his use. He held court
from there these days, propped up near the window where his devotees
could pass and get a reassuring glimpse of their now frail leader and
guide.

Yakov felt frail and old himself, though he was barely twenty-three.
His body was strong; his frame lanky, long and lean. The nondescript
uniform of the Chasid, the formless black suit and plain white shirt billowed about his body, but didn't disguise the grace with which he held
himself and moved. Of course he wasn't delicate at all, and his mind was
sharp but emotionally he felt ready to crumble, as if he'd endured something for a very long time and yearned to finally surrender to a long rest.

In a few hours he would be sitting at the Shabbes table across from
yet another suitable girl, in a long line of suitable girls. Underneath the
effort to make polite conversation with her and her family was the tacit
agreement that they were all checking each other out. His Uncle Yossi
would accompany him as usual—though it was his grandfather who had
set this meeting up, as he had all the others—and while the girl herself
would say little, it was understood that the evening was all about her and
whether she would win Yakov as her prize of a husband.

He'd met with no fewer than seventeen girls over the last four years.
It began when he was eighteen and stopped only for a period of four
months after his father died the year before. It began again with renewed intensity when the Rebbe announced to the family and stunned
community that he expected Yakov to succeed him in his work, to become the next Rebbe, the leader of their growing community—their
spiritual guide, interpreter, and protector.

Their sect of Chasidim, concentrated in Crown Heights but spread out all over the world doing the work of Jewish outreach, had become comfortable with the idea of Yakov's father, Moshe, as the Rebbe's right-hand man and natural successor. He had many of the qualities the Rebbe possessed, even if he had not proved himself to be as visionary or charismatic a figure. Perhaps he would grow into that. He was kind, studious, devoted, accessible, and patient. He had the lineage and the human potential to be, if not what his father was to the community, at least a comforting and stable force when the time came.

When Moshe died unexpectedly, the community felt a tremendous loss, not only in the present, but also for its future. The Rebbe's other son, Yosef, or Yossi, was an enigmatic man, not easy to know, and not well loved. The idea of his taking over the role as community and spiritual leader was generally dismissed. Not much was known "officially" about the failure of his marriage, which ended with a get, a rabbinically-sanctioned divorce, in less than a year. The gossip ranged from rumors of abuse—blaming him—to speculation she was barren—blaming her—to interpreting it all as a sign from God that Yossi was certainly not to be considered for a leadership role. Even so, a furor arose in the wake of the Rebbe's declaration after Moshe's death, that he was now certain God meant for Yakov, his grandson, to be the greatest leader the community had ever had.

Part of the outcry against this choice had to do with the fact that the community did not want to face the reality of a time without their Rebbe. Certainly it was premature to even think about it—he was only sixty-eight! A fringe group of the community believed that discussions of succession were a moot point because they were convinced the Rebbe was the Messiah, the long-awaited Moshiach, himself, and that it was only a matter of time before his true identity was revealed and the Messianic age, long-ago prophesized in the Torah, would begin. God would inhabit the earth, and the Jews would take their rightful place of leadership in this divinely ordered new heaven on earth.

On the other hand, a good portion of the dissent centered on the young Yakov and his ability to be a credible and accepted leader. Thus, the boy was suddenly thrown into public scrutiny, as he never had been before. He was so young, unmarried, and for all intents and purposes, seemed to be avoiding that next obvious step in his life. In this community a man could not reach any status as a leader or teacher unless he was married. In their eyes and God's, a man could not transcend to heights of enlightenment, nor master the earthly mundane, without the steadying influence that came from this important partnership.

And with all this, there was Yakov and his undeniable gifts. He was a breathtaking artist. A pencil, a crayon, a piece of coal, was like an instrument of the angels in his hands. He could draw anything, bring it to life on the page, and portray the subject's lingering thoughts, inner pain, or ecstatic joy with the turn of his wrist. An ink portrait he'd done at age sixteen of the Rebbe at prayer hung in the entryway of their house and a numbered lithograph of it hung in practically every shul of their sect throughout the world. This talent, staggering as it was, was considered secondary to the talent he had for study and interpretation, memorization and understanding of the texts by which they lived their lives. He wasn't simply a bright or diligent student like his father. It was more like the drawing—a gift from God—this ability to feel the meaning, elicit the teaching, free with simplicity the mystical truths locked within the Torah, the Tanya, and the Talmud. The Rebbe saw it as further proof that Yakov was "chosen" for the role. His uncle, Yossi, felt it as a slight. Yakov felt it as a burden.

Yakov turned from the window and sat heavily at his desk. From the drawer he pulled out a sketchpad and a handful of pencils. He flipped through pages and pages of starkly beautiful studies of the male form: a muscular and veined forearm and hand, the curve of a back, the line of a jaw as an extension of a taut neck that seemed to reach for the heavens. He found an empty page and began to tear lines across it that seemed random, but would eventually reveal itself as something. He rarely drew faces during these solitary sessions because if he did, someone might see, and he'd have to admit to himself that all these drawings were of Daniel. Yakov could not remember a time in his life when he wasn't with his friend. Nursery school to seminary, toys to Talmud—they'd always been inseparable. In a few weeks, Daniel's wedding would change that forever.

Yakov was not aware of the passing of time while drawing, except when he sometimes noticed the draining of light from the room or a small knot of tension above his eyes that meant he had been squinting for too long. He usually stopped in time to keep his Uncle Yossi from climbing the stairs to retrieve him. He didn't like being alone with the man. When the sharp knock erupted and his uncle's voice needled him through the door, Yakov was startled enough to jump and cry out, as though he'd suddenly been pushed from behind.

"Yakov, while you are doodling around in there, Shabbes is practically on our doorstep. Or maybe you want to just keep drawing all through Shabbes?"

Yossi seemed to savor the private moments when the Rebbe was not around in which he could deliver some punishing bit of malice to his nephew. And now here he was just on the other side of the flimsy door, braying on about Yakov's "doodling." He neglected no opportunity to deride Yakov's drawing as a frivolous or unseemly pastime.

"It's only four o'clock." Yakov raised his voice above his uncle's aggressive jiggling of the doorknob. He moved quickly to clean up the scattered and discarded drawings before the old lock gave way and he was confronted with Yossi's bulky presence.

"The Rebbe wants to see you. You're meeting that Fine girl tonight, and he wants to talk to you about it so you don't make a fool of yourself."

The big man was in the room. Yakov was on his knees, retrieving a sheet of drawing paper that had slid under the desk, feeling as if he were about to cry. He wasn't afraid of his uncle—he hated him, and hated that, in a moment when he felt so immersed in beauty, he could be so cruelly plunged into this ugliness. If only his father were still alive! His father had made it possible for Yakov to live a buffered life, untouched by such moments. Moshe Rubinstein was a man who made room in his life for beauty and its appreciation, even if his own wife and brother were oblivious to it. This he shared with Yakov, his only child. People said what a shame it was to have had only the one child. While his mother seemed in constant mourning over this fact, Yakov's father always behaved as if it were the highest of honors to shepherd Yakov—so talented, so gifted, so sensitive—through this lifetime, unfettered by concerns for other children. But where was his shepherd now?

Moshe's flawed heart—a congenital defect—had simply stopped beating as he sat at the dining room table, listening to music and reading the paper. He lay in an unmarked grave; the headstone would be dedicated and put in place next month on the first anniversary of his departure from Yakov's world. He left it as inconspicuously as he had lived his life, as gently as he had loved his son.

"The Rebbe didn't say that." Yakov hadn't made a fool of himself with all those other girls. He just hadn't wanted to marry any of them.

"He doesn't have to say it, it's what he thinks, believe me. It's what everyone thinks. 'What's wrong with Yakov? He thinks he's too good for any of our girls?' Or maybe..." Yossi bent down to pick up a sheet of paper on the floor, a sketch Yakov had tossed aside as imperfect, a rough outline of shoulders and back fading at the hip line. "Maybe you're too busy scratching out these filthy pictures to think about getting married." Yakov fought the urge to scream.

"Please, leave my room."

"Oh, why? So you can be alone with all your boyfriends?"

"I'll be down in a minute."

"Yes, let's give the little *faegella* a moment to say 'Good Shabbes' to his beauties." He turned to leave but not before crumpling the drawing he held into a tight ball and throwing it to the floor.

"Disgusting," he muttered as he took to the stairs, now creaking loudly under the weight of his unconcealed and hurried steps. "The Rebbe's waiting for you. Then we'll leave for shul!" he yelled upward.

Yakov gathered himself and his scattered work, wishing he could hide in the slim drawer with his pencils and papers. Instead, he took the stairs slowly, each step bringing him closer to reality, to meeting with his grandfather and speaking with enthusiasm about finding a wife. Then, he'd stand with his uncle at shul, pretending to all who would greet them that nothing at all was amiss.

CHAPTER THREE

No one ever found out about the wine. Lark retreated to a corner of the lunchroom and assumed as sober a posture as was possible given the sequence of events she had just witnessed. She thought it best not to be among the girls who helped Rachel up to her feet and down to the school nurse's office. An agitated Rabbi Mintz trailed along at a safe distance, looking on while Rachel had her temperature taken and her bleeding tongue tended to by Mrs. Rosen. "Ma Rosen," as they all called her, was a fixture at the school. No one was really sure if she actually was a nurse, but she certainly was the resident Jewish Mother, dispensing Band-Aids, sanitary pads, ice packs, and aspirin while lending a sympathetic ear.

The walk to the musty basement, surrounded by her solemn classmates exchanging meaningful glances, allowed Rachel to compose herself. The thermometer under her tongue, then the ice chips she sucked on to bring down the swelling kept her from confessing all, despite the remorse she felt and her absolute certainty that God had dramatically interrupted her rebellion to let her know just how He felt about it. When, at last, she could speak, she mumbled something about dizziness and cramps, causing Rabbi Mintz to withdraw hastily from the doorway where he was hovering. Rachel's parents were not called. Everyone knew her father was at the store and her mother couldn't be running around picking her up at school on a Friday afternoon—there was too much to do before Shabbes. The girls at school were from large families, seven, eight, thirteen children, one girl from a brood of seventeen. They didn't expect their parents to come running every time they had a tummy ache or stubbed toe. At their age, almost or already eighteen, they had acted as mother to the many siblings that came after them.

The bell rang, signaling the end of the lunch period. The girls left Rachel reluctantly, not so much out of concern for her condition as out of curiosity for the source of this round of drama. Rachel had a reputation for being quirky and sometimes comical, and there was her friendship with Lark. The girls rushed away, but Rachel could hear them whispering and giggling and shushing. Suddenly she was very tired, too tired to care.

"You must be nervous about tonight. It's understandable."

Mrs. Rosen smiled knowingly and leaned over her to place a damp washcloth on Rachel's forehead. Her massive bosom pressed into Rachel's shoulder and along with the fleshy warmth came her blend of smells—a not unpleasant sour sweatiness trapped in folds of flesh, rubbery latex from the girdle that held those folds in check, and a hint of some sweet old-fashioned perfume.

"You shouldn't worry about it. He should worry. Not you." Ma Rosen patted Rachel's arm. She had no idea what the old yenta was talking about.

"Excuse me?"

"Your mother told me; you don't have to pretend."

"My mother told you?"

"Rochella, when the Rebbe decides, out-of-the-blue, to send his grandson to you for Shabbes dinner, and he agrees to come even though he has already turned down more than a dozen other girls and is driving the Rebbe crazy because he wants him married already, it's something, believe me!" Mrs. Rosen took a long breath, having delivered all of that without bothering to stop for one. "So, your mother was excited about it, so she told me, but I told no one." Rachel knew Mrs. Rosen's "no one" really translated into everyone in an eight-block radius.

"The Rebbe's grandson is coming to my house for Shabbes? Are you're saying he's coming because of me? To meet me? That's impossible."

"Why should it be impossible? You're gorgeous." she quickly made a "V" of her index and middle finger and spat dryly between them in a machine-gun fashion, to mow down the evil eye, the stealer of dreams and children, who might be drawn in by the compliment.

"I'm surprised it took him so long to get around to you. You're from a good family, smart, a little *meshuga*, but maybe that's what he's looking for, that boy. He's a little crazy himself—can't make up his mind, upsetting everyone. He's lucky you would even consider him—thinks he's a prince! Eh! In a way I guess he is, since someday, God willing, he'll take the Rebbe's place, when, God forbid...well, you know." Mrs. Rosen waved her chubby hands in the air to erase the words and the notion that the Rebbe would need replacing.

Rachel's head was spinning, but now it wasn't from the wine. The Rebbe was the feared, loved, and venerated leader of their community. He was the man some believed was God's personal instrument to prepare the world for the Messiah, if not the Messiah himself. He was sending his grandson to her house to consider her for a shidduch, a match? To Rachel, this was unthinkable, and not because Rachel felt she was not a "catch," but because she didn't want to get married. Not now, anyway. Though Rachel had been raised to expect this outcome—this inevitable matching and marrying and mommy-ing—she felt shocked by its insistence, its intrusion into her life just now. Her head ached and she happily sucked on the orange-flavored children's aspirin Mrs. Rosen gave her.

"So you have to take eight of them at your age—they taste like candy, and you can feel like a little girl for a few minutes while you are here."

Was that it? Was Rachel afraid to grow up, to assume the huge responsibilities that awaited her as a Chasidic wife? That didn't feel like
the answer. Her resistance didn't feel as though she were just trying to
avoid something, but more like she was searching for something else,
something bigger. It wasn't about wanting to remain a child—she always
felt impatient about being young, and wanted to grow up faster, to be
older, taller, and have more freedom. She enjoyed the company of adults
over most girls her age and participated whenever she could in lively
discussions at the dinner table with her father and various guests. Why
did the idea of tonight's purpose, to look her over as a potential wife for
the brilliant son of their pious leader, leave her with a tightness in her
chest that made it hard to breathe?

Rachel must have dozed, because when the bell rang at three o'clock,
signaling Friday's early dismissal, she sprang up and swung her legs
around, nearly toppling over the narrow cot she had been lying on.
Overhead, she heard the thunder of feet as the girls burst from their
classrooms and stuffed their books into lockers, where the thick volumes
would get their rest on the Sabbath, too. No one lingered on a Friday
afternoon. The girls were needed at home to help with-last minute
preparations for Shabbes: bathing and dressing the young ones in their
best, setting the table with the good china, the silver flatware and can-
dlesticks that waited all week in the dark mahogany cabinets. Food had
to be prepared in advance that could be eaten on Friday night as well as
the next day without additional cooking. Lighting a fire was forbidden,
as was any other work or any activity that could be loosely interpreted as
work. No driving, no carrying anything outside of the home—not even
the house keys, which could be worn on a chain around your neck but
not held in a pocket or a purse. You couldn't carry those either. No
money could be held or exchanged, no pushing, pulling or dragging,
unless you were within the boundaries of the eruv, an inclusive territory
created by running a high thin wire or rope around a neighborhood and
its shul. It served as a literal and metaphoric enclosure, making the area

like a "home" in which the observant inhabitants could push a stroller or carry a baby to shul or to the nearby park. Their observances were full of tricks like that—ways of making a life heavy with rules and rituals workable in a modern world. Rachel wondered often if the layers and layers of obligations were really what God wanted. Was all this necessary to know God and for God to know us? Lark had a definite opinion about this subject.

"If you can believe the whole thing about Moses talking to God at Mount Sinai and getting the Ten Commandments and all that, then that's really the last time we heard from God himself. Everything else is just the mental masturbation of a bunch of beards."

"What does that mean?" Rachel often needed clarification when it came to Lark's theories.

"It means these old-time rabbis were just sitting around stroking each other over what this means and what that means and making up stuff so they can feel like they have the inside scoop on what God really, really meant. Take, for instance, the reason your mother and my mother and every other hypnotized woman in this place cuts off her hair when she gets married and wears a wig. It's because someplace in the Torah it says some girl, I forget who, wore a scarf on her head when she went to greet some guy at a well. Bing, bam, boom! These rabbis then decide that she was a role model for the ages and did it out of modesty, and every woman from now on has to cover her hair, forever! And they buy it! Everyone buys it and does it like their life depends on it. What if it had nothing to do with modesty? What if she was having a bad hair day? What if she just washed it? Or hadn't washed it for a week, or just put some camel oil on it or something? What if the real point of the story is not the hair thing but that the best way to meet guys is over a drink? What if God does not give a shit what we do with our hair! But the rabbis decide what it really, really meant, and then they get to control women and who they show their hair to and say it's what God wants!"

Lark walked up and leaned into the doorway without entering Mrs. Rosen's office.

"Hey."

"Hi."

"Can I help you, Miss Shulman?" Like every other adult in the building, Mrs. Rosen didn't trust Lark.

"It's okay, Mrs. Rosen. Lark and I walk home together. She lives right near me." Rachel didn't want Lark to get into a conversation with the nosy matron. She wanted to get out, talk to her friend in private, and get some air. Her thoughts and the basement were closing in on her.

"Mmm. Does your mother know about this?"

"My mother? My mother knows everything!"

"How true!" Mrs. Rosen laughed and shared Rachel's little diversionary joke.

Lark stood in the doorway and waited for the two to conclude their bantering. She was offended that the old woman would question Rachel's friendship with her, but she understood; Rachel was a cherished part of this world, and Lark was an interloper. Though Lark didn't want to live the life they were so cocooned by, moments like this made her oddly envious of the idea of such a cocoon—of being so included, so protected, so certain of the outcome—just as a caterpillar is certain it will emerge from the dark to fly, simply as a function of its innate destiny.

By the time the two friends got ready to leave the school it was empty and quiet except for the slow rhythmic swishing of the mop. They saw Carl, the school custodian, a dark, lumbering man of indeterminate age—Rachel thought he could just as soon be thirty-five as fifty—mopping the floor. She had little experience with close examination of the blacks that closely inhabited her world. They were cohabitants with the Jews of this little corner of Brooklyn, New York, called Crown Heights, but not exactly neighbors, and definitely not friends. Everywhere in Crown Heights, but nowhere in her life, except as a group she was trained from childhood to ignore or fear.

"Bye, Carl," Lark shouted behind her shoulder as the girls walked down the hall toward the front door.

"Huh?" It had startled him to have one of the girls speak to him. He was more accustomed to being invisible, being passed up by these people in the halls and on the street, with their eyes focused ahead, looking through him as though he were not there.

He squinted down the hall at the silhouette of the two girls, who were backlit by the afternoon light coming in the open front door.

"Oh, Lark, it's you. Well, have a good Shabbes, girls." His tone was deep and musical. Rachel realized she had never heard his voice before, though she couldn't remember a time when he hadn't been there, mopping, emptying trash cans, and washing down the blackboards in straight even lines.

They walked halfway down the block without talking. Finally, Lark said flatly, "What happened?"

Rachel had been posing that exact question to herself, but was not ready with an answer. "I don't know. It got confusing, with the wine, you know? I couldn't think. I couldn't remember the brachas. I got scared."

"Of what?"

Rachel was reluctant to say; she knew Lark would disapprove.

"Of God?" Lark guessed.

"Well, sort of. Actually...yes. I had this feeling I was being watched and then...punished."

"Man!" It was all Lark could say.

"What?"

"This is why I don't have anything to do with all of this crap!"

"What do you mean?"

"This God—you know, the guy in the white robes that sits up on a throne somewhere, with a nasty mean streak just waiting to trip up bad little Jewish girls? Is that what you think He is?"

Rachel could feel the tears rise up and burn her eyes. How could she answer her angry friend? Rachel didn't know what she thought about God, exactly. She wasn't raised to sit among her friends and casually discuss such things. God was God. Unexplainable, unfathomable, all encompassing. She knew the ancient mystic texts taught that God was intimately involved in every aspect of creation and the Almighty created the world newly each day. They were taught that even a blade of grass had its own personal angel whispering at it to grow, so why shouldn't she be tripped up by such an emissary of the divine—if not by God Himself—if he found her going astray?

They walked a few more blocks without talking. The clamorous pre-Shabbes activity of the neighborhood was enough to temporarily fill the tense void between them. Rachel felt bad about everything: about stealing the wine from her basement and sneaking it out; about drinking it; about being drunk; about forgetting the bracha for washing, and falling and making a fool of herself in front of everyone. Everyone would talk about it. They'd go home and tell their mothers, sisters, and cousins over dinner. Tomorrow, women would come over to her in shul and ask politely if she'd recovered from her little "accident." She wouldn't have to say, "How did you know?" She'd know how they knew—wildfire spreading even on a day when you couldn't light a match or use a phone.

She felt the worst about Lark. Their friendship was like a tear in the tightly stretched canvas of Rachel's life—a tear that allowed a flood of light and air and color to come through. But it was a friendship based on Rachel's willingness to rebel against convention in thought and deed. She stole a glance at her friend walking stiffly to her right, chin pushed out, lips clamped and twisted to the side. Rachel had seen this face before; the barely perceptible shaking of Lark's head was the only outward expression of her inner argument. She's disappointed in me, Rachel thought. She's thinking I'm just like all the other "skirts." And then it occurred to Rachel. How could I be anything else?

* * *

Rachel closed the heavy front door as gently as all its various locks and bolts and latches would allow. She removed her shoes and held them to her chest. If she could possibly postpone her mother's knowing she was home for just a few minutes, rinse her face with cold water, brush her teeth, smooth her hair, and have a moment of quiet solitude, separating the turmoil of the day from the expectations of the coming evening, she could—she hoped—present herself as unchanged in any way.

Rachel paused in the foyer to see if she could determine where her mother was in the sprawling house. It was an old, wide, four-story brownstone, nestled among others just like it, in the most desirable section of Crown Heights. From the sweet and savory smells making the air thick and warm around her, she could picture the strudel on the counter, a couple of chickens roasting in the oven, and warm potato kugel on the sideboard.

From the small foyer sprung two long picture-lined corridors, one leading to the dining room, the kitchen—with its tiny maids' quarters—the living room and her father's den, and the other hall leading to the stairs and the first floor of bedrooms. Her father named the hallways "What Was" and "What Is." One was a gallery of long-dead relatives—the sepia-toned smiles and yellowing eyes of people whose names Rachel knew but had never met, many of them dead before she was born. These photos were part of the small and precious legacy her grandparents were able to smuggle along with them when they escaped escalating danger in their homeland and inhabited a new and unknown one in America.

The other hallway paraded years of baby poses and school photos of her and her sisters. Plain wooden frames for the most part and gilded, ornate ones for the special occasions. The newest editions were the large family photos staged at the weddings of her sisters. These photos were almost identical except for the groom and the in-laws, and Rachel often thought privately that there wasn't much difference there either. The men in their black coats and preponderantly brimmed hats, their faces buried in beards of various lengths, the women in dresses that were expensive and tasteful but, above all, modest, were all crowned by their helmets of hair—the too-perfect pageboys and the rigid hairlines of their well-made *sheitls*, or wigs. Their natural hair, shorn short just before their weddings, was only for their husbands to see behind closed doors. To Rachel, and certainly to Lark, who had railed against the whole custom time and time again, the ritual geared to guard a woman's beauty for her husband's enjoyment alone was a paradox.

"My mother has this gorgeous, thick red hair," Lark ranted. "My father, who is the only one now who is supposed to actually see her hair, doesn't get to see it because she keeps it chopped off so the wigs will fit, and she always has some *schmatte* on her head to cover it at home. When she goes out, she wears the wig that looks just like her real hair. So what is the point? She is supposed to 'save' her beauty for my father, but she looks better out in public with the wig on than she does at home. At home she looks like a damn refugee or some holocaust victim or something."

As usual, Rachel had not known what to say. She had never seen her own mother's hair long and certainly never contemplated her mother's relative sex appeal or lack of it. Routine answers to such questions, answers that Rachel had always accepted as sufficient, like, "God wants us to, so we must," would just make Lark madder and even more determined to reveal the ridiculous ironies of religious life.

Rachel slipped into the bathroom nearest to her bedroom. She closed the door gently, flipping on the light but careful not to touch the switch for the noisy exhaust fan that would rattle her already shredded nerves and telegraph her presence there. She refused to look at her face in the mirror until she had rinsed it with water and dried it roughly, careful not to use the dainty guest towel that was already in place for the Shabbes guests.

When Rachel lifted her face to the mirror, she felt mostly relieved. Her eyes were a bit bloodshot, more a function of crying and rubbing them than any effect of the alcohol, lips a bit swollen from a habit of chewing them when nervous. Other than that, she looked like Rachel. Her thick dark hair, in need of a good brushing, still tumbled around her shoulders and framed her angular jaw line; her dark brown eyes brightly reflected the bulbs that lined the top of the mirror; her teeth, still perfectly white and straight, were revealed by a smile, which, when tested, was her same smile. "Baruch Hashem," she whispered and tiptoed down the hall to her bedroom.

"You were in the bathroom so long, I was about to come and see if you fell down the toilet."

Miriam stood with her back to the room, quickly examining one dress after another hanging in Rachel's closet. Rachel let out a startled gasped at the sound of her mother's voice.

Miriam ignored her and continued her frantic pace at the closet. Rachel sat on the edge of her bed and watched her.

"Ah-ha, this is the one I was looking for. I was afraid it was at the cleaners. Mazel Tov! This is the one." She held it out for Rachel like a prize.

"The one?" Rachel cocked her head like a confused spaniel.

"For tonight. To meet the Rebbe's grandson, Yakov! Don't tell me you don't know. I know you know because Channi Rosen called me from school to tell me that she was 'soooo sorry' that she ruined the surprise, but she thought you already knew. She couldn't keep a secret if it was sewn on, that woman. Anyway, now you know! They only called a few days ago with the interest, but never mind. I didn't want you to be nervous and chewing your lip all day; I just wanted you to meet him when he came, nonchalantly, like a regular Shabbes guest, and it would all be fine. Don't be nervous, and wear this dress with your nice black pumps and light hose, and he won't be able to resist you. Of course, there is more to you than your looks, but it doesn't hurt. Life is hard enough without being homely, so thank God he made you beautiful— *kehnynah hora*—and make the most of it." She tossed the dress on the bed and sailed out of the room.

Rachel felt helpless. She lay on the bed staring at the ceiling, with its overhead triangle of light bulbs concealed by a square of milky etched glass. The burning bulbs reminded her of something.

When she was little, maybe four years old, she believed that God lived in the clear, flame-shaped light bulbs topping the fake candles on the electric Chanukah menorah they kept on their windowsill during that winter holiday. The burning filaments seemed like halo-ringed holy men in long robes, glowing with divine light. The staccato electrical movements of the tiny gods made them look like they were davening, swaying and dipping like she saw her father do when he prayed. She would stare at the synthetic flickering of flames until her mother would make her stop.

"You want to go blind for Chanukah?"

Then, she'd close her eyes quickly to capture the points of light, embossed as they were on the inside of her eyelids. The game she played then was this: If she could complete the entire *Sch'ma*—the first prayer she had been taught and the only one she knew by heart—before the image faded, God would grant her most-pressing wish.

Rachel had long forgotten this game of bargaining with God, and her formal schooling, which began not long afterward, dispelled her childish notions. God was everywhere, she learned, in everything, omnipresent and omnipotent. So then, she reasoned as she lay floating on her bed, adrift in confusion about her future, her desires, her destiny—God is in light bulbs, too. She stared intently at the light above her, stretching her eyes wide, trying not to blink for as long as she possibly could. Finally, when her eyes burned and tears collected and ran from the corners, she shut them tightly and focused on the pulsating trick of light wavering before her. Rachel prayed, moving her lips, *Sch'ma yisrael adonai eloheinu adonai ehad.* Hear O' Israel, the Lord our God, the Lord is one. Baruch shem k'vod malchuto l'olam va-ed. Blessed is He who created our world. V'ahavta eit adonai elohekha b'khol navshecha, b'khol meodecha... Thou shall love thy God with all thy heart and all thy soul and all thy might.

She raced against the fading image, no longer a stumbling child, reciting with speed, accuracy, and a sense of desperate urgency. When she finished the prayer with the ghostly light still floating there in the dark, her eyes sprung open and she drew in a sharp breath. What was her wish, now that she'd won it? Toys and sweets were the stakes the last time she held this contest. What do I need from God today? Her hands covered her face and she said in a whisper, "Please, tell me what you want from me. Show me. Send me a sign, a definite sign."

At that very moment the door buzzer sounded, a sizzling electric sound, and Rachel burst out laughing.

"That was quick!"

But it was no sign from God, only a delivery boy from the grocery store laden down with last-minute specialties for tonight's special guests.

"Would you mind going to the service door." She heard her mother directing the boy. "Rachel, where are you? Can you help me with these flowers?"

Rachel followed her voice into the kitchen where a young black man unloaded a handcart stacked with paper sacks, one foot inside the kitchen, one foot on the back porch, which the service door opened to. Her mother stood over him and inspected the sacks.

"That's mine, that's mine, this one is not mine—we don't use gefilte fish from a jar—that one is mine and that one, too."

Miriam placed a folded dollar on the counter, indicating the money with a nod, and then turned away from the boy. He looked at the dollar then back up at Miriam who was already busy with the next task. The boy caught Rachel's eye and shook his head, taking the money and backing out of the door. He knew, and Rachel suddenly realized, that Miriam put the bill on the counter because she didn't want to touch him accidentally or even indirectly through the bill. Rachel could feel her face redden as she looked intently at her feet. When she looked up, the boy was gone. She heard the back porch door bang shut and turned to help her mother get extra vases down from their place above the kitchen cabinets. Candle-lighting time was in forty-five minutes. There was still much to do before their world stood still for Shabbes.

CHAPTER FOUR

It was his eyes, lifted and steady, that she noticed first, as he emerged from the dark hallway into the brightly lit dining room. Rachel's experience with boys was limited, and what little she had was characterized by a painful shyness that kept her eyes glued to the floor or searching her cuticles. Once they reached school age, boys and girls were kept apart. Boys were warned early on about the dangerous distraction that females represent. They were taught that even the most casual encounter was a threat to a man's ability to concentrate on matters of holy importance. A handshake was benign enough to the rest of the world, but the Chasidic sages must have believed it could lead to more, so they decreed all contact to be off limits. Sexual feelings were to be controlled, suppressed, ignored, overcome, and atoned for.

When Rachel's sister Ahuva came home from one of her early arranged dates, she was giddy with gossip as she instructed her younger sister. "First of all, you can really take your time and look at them as much as you want. Inspect them from head to toe! They'll never notice, because they're always looking down or suddenly very interested in their tie or napkin." She demonstrated with an exaggerated pantomime that had Rachel rolling on the bed, holding her stomach against the waves of laughter.

"I could count every stitch on his *yarmulke* twice over before he'd look at my face!" Yet, despite this inauspicious first meeting, Ahuva was encouraged enough to see him again. Whether he ever looked up to see her laughing eyes or not, he decided that they should be married after only four more meetings, and Ahuva agreed.

So it was Yakov's eyes that surprised Rachel most in the first moments after he arrived. The soft blue of them, the steady gaze in which he held her suspended for a few moments until he had taken her in. *I know the story of your life*, they seemed to say.

"Rachel." She realized her father was talking to her. "You know Yossi Rubenstein and his nephew, Yakov, of course?"

"Yes, of course. It's good to see you again. Good Shabbes."

"This is Rachel?" Yossi growled, stretching out his long arms until they hovered too close to Rachel's shoulders. "It can't be. Let me look at you. You've grown into quite a *maidela*. A future woman of valor, no doubt!" He nudged Yakov a bit too hard. Now it was Rachel who searched the floor, color rising in her face. She looked up to catch Yakov's eyes again, this time a harder, glassy blue that said, "Now you know the story of *my* life."

Miriam swept in from the kitchen. "It has been too long since we've spent a Shabbes with you, Yossi. Welcome! Sit. You must be starving now that Shabbes is coming later and later. Can you believe it's May already? Where does the year go? I wish I could get rid of a few pounds as easily as I seem to lose track of the years!"

Her father's soothing baritone floated above the table where he took his position at the head, *"Shalom alechem, malachai a shoreis, malachai el yon..."* They joined in the song that welcomes the angel of Sabbath, the men's voices booming, their hands pounding the table in rhythm, while the women sang discreetly or not at all, as modesty dictated.

Mr. Fine poured the wine so that it overflowed the silver chalice used for the kiddish, and splashed onto the saucer under it. As the wine spilled over, so would their blessings. They said the bracha over the wine, and drank; washed their hands, then blessed the two golden *challahs* and broke bread. Tearing off a hunk of the soft egg bread for himself, Rachel's father pressed it into the salt he'd sprinkled on his plate and took a bite.

Rachel and Miriam busied themselves bringing course after course to the table and Rachel was glad to be distracted. At noon she'd been drunk on wine and rebellion—Lark had been the fiery comet whose tail she would happily ride into uncharted galaxies. Tonight she felt grounded. Familiar songs punctuated each comforting course—the airy matzo balls floating in golden broth, the handmade gefilte fish, garlic-roasted chicken and sweet *tzimmes*, the potato kugel, the sherbet, the flaky strudel, and strong tea. In between, the men, at least Yossi and her father, found several perfectly good reasons to fill a shot glass with aged scotch and drink "*l'chaim*," to life—this blessed Chasidic life.

Rachel stifled a yawn. She would have liked nothing better than to crawl into her bed and drift off into a dreamless sleep. Escaping to her bedroom seemed like a better idea each minute that passed with Yakov staring at her like she was an exotic animal in a zoo. She knew she was on display for him but didn't like it. He was studying her from his seat near her father, his eyes clearly focused, his hands drumming on the table. Ahuva had given no instruction for what to do with such an odd, bold suitor.

Rachel started feeling self-conscious—was there something wrong with her, was her hair a mess, her zipper undone, food stuck in her teeth, something hanging from her nose? Her mother would have dragged her into the kitchen and had her fixed up in a second if that were the case. Knowing that, she still couldn't relax.

Why was he having this effect on her? She wasn't interested in him. *Too tall, too thin, too quiet. Look at him fidgeting!* But he was the Rebbe's grandson; a celebrity of sorts in their midst, and everyone had heard the stories about him—his extraordinary mind, his undeniable talent, and the sudden loss of his father not long ago. Everyone knew the stories, but few knew him well. Her thoughts were interrupted by the booming, slurring voice of Yakov's uncle.

"Look at the two of them, not a word! How long have we been here tonight, Dovid, and they haven't said a word to each other!" Yossi Rubenstein snickered. "Miriam, when we were young we knew how to have a conversation, no? What is it with a boy who is twenty-three, who should be married by now, who can't even talk to a girl? It's not for the girl to speak up, naturally, but what can she do if the boy doesn't even talk to her?"

Miriam chuckled uncomfortably and shook her head. "Normally, I can't get her to be quiet; this is unusual for her..."

Rachel looked at Yakov who was no longer staring at her but examining the teacup in front of him, clutching it with both hands. Rachel was surprised by the sound of her own voice and its angry tone. "Please don't talk about us as if I weren't even in the room, as if we can't hear. We are not plants or babies...or something!" She stood up abruptly as the three adults just gaped at her. Yossi's face darkened, but before he could say anything, Rachel looked at Yakov and said, "It's very warm in here...we should go to the roof, get some air." He nodded, stood up and quickly followed her without looking at his uncle. As they reached the door leading to the back stairs, they heard Miriam smoothing things over.

Rachel ran up the stairs, past three floors of bedrooms, to a narrow door leading to the roof. The effort of climbing the stairs began to clear her head and give her a second wind. Her legs ached and her lungs burned by the time she pushed her shoulder into the heavy door at the top of the house. Pushing just a little too hard, she stumbled onto the tar-coated surface of the roof and into the night air. She hadn't looked behind her to check if Yakov was following, but now as her breath eased, she could hear his steady footfalls rising on the steps. He was taking his time. Rachel took up a position at the roof's railing and stared out at the street below and beyond, not wanting to appear as though she were waiting for him. And she didn't want to be looking right at him. His eyes were making her feel funny.

"It's nice up here," he said quietly from somewhere behind her.

"I love it." She took on a bright, chatty tone she hardly recognized. "No one really comes up here much." She walked to a corner of the roof, and from there she could watch the traffic lights change down the wide avenue below, falling away from her like so many green, yellow, and red dominoes.

"I think I am afraid of heights."

She spun around to look at him now. His hands were dug deep in his pockets, his arms clamped to his sides against the cool air. He smiled for the first time that evening.

"So am I," said Rachel, "but you can handle standing at the edge if you look out, not down."

"Like, where you are going, not where you've been?" Yakov said as he stepped toward the railing where she stood. They stood side-by-side but not touching, their arms dangling over on the chest high guard railing.

"That's one way to think about it," replied Rachel, feeling the stupidity of her reply the moment it left her lips. She really had no idea what he meant.

"I think about it all the time." He spoke so softly she could hardly hear him above the street sounds and the wind up there.

"Think about what?" *Sounding even more stupid or deaf!*

"I think about where I'm going, what I'm going to do with my life." He raised his voice a bit now. She turned to look at him, to see if he was joking. Everyone knew what he was going to do with his life; the Rebbe knew, so what was there to think about? She looked at his profile, his upward turned face and long neck, a lean, sparsely bearded jaw, his pale skin ruddy at the cheeks. He wasn't laughing, but was on to the next subject. "You can't really see stars in the city. Too much light," he said.

"Wait a minute—everyone knows what you are going to do with your life; the Rebbe already said..."

"That's what everybody wants me to do with my life. But that might not be where I'm going." He suddenly grabbed hold of the wide railing; his hands spread shoulder length apart, and hoisted himself up. Supporting himself with rigid arms, his long legs dangling, his black coat flapping in the wind like a cape, he peered over the top of the railing and down toward the street.

Rachel cried out, "What are you doing? Don't do that! You'll fall! I thought you were afraid of heights."

Yakov concentrated to keep himself propped up. His arms trembling, he forced himself to keep looking at the street below. "I am afraid. But I don't want to be." After a few seconds he pushed backwards off the railing and landed on his feet. He brushed the soot from his hands and stuck them back into his pockets. He leaned one shoulder against the railing and faced her with those eyes again. They were lit up now with mischief.

"Why did you do that? Are you crazy?"

"Think about it, Rachel." He pushed his face closer to hers. "Why just stop something because you're *supposed to*, because someone says you should? Why did you get up and yell at your parents downstairs? Why?

"I don't know. I think too much, I mean, I talk before I really think."

"No, it's *because you think* that you said it. You were thinking. You were right. They were talking about us as though we weren't there, as though we had no feelings that would matter. I was shocked when you said it, not because it was wrong, but because I didn't expect it. You stood up for yourself. And me."

For a moment they just stood like that, very close. His eyes were searching hers for her reaction to his speech. When he finally turned and walked away, Rachel let out the breath she had been holding onto and again faced the steadying timing of the traffic lights. Yakov strolled around the perimeter of the roof, peeking over the edge, then joined her back at the railing.

"I think about it, too," she said, almost whispering. "What I want to do with my life."

"I know," he said. They looked out at the street for a while without speaking, then Yakov walked to the door and Rachel followed, taking the stairs slowly. When they reached the main floor of the house, Yakov said, "I'm sorry if I was staring at you at dinner. Your face, it's...well, very...interesting. I would like to sketch you. Maybe we can meet again sometime."

"Maybe," Rachel said just loud enough to warn the adults they were back. And the murmuring they'd heard from the hallway stopped abruptly. When the two of them walked into the dining room everyone was conspicuously silent, but the look of hope in Rachel's parents' eyes spoke volumes.

CHAPTER FIVE

Most mornings, Rachel had to be awakened by an alarm. Her room's windows faced the narrow strip of pavement between her house and the identical one next-door, and little sunlight reached in to interrupt her sleep.

This morning Rachel lay awake listening to the sounds of her household and neighborhood slowly stirring. Trying not to think about Yakov, she focused on what to wear to shul, which quickly brought her around to thinking about him again and wondering if she'd see him there. Tangled up in her blankets from so much tossing and turning, she fretted about meeting Lark before shul, as usual, and about how to describe what happened last night. Then, finally giving in to it, she went over the evening in obsessive detail.

She'd practically screamed at her parents in front of guests, very important guests by her parents' standards, rudely left the dinner table, practically dragging Yakov, someone she hardly knew, up to the roof, where she proceeded to have a strangely intimate conversation with him that left her feeling even more off balance than she had after falling over her lunch at school. He asked to see her again and, while hours earlier she would have guaranteed her answer to that question to be a resounding no, she had instead answered him with a coy "Maybe." *What does this all mean?* The question reverberated in her head.

"Ahhhhgh!" She groaned in frustration, sweeping the covers off and jumping from the bed, determined to get on with the day and drop her trademark over-analysis of everything. She could hear her mother, "You think too much, Rachel. Why analyze? Are you a Torah scholar? A holy *tzaddik*, like my great-great-grandfather, may he rest in peace? No, you are not. You are a girl. With everything you could possibly want and need, what is there to think about?"

Rachel washed her face with cold water, since using the hot water could turn on the big boiler in the basement, and that would be lighting a fire—prohibited on Shabbes. Dressing quickly, she refused to change her outfit, when a thought crept in about whether Yakov would like the mauve suit that had been her favorite up until that moment. She walked toward her parents' voices in the kitchen. Her father would be ready to leave for shul, wearing his knee-length black coat with its sash across his broad middle. Rachel would go to shul later and her mother would go even later or not at all. Davening in shul was not mandatory for women, especially married women, whose most important role was in the home. Her mother would be home supervising Maria, watching her put out a lavish cold lunch for Rachel's father and the guests who would inevitably make their way back to the house after shul, hoping to spend the afternoon in good company with perhaps a little debate or discussion of the Torah portion for that week.

Rachel entered the kitchen prepared to get "the treatment" for her behavior of the night before. The "treatment" was different from each parent. If her father became annoyed with her, he would simply ignore her, squint right through her, like a dusty screen window, until she could no longer stand it. Then she'd erupt in explanations and apologies. Her mother, on the other hand, would look directly at her, giving her the "eye"—a look that managed to point downward and upward simultaneously, eyebrows arched athletically toward her hairline, chin pressed nearly to her chest, while bulging eyeballs pointed accusingly. An imperceptible shaking of the head would rub it all in good. Rachel had given her parents little time to chastise her the night before, rushing off to her room while they chatted at the door with the two Rubenstein men. Rachel climbed into bed and pretended to be asleep before they could get to her.

Rachel steeled herself for the worst and entered the kitchen. Her father stood at the counter, wiping coffeecake crumbs from his beard, her mother hovered beside him scooping up the crumbs as they fell to the counter. When they saw her they both froze, mid-wipe. After a beat, the oddly uncharacteristic smiles leapt to their faces—a matched pair.

"Good morning, Rochella" they said, nervously talking over each other.

What is going on here? As she got some hot water from the big kettle that stayed on a low flame all through Shabbes, and made some instant coffee, the three of them talked about everything except last night. The dress she had on, "just lovely," though they'd seen it before; the weather, "so warm, you won't need a coat," the relative moistness of the coffee cake from Schlachter's, as opposed to that from Bernie's Cake Corner, the letter they received late yesterday from Sara, but couldn't open until sundown. When it seemed as though her mother was about to burst, she finally spoke about the evening.

"Well, what did you think?"

Now it was Rachel's turn to freeze in mid-sip.

"What did you talk about on the roof? You came back. He was smiling a little, I noticed?"

Her father stood stock-still, his eyes forming the same questions.

Rachel realized that not only weren't they mad at her, they were practically congratulating her on her ingenuity! That somehow she had been clever enough to get herself alone with Yakov and then impress him enough to want to have a second meeting.

She was caught between her tentative excitement about the evening and resentment for her parents' assumption that she contrived the whole episode to impress the boy. They were acting as though her fate as his wife was practically sealed. Rachel looked at her parents, eagerly waiting for her answers, and realized they were *kvelling*, practically oozing with the delicious fantasy that their least-likely-to-marry-well daughter could end up with the grandson of the Rebbe. Imagine! She wanted to burst their little airtight bubble, the one that contained the neat package of Rachel's life from now on. Instead she just said, "Nothing happened. We went to the roof; we looked at the view."

"And...?" her mother prodded.

"He talked a little. He's strange." *He looks right at you with those eyes until you have to look away*, she remembered, but didn't add.

"What's so strange about being the grandson of a great man, from a great family, destined for greatness? Hmmm?"

"Miriam!" Her father interrupted. "Rachel, walk me to the door, I don't want to be late for shul." She followed him down the hallway to the foyer. He opened the hall closet and retrieved his good Shabbes hat with its wide brim. He took a moment in the mirror that hung by the front door to position the hat over his broad *kipah*, the skullcap he was never without, then turned to Rachel and held her chin gently with one hand. Rachel smelled the mixture of soap and coffee cake on his fingertips.

"Rochella," he started. "Make no mistake; if you become Yakov's wife, it will not be because he chose you or you chose him or what you said on the roof or what he said. It will be because God has already written it, already chosen you for him, and has in mind for you a great task. And God would only choose a woman who could handle it. You understand?"

He gripped her chin a bit tighter then let his hand fall. As an afterthought he brushed a stray hair from in front of her eyes and put it back in place, then turned and walked out of the front door before she could reply.

CHAPTER SIX

From her bedroom window Lark could see the playground across the street through the green mist of budding trees. The park was empty except for a few old men sitting around a concrete chessboard, chain-smoking and drinking beer hidden in crumpled brown bags. With the weather warming, this crowd of cronies, along with boom-box toting teenagers and stroller-pushing young mothers, would be regular fixtures until it turned cold again.

Lark scanned the small park, which was really just a triangle of asphalt between two converging streets—some gnarled trees, worn benches that lined the iron fence around its perimeter, a set of heavy, city-issue swings and monkey bars, a tall slide, and a lone brass dome that looked like an odd bump in the ground now, but in the heat of summer sprang to life as a fountain for children to run through. *Some park.* Lark thought about the big sprawling county park near their old house in New Jersey. She used to love riding her bike on the miles of trails, wading in the mossy stream, navigating the playground that covered at least two acres, and re-visiting the tiny zoo and petting farm so often she knew the animals' names by heart.

Brooklyn! She leaned her forehead against the window. Even after four years, she was still not used to apartment life. *Why do people live this way? Someday I'm going to see the sunset from my bedroom. I'm going to fall asleep to the sound of ocean waves crashing in the distance.* Her heavy sigh fogged a large circle on the window before her. She drew a quick frowning face in the mist there then watched it slowly fade.

"BTI," or "Before The Insanity"—as she referred to her life, nearly four years ago, before her father, Abe "Abby" Shulman, made the decision to become ultraorthodox and move to Crown Heights—they lived in the suburbs of northern New Jersey, a fifteen-minute ride to half a dozen farm stands and four different malls. They had a backyard with a patch of woods that turned into whatever she and her older brother David decided it was on any given "adventure"—swamp, war zone, jungle, maze, or fairytale forest.

The family went to the Jersey shore every summer on long day trips, crowding into the car with towels, beach toys, and an oversized cooler filled with Italian subs, Yoo-Hoos, and beer. Straining along the Garden State Parkway in their old, vibrating VW van, slowing down and lining up at the tollbooths over and over again, her brother and she would take turns throwing the coins into the gaping mouth of the toll bin. Her mother Sarah's red hair blowing wildly from the open window made her look like a hippie medusa. Though by then it was the early eighties, her parents never let go of their glory days' look—long uncoiffed hair, peasant skirts or flannel shirts, t-shirts and jeans, Birkenstock sandals through the summer, construction boots through the winter.

Her father sang badly at the top of his lungs on these outings, punching the radio buttons and searching for rock and roll amid the proliferation of punk and top-forty hits. Finally, coming into range for a "classic rock" station, he'd crow, "I love this song!" and launch into an off-key rendition while beating the rhythm on the steering wheel with both hands. The songs often triggered memories for her mother, and she'd tell the stories they'd all heard before—when she first met Abby in college, the time they went to that protest and got arrested, or that trippy Werner Erhard thing they did in the woods for six days.

Her parents were always following some guru into the woods, searching for God, or at least the next spiritual high. Not that any of it eliminated her father's sometimes explosive temper, or kept him from drinking or getting high, but Lark and David knew that with each "path" their parents pursued, their father's most unpredictable traits would be subdued for a while. The family could count on at least a couple of months of the "mellow" version of Dad.

When Lark was in seventh grade, the newest guru on the long list was a young Chasidic rabbi they stumbled upon driving around upstate New York one beautiful spring Sunday. They saw a homemade sign for a Purim festival and despite protests from Lark and David, they piled out of the van at what turned out to be a pretty rinky-dink affair behind a private home that housed a small synagogue. They didn't even realize it was a Jewish holiday. The rabbi charmed them with his good humor and "no-pressure" approach. In the masquerade tradition of Purim, he wore a tie-dyed "hippie" outfit, his long beard fitting in perfectly with the charade. Now, here was a rabbi her parents could relate to!

Her parents accepted the rabbi's invitation to return for a Friday night Sabbath dinner, where the sixties garb they'd first encountered on the man were replaced by the long black coat and black hat of the Chasid. The food that came in wave upon wave from their tiny kitchen was homemade, and the atmosphere warm and welcoming. This first dinner led to many more and the Jewish food-and-philosophy-filled nights led to whole weekends sleeping over at the rabbi's cramped house. A dormitory of sorts had been set up in his damp basement so secular folks like the Shulman family could share the whole observant Shabbes "experience" along with the rabbi, his nine children, and his wife who was thirty-five, but looked fifty from churning out a child every eighteen to twenty months from the time she was nineteen.

At first, it was a novelty for Lark and David, sort of like being on an anthropological research trip. During those long, tedious Sabbaths, without TV, radio, or any other familiar distractions available, David entertained himself and Lark by pretending he was a big-shot broadcast journalist, shooting a groundbreaking documentary on these "tribal peoples." He'd frame a particular moment, with his hands, then lean over to Lark with some cynical and hysterical "voice-over" to the shot.

"Notice how the leader of the clan, the hairy one, manages while eating, to never, ever fully close his mouth or stop talking. In our culture we might consider this rude, even repulsive. In this case, however, it is a technique, evolved over thousands of years, for storing food in the beard, to be eaten later. You never know when you might have to spend forty years in the desert or a few months floating around in an ark. Darwin's theory of adaptation was never so evident."

After a few months, it wasn't funny anymore. They realized their parents weren't letting up. Lark's father, who was never that industrious—working sporadically as a landscaper, construction worker, a not-to-handy handyman—started working even less and spending more time studying at the Jewish Learning Center in Monsey. Their mother started taking classes too: "Holiday Menus," "The Jewish Mother, 101," "Keeping Kosher Basics." Once a month, she drove up there to visit the *mikvah*, the ritual bath, to "cleanse" herself after her period. A nurse, Sarah kept up her hours at the hospital, though she switched to a schedule with Friday and Saturday off.

By the time the following summer rolled around, her father declared that they wouldn't be going to the beach anymore. "Jews don't wear bathing suits and parade around half-naked for the world to see," he told them on a brilliant and balmy Memorial Day, a day they traditionally started by rising early to beat the traffic and have their Hawaiian Tropic slathered on and toes in the sand by ten o'clock.

"But we were Jews last summer, and we went to the beach," argued Lark. Her mother had a habit of tanning with her top off, for that matter.

"We weren't really Jewish then."

Her brother David left home at the end of that summer. He was eighteen and wanted to go to college. Always proud of David's academic achievements, they were suddenly against "needless secular education." They thought that with his mind he should become a Torah scholar; study at the seminary in Monsey or, even better, Crown Heights, where they were actually thinking of moving now that their rabbi relocated there to teach and be closer to his Rebbe.

"I can't even read Hebrew anymore. How am I supposed to become a Torah scholar? And why would I want to?"

David was right. Until their parents' recent foray into ultraorthodox Judaism, the last time they entered a synagogue was the day David had his *bar mitzvah*. Nine months before he turned thirteen their grandparents collectively put the pressure on her parents to make David go through the Jewish rite of passage. Large amounts of gift money were promised if David went through with it, so Abby and Sarah caved in. David took a crash course with a reformed rabbi in Paramus, memorized his *haftorah* from a tape, and "became a man in the eyes of God" in front of all the congregated relatives, neighbors, and most of his eighth-grade class.

Abby Shulman was not amused that the bar mitzvah gift money they were expecting from their parents was going to be held in a trust account established for David to be used exclusively for his college education. David laughed out loud when he found out, appreciating the irony of it. His father had already prepared him for the fact that any gift money wouldn't be David's to just spend willy-nilly—they were laying out a lot for the lessons and the party afterward and they expected to be reimbursed from that gift money. David had a whole new respect for his grandparents after that, but no love lost on Judaism. Disgusted by the whole debacle, their father barely paid attention to any Jewish holidays after that. That is until the rabbi from Monsey came along with the secrets of Kabbalah, the new improved directions—or so it seemed—to the Emerald City. It was a shiny new yellow brick road to follow.

But David had had just about enough. Lark knew he'd long outgrown the backyard woods. He wanted to be a journalist and travel the world, report from the real trenches, wherever they were. His expansive dream didn't jibe with his parents' plans to shrink their existence into a world they were now sure was "the true and only way to God." Abby declared he wasn't going to pay for David to go to college—a moot point since they didn't really have the money—but there was the bar mitzvah account and David had won a substantial scholarship to Rutgers. Along with his Merit Scholarship and other state funding, David could swing the balance of the state-school tuition and room and board on his own. One morning, in mid-August, he was just gone. He left Lark a note. *I'm leaving them, not you. It's not your fault. You'd leave too if you were my age. You only have four years to go. Don't get brainwashed. I love you.*

Lark couldn't blame him for leaving, but she cried for weeks out of sight of her father. David's decisive departure and the arguing that went on for the weeks before left her father dark, unpredictable, and less sober again. He wouldn't allow any outward grieving over David's absence. On a drunken tear, he ripped down pictures of David from the walls, and was about to purge his image from the photo albums, when her mother finally intervened. He wanted them thrown away, but Sarah Shulman simply packed them in a box and hid them in the basement, pretending it was a perfectly normal thing for a mother to be doing. David wrote to Lark a dozen times before he gave up—she found out years later—but she never saw the letters. They, too, ended up in the basement.

"David has chosen to be out of our lives," her father declared, absolving himself from any blame. "We'll say *kaddish* for him."

"That's the prayer for the dead! I'm not saying it! Mom?"

Lark pleaded with her mother to restore some sanity to their household but knew as she said it that she'd have little luck getting her mother to take any action opposing her husband. He was her fearless leader. And Lark, who was fourteen at the time, could do nothing about it except wait for this phase to pass like the ones before it. Only it didn't. Within a month they moved to Crown Heights. This "phase" was now in its fourth year, and going strong.

As soon as Lark turned eighteen she'd be able to take control of her life. Then what? She had nothing holding her in Crown Heights, except maybe Rachel. She was her only friend, the only one among the skirts who really let her in, let her be. Lark had hope for Rachel; hope that she would break out of the mold, though the little "I'm so sorry" demonstration at school when they drank the wine was definitely a setback. She wished for Rachel to wipe her whole slate clean and reinvent herself without all the superstitions, the rules, the guilt, and the heavy-handed, micromanaging God that came along with her brand of religion. It was the same hope Lark had for herself: escape. She knew what she had to do to get out and she fantasized about saving Rachel along the way.

With or without Rachel, Lark would leave Crown Heights soon. But, to where would she go? What would she do? Unlike David, she had no bar mitzvah account and her chances of a scholarship were slim since she was attending a school whose curriculum was hardly "college prep." With half the day spent on religious studies, the minutia of *halachah*, the painstaking rituals of family purity, *Mishna*, Torah, prayer, and more prayer, Lark felt her life and mind were being wasted. Why obsess over something that was already established, namely, one's relationship with the creator of the universe? As far as Lark was concerned, by just being alive you had a connection to that force. She couldn't understand why people throughout the ages felt they had to figure out what "it" was, name it and write volumes about what "it" wanted. History, geography, physics, chemistry, calculus, literature, and grammar...she could use some work on those subjects if she was ever going to get into college.

Lark tried to keep up with the real world, but it was a challenge. Being in school from morning until early evening, immobilized for most of the weekend by Shabbes, and watched carefully by her parents, she had little chance to broaden her horizons. The last novel she read openly was *The Catcher in the Rye* and that was in eighth grade back in her New Jersey public school. Since then, when she wanted to read literature she would take a train to Prospect Park or Brooklyn Heights and sit in the library there. She never brought books or magazines home anymore. Her father routinely searched her room and destroyed any "contraband." Lark stopped bringing books home after he tossed *Atlas Shrugged* into the incinerator and then tossed her around the apartment to further make his point about her indulging in such "Godless" material. She didn't want to think about the late fees she owed for that one.

Lark had a few more months before she turned eighteen and had to figure out what she would do next. Graduation was in six weeks. Then she just had to get through the summer and the High Holidays, and she could take control of her life. Her parents were in their own special denial about it, busily trying to rustle up marriage prospects for her inside the fold. Engaged or not, they planned for her to attend seminary, the Chasidic version of higher education for girls.

Getting Lark married off would not be an easy task. Good families didn't want their sons marrying *bali teshuvas*. They wanted girls from a long, unblemished line of Chasidic stock. So Lark's parents had to find young men who were willing to consider her, either because of their family's own weak status in the community or because they had already been rejected by too many girls. Lark didn't formally consent to meet anyone for the purpose of considering marriage, but that didn't stop her parents from hosting a string of misfits for lunches, dinners, and teas over the past few months. Izzy the Overweight, Schlomo the Schlepp, Baruch of the Eternal Bad Breath, Natan with Nothing to Say.

Her parents lived so tightly in their newly constructed world, they were so vested in being an accepted part of the community, that they ignored their daughter's feelings (her mother) about their life, stifling it whenever it floated to the surface (her father). Lark had become pretty good at submerging her impulse to argue with them—learning well that it wasn't worth the trouble. She was determined not to expose herself to her father's rages if she could avoid them by keeping her mouth shut. It made her feel more powerful, more in charge of her life, when she realized she could control him by controlling herself. A recurring nod, to seem as though she were listening intently to his latest, greatest insight, and jumping up to do the dishes in order to get away from the dinner table (the most dangerous place in her house) as quickly as possible, could save her from a lot of drama. After three or five "l'chaims" of vodka on any given Shabbes, Lark learned that she didn't want to get in his face about the contradictions of religion, as she saw it—not unless she wanted to end up in the emergency room, making up stories about how she slipped on the stairs or walked into a kitchen cabinet to explain away the black eyes and split lips. On top of that threat, Lark couldn't handle her mother's hair-trigger tears and uncomprehending looks whenever she tried to question the life they were leading or talk about her future. So she didn't. She kept it to herself, or talked to Rachel about it.

Outside the window, a flash of yellow caught her attention. Focusing her eyes back across the street to the park, Lark saw a long yellow slicker trailing in the wind as the young man wearing it sliced through the air on one of the swings. He was pumping his long body hard, as though he were in a race to catch up with the clouds blowing across the sky. The chains that held the swing began to buckle as he reached higher and higher. Then he just stopped pumping and rode out the ride. He was waiting. She had better go.

Lark ran out the door, letting it slam, not bothering to lock the top lock since it was Shabbes. Her parents were already at shul. Her father needed to be among the first to arrive, but they allowed Lark to come later. She took the stairs two at a time and hit the street running, crossing the street without having to wait, since there was little car traffic in

Crown Heights on Saturdays. As she entered the gate to the park, he was just slowing to a stop on the swing, and saw her. His face brightened, then quickly recovered, but not before she got the heart-stopping effect of his perfect white teeth against his luminous black skin. His face was framed by the long dreadlocks gathered into a thick tail that hung between his shoulder blades. She walked to the swings and sat on the one next to him. She looked straight ahead.

"Hi."

"Hey," he answered, looking straight ahead, too.

Lark started to move the swing from side to side, swinging away from him then ever closer. He followed her lead, but in an opposite way so that they almost collided in the middle with each swing. Each time they came together he whispered something: "Hey beauty," "Hey mama," "Hey girl." Lark looked down at the blur of asphalt below her, smiling, blushing. He suddenly reached out and grabbed her swing, trying to pull it to him, but lost his balance and nearly fell off his. They jumped off the moving swings and walked toward the benches—she laughing at him— he trying to maintain his dignity.

Lark kept an eye over her shoulder toward her apartment building. She was conscious of the streets filling up with people walking to shul, worried as usual about being seen with him, yet taking more and more risks. Her father would kill her. She'd end up knocked around and locked up in the house for the next three months or forever. But she had to see him.

She sat on bench. He sat also, but not too close. This way she could always say she was just waiting for Rachel and this guy sat next to her and was bothering her. Since he was black, everyone, especially her father, would believe it.

"Are you going to be there tomorrow?" he asked her. His voice was like melted chocolate. Smooth. Sweet.

"I'm pretty sure. There's this wedding. The whole neighborhood goes, practically. It's a frenzy once things get going, and then I can get away. My friend will cover for me."

"That's good. The Rain Man needs to see his Bird."

Lark, she was his "Bird"—he'd called her that the first night they met and the name stuck. Everyone called him Rain Man because he always wore that long, yellow coat—a cowboy duster kind of thing. A silly garment for this neighborhood—he ordered it from a catalogue that had rambling romantic descriptions and hand-drawn illustrations of its worldly wares. He made it his trademark and had the right amount of swagger to make it work. The coat had deep pockets he used to hide his hands in, stained blue/black with ink. After she'd known him a while, and Lark teased him about his dirty fingernails, he reluctantly told her did graveyard shifts at a printing press down on Joralemon Street near the courthouses that churned out legal documents and triplicate municipal forms day and night. He hadn't wanted to admit the job. Lark guessed that this mundane and dirty work somehow didn't jibe with the cocky outlaw image he like to project. After that she didn't ask him much about his life and she tried not to talk about hers. He could be her mysterious Rain Man and she could be his free-flying Bird during the short times they had together and that was fine with her.

She met him for the first time one late afternoon the previous fall when she followed the scent of burning marijuana to a corner of the little park. She spent a lot of time there when weather permitted. It wasn't her old park in Jersey, but at least it was outside and at least she wasn't home. That afternoon the park had been fairly empty, with dusk not far behind their school dismissal at nearly five o'clock and the temperature dropping with the sun. The small circle of young men, around her age—maybe a little older— lighting up and passing around several joints had the park to themselves, except for Lark, who sat perched up on the tall slide, a spot she liked to take over when there were no kids around.

Lark was familiar with the musty smell floating across the park that evening. Years ago, her parents had introduced both her and David to what, they were certain, were the mind-expanding properties of the wacky weed. By the time she was twelve she was the house expert on rolling tight little numbers for her parents and their odd assortment of friends. David rarely partook. He hated the out-of-control feeling the drug gave him and everything else his parents seemed to live and die by. He tried to get Lark to refuse to smoke with them, but she liked the way it turned her father into mush—it wasn't like what happened with alcohol. On pot, her parents got all huggy and they listened to music and danced and made three things of Jiffy Pop and gobbled them up, laughing at nothing. It was real family time, according to Lark's warped sense of family. David never bought into it.

Her parents gave up drugs along with every other thing that seemed fun to Lark when they had their "big matzo ball of an epiphany," as David once described it, and jumped into Chasidic-brand Judaism full-time. Lark missed everything about their old life, David the most. But that afternoon when that sweet smoke drifted her way, she remembered something else she missed: getting high and laughing her ass off.

She slid herself slowly down the slide, controlling her descent with her heels, then drifted over to the circle of rough-looking black boys in their late teens or early twenties, whose loud back-and-forth banter was stopped dead by the pretty yeshiva girl asking them if she could have a hit.

"Girl, don't you have to be home for Shab-biz?" one of them said, while the others behind him high-fived each other and laughed.

"Shabbes is Friday night. This is Wednesday," she said matter-of-factly. She realized what she must have looked like to them. Inside she was Lark, the same normal Lark she always was. On the outside she looked like any one of the skirts that wouldn't think of talking to, coming near, or approaching a group of black boys standing around in a park at dusk, let alone invite herself to their party.

"Oh, yeah," another of them chimed in. "Well, what is Wednesday then, Hebrew Weed-Smoking Day?" making them all crack up again. She turned to walk away.

"Pee Cee, you are being rude to the young lady. What's your name?" One of them, one she hadn't noticed, broke through the knot of boys. Maybe he'd been behind on the bench, but he seemed to come from no-where. He wore a long yellow raincoat that nearly brushed the ground when he walked even though he was taller than she was and she was nearly 5'10". He stopped her with his question and the liquid sound of his voice. Lark turned to get a look at him.

"My name's Lark."

"Let the little bird have some of that seed, Pee Cee," he instructed his less-friendly associate as though the dour boy were his personal assis-tant. "Can't you see she's hungry?"

Lark walked back toward the circle. Three glowing joints were ex-tended toward her by the other grinning youths and she had her pick. They laughed again, but this time she did too. She reached for the fat roach held out by the one in the yellow coat and took a long hit, the heat of it nearly burning her lips. Holding her breath and then letting it out slowly, she reacquainted her mouth with the good, familiar taste. She began to feel a good, familiar feeling as she took another toke and then one more.

"What's a nice Jewish girl like you doing in a place like this?" he flirt-ed with her.

"What's a black boy from Brooklyn doing wearing a frigging cowboy raincoat?" she flirted back.

She should have been afraid, but she wasn't. Her heart was beating; her mouth was dry, her breath shallow and quick. But that wasn't fear. It was excitement. Standing there in the park, in the darkening fall after-noon, she was cold, high, and her face ached from laughing as each of the boys took their turn clowning for her benefit. The one in the rain-coat stood back and just watched her. Lark felt his gaze like a soft breath on the nape of her neck. Her fingers and toes tingled. The pot made her feel as if she could see more sharply and hear everything more keenly. It was as though someone had suddenly stripped the filter off of the lens she'd been looking through for nearly four years, a filter covered in gauze, smeared with grease, placed there to make everything seem soft and tolerable. On that evening in the park, in those few minutes, she was practically knocked over by the rush of aliveness, the gushing energy of the present moment and the power of the enormous pleasure she felt. She'd been almost dead, dormant for all these years—living here, a way of life pressed on her, pressed down on her. She'd been waiting to live. Waiting until she was eighteen, waiting until her parents woke up. Waiting for Rachel to wake up, too. Waiting for David to find her and rescue her. Waiting. For those few minutes, the waiting was suspended and she felt alive to the very moment she was in.

All but one of the boys eventually took off, and she was left standing with the raincoat guy and the unsmiling, densely muscled "assistant," who hovered between them like a bodyguard.

"Pee Cee, I'll catch you later."

"Man, you do not want to mess with this shit," Lark heard him say out of the side of his mouth to his friend. A warning to both of them.

"Cousin, you are insulting the lady here and I know you don't want to be telling me what-the-fuck to do or not do. So...I'll catch you later, Pee Cee..." He danced around his gloomy friend, yellow coat sailing behind him like a cape, jabbing him and punctuating his words with mock punches to his clenched jaw. The protesting boy shook his head in disapproval and backed away from the punches. After a few steps backward, he turned and quickly left the park.

"Pee Cee's my cousin. He's very serious," he explained, keeping up the little jabs but now playfully directing them toward Lark.

"I can see that." She noticed him now, stationed on the far corner just beyond the park gate. Watching them.

"I don't think he likes me."

"He's family, you know? Like, if I walked you home right now, you think your mama would like me?"

She didn't laugh. It was beyond true.

"What's your name?"

"Rain Man. That's all. Rain Man. And you the Bird." He held out his hand and offered her a fresh, unlit joint. "You might be hungry later."

"No. I better not."

"See you around, then Birdie. Fly home. Shoo!" He started in dancing and punching the air again, and she just laughed and walked away. He stood and watched her cover the long stretch of park to the street. At the door to her building she turned and saw him there, standing finally still, just watching her.

After that it seemed as if he was everywhere she went. With alarming ubiquity he populated her life. There he'd be standing with his back to her, not twenty feet from the entrance to her school, the long coat wagging at her; or leaning against a car as she rounded a corner on the way home from the store on any given afternoon. Once, when she saw him and the stone-faced Pee Cee from the window of the ladies' bathroom at shul, where she spent a good portion of the morning service, she knew he was following her.

Often Rachel would be with her when she spotted him. Lark would look anywhere but directly at him, inevitably blushing and stammering mid-sentence as they passed by. Rachel, so programmed to ignore his type on the street, wouldn't notice the small, wordless exchange between them or the effect it had on her friend.

After weeks of this, Lark got used to seeing him and, in fact, became obsessed with his absence, when, for a week in late December, he was nowhere to be found. Finally seeing him again, she was so relieved that she lost her last bit of reserve and met his gaze steadily, confidently. It felt good. It felt like she was getting a little piece of herself back with that look.

At thirteen she had been confident and comfortable with boys—she liked them. Maybe because of David or maybe they were just fun in a less complicated way than girls her age. After nearly four years of practically zero interaction with boys in Crown Heights, the energy of this game with Rain Man was intoxicating and electric. And she wasn't thirteen anymore.

Once, walking with Rachel, she spotted him leaning against a chain-link fence that surrounded an empty, overgrown lot. She ignored him until they were just past, then quickly turned and gave him a broad wink, surprising him and herself. She heard him laugh out loud as she kept walking. Rachel, oblivious, missed the bright green light Lark had just given her Rain Man. The next time she saw him he said loudly to his friend as she passed, "Yeah, I'm gonna be at the Third Street park tonight after seven." She knew it was a personal invitation for her to show up.

And show up she did. She soon learned that it wasn't hard to deceive her parents. As strict and as crazy as they could be, they were very self-involved. If she played into their little fantasy of what they thought she was becoming, Lark could get away with a lot. She could always get out by saying she was doing something with Rachel—the perfect "*Yiddishe maidela*" as far as they were concerned. Any time spent with Rachel was above reproach or suspicion, and especially foolproof because the Shulmans felt too intimidated to call Rachel's parents and question them about arrangements.

So, over the next few months Lark was, as far as they knew, spending a great deal of time with Rachel to raise her grades and prepare for final exams in the spring. Lark's ambivalence about school until that time showed in her grades, so her parents were delighted that she was suddenly developing a desire to remediate her past performance and graduate on a high note. They were thrilled, and Lark was thrilled to be out on the streets for those delicious and dangerous stolen hours.

She met him that night and many others. They met in the park if her parents weren't home, keeping to the shadows to sneak a smoke and a laugh; sometimes in an alley between buildings in his neighborhood where she'd let him wedge her against the wall and kiss her until her lips were swollen and red, and rub her breasts under her coat until they ached. He'd coil himself around her; grind himself into her so hard that she'd feel bruised the next day along her pelvic bone or hip. That's as far as it went. They were often interrupted by the ever-watchful Pee Cee, who acted as lookout and wet rag. She could hardly breathe when she left him on those nights. He was so hungry for her, and she liked it, even if she wasn't sure she wanted what he wanted or what would come of it if they went farther. It didn't matter; she couldn't stop it now. Why should she? What else was there?

Here it was nearly summer, and after nine months of these meetings, Lark found herself relying on the Rain Man more and more for the release she needed from her parents' tight little world. Lark had gotten some relief through her relationship with Rachel; a chance to let off verbal steam, to dabble in mischief, to dream of future freedom, but that was changing. The whole incident with Rachel and the wine at school had sobered and saddened Lark because it confirmed something she suspected, but didn't want to think about: that Rachel was too sucked into the whole God-is-watching-my-every-move mentality to ever break out. It hit Lark that afternoon in the nurse's office that she was kidding herself if she thought Rachel would ever be able to leave it all behind, to run away. It wasn't going to happen! Rachel was as much *inside* the ultraorthodox world as Lark was on the *outside*, and whatever middle ground they had managed to find to play out their little fantasies was just that—middle ground. In a way, they used each other all these years. Rachel got to taste, vicariously through her rebellious friend, a bit of the forbidden world, without risking anything. And Lark got to be included in Rachel's well-ordered, predictable, and privileged world, a world her own parents had never been able to provide, without the lifelong commitment this life of faith required. Lark wasn't going to step over that line and enter Rachel's world completely and Rachel wasn't capable of crossing that line into hers either. Rachel's drunken apologetic bellyaching on the lunchroom floor proved it. So, Lark really was alone; she had to face that. She was alone, except when she rounded a corner or peeked out her window and saw that flash of yellow, that flag-of-a-coat waving at her, winning her over, welcoming her, wanting her so bad that it was good, so damn good.

CHAPTER SEVEN

Walking the three blocks to Lark's building did nothing to clear Rachel's mind, in spite of the warming air, the crisp cloudless sky, and the white brilliance of the midmorning sun. Rachel couldn't stop thinking of her encounter with Yakov the night before or her father's words to her that morning. Was she destined to be Yakov's wife? Was God choosing her for some important role? How was she supposed to know for sure? She'd had no visions, dreams, or premonitions to prepare her for contemplation of such a matter. Even her little "bargain" with the light-bulb God the afternoon before hadn't given her insight or warning.

Rachel felt exasperated with herself. Why was she always looking for some definitive sign from God about life when she knew that He didn't work that way? Mostly, He just plopped things down on you without flashing a yellow light or printing out instructions. She felt totally out of control. Hurrying her pace, she was almost frantic. She wanted to run to meet up with Lark, as though being in her company, surrounded by her certainties, would protect her from the barrage of conflicting emotions that swirled around her sleepy head. Lark could cut through it. She'd see it for what it was, state it simply, and get Rachel to see it that way, too. Then her stomach could stop flopping around like a hooked fish and she could just go back to normal. In the past twenty-four hours, the budding confidence she'd felt about taking control of her life, making of it what *she* wanted, was shaken, to say the least.

With Lark she'd begun to faintly sketch an outline in her head of how her life could go if she had the courage to pursue it, but forces seemed to be at work to derail her. Or her other thought was, maybe these forces were trying to get her back on track—a track that was better, the "right" track according to everyone she knew, except Lark. That's what she had to figure out. She had to know! Was this a test for which she had no clue to the correct answers? If it was a test, it seemed to Rachel as though it was one of those tricky multiple-choice nightmares. Every answer seemed plausible but there was no "all of the above" option. How could she choose? Then there was the matter of the questions—was she even asking the right questions of life? Was it "What do I want?" or "What will make me happy?" or should she be asking, "What does God want of me?" And why do the answers to these questions feel so diametrically opposed to one another?

She sped along to find Lark so they could make an appearance at shul. Both their parents would expect to see them there at some point. "Ugggh!" she said aloud to no one as she felt the frustration of her endless circle of thoughts. She was sure life was much simpler for normal people who didn't over-analyze everything the way she did. Rachel noticed no evidence of this kind of tortuous mind play before her sisters had married, or in any of her classmates, girls she'd been around daily since nursery school. That's why she'd been drawn to Lark. That girl had questions! She questioned everything. But more important to Rachel, she seemed to have answers she was sure of. Rachel wanted that, even if at this point, it was merely through association.

When she finally reached Lark's street, she quickly checked down the row of narrow apartment buildings to see if Lark was waiting out in front for her. If she wasn't there, she knew to check for her across the street in the park. When she spotted her on the opposite end of the park by the benches, Rachel broke into a trot, crossing the street—she was so happy to see her, even though she worried that Lark might still be mad at her because of the way she messed up the whole wine-drinking thing. They had planned it to be this daring, hilarious scheme and Rachel had turned it into an embarrassing guilt-ridden mess. She was relieved to see Lark smiling at her as she approached. Rachel waved, but Lark didn't wave back. She seemed to look right past her and then suddenly turned away and ran toward the monkey bars. Rachel was about to call after her when she saw that a guy was chasing her, some black kid in a long coat. *Oh, my God! What is happening?* Rachel nearly tripped over her own feet as she scrambled between the parked cars that stood between her and the park. She snagged her hose on a rusty bumper but didn't stop running to get to her friend who was obviously in trouble. She heard Lark squealing as she quickly dodged her assailant and forced the boy to chase her in circles around the maze of metal.

Rachel frantically looked around for anyone who could help, but on Shabbes morning the park and surrounding streets were as empty as the shuls were full.

"Leave her alone!" Rachel screamed as the boy caught Lark by the coat and pulled her toward him. It was then she noticed that Lark had a big grin on her flushed face and, instead of fighting off the boy, she'd locked her arms around his neck. She looked absolutely goofy.

The boy let go of Lark, but Rachel could see that he had been laughing until her histrionic interruption in what—it dawned on her—was some flirty game the two of them had been playing.

"Lark?" was all that came out of her mouth, as if, given what she thought she was seeing, the girl in front of her couldn't really be her old friend.

"Rachel, I'm okay. This is Jamal. He is a friend of mine. We were just...talking."

"Oh." Rachel was about to explain what she thought was happening, but she knew that they knew that already. The way the boy looked at her now, she was certain of that.

"Wait a minute, okay? We'll walk to shul in a minute, okay? Are you all right?" Rachel nodded, she could only imagine how she must look for Lark to ask her that. She watched as Lark walked with the boy to the gate nearest them. He was chuckling and still plucking at her coat, wanting to resume their game, but Lark had become serious and kept looking over her shoulder to check on Rachel, shooing him away from her. At the gate they exchanged a few words and a lingering high five, their hands meeting in the air and floating slowly down.

Rachel stood there, shifting from one foot to the other, wanting to simply disappear into thin air or sink into the ground or rewind herself out of the park—as if by entering newly, she would find the previous scene erased and her comfortable reality returned to her.

Lark walked toward her now. Rachel didn't like the look on her friend's face. There was something foreign there. Something defiant and impenetrable, reserved for teachers or rabbis before this, but never directed toward her. It made Rachel look away.

"We better get to shul." Rachel turned to walk out of the park.

"That's all you can say? 'We better get to shul?'" Lark saw the horror on Rachel's face and felt her own resentment rising.

"Well, what do you want me to say?" Rachel felt choked by the emotion that was burning in her throat.

"Nothing. Forget it, look, I'm sorry. I should have told you about him a long time ago."

"A long time ago?" Rachel echoed. How long had this been going on? She felt like she was falling. She looked around for the nearest bench, but couldn't move. Lark gently took her arm and began to walk with her. Rachel wanted to pull away, but somehow couldn't do that either. They sat for a moment on the wooden bench, already heated up from the morning sun, but Rachel jumped up before Lark could start her explanations.

"I really think I should go to shul now."

"What? Suddenly you've got to hurry to shul? Oh, yeah, you better not stick around here with me 'cause I'm about to get struck by lightning! Ahhhh!" Lark hopped madly from side to side, dodging imaginary lightning bolts, clutching her leg, her arm, and her stomach as they "hit." "Ooooh, watch out, she touched that dirty black boy! It's worse than you think...she kissed his big 'ole lips, too. Eeeeek! She's gonna fry now, *schvartze*-lover. Burn her ass!"

Rachel turned to leave, but Lark jumped in front of her. "Stand back, I'm hot, I'm burning up!" Rachel spun around in the other direction, but again her possessed friend blocked the way. "I'm melting, I'mmmm mellllting!" Lark's "Wicked Witch of the West" imitation was lost on Rachel, who had never seen the popular film.

"Stop it!" Rachel screamed, and the tears came, the phlegm rose in her throat, and she nearly choked as a sob exploded from her. "Stop it!" she said again, even though Lark had already stopped mid-melt and was backing away, hands in the air, like a surrendering prisoner. "Okay, okay," she repeated a few times as Rachel tried to recover.

"It's not what you think," Rachel protested. "It's not about that—I'm not a bigot! It was a surprise, that's all. It's just surprising to think you know someone and then you find out you really don't." Another sob erupted despite her efforts to control her trembling chin and swelling lips. She turned her back on Lark. She didn't want to slobber in front of her. Like a child, she wiped her eyes and nose with the back of her hand and wiped her hand on her coat. She always carried tissues—a victim of a constant dripping winter nose—but on Shabbes she emptied her pockets before leaving the house. No carrying today, not even a tissue, so how she wondered, would she carry the weight of what she'd just discovered about her best friend?

Rachel felt betrayed by the obvious deception that had to have taken place over a long period—through months of talks and walks and secrets and notes and knowing looks passed between them. It all seemed now to be contrived, inauthentic. She felt cheated on, jealous.

She also had to privately admit she was totally horrified. It was wrong, what Lark was doing. All her training, her entire upbringing came to bear on her now with this instant, utter rejection of Lark's association with this boy. It was a physical relationship, obviously. *That was wrong.* He was not a Jew. *That was wrong.* That he was black was unacceptable, outside the realm of possibility for a white Jewish girl from Crown Heights. These were not intellectual ideas that Rachel summoned as part of some thought process. They were completely visceral, a part of her. The feelings were there in an instant, on her like a swarm of bees, obscuring her vision, stinging relentlessly and causing her to swell with righteous indignation.

She could feel Lark approaching behind her.

"Rocky, listen. Please. I am so sorry. You have to believe me. I just couldn't bring it up to you. I wanted to so many times. But I was afraid you'd, you know, freak out."

I am freaking out, thought Rachel. *I am freaking out.*

"Will you still walk to shul with me?" Lark gently pleaded. And with that a truce was tacitly agreed upon. They walked the familiar route to shul and stayed on familiar ground with the few words spoken between the park and their destination. They would leave the subject alone for now. Maybe some other time Rachel would want to or would be able to hear the details, or maybe not. She didn't feel like telling Lark about Yakov anymore. Anyway, the anxiety she felt about that whole subject was pretty pulverized by the events of the last fifteen minutes. One confusing dilemma was now replaced by another. She hadn't reached any decision about Yakov, but somehow she knew the answers she hoped to get from her friend would have to be gotten somewhere else.

As she crossed the threshold of the old shul, the familiar smell of dusty, yellowing prayer books and the soft murmur of melodic prayers washed over her.

"I'll be up in a minute," Lark said, as usual, and headed to the girls' bathroom, where she spent a good part of the service most Saturdays. Rachel would always join her in the mirror-lined ladies' lounge after a while, to gossip about who was there and what people were wearing, and to hear Lark's diatribe on whatever the sermon was about. But today would probably be different. Still, she pretended along with her friend that everything was the same between them.

"Okay, I'll see you later."

Rachel climbed the narrow stairs to the women's section and then searched for a place to sit among the women and squirming children. Her mother waved to her from the far side of the balcony, pointing to a saved seat beside her, but Rachel pretended not to see and took a lone seat on the edge, near the entrance. Her view of the main gallery below was obstructed. She could only see the tops of heads bobbing around the *bima*, a group of men surrounding one of them who was chanting from the open Torah scroll. The voice rose up to her. Rachel's erratic breathing fell in step with the steady rhythm of the ancient chanting and she felt, all at once, the true meaning of the word *sanctuary*.

CHAPTER EIGHT

The dark empty hall rang with his footsteps. Yakov walked toward the switches on the nearest wall, but thought better of it—as if waiting to turn on the bright overhead lights could somehow postpone the evening's imminent festivities. In a few hours, the long tables pushed up against the walls, dressed in long skirts that brushed the floor, would sag under the weight of a local caterer's best efforts. The bride's dress might be borrowed—it was considered good luck—but no expense would be spared on the food or drink. Full plates and full glasses would set the pace for abundance for the young couple being ushered into married life—a future with much happiness, prosperity and more importantly, rooms overflowing with children. Soon the polished floor would disappear under hundreds of polished shoes and flowing skirts belonging to the evening's wedding guests.

Weddings in general made Yakov melancholy. They were excessive according to his sensibilities—*too* much food, *too* much drink, *too* many drunken, sweating men too close together, whirling and spinning and jumping to music that was too loud. Then, there was the promise that weddings held. For those not yet married, the promise was a shout, a breathless beginning, a door opening up into pleasures once forbidden but now blessed, and a rise to status and visibility within the close circle of their community. For those already married, the promise was a whisper—a chance to relive that innocence, when all of married life lay before you and you believed it could be holy and sacred and important—a time before all the years and all the babies had taken their toll. All of this, so intoxicating for others, was sobering to Yakov.

He continued across the cavernous room to a raised platform where a *chupah*, the wedding canopy, stood vacant, expectant. Yakov looked around the room, nothing more than a big box built adjacent to the old shul—housing this catering hall, a few private rooms used for prenuptial rituals or as dressing rooms, and a kitchen—which was built before Yakov was born to accommodate the almost daily need for their growing community to come together and celebrate various life-cycle events and holidays. How many celebrations had he attended in this very room? The countless *bris meilahs* with the infant's mother surrounded by sisters and friends, clutching an arm to steady herself, a handkerchief pressed to her mouth, nervously waiting for the *moyel* and the men to be done so she could hold her wailing baby boy and kiss his confusion away. And the bar mitzvahs, too many to count, a blur of affairs spent racing around, playing tag with the dozens of other boys present, while the adults compared this caterer's spread to the last one's.

He had his own bar mitzvah party here, too. Yakov remembered making his requisite speech to the congregation, nervously enunciating his terribly profound insights into the *haftorah* he had chanted that morning as part of the ritual. As grandson of the Rebbe, expectations were high, but his squeaky voice was low, barely audible. His father sat beaming, his mother worrying over every detail that the community would judge her by, and trying vainly to signal him to speak up! Speak up! Then the Rebbe talked for an hour, extemporaneously, about what it meant to be a man in the Chasidic tradition, in their way of life. The room had been unusually hushed as the Rebbe spoke that day. Everyone sat still, quietly measuring his or her location on the Rebbe's clear and inspired roadmap for living a righteous life. Yakov, sitting behind the

Rebbe on the platform as he spoke, stared at his then upright back and his waving arms, certain that the message was meant for him and him alone. It was as though the Rebbe were pointing to a big red "X" on his map and saying to Yakov, *this is where you are...this is your destination.*

As Yakov stood in the shelter of the chupah, he knew that this was one of the major destinations intended for him, written on the map long ago. Even the word destination implied it was his destiny, his fate to stand there someday with a young girl beside him. A girl like the one he met the other night. A girl with a face you wanted to draw, wanted to capture. But could one build a life on that? Yakov thought of Daniel, his lifelong friend, who would stand here in a few hours and marry a girl he hardly knew, simply because of the way she had looked at him.

"What is there to know?" Daniel had shrugged off Yakov's doubts the day he announced his intention to marry her. Standing there, in the near dark, Yakov couldn't even recall her name, though Daniel had annoyingly spoken of little else in the last two months. Was it Ariel? Maybe it was Yael? Or Gavrielle? Yes, Gavrielle, named for Gabriel, the angel that God sent to Daniel in the Torah. How perfect.

"She *is* an angel. I'm telling you," Daniel had said. "I don't know...it's the way she looks at me...like I know something. She makes me feel strong and good. Better than I am. When I'm around her I feel like I can be what Hashem wants me to be."

Yakov had little faith in Gavrielle's transformative powers or in what Daniel believed was God's plan.

"You're a little early," a voice travelled softly from across the room—Daniel's unmistakable, radio-announcer voice. Even at a whisper, it carried like music and demanded your attention.

"I'm too late, if you ask me," Yakov shot back, but regretted showing his hand so quickly.

"Oy, here we go again." Daniel walked over to the chupah platform, where Yakov now sat along the edge, head in hands, searching the floor. He sat down and swung his heavy arm over Yakov's bent shoulders. The two of them were like a mismatched set of bookends. They wore the same Chasid uniform, but Daniel was the more robust of the two—taller, long-legged, broader in the shoulders, thicker in the chest, with some extra flesh that was the result of several months of being wined and dined by his future in-laws. While Yakov had a ghostly translucent beauty to his face, Daniel always had a splash of color in his cheeks that rose above his beard line like a morning sun. They had been inseparable as friends since their days in nursery school. As time went on, the boys became study partners. They were an obvious match with their sharp minds and instincts for each other's next sentence. They thrived, arguing and sparring and unraveling the riddles of Torah and Talmud, digging and uncovering the semantic secrets of the mystics, as well as very personal secrets of their own.

"You are going to start nudging me now, on my wedding day? Why? Why can't you be happy for me?"

"You know why. I came over early on purpose, to talk to you, to get to you before..."

"Before what?"

"Before it is too late." Yakov shrugged off Daniel's arm and stood so he could look directly at him. They had to talk about it, and he wasn't going to let Daniel avoid it this time. Everything was at stake.

Daniel rose slowly, as though thirty years had just drained out of him and he was suddenly old and heavy. He approached Yakov and touched his face lightly with the back of his hand and let out a sigh that held some regret despite his wedding-day enthusiasm. Yakov reached up quickly to capture Daniel's thick hand and covered it with his own. He then pulled his warm, moist palm toward his nose, taking in his familiar smell.

"There you are," said Yakov, inhaling. "I miss you."

Daniel pulled his hand away. "Be happy for me, Yakov. I'm here today because of you." His tone was patient, measured.

"Because I was a coward that night, that's why you are here." The night they never spoke of...pretended never happened. Whether they spoke of it or not, a day did not go by that Yakov didn't think of it, didn't wonder what it meant about them. Each moment of that evening played out in his mind like a film that ran both comically fast and dramatically slow, more real than anything he'd ever experienced and yet, surreal and dreamlike.

Four months earlier, it was a night like many other nights they'd spent, holed up in Daniel's room, studying. They spread out on the floor or the bed, bent over books and papers, their shirts untucked, sleeves rolled up, crumbs of some late-night snack snagged in their scraggily young beards. During a break in the studying, Yakov was sprawled on Daniel's brother Ruvi's old bed, staring at the ceiling, trying decide whether to go home or just fall asleep where he was, as he had done so many times before. With Ruvi married and living in his own apartment, they had the room to themselves.

"Have you seen one of these?" was how it all began. Daniel, on his knees between the two twin beds, pulled a flattened newspaper out from between his mattress and box spring.

"What is it?" Yakov propped himself up on his elbows as Daniel waved the thick newspaper at him like a flag.

"It's the *Village Voice*. You *have* to see this." Still on his knees, he slapped the paper down on the bed where Yakov sat and began flipping the pages, starting from the back. He stopped at the page he'd been looking for, and ran his hands over it to smooth it out.

"Can you believe this? Look at these guys." There was a two-page spread of ads, large and small, displaying pictures of muscular men, leering out, inviting you to call. Their shirts were off or in some cases they were totally nude, except for some small token of something covering their genitals.

Yakov's first reaction was to look at the door of Daniel's room to see if it was shut, even though he knew that his parents were not home.

They were visiting with Daniel's sister in Atlanta. Yakov turned back to look at the pages laid out for him by Daniel and then at Daniel's expectant face.

"Daniel, why are you looking at this? It's totally forbidden. So is this newspaper. You know that."

"It excites me," he said plainly, the smile fading from his face as he stated that simple truth. He flipped over a few more pages and stopped at another spread of photo ads, these displaying half-naked women in various poses and positions.

"Schmuel Beiler gave me this copy a few weeks ago. He told me to 'check out the *shikses* on page 157.' I go to 157 and think 'Eh, so what?' Then I found page 203." He flipped back to the pages of men, his grin returning.

Yakov sat staring at the pages without speaking. His breathing became a bit shallow and he was aware of a feeling spreading over him that he recognized, an ache that he felt while he drew his countless male figures, alone in his room; an ache he felt each morning as he sat in the dressing room of the mikvah while his classmates passed around him in various states of undress, getting ready to dunk themselves in the purifying waters as they did each morning before prayer. The feeling that made him stay longer in the water and longer still in a cool shower afterward, to avoid watching his fellow classmates dressing, to avoid that pulsing, aching feeling.

"Why are you showing this to me, Daniel?"

"I see you in the mikvah, my friend. I've sat head to head, knee to knee with you all these years. I know you like I know myself. I'm trying to tell you I understand how you feel. How *we* feel."

Daniel closed the paper and replaced it under his mattress. He walked over and switched off the overhead light and then turned off the lamp on the nightstand between the beds. Two rectangles created by the streetlight coming in from the windows hovered on the wall behind

Yakov, who sat motionless on the bed, holding tightly to a pillow that he'd gathered to himself.

Daniel stood at the foot of the bed and slowly unbuttoned his white, wrinkled shirt, slipping it off and throwing it on the other bed. He then lifted the *tzitses*, the bib-like prayer shawl with its long strings that they were required to wear, over his head along with his undershirt and let them fall on the bed, too.

Daniel knelt down on the floor, near the edge of the bed at Yakov's feet. He pulled at the pillow he was clutching, extracting it from his grip one hand at a time.

"Yakov, take off your shirt."

Yakov followed his directions like a simple, obedient child, never quite meeting his eyes, his pale skin raising goose bumps in the suddenly cool room. Daniel sat down on the bed then, lying down on his side. The stronger by far of the two, he pulled at Yakov's arm, leading him to lay down facing him, until finally there were only millimeters of air between their bare chests.

"I want to feel how you feel, okay?" Daniel asked, but had already begun reaching.

Yakov kept still, neither giving nor denying permission. Daniel ran his damp, trembling hand slowly over Yakov's chest and upward to his neck and shoulders and down his arm, lying rigid at his side. When Daniel ran his hand to Yakov's back and pulled him closer, their chests pressed together. Yakov felt the breath catch in his throat. Daniel moaned softly.

"Look at me, Yakov." Yakov's eyes had been squeezed shut.

"No, I can't."

He wouldn't look, but he felt his friend's sweet breath on his face and then his dry lips and beard as they brushed his cheek and then his lips with his own. Yakov extracted his arm from underneath Daniel's and touched his friend's face. Daniel hungrily pulled Yakov's hand to his lips and held it there, inhaling to capture his scent.

"There you are," he said as Yakov slowly opened his eyes.

Daniel pushed Yakov on his back and climbed onto him. Slowly, as though testing, then more quickly, he began pressing, pressing at the ache there, so that it hurt, so that it could stop hurting. He leaned to the side, managing to undo his pants, to undo Yakov's, too.

"No, Daniel," Yakov said quietly, but his body had already responded otherwise. With one hand he gripped Daniel closer. The other was wedged between them at the hip, trying weakly to push him away, to stop the rhythm that was gaining momentum there. As Daniel pressed his body downward into Yakov, over and over, a feeling rose upward into Yakov's chest—a feeling that replaced all thoughts because he could think of nothing but meeting Daniel with his own body. But within a minute or two the acute pleasure rising in him was infested with panic—an absolute panic like that which comes when you are falling or have lost something precious, or know you are about to die. And this terror made his body suddenly rigid, his arms suddenly strong. The panic, like the pleasure, rose upward, too, into his throat and made him scream so that he barely recognized his own voice, "No! No, I said!" He pushed Daniel off of him so forcefully that they both ended up on the floor, but at opposite sides of the bed. Daniel banged his forehead on the corner of the nightstand on the way down.

Yakov jumped up from the floor and turned his back on Daniel, pulling his pants up from his knees, waiting for his body to regain composure, to catch up with his mind.

Daniel lay on the floor. It sounded like he was crying, but Yakov wouldn't look at him to find out.

"I think my head is bleeding," he whimpered.

Yakov located his tzitses and undershirt without turning on the lights. His shirt he found jammed between the mattress and headboard of the bed. He heard Daniel moaning as he lay in the shadowy canyon between the two beds.

"I hit my head," he said and stuck up his hand, smeared with blood.

"I'm sorry." Yakov was putting on his shoes. "I just...." *I just can't feel this.*

"I know." Daniel's leaden voice rose up from the floor. "It's okay."

Yakov finished dressing and left without saying another word. The next day at the yeshiva, Daniel appeared with a bandage over his right eyebrow. He told everyone he had walked into an open kitchen cabinet door while getting a late-night snack, and suffered through the requisite teasing. He and Yakov went on as usual through the day, though Daniel excused himself before the time for partner study, citing a bad headache, most likely due to his "battle wound." There was more teasing, but Yakov could see he was relieved to go. He studied alone that day and felt relieved, too.

Within a few days the incident passed as if it had been a dream. They never spoke of it. It might have been as though it had never happened, except that Daniel stopped touching Yakov in any way, whether it was to drape an arm over Yakov's shoulder or sit with his knees brushing Yakov's during their study sessions. And while the nighttime study sessions continued when needed, they kept now to the dining room table and ate more snacks than before.

Yakov joined an esoteric prayer group on Wednesday evenings designed to help suppress uncontrollable urges. The men all sat in their creaky wooden folding chairs close together in a small room lined with a half dozen room heaters. The temperature in the room would hit 105 degrees. They sweated through their clothes as they chanted and swayed, praying their prayers, begging God for the strength to cool the heat of their unspeakable urges. Yakov barely looked at the faces of the men in the room. He didn't want to look into their eyes or know who they were. He didn't want to see what they were struggling against or let them see his demons either. Those who recognized him thought only how righteous he was, the grandson of the Rebbe, participating in this arduous ritual, someone so learned, so wise for his age, so obviously unblemished, seeking even higher levels of connection with the divine. If they only knew! If they could only see into him, they'd understand that since that night when he shouted the irrevocable "No!" every ounce of him had been wondering if he should have said yes, if he wasn't meant to say yes. And the sweating was not helping. He could feel the power of the pleasure that had run through him, and understood he would want to know that power again, if he didn't somehow learn to control it.

Within a month, Daniel began talking loudly in the hallways at yeshiva and shul about this girl or that he was meeting for a possible *shidduch*. Yakov said nothing, kept his distance.

After Daniel had a second, then a third meeting with Gavrielle, and decided for himself that she was the "one," he pulled Yakov aside in the hallway at shul and unfolded his highly polished reasoning.

"I want to thank you. Everything that has happened to me in my life has led me to this moment. Everything has its purpose and meaning. Now that I have found Gavrielle, I see that. All of it, all we've been through will make me appreciate her, honor her in the way Hashem meant for a man to honor a woman." That was the closest they'd come to reflecting on that night, on the window of opportunity that had opened up, that let the air flow around all those years of unspoken, unheard-of desire, a window that had slammed shut with Yakov's resounding "No!" and could not be pried open.

Now, on Daniel's wedding day, Yakov woke up with a sense of dread. Was everything, as Daniel said, truly leading him to this moment, to have some inevitable wedding to some inevitable girl, and leading Yakov to do the same? Or did that night have some other meaning, some other clear message for them both? It was a message that frightened Yakov and sent him into a panicked flight, sealing Daniel's feelings up as tightly as the wound over his eye had healed. *That* message, *that* information, they were choosing to ignore.

But where did that leave them? Where do those feelings go? Would they eventually evaporate in the heat of the prayer room? Would they vaporize in the presence of Daniel's personal angel on their wedding night?

Behind him Yakov could hear voices and shuffling down the hall leading to the kitchen. The caterers were probably arriving. Yakov's stomach tightened at the thought of time and opportunity slipping, slipping away.

Daniel spoke quietly but quickly as if keeping pace with the fast-moving train he was on and couldn't get off now.

"It was not you who was a coward that night; it was the opposite, really. I was fooling around with something, something very...wrong. I see that now. How you reacted that night was *beshert,*" he used the Yiddish word for destiny, God's will. "It was a test I almost failed, if it hadn't been for your strength, your holiness."

Yakov searched his friend's moist eyes. He saw that at this moment Daniel believed what he was saying. "And even the cut on my head was a blessing. It was a wake-up call. 'Wake up!' Hashem was saying, and now I have this little scar to always remind me." He took off his wide-brimmed fedora. "See?"

Yakov stepped toward him to see the shiny stripe of raised and shiny skin above Daniel's eye. "I see," he said. Some other day in their lives, a few months ago, he might have touched it, touched him.

"So you see," Daniel went on, "it's beshert, and here I am today with an angel delivered to me. I thank you for what you did...that night. You saved my life."

In the months that passed since that night, it seemed that Daniel had turned himself inside out. *No,* thought Yakov, *more like outside in.* He looked for the telltale seams along the perfectly cut cloth of Daniel's new outlook. Maybe there was a loose thread he could pull to open a hole in this expertly tailored garment he called his "saved" life.

Three months ago, in his bedroom, Daniel would have had Yakov as close as his own breath, the two of them, one body. Today he placed him on a towering pedestal as a hero, a holy man. A savior.

"What did I save you for? And me, what am I saved for? A life of wondering, pretending?"

"Who's pretending? I'm not pretending." Daniel was losing patience. "I am living as what I am. I'm living as a Jew. The only way a Chasid can live." Resignation flickered across his eyes, then a pleading for Yakov to let it rest. Let it rest.

There was nothing Yakov could say to that. He knew well what the Torah said explicitly. Leviticus 18:23: "Do not lie with a man as one lies with a woman; it is an abomination." *Toyevah.* There was no equivocation, no *Halachic* interpretations to mitigate its decisive meaning. In the days of the Holy Temple in Jerusalem, when a Jewish holy council of judges enforced law, The Sanhedrin, it was a crime punishable by death. Today, living such a life meant another kind of death—complete ostracism by the community, utter rejection by family, friends, the Rebbe. It would be like death, he knew. He thought of his mother, his uncle, his grandfather. They would rant and tear their clothes and say kaddish, over him, the prayer for the dead, as someone lost to them, lost to God.

"But what about Gavrielle, Daniel? Can it be fair to her?" Yakov wanted to know. He had to know. He wasn't sure. Maybe it could work. He himself gave a *dvar torah* to the congregation just yesterday, extolling the sacred nature of women, describing their very beings as an extension of God's creativity on earth, of holiness incarnate. Was he preaching what he needed so desperately to believe in? He wanted to be convinced it was true. For him. For Daniel, too. "Will it be fair for her to be married to a man for the rest of her life who can't really love her completely?"

"I can love her!" He looked away. "I mean, it's...just the beginning. My love for her will grow...over time. It's a shidduch, Yakov, not a Hollywood movie. We will have a life. We will have children. They'll surround me at the Shabbes table. That's what I want. The love...will grow. It will grow."

Yakov impulsively reached out, grabbed Daniel's belt buckle and yanked at it. "And what about what's in here—will that grow for her, too?"

Daniel looked at him, momentarily shocked by his friend's bold remark and gesture. Then he threw his head back and laughed in a way Yakov hadn't heard in some time. "I don't know!" He laughed again. And Yakov found himself laughing, too. There was a relief in the laughter, and he felt closer to Daniel than he had in months.

All at once, the fluorescent lights above them blinked on and the color and smiles were drained from their faces by the flat white light. Yossi, Yakov's uncle, stood taking up a good portion of the arched entrance to the hall. He dwarfed Raphael, the skinny Jamaican janitor at his side, whose dark face reflected the long tubes of light.

"Am I interrupting? Having a little wedding rehearsal? Which one of you is the bride?" Yossi laughed at his barbed humor. Daniel chuckled nervously. He had always felt uncomfortable around Yossi. Though nothing illicit had been going on, Yakov's uncle always had a way of making him feel caught, making him feel as though his secrets lay on his sleeve for him to pluck and let fly like so many chicken feathers in the wind.

"Where is the ramp?" Yossi boomed. "How am I supposed to get the Rebbe's wheelchair up to the chupah? Either I have a ramp or the whole thing has to be dismantled and put on the floor."

Now Yakov remembered that he'd left the house early with the excuse that he'd see to setting up the room for his grandfather's arrival. The Rebbe had been getting stronger these last few weeks and insisted he would make his first public appearance since his stroke by officiating at Daniel's wedding. Daniel was, after all, Yakov's oldest and dearest friend. The Rebbe didn't normally "do" weddings, but he had been very excited about Daniel's engagement. And, of course, Daniel and his family were beside themselves with the honor. Another sign for Daniel, Yakov supposed, that God approved, that God loved him even more for his change of mind over the past months.

"You will be the next *chassan*, the next groom; the way is clear now," the Rebbe told Yakov, when he received the formal letter from Daniel's parents, asking for his blessing for the match. No one in their community would proceed with such an event or other life-changing decisions without the Rebbe's express permission or his learned and holy interpretation of any given situation. Such was the dependence of the Chasid on his Rebbe that it was a common practice for many to also visit the graves of past Rebbes, here and abroad, and pray for blessings, answers, and heavenly intervention on their behalf in matters of health, happiness, and mortgage approvals. The graves could be seen littered with scraps of paper; cracks in the masonry of the mausoleums would be stuffed and overflowing with Post-it note invocations for holy guidance.

What had he meant when the Rebbe said that the way was clear for Yakov to be married now? He wondered about that and whether, in his wisdom, the Rebbe knew the truth about Daniel and him. *No. No,* thought Yakov, *that isn't it.* He simply meant that the friendship was so close and we had done everything together, so naturally I would probably marry, too, now that Daniel, another "old" bachelor at twenty-three, was making the leap.

"Dat ramp, she unda the platform. Just slide out da back," Raphael said matter-of-factly.

"Well, get it out of there and set it up," barked Yossi. "We pay you to work, not state the obvious. Yakov, if you can fit it in to your rehearsal schedule, the Rebbe wants you back upstairs. He will not come down without you and he wants to be here before the crowd."

"Of course, I'll go immediately." Yakov turned and extended his hand to Daniel. "Mazel Tov, my friend. I'll be back to dance at your wedding." As they grasped each other's hands, strongly, meaningfully and then let go, Yakov felt all that he'd hoped to accomplish with Daniel before his wedding slip away. And suddenly he couldn't quite put his finger on what it was he had hoped for—to convince Daniel of what? And then to do what? Leave the community, turn their backs on everything, and run away as lovers? It was all unthinkable. *Maybe*, Yakov thought, as he left his friend and walked out of the room, *maybe Daniel was right about everything. Maybe everything, God willing, would turn out for the best.*

* * *

This would be the zillionth wedding Rachel attended in this hall, yet each time she passed through the wide archway into the shimmering room, she was filled with the sense of excitement that new beginnings bring. Having seen the room during the day for lectures or community meetings, with its uncompromising fluorescent lights and peeling paint, she always marveled at the transformation that took place, when only the two rows of dimmer-switched chandeliers were lit. The white rectangles of industrial light, the water-stained drop ceiling, along with the other flaws of the room, retreated into the shadows above the hanging, crystal-laden lamps. Below them, romance happened. The marriages in her community were largely arranged, and most of the couples had only spent a collection of hours together before deciding to marry, but there was still a breathless romance to it all. Everyone there was in love with the idea of the marriage, what it meant. Even Rachel, who, for the most part, felt ambivalent about the inevitability of marriage, could easily be swept up in the frantic celebration that took place with each wedding. The weddings were a giant community love fest—a colossal affirmation of their way of life. A wedding reached back to touch the ancients who created the institution with its intricate laws of order, purity, and ethics governing everything from intimate relations to the division of property. A wedding reached forward to insure their future as a people.

Rachel knew this wedding would be extravagant. The bride's family was wealthy, in the diamond trade by way of South Africa. And with the

Rebbe's decision to officiate, they would have pulled out all the stops to make it an even more impressive event. Everyone would be there.

At least 300 silver and gold balloons covered the ceiling above the chupah, creating a second, higher canopy with their shimmery, pearlized ribbons streaming downward like so much moonlit angel hair. *That looks amazing*, thought Rachel, filing the effect in her "my wedding" mental file, a collection she would never admit she kept, but pulled out during these occasions. Even the *mechitza*, the tired and wobbly lattice divider that separated the room into a men's side and a women's side during the ceremony and during the music and dancing that would go on late into the night, was dressed up with another hundred or so of the shiny metallic balloons. Their ribbons wove through the whitewashed lattice, all but hiding the dusty silk flowers and plastic ivy that usually served as camouflage between the sexes.

The room was packed. The roaring noise of conversation, laughter, children squealing as they ran about, circulated like a tornado around Rachel. She could hear bits of conversation as she scanned the faces, almost all of them familiar. If she couldn't tell you everyone's first name, she could at least place the family: That's the youngest Schwartzberg; that's what's-his-name, the butcher's oldest son; look at Channi Weissman, or is it Weissbaum, with that peach-colored suit? Didn't I see that on Sarah Silverman at the last wedding? And there are Avram and Sarah Shulman, Lark's parents, looking slightly self-conscious, her mother always touching and checking her sheitl, as if it might fly off her head at any moment, her father twisting a strand of his beard between his thumb and forefinger. Rachel tried to picture them as Lark had described them to her—her father with his long hair tied back in a ponytail, her mother, braless and shoeless, dancing around the house with the stereo blasting to some rock and roll music. She couldn't. She didn't have to picture where Lark was at this moment. She knew she'd be in her unofficial headquarters—the ladies' bathroom.

She hadn't seen Lark since shul yesterday. As stimulated as she felt by the festivities, she ground the heels of her hands against her tired eyes and stifled a yawn, having been up half the night, running over the events of the past two days in her head. She couldn't help it. It all seemed to play out on a loop in her brain, disturbing her on some core level, making her second-guess herself about everything.

Friday at school had been unnerving enough for Rachel, but after the scene with "Jamal" in the park, she and Lark were both rattled. Once at shul, Lark had stayed in the bathroom most of the service, then joined Rachel in the balcony only at the tail end, in time for the *dvar torah*, a talk reflecting on the day's Torah portion, given by, of all people, Yakov, the Rebbe's grandson! She couldn't remember the last time she'd heard him speak, though she knew he spoke often. Maybe she'd spent more time in the bathroom with Lark than she thought. Or maybe she'd never paid attention to the Rebbe's grandson as she had in the last twenty-four hours.

Rachel had felt her face flush as he walked forward to the bima, where minutes before a group of men crowded around, taking *aliyahs*, or "going up" for their turn at blessing a reading from the week's Torah portion. Each man swooped up to the platform, his long tallis bellowing behind him like a superhero's cape, to take the honor. Grasping the corner of the tallis where the fringes fell, he touched the corner—not his fingers—to the point on the Torah parchment where the reading began, then brought the fringes to his lips, kissing the place that touched the words that God gave him to live by. He blessed the opportunity and praised God...*praised be Adonai, the exalted one...throughout time...praised be Adonai who rules the universe....praised be Adonai who gives us the Torah.*

"Emor." Yakov began with the name of the portion and a kind of confidence that Rachel had not seen in him the night before. As he spoke he was transformed from the previous evening's silent, sensitive boy into a young man who took hold of the words he spoke, and the crowded room, with an innate power.

He quoted from the portion, "And you shall not desecrate my holy name; and I shall be sanctified in the midst of the children of Yisrael. I am God, who sanctifies you, who took you out of the land of Egypt to be a God for you." Whatever miscellaneous noise could be heard—feet shuffling, women whispering and children whining, old men endlessly coughing and sniffling—slowly died down, as if on a dimmer switch activated by the sound of Yakov's now commanding voice.

He looked down for a moment at the podium's surface, but Rachel saw from the balcony that there were no papers there, no note cards to which he might refer. He looked only at his pale hands that gripped the brass railing across the podium's edge, as one might grip the railing of a ship being tossed at sea. He seemed to be holding on, or holding himself down, as though he might float away on a passing wave.

"In this passage, Rashi explains, Hashem is conveying that He rescued us from Egypt on the condition that we sanctify His name. As Jews, we are commanded to bring greatness to Him in the eyes of the world through our dedication to Him, even if this means making the ultimate dedication—giving up our lives if particular circumstances call for it." He paused, stretched his fingers, and then resumed his white-knuckled grip.

"Does this mean that Hashem wants us to go out and sacrifice our lives for Him? Well, the answer is yes..." A quiet murmur rose from the crowd, skull-capped heads nodded, women clutched their sleeping babies a little tighter.

"...And no," Yakov continued, relieving and building the tension at the same time. "Hashem doesn't want our death in celebration of His name. But He demands our life. He demands that we give our life, the 'entire House of Yisrael' gives its life, to sanctify, to make holy his name and his people.'" Rachel shifted in her chair. Lark groaned under her breath beside her, "Oh, pah-leese!" Rachel kept her eyes focused on the top of Yakov's head. She didn't feel like joining Lark in the usual eyeball rolls and pot shots they took during the weekly sermon. Things didn't feel usual today.

Abruptly, Yakov lifted his face to the gallery, as though speaking directly to the women. "Rabbi Moshe Chaim Lutzatto writes in his book, *Path of the Just*, 'We are placed in this world where many are the things which distance us from God.' It is up to us to recognize the distractions placed in the way of our having an intimate, holy relationship with Hashem. These distractions can be a potent elixir, a seductive, intoxicating diversion from true good. Sanctifying the name of Hashem, as commanded in Emor, sanctifying our presence in this life, means declaring a personal pledge of sobriety from these distractions; waging a personal battle against that which lures us away on a daily, sometimes moment-to-moment basis." Was he looking straight at her? Rachel felt frozen in her chair, frozen in place by the intensity of those blue eyes, which seemed locked on her as he continued.

"I speak to the women, not because they have the most to glean from these words, but because they are the embodiment of this principle. Hashem demands less from them in prayer and daily devotion, not because of their diminished status amongst us, but because of their innate holiness, a state that need not be reinforced so rigidly all day long, as is the case with men. While men are easily distracted by unholy pursuits, women routinely live their lives for the good of others, for the good of the community. They naturally give themselves over to the highest of vocations, which has little to do with accumulating wealth or perpetuating beauty, indulging in pleasures or establishing power, but everything to do with the continuum of our people, of our faith, of our tradition. They are the source of creation on earth, the garden that nurtures our children, the sowers of the seeds of our bond to Hashem."

Lark snickered and leaned in to whisper to Rachel, "Oh, is that why they treat us like we have the cooties for two weeks out of every month? If we're so holy, why do we have to soak in the mikvah like dirty dishes before they can touch us?"

Rachel barely heard what her sarcastic friend said. She instead kept her eyes trained on Yakov even as he moved his gaze back toward the men in the sanctuary below, concluding his message with a call to action that seemed to reach up to her high seat and grip her around the throat. He asked for all congregants to look within, to look to their lives and name their obstacles, the shiny trinkets of worldly pleasures, for what they were: impediments to living an ordained and holy life, roadblocks on the path to righteousness, interruptions in a lifelong conversation with God.

Rachel's mind whirled even as she went through the motions of the closing prayers of the service, even as Lark chatted nervously as they descended the stairs and entered the large social hall to partake in a kiddish sponsored by the family of the following day's bride. Juice and coffee and cake. Cookies and tidbits of gossip. Rachel felt as though she were floating apart from it all, apart from Lark, apart from the various girls that swirled around them, from the mothers who had, as predicted, heard of Rachel's mishap at school the day before. It all occurred in a blurry sequence with only one sharp image coming back to her again and again, creating a tight feeling in her stomach, a catch in her breath: the image of Yakov speaking to her, looking directly at her, from the bima. His eyes saying to her again, as they did the night before, *"I know you, I know what your life is all about."*

"I said what time are you going to the wedding?" Lark looked at her like she was examining a bug on the tip of her nose. "Are you okay? You don't look so good."

"I'm fine. Um...I was just thinking about the dvar torah."

"Are you kidding? Why? Oh, wow, wasn't he supposed to come over to your house for dinner last night? Did he? What happened? I can't believe you didn't tell me everything."

Rachel couldn't believe that Lark was acting as though nothing had happened that morning to alter the normal rhythm of their friendship. *So what? You've had a black boyfriend from the neighborhood for the past several months without telling me, but let's just girl-talk about my "date" with the Rebbe's grandson anyway. I feel confused about my feelings for him, any ad-*

vice? Maybe we could double date? The cynicism died on her lips. Rachel didn't have the confidence for a confrontation with Lark and she was too shaken by all the events of the past twenty-four hours to really know where she stood.

"He came over with his uncle."

"That guy? What's his name, Yossi? He's scary."

"Do you want me to tell the story, or no?"

"Go ahead, I'm sorry."

"They came over; it was fine. He...he wasn't what I expected. He was shy, but then, I don't know. We went up on the roof to talk."

"Alone?"

"Yes."

"And?"

"Well, we just talked. He didn't sound like, you know, the Rebbe's grandson, like he sounded today. He was...interesting. Different than I thought he would be. I don't know what I thought."

"So, what do you think now? That was some performance he gave today."

Rachel was suddenly hot with anger. She felt as she had the night before, like she wanted to defend Yakov—defend herself, too. Why did people around her feel like they could just ride over her, insult her, and expect her to just spring back, bouncy and wholesome as a well-made matzo ball?

"That was some performance you gave in the park today, too," was the best Rachel could do.

"Touché." Lark decided to head for neutral ground, figuring that today was not the day for her to offer her opinion on who Rachel should or shouldn't have a crush on.

"So... of course, you are going to the wedding tomorrow? What time are you going? My parents will be there early, as usual—apparently my mom home-nursed a relative on the bride's mother's side, something like that—so I have to walk over with them." They set a time to meet, and then Rachel was swept into an interrogation by Mrs. Rosen, the school nurse, who wanted to make "double-sure" her favorite patient was feeling better.

*   *   *

Rachel pushed the heavy swinging door to the ladies' lounge with her shoulder. She held two crackers piled high with cream cheese and smoked salmon, dotted with capers, one in each hand.

"Are you coming out? The ceremony is going to start in a few minutes. Your father is looking for you."

Lark sat cross-legged on the vanity counter that ran the length of two converging walls in the ladies' lounge. She sat with her back to the corner. Behind her were counter-to-ceiling mirrors that also ran the length of the walls, creating a long reflected chorus line of Larks behind her. She was always fascinated with that effect and told Rachel it reminded her of the black and white musicals you could see on cable TV. Rachel had never seen one, so the reference was lost on her, but many hours in this very lounge were spent with Lark acting out, for the benefit of Rachel's "culturally malnourished" mind, entire scenes from popular movies, or television shows, or novels that Rachel had never heard of. "You can't not know who Archie Bunker is!" she'd demand, then launch into a particularly memorable episode, doing all the parts and the voices that, according to her, had more of a moral and ethical impact on her than the entire past few years of religious studies. Rachel had been a delighted audience. She received an abridged yet highly individualized education on pop culture that ran the gamut from *I Dream of Jeannie* to *I Love Lucy*, from *The Graduate* to *The Godfather*.

Rachel handed her the crackers and watched as Lark made them into a fat sandwich that she devoured in one bite. With a full mouth and crumbs flying she said, "Is this all there is...friggin' lox? Oh, right, the important food happens after they determine that the bride is actually a virgin, I forgot!" She sent herself into a spasm of laughter that nearly choked her.

Two women talking loud and fast nearly knocked Rachel over as they barreled into the lounge.

"Oh, Rochella, so sorry! What a beautiful suit. I loved it when I saw it at your sister Sara's wedding. And it still fits you beautifully after all this time. So, when are we going to dance at your wedding already? Mmmmm?"

They didn't wait for an answer, and Rachel only offered a tolerant, embarrassed smile as they passed by her and through the door to the bathroom area.

Lark rolled her eyes in response. Rachel just shrugged. She was used to it.

"Listen," Lark said, waving her over, "I have to talk to you, seriously." She hesitated, knowing she was on a bit of shaky ground with her friend. "I know that you were upset yesterday, you know, with Jamal and everything. How could you not be? I mean, it was a shock and that is totally my fault. I am so used to being paranoid, my parents and everything. But I know I should have trusted you...that part was totally unfair and I am so sorry about that..."

"It's okay," Rachel offered as an automatically comforting response, but she didn't know how okay she was about it.

"No, really. It's not okay, but I guess I want it to be okay because you're my best friend. I really care about what you think. Maybe that's why I was afraid to tell you." Lark took in an audibly deep breath and continued, "But I want you to get that I really care about him, too. He's, well, he's...incredible. He's so...real." She said it as if it was the ultimate defining word. Rachel had no idea what she meant.

"He's real?"

"I don't know if you can understand. No, wait, I know you can and I want you to." She spun herself around to look at her gallery of reflections, as if she were signaling them all to come to her rescue, to help her find the words to say what she wanted to say. She continued, making eye contact with Rachel's image in the mirror. *I can face you better this way*, her eyes were saying.

"I feel so real with him, so myself. I'm not following a bunch of rules that someone is imposing on me. I'm just feeling and moving and doing Lark's thing. And he's not looking at me and saying, 'I can't like you because you're white or Jewish or not Jewish enough' or whatever. He just wants me around as me. Do you understand?"

"I guess so," Rachel answered, but she was feeling impatient. Normally, she had unlimited capacity for Lark's philosophizing, but at that moment she wanted to just get out of that perfume-y, windowless little room. She suddenly didn't want to miss today's ceremony. She wanted to see the Rebbe, shrunken and small as he seemed in his wheelchair, and she wanted to see Yakov, constantly at his side like a power source the withering man could plug in to. Lark went on.

"Listen, Rocky, I've been trying to, you know, meet up with Jamal, to have a special sort of date, where we could be alone and just have some time together, but it never works out. I mean he could hardly just come over to my house or anything. Anyway, we made a date to meet tonight and it's perfect because this wedding is going to go on until two a.m. and no one is going to notice if I'm not here, especially my parents. My father will be drunk by midnight and my mother will be too busy worrying about who's talking to her and who isn't and her wig and everything. But, what I'm saying is, I need you to cover for me just in case. You could just say I'm in the bathroom or, better yet, say I got my period and didn't feel good and went home. I'll be home before they get there."

The two women came bursting out of the bathroom at that moment, still talking fast and furious, and shaking the water from their manicured fingers.

"Rochella, you are going to miss the ceremony hanging around in here," one of them said as they both threw a sidelong glance at Lark.

"I'll be right out," she assured them as they rushed out the door, then turned back to Lark and her infinite reflected incarnations.

"Lark," her voice sounded whiny, "I wish you didn't tell me. I wish I didn't know anything. I wish I didn't even see you at the park yesterday. I don't want to lie to your parents, and I don't know if this whole thing is a good idea. I'm afraid for you. Where are you meeting him? Is it safe? Do you know if it is safe to be alone with this guy? What do you really know about him? What are you going to *do* with him?" She emphasized the "do" in a way that made it seem like an accusation.

Lark chewed her lower lip, as though she needed to stop some answer from spilling out; stop some unretractable something from ricocheting off of all those mirrors and piercing, laser-like, through everything, every tenuous line that connected her and Rachel, every feeling they had for each other. She could feel the moisture rising in her eyes as she realized that in the next moment Rachel was going to become part of "them" for her: those she couldn't trust, those who were a part of what she had to tolerate until she wouldn't have to anymore, those who she'd lie to and pretend around. She'd been doing that for months with Rachel with regard to Jamal, but now the rest of her would have to be tucked away too, wedged somewhere behind her tightly folded arms, her set jaw, her cynical eyes.

"Forget it," Lark finally said. "You're probably right. And the truth is I don't really feel that well. Maybe I am getting my period. Maybe I will go home." She swept herself off the slick Formica and passed Rachel on her way to the bathroom door. "You better get out there; it sounds like it's starting. See ya, Rochella." Rachel knew she was being mocked with the endearing Yiddish version of her name, but before she could say anything, Lark slipped through the door and left her facing her own chorus line of Rachels staring blankly back at her from the mirror.

CHAPTER NINE

Y es! The bag was still there. She could see the brown paper edge of it sticking out from underneath the mailbox on the corner. She walked directly up to the box, pulled open the little door, and pretended to mail a letter. *Why am I pretending? Who cares?! Who's looking?* She quickly squatted down, snatched the crinkled bag, and, pressing it to her chest, walked half a block before she realized she was headed the wrong way. *Oh, smooth,* she congratulated herself. *Real smooth...just mailing invisible mail and picking up my special delivery from under the mailbox. No problem! Not at all nervous.*

She was laughing at herself, but she was nervous. Leaving the wedding unnoticed was easy. When she was wandering out the door, trying to look as nonchalant as possible, the major buffet line was forming, the Klezmer band was kicking in, and the vodka and wine were flowing. By the time the dancing began at around eleven p.m., no one, not even her parents, would give her whereabouts a thought. The rest of the evening would require more of her.

First of all, she had the brilliant idea that she wanted to dress up for the occasion, and she didn't mean the suffocating little number she was currently wearing with its nearly ankle-length skirt and long sleeves. *What's wrong with these people? Don't they know it's practically sum-*

mer? She was sweating through the dress, but it had little to do with the balmy night air. In the bag she had a few wardrobe items that would hardly fit into the Chasidic dress code: an off-white, lacey halter-top that tied around her neck and fit nice and snug because of the Lycra. She was in love with Lycra—it made her boobs look really great, or at least that's what the tattooed sales girl said to her when she tried it on at that tiny shop in the village a few days earlier. Is there anything wrong with great-looking boobs? The black leggings had Lycra, too. What's the point of having a great tush if you can't even show it off? She wanted to show it off, wanted to see the outline of her own body, and wanted to surprise him with it, too. It was still a mystery to Lark what he actually saw in her, what he wanted with the Jewish girl in the boxy skirts and thick stockings. Her mother, Sarah, insisted she was beautiful, but that was her job, wasn't it? Lark only felt awkward much of the time, too tall at almost five foot ten, too much auburn hair that circulated wildly around her face, a face that was a little too round in the cheeks, pointy at the chin, a host to freckles, and green eyes that gravitated toward her nose, giving her a vague crossed-eyed look when she was tired or refused to wear her glasses. It didn't exactly all come together as beauty in her mind, in her mirror, but it seemed to work for the Rain Man. The way he looked at her gave her startling information: she was desired. Whatever he may have felt about her looks, it was clear he wanted her, needed to be with her. If what had compelled him toward her was the excitement and danger of tasting forbidden fruit or a longing to get at what lay beneath all the propriety, she was going to let him have it at last. She wanted to see his face when she walked up to him in the new outfit, watch as his eyes and mind registered just what she had waiting for him under the long skirt.

Lark looked at her watch. They were supposed to meet in twenty minutes. Jamal had set the meeting place as the entrance to a dance club a friend of his ran. The place was at least a ten-minute walk from where she was, giving her ten minutes to figure out how to get the outfit on and stash her "good girl" clothes so she could change back later on her way home. She couldn't have risked hiding the clothes in her room or wearing the outfit under her clothes. So she took a chance with the mailbox. Somewhere, girls my age are living normal lives, but not here, not tonight. Not me. Now, she just had to find a place to change.

Lark scanned the street. A liquor store. Forget it. A kosher Chinese take-out. They have a bathroom, but I could be recognized there. A convenience store. Worth a try. She crossed the street and pulled open the door. The place was empty except for the cashier who sat smoking and staring at a small TV screen behind a wall of three-inch Plexiglas. It reminded Lark of those exhibits at the Museum of Natural History she'd seen years ago—tableaux of life behind glass. Dusty mannequins with bad wigs in their fake natural habitats, populated with glass-eyed animals and plastic insects, papier-mâché mountains and cellophane streams.

If I knock on the glass, will the cashier respond, all three hundred pounds of her, or will she just gaze forever at the little TV, eternally poised to purchase, for only six easy payments of $14.95, the complete set of top-ten hits of the sixties, seventies, and eighties?

She responded, but barely, smoke streaming from her nostrils, making the little cage cloudier still behind the already cloudy and scratched plastic.

"Yeah?"

"Can I use the bathroom?"

"Bathroom's for customers only."

"Hey, listen, I really gotta go. I don't have my wallet with me, but I'll come back tomorrow and buy something, really. I live near here. I'll buy something tomorrow."

"If you live near here then go use the toilet at home."

She turned back to the TV and the conversation was clearly over.

"Bitch," Lark muttered as she walked to the door clutching her drooping paper bag. As an afterthought she ran her hand along the display of gum that lined the shelf under the partition. With one slow sweep she upended box after box and stepped daintily around them as dozens of the soft rectangles clunked to the floor.

"Bitch," she said louder this time and walked back into the night.

It was as welcome as the sun rising after a long, sleepless night when she spotted the golden arches beaming at her from the next block. Not much chance of being recognized there. Cheeseburgers. Bacon burgers. Bathrooms. Bingo!

There was no mirror in the bathroom, but she knew she looked good. She felt good. The low-heeled shoes she had on weren't exactly right for her new look, but new shoes had not been in the budget, since her savings consisted of money she lifted from her father's wallet whenever she could, and the few dollars her mother would push at her when she cashed her paycheck twice a month. Anyway, she doubted her shoes would be the center of attention this evening. She batted around the bottom of the bag to find the little pot of lip-gloss she'd palmed at the checkout counter when buying the clothes. Lark justified her occasional shoplifting habit—how else could she ever have anything nice? Anything normal?

Carefully, she dabbed some on, managing to get a look at her lips in the aluminum surface of the toilet-paper holder. She rolled her lips to smooth the goop out, puckered, kissed the pungent air, and giggled. She was a nervous wreck, but the adventure tickled her all the same. She walked back the two blocks to the mailbox. This time she didn't bother to mail any imaginary letters, but she did do a quick check to see if anyone was watching her before she nestled the crinkled bag containing her clothes in the shadowed area under the box. Lark needed them to be there when the evening was over—even if she hated the dress, she didn't want somebody taking off with it.

Checking her watch, she had eight minutes to be on time to meet him.

How strange it felt to have the silky night air on her bare back, her thick hair swaying across her shoulder blades, and to watch the outline of her legs scissoring, reflected on the dark glass storefronts she passed as she made her way to the club. She felt naked, but clean. It hit her that all the layers of clothing she'd been forced to wear the past few years made her feel dirty, like she had something that needed to be concealed. With nothing to hide, she felt honest.

There was a crowd on the sidewalk outside the club. A big, muscular black man with dreadlocks that stuck out like a small explosion from his head controlled the flow and the velvet rope that only moved aside at his discretion.

She spotted him right away—the wave of yellow in a sea of brown and black. His back was to her, the long coat scraping the ground, floating above his thick cowboy-boot heels. She stopped, suddenly self-conscious about just walking up to him through the middle of the crowd. The white girl. The Jew. No, that wasn't it...that didn't matter. She just wanted him to come to her. To welcome her. She recognized a few of his cronies around him, including the ever-present Pee Cee, but not the girl who hung on his shoulder, waving her long red nails and laughing.

Turn around. Turn around, she chanted like a mantra in her head. She worried that he might not recognize her, that he'd be waiting to see the skirt, the cardigan, but she shrugged it off. He knows I'm no yeshiva girl. He's had his hands on me enough times to know my body when he sees it.

Turn around. Turn around. And so he did. And his face at that moment was worth waiting for. With his utter surprise and unguarded approval she felt her confidence drop back into her like a missile falling from the sky. She walked toward him and he toward her, leaving the slack-jawed fingernail girl behind him.

He didn't even try to stop smiling. Lark didn't look directly at him, but focused on his left ear, counting the little hoops that decorated it, in an effort to control a rush of blood that rose from her feet and heated up her whole body. She heard catcalls from behind him as his friends realized who she was. She had to laugh.

"I was looking forward to being alone with you, but now I'm going to have to show you off for a little while first." He wrapped an arm around her waist and brought her through the crowd to the velvet rope. A knowing look passed between the bouncer and Jamal. The rope clicked behind them as they entered the noisy club.

The place was cavernous and dark. He held her hand now and walked ahead of her, pulling her through the crowd. They passed the bar and a series of low tables and couches with couples sprawled across them, talking, drinking, smoking joints, a few wrapped around each other, kissing deeply. He made his way to the dance floor, dense with bodies. The music was throbbing with an insistent bass line, thumping from ceiling-high speakers in each corner. She felt the pulse of it in her chest—even if she were deaf, she could have kept the beat and kept up with the dancers closing in around her.

They made their way to the middle of the floor. He slipped off his trademark coat, revealing a simple black t-shirt that clung to his chest and arms but hung loosely around his narrow torso. He folded the coat into a bundle and threw it overhead across the room to Pee Cee, who seemed poised at the edge of the dance floor for the express purpose of catching it and throwing back a scowl of disapproval. She saw the Rain Man's bare arms for the first time, after months of being around him outside, with that coat on. They were chocolaty brown, smooth, sinewy, Chinese characters in dark indigo ink wrapped around his bicep like a garter. She brushed the tattoo with her fingers, and he pulled her close then gave her a little push away. Dance for me, he seemed to say. He began to dance, keeping his eyes fixed on her. Instinctively, she moved to the music.

The last time she danced with a boy was her seventh-grade spring dance sponsored by the PTA of her public school back in Jersey. Even then, her father hadn't wanted her to go, but it was still the early stages of "the insanity," and her mother hadn't quite jumped whole-hog on the bali teshuva bandwagon yet. That night she had danced mostly within a circle of her girlfriends and occasionally, reduced to a giggling mess, she'd agreed to dance across from one of the stiff and awkward boys in her class.

Now this was an altogether different experience. Inches away from each other, pressed in on by the crowd, they moved. He was a natural dancer, but she could tell he worked at it, too. He loved moving his body and he liked having her watch him move it. His hips waved as if unattached to his rib cage, his arms went up into the air then came down slowly, hands caressing his hair, his chest. Lark mirrored his movements, or caught glimpses of women dancing around her and tried to copy what they were doing. She was a natural, too, but certainly not practiced. In his eyes, she could see that she was getting it right.

*　*　*

There was a quality of relief on Daniel's face as he brought his foot firmly down to crush the wine glass that had been carefully wrapped in a cloth napkin and placed before him on the floor under the chupah. The ritual signaled the end of the long ceremony, made longer by the slow pace the Rebbe took to complete it. He had paused often, breathing irregularly—at one point he had just stared off into nowhere while a concerned and horrified crowd held their breath, waiting for him to continue. Yakov, his hand on the Rebbe's shoulder, shook him imperceptibly and bent to speak softly in his ear. The old Rebbe resumed, his one-time bellowing voice at just above a whisper.

Daniel and Gavrielle were whisked away to spend their requisite first moments alone and the room erupted in a cacophony of conversation.

The six-piece band of bearded men took their place on a platform and began to play.

Yakov took his place at a table set expressly for the Rebbe and himself, and Yossi, who was arranging for food to be brought to them. But Yakov had no appetite. He did not, however, refuse a healthy glass of vodka, and sipped it slowly as he scanned the room. Already some of the men and women began dancing in circles on their respective sides of the floor, others standing along the outskirts, clapping and moving in time to the music, anticipating the return of the bride and groom, when the real dancing would begin. The Rebbe's veined and trembling fist lightly pounded the table in time to the beat too, while his other hand scooped at the air in front of him, a gesture of revelry, encouragement. My body may be stuck in this chair, he seemed to be saying, but my soul dances. His eyes brightened and glowed outward from the wrinkled folds of his face. Yakov watched him and suddenly felt overtaken by the depth of his love for his grandfather. He had spent his whole life in the aura of this man, in the circle of his protection; now he felt as though he wanted to protect him—would do anything to protect him.

The band abruptly stopped playing. A drum roll sounded and then someone announced, "Let us welcome the chassan and kallah, Mr. and Mrs. Daniel Adler!" Daniel had a kind of deer-in-the-headlights look on his face, but Gavrielle was smiling broadly, as they were swept into the dancing swirls on separate sides of the room.

Yakov knew he would have to join the dancing soon, to link himself arm over arm with the other men and boys who were now throwing off jackets and whipping ties over their heads, opening shirts a button or two, stopping their momentum only to quickly throw-back little plastic shot glasses full of vodka, or to wipe the dribble off their chins or sweat off their brow. Circle within circle of the dancing men formed, with the innermost circle comprised of Daniel, his father, uncles, brothers, along with the new members of his *mishpucha*, the male in-laws.

Yakov had the Rebbe as his excuse not to dance, but now the revered old man was surrounded by young boys, either pushed over by their parents or just drawn to the old man's kind smile and his pocket full of dollar bills. He patted each child's hand or cheek and said a word or two before pressing a crisp bill into each of their sticky little palms. He would be occupied happily for some time. Yakov was superfluous just sitting there. Still, he sat, sipping his drink.

"Yakov!" He heard his name from the dance floor. Ruvi, Daniel's oldest brother, was waving to him with one arm and holding a wooden chair in the other. "C'mon!" Yakov gulped back the rest of his vodka and jumped to his feet. He made his way to the inner circle, his back being slapped along the way, teasing words of encouragement, "It's about time!" "You're next, my friend." "Get used to it..."

Ruvi grabbed his arm and drew him in through the whirling circles. "Let's go!" He held the chair aloft for a second as a signal to the group. With the help of the others who stopped their dancing, they converged on an already drunk Daniel and muscled him onto the creaking chair, lifting him above their heads and chanting along with the music now escalating in both volume and tempo.

Yakov was directly under the chair, his right hand helping to support the seat below Daniel. He was crushed on all sides by the now nearly frenzied dancers and others helping to keep the groom aloft. Daniel held on for dear life, as the chair bounced and swung from side to side. Yakov studied his friend. Glassy-eyed from the vodka, he seemed happy, supremely at home. Something in his eyes, when they looked down momentarily and found Yakov's, telegraphed, I made it; look, I've really made it.

Someone tossed a scarf made of several cloth napkins tied together to Daniel and they lifted him higher still as they approached the mechitza that separated them from the women. On the other side, Gavrielle bobbed about on her elevated chair, the reveling women straining below her. Daniel tossed one end of the scarf across the divider and between the balloons that floated up there with them. Gavrielle caught it and they "danced" connected this way for several minutes as everyone, including those at tables sitting out the rigors of the ritual, cheered them on.

Yakov felt he couldn't keep up his arms a moment longer and, as though by silent consensus, the chair holding Daniel abruptly plunged to the floor. On the way down, Daniel grabbed Yakov's forearm. As his feet hit the ground, he held on to him, grabbed his other arm, and began to spin him around, keeping time to the Klezmer beat, the buzzing violin. Someone came up behind Yakov and tugged at his coat, which he let slip off, one arm at a time. Someone else passed them sloshing cups of vodka, which they gulped on the fly. Around and around they spun. Yakov waited to feel dizzy, but he didn't as he focused on his friend's laughing face, as he felt Daniel's thick, strong forearms tightening under his grip. Yakov laughed now, too, and the rest of the room seemed to evaporate in a blur, the music withdrawing into the distance. He was just there with Daniel, suspended in some private place. Eventually, Yakov's lungs burned and he could barely catch his breath. Daniel, too, panted and dripped with sweat. As their whirling slowed, slowed and then stopped, they collapsed in on each other, bowed head pressed to bowed head, hands clutching opposite shoulders. They wobbled there for a moment, the clapping and stomping men around them, and they simply held each other. Then someone, perhaps a new in-law, after all, there was so many of them, cut in, "What, tired already? This is just the beginning!" And he funneled Daniel back into the crowd, back into the forming circles, back into the rhythm of the evening.

Yakov retrieved his jacket, which lay in a heap on the floor near the buffet table. He methodically rolled down his sleeves and tucked in his shirt. He buttoned his buttons, shook out the jacket, and put it back on.

"Your collar is all *fahmished* in the back."

"Huh?" He was startled, and turned to see that dark-haired girl from the other night, from Shabbes dinner. She was the most recent in the long line of those he was meant to consider for marriage but never could. But then he remembered the conversation on the roof. She had come to his rescue.

"It's half up and half down." She pointed to her own collar and then at his.

"Oh." Rachel. Her name was Rachel. He fixed the collar and brushed invisible dust from his sleeves. "Thanks."

"Oh, no problem. I notice things like that. My mother says I always notice the things that are wrong first. In the Garden of Eden, she says, I'd point out the snake, then notice the flowers."

"I know what you mean."

"What, that I'm negative?"

"No, just that I know how it is. Seeing the world a little differently from one's mother, or other people in general."

She nodded but couldn't think of what to say next. She couldn't believe she'd had the nerve to walk up to him, but she came to the buffet table to get her mother a plate, and there he was. He was staring out at the dancing men. Sweat trickled down the side of his face and mingled with his spotty beard.

"How do you see this wedding?" he asked her, without looking at her, intent on some point across the room.

She felt like it was a trick question. What was the right answer? Who wanted to know, the boy from the roof or the one at the Shabbes pulpit? And what for? Was God listening? He turned to look at her now, his eyes, those eyes, expectant.

"Hmm? What do you see in all this? I'll tell you what I see. I see that it is all inevitable."

"That's not very romantic." Rachel knew romance wasn't the point, according to everyone, but she couldn't resist the notion.

"Oh, that's not true. It is romantic in a way, because it's as though there is some force stronger than anything, stronger than fear, stronger than desires, stronger than intellect that makes it irresistible, that makes it..." he trailed off.

"Makes it what?" She wanted to know.

He looked at her, her unusual face, smooth skin, soft curves, tiny almost invisible golden hairs that hugged the hollow of her cheeks and the slope of her neck below her ears.

"...makes it right," he finished. "That makes you want to." He turned to her. He wasn't touching her, but it felt as though he was. "I think I want to. Do you?" He took a deep breath and held it, knowing what he was asking, realizing, incredibly, what he was doing.

Rachel was glad she wasn't holding a plate full of food because she would have dropped it then. What was he asking? Did he want to know if she wanted to get married someday or was he asking her to marry him? She searched his eyes for a clue, so she could come up with an answer that wouldn't embarrass her or him. Then she realized, as all her feelings and questions over the past two days flashed across her mind, that her answer to either question was the same.

"Yes," she said holding his gaze. "I want to."

* * *

How could it be closed? But it was. A lone pimply-faced employee could be seen sweeping the floors, making little piles of French fries and balled-up napkins. He refused to even look up as Lark pounded on the glass doors and begged to be let in to use the bathroom. He turned his back on her and dragged the long broom to the far corner of the store. He snapped off a row of lights to make his point: Go away.

It was a quarter to one. She had to be home by one, one-fifteen at the latest. Her parents would stick it out to the bitter end—they wouldn't want to offend anyone—and her mother would have a hard time getting her father to leave. He was still the hearty partier, even if he did his partying now with the holier-than-thou crowd. To Lark it was all the same.

Getting fucked up was getting fucked up—just now he thought he had God pouring the shots, so he could be all superior about it.

Lark was suddenly tired from the enormous effort it had taken and was still taking to pull off the evening, and it was exhausting trying to focus through her own substance-induced fog. At the club they had smoked something that was like pot on steroids. She was flying within three tokes. Really flying. But she didn't freak out; she liked it. The music became fluid around her, like a thick gel that slowed everything down and allowed her to observe it in this magnified way. Her skin became hypersensitive—she remembered thinking that at one point she could feel the air in the room as though it were velvet brushing lightly across the little hairs on her arms.

Right now the little hairs on her arms were standing at attention atop some serious goose bumps. She was cold. The temperature had dropped. It had rained. She wanted to get changed and get home and crawl into bed, way before her parents got home. She turned up and down the street. Everything looked closed except for the convenience store and that was not an option.

Lark started walking in the direction of her street. When in doubt, keep moving, she thought and trusted she'd come up with a plan along the way to get back into her "good-girl" outfit before anyone recognized her. Before she knew it she was staring at her building across the expanse of the park where everything had started, where she first met the Rain Man. It was deserted. The park had been many things to her, a patch of green in the grim and grimy landscape of Crown Heights, a refuge, an escape from the claustrophobia-inducing atmosphere of their apartment, and a playground of the sort that had nothing to do with the swings and the slides and the seesaws. Tonight it might as well take on a new incarnation: dressing room.

She sought out the dark triangle of darkness below the longest slide. She banked on the idea that it was a blind spot to anyone who happened to be looking, and that it was late enough that most of the people living within view wouldn't be searching the shadows of the lonely little park at this hour. She pulled her damp and wrinkled dress from the nearly dissolving paper bag she'd been relieved to find in its hiding place, shook it out a few times and draped it over a rung on the slide's ladder. She started to untie the halter from her neck and thought better of it. Although confident that she was well hidden beneath the slide, there was no sense in standing there half naked. She decided it would be smarter to slip the long and baggy dress over her current outfit and then shimmy it off under cover. It was proving a bit more difficult than she thought, everything was damp, her fingers were numb and cold, and she struggled with the double knot she'd made to secure the halter around her neck. Her heart stopped as she heard voices, shouting from somewhere behind her, echo across the empty street. Were they talking to her?

She spun around to see her mother walking determinedly down the block toward their building. Then she heard her father bellow from behind, "Don't you dare walk away from me, you bitch. I'm the man, do you understand. I AM THE MAN." Her mother whirled around and answered him, "YOU ARE THE DRUNK!" She continued down the block at an angry pace.

Oh shit, thought Lark as panic gripped her, and her hands fumbling with the damn knot, began shaking. Suddenly sober, she tracked her parents' progress down the block and simultaneously took in their respective distances from the front door to the apartment building. Her heart was racing as she came to a decision like a reckless driver suddenly deciding to cross the railroad tracks despite clanging bells and lowering gates. Fuck it, it's now or never. She kicked off her pumps, scooped them up, and nearly fell over as she burst from under the cover of the slide. Her dress clung to the leggings underneath, so she hitched up the skirt as she ran. There was more shouting to her left now.

"SARAH! SARAH! HELP ME." Apparently her father had just this moment reached the blubbering stage of his binge. Lark almost laughed out loud at the utter serendipity of it. Thank you, God! she thought to herself and laughed at that thought, too. My God is arranging for my butt to be saved right now. How would the rabbis explain this? As she quickly glanced toward her bellowing father, she saw her mother turn on her heel and walk slowly back toward his slumped figure on the sidewalk. His own, once-athletic legs had betrayed him and landed him on his ass. Again.

Lark continued her sprint toward home, taking advantage of her otherwise engaged parents and the good graces of the moment. She negotiated the outer door, the lobby lock, and summoned the elevator. Alone inside, she stripped off the leggings, the shredded knee-highs, and nearly broke her neck getting the halter off without being able to undo the knot. She rolled the outfit into a ball and stuffed it under her arm. Letting herself in the apartment she relocked all three locks behind her. That would give her another minute or two. No lights, don't turn on a light, she decided and headed straight for her bedroom and the window that overlooked the street in front of the building.

Down below, her father hung over her mother as they slowly made their way the last fifty feet to the entrance. His head was bowed and shook, which meant he'd be crying and apologizing and moaning to God and his ancestors to forgive him. She couldn't see her mother's face but imagined her tight-lipped determination and tired eyes.

Lark wished she could take a long hot bath. She felt sore and sticky, but there wasn't time. She needed to be in bed and feigning sleep by the time her parents stumbled in. Still, she had to pee badly and she had to clean up. There was blood that she had been prepared for, sort of. That was all part of the romance, the mythology of losing your virginity. But she hadn't realized how really messy it would all be—that she'd be left with the gluey results of the evening soaking her underwear and running down her leg.

She quickly rinsed out her panties and hung them to dry on the showerhead. If her mother asked, the drying panties would jibe nicely with the "I-got-my-period-so-that's-why-I-left-early" excuse. Running the tub water, Lark squatted over the drain to give herself a perfunctory wash and rinse. The hot water and soap burned her soreness, but soothed it at the same time. She pulled her nightgown down from the hook behind the door, slipping it over her head and still-damp body. Opening the bathroom door, she cocked her ear and could hear her parents in the hallway down by the elevator.

Back in her room, she went to the window and opened it. The cool breeze, or maybe it was the realization that she'd made it—by a hair, but still—gave her a shiver. Lark picked up the tight little ball of clothing that was her illicit outfit and checking to make sure there was no one below, or no one watching, she tossed it out and to the far left, so that it would drift and land anywhere but directly under her window. The door to the apartment slammed shut and her parents could be heard bumping about in the foyer. Lark dove onto her bed and pulled the covers up to her neck. She closed her eyes and waited.

In about ten minutes her door creaked open. "Sweetie?" It was her mom. "Lark?" Lark concentrated on relaxing her face, remaining still. She couldn't talk to her mother now. She didn't want to hear her whining about her father, or kvelling over the wedding. She heard her mother shuffle in her slippers across the floor to the window.

"Why is this open?" She asked no one. "You must be freezing." Lark could feel her mother standing over her now. Sarah bent to kiss her forehead, and Lark wished she could just sit up and have her mother hold her and stroke her hair and sing folk songs in her ear the way she had when she was much younger, worlds younger. Instead she lay there, stiff with the knowledge that those days were lost to her now. She held her breath and listened as her mother gently closed the door behind her.

CHAPTER TEN

The adults involved wasted no time in discussing a wedding date for late August. A Thursday would be the most auspicious day, of course, and as luck would have it, the third Thursday of that month was free for everyone and coincided with the perfect time of the month for Rachel to visit the mikvah, a detail discussed only between the women. It was May, so that would give them plenty of time. Long engagements were considered unnecessary in their world, and what was the point in delaying marrying the Rebbe's grandson! He was the catch of the century as far as everyone was concerned, and there was no question about the standing of Rachel's family, the Fines, whose religious lineage, their *yichus,* was impeccable, with a genealogy that revealed Rebbes on at least one side, a fact Mrs. Fine reminded everyone as often as possible. There was even the serendipitous association between the current Rebbe and some relatives of Rachel's father before the war—they had in some way been obliquely responsible for helping to get the Rebbe out and to America, while they themselves had stayed and perished. It was a match made in heaven, and now that it was agreed upon, they wondered why they hadn't realized how really beshert bringing Yakov and Rachel together was to begin with. It was obviously meant to be.

And that was how Rachel supposed she felt from that moment, on the night of Daniel's wedding when their enigmatic agreement had been struck, that her destiny was demanding to be played out, and that Hashem himself had contrived the events of the previous forty-eight hours to broadcast his intention for her. So, now Rachel felt not as though she were making a crucial decision in her life, but more like she was simply following an itinerary carefully laid out for her. The fact that just days before she fancied herself the renegade and entertained thoughts of college and a modern life outside the community took on a blurred quality, like a reminiscence of some distant time. All the positive attention she was getting from her parents helped make her reasons for rebellion drift out of focus as well. "Little Rochella," the over-analyzing, the moody, the exasperating, had suddenly stepped into the light, as far as her parents were concerned, and Rachel could feel the glow, too. Then she talked to Lark.

"You agreed to what?"

The normally unfazed Lark stood slack-jawed on the street in front of Rachel's building where they usually met to walk to school. Rachel had blurted it out before she even said hello.

"I agreed to the *shidduch*. I agreed to marry Yakov Rubinstein."

The realization that she would have to tell Lark the news and suffer through her reaction crept up on Rachel once the initial excitement of her acceptance had passed. The anticipation of that moment kept her up most of the two nights that had passed since the wedding, along with the utter vertigo she felt during the day at having taken such a leap to begin with.

"Tell me you are kidding. This is a joke. A cruel joke. In a minute we are going to be laughing about it, right?"

Rachel shrugged, her palms turned up to the heavens, as if to say, "I couldn't help it." There was no laughter forthcoming.

"This is what happens when I leave you alone at a wedding. Tell me everything, every detail."

Rachel did not have to work hard to summon up the specifics of that night, since she'd been running the roughly eight-minute conversation over and over again in her mind until it had reached mythic proportions: The Eight Minutes That Changed My Life Forever!

When Rachel had uttered her "I want to" to Yakov, he simply nodded. He turned to the room as if looking for someone, then back to her. "Rachel Rubinstein," he said, trying it out. Rachel blushed instantly and tried to suppress a stupid grin that was fighting to take over her face. She liked the way her name sounded joined with his. Forever alliteratively spoken, forever knowing what her path would be, never having to be confused, confounded or adrift. Initials RR, like a railroad car, eternally on track.

"Our parents will talk. Arrangements will be taken care of," he said, suddenly adopting a confident tone. Then he bowed his head slightly to signal the end of the conversation and walked purposefully away from her and across the room. Finding his mother at a table with six or seven other women her age picking at the remnants of their food, he bent his willowy frame down and whispered something in her ear. Rachel laughed out loud as she saw the perfectly coifed and designer-dressed matron nearly choke on whatever it was she had in her mouth, once her son's news had registered. Then, clutching a napkin to her lips, red-faced, she scanned the room and locked her eyes on Rachel, who braced herself for the moment of recognition. Rachel smiled weakly and gave what she now described as her "stupid little wave."

Then a chain of events unfolded that made Rachel feel as though she was watching some clandestine operation, a delivery of a secretly coded message that needed to reach its destination behind enemy lines before it was too late, before anyone changed their minds.

First, Yakov's mother, having swallowed and recovered, threw her napkin down on the table, jumped up from her chair, not a far jump considering her under-five-foot stature, and bolted across the room toward the lattice divider. She left the other women at the table murmuring, leaning over each other to track their friend's trajectory, wondering and whispering about the possibilities for her sudden departure. Leaning around the end of the mechitza, the tiny woman fairly bounced as she waved at and waved over Yakov's uncle Yossi. It took Yossi a few minutes to realize he was being summoned and then another few minutes to negotiate his way across the crowded dance floor, a challenge even for someone half as drunk as he currently was. He had barely reached his sister-in-law when she began talking rapidly, stabbing the air in Rachel's direction with her manicured and jeweled fingers. Rachel felt glued to the spot, on display like a mannequin who would have to wait for someone to come along and move her. At first Yossi looked as if he believed Yakov's mother to be joking, chuckling and shaking his head at her words, but the little woman stamped her high heels into the floor, a tantrum-like tactic that signaled her complete seriousness and a demand for the lumbering giant's attention.

Convinced, Yossi too fixed his gaze momentarily on Rachel, and she, again, forced a smile to meet his almost suspicious perusal of her. Then he bolted forward and the effects of the vodka seemed to evaporate as he strode around the room, avoiding the revelers, toward the front door, where a group of men that included Rachel's father, stood just outside, smoking cigars. Rachel moved over a bit to get a better view of the hallway leading to the door and saw Yossi and her father making their way back into the room. At that point they split up, her father on a mission to deliver the news to her mother, and Yossi headed toward his final destination, the Rebbe, who looked as though he about to doze off in his wheelchair, despite the men and boys who had taken up permanent residence at his table just to be near him.

All this had happened in less than five minutes, though Rachel felt as though she had been standing there for hours since she spoke to Yakov. And where was Yakov? He had set this clockwork operation in motion and then disappeared.

"Is it true?" Rachel's parents had materialized beside her. Her mother took her daughter's ice-cold hand and held it in both of hers. Tears! She saw tears welling in her mother's eyes!

"Is it?" Her father repeated, both impatient and hopeful.

Rachel could barely find her voice, so she nodded and squeezed back at her mother's vise-like grip on her hands.

Her father placed his heavy hand on the crown of Rachel's head, as though bestowing a benediction, and briefly closed his eyes. When he opened them they shone with a light of approval, the likes of which Rachel was certain she had never seen directed at her before. Now she felt her own tears rising.

Her father left them standing there dabbing their eyes and he joined Yossi, already in close conversation with the Rebbe, completing the circle and now making it all irrevocable. Rachel Rubinstein. Though the wedding wouldn't be for months, Rachel knew that this is whom she would be from that moment on.

Despite Rachel's fairly enthusiastic retelling of the evenings events, Lark did not quite embrace the situation as a *fait accompli,* because she spent the entire walk to school ranting and trying to convince Rachel that this was a huge mistake. She passed notes to her during classes all morning, little fortune-cookie messages like, *Rachel Rubinstein, age twenty-five, mother of five,* or *Missing: clear-thinking, interesting individual. Kidnapped and replaced by stranger with sheep mentality.* When Rachel got to her locker after the last class that day, a small note taped to the door read, *You Can Still Change Your Mind!*

"I don't want to change my mind Lark," Rachel said simply, punctuating her stunning remark with the slam of her locker door. She spun the lock, as though putting an exclamation point on her statement. Though Lark's daylong campaign had irritated her, she felt strangely confident. Normally, she would break down under the force of a Lark harangue. She'd be launched into confusion, plagued by uncertainty. She felt none of that now. She hardly even felt the need to convince Lark that she was making the right choice *for her*. Part of that confidence came from the waves of support, attention, and approval she had received and continued to receive from every quarter of her life since the announcement a few days before. She was no longer just the third daughter, the quirky, dark-minded girl who lived on the periphery, an outsider befriending outsiders. She was enjoying the status of favorite child, most popular girl, luckiest bride-to-be, and it was just the beginning.

The other measure of her almost smug certainty came from Lark's change in status in her eyes, her fall from grace, as it were. Since Rachel had discovered Lark's involvement with that guy from the park, the dynamic of their relationship had changed. Lark was no longer the fearless leader of harmless rebellions. She had gone too far—beyond where Rachel could follow or comfortably cheer her on.

"You're sure you want to marry him? Do you even know what you are getting into?"

Rachel thought of her mother. She thought of her grandmother and the sepia smiles of the women that decorated the walls and side tables of her home. She looked at Lark squarely.

"I know what I'm getting into. Do you?"

Lark knew what she meant and took a beat to answer.

"No. I guess I don't know exactly what I'm getting into. But that's the point of it, Rocky. That's exactly the whole point."

CHAPTER ELEVEN

Lark took a circuitous route home. She told herself it was because her father was out of work again, and she was in no hurry to get home. He was home most afternoons now, ambling around, bored, looking for something to pick on, pick over. Like most Chasidic families they had no TV, but her father played the radio incessantly—not tuned to the classic rock stations he once loved, but to various call-in talk shows where equally under-stimulated men and women had nothing better to do than spend their afternoons speed dialing and redialing to get through to some cocky so-called expert and rant their self-important ravings on the airwaves for all to hear. *Who cares?* That's all Lark could think when she heard Sheila from Bayside trying to sound intelligent about the recent bridge and tunnel toll hikes, her Queens accent as thick as her skull, or Clarence from Harlem losing it over what he imagines is the racial issue behind alternate-side-of-the-street parking. Yet her father interacted with these people as though they were in the room. "That's a bunch of shit!" he'd yell, slamming his hand down on the small, worn kitchen table, tucked against the wall near the only window in the small kitchen. He'd sit there smoking, ashtray overflowing, the window open to let the blue haze and his bellowing carry across the alley. His various books were piled up there too, his "studies."

127

This is what drove Lark crazy—he perpetuated this charade of being a serious Judaic scholar, the main reason why he didn't want to or couldn't hold a job for any length of time. He was too preoccupied with his studies! How could he merely function in the mundane world, when a loftier world beckoned him? *Oh, yeah, real lofty*, thought Lark: Him, the Talmud, and the crazy cast of talk-radio characters that floated in to aggravate or validate him each day. He used to go to a kind of part-time yeshiva designed specifically for newcomers to Chasidic life like him, to study and receive instruction, but something about that didn't work out. Lark never got the story. Her father insisted he didn't belong there, that he belonged in the "serious," "real" seminary and it was just a matter of time before a spot would open up for him there.

So, when Lark left Rachel off at her house, she just walked around instead of heading home. While she was walking, she figured, might as well just go by that Jamaican deli that he frequented and the vacant lot, that check cashing place where Pee Cee worked part-time and the basketball courts he'd pick up games occasionally, even though that was really out of the way. She felt like walking! Why not? It was a beautiful day. She wasn't exactly looking for him, but if she ran into him...*It wasn't like he could just pick up the phone and call her or send her flowers or whatever guys are supposed to do after the first time.*

Eventually, she faced the park across from her building and decided to walk through it, instead of around it. It was just shorter that way. Kids and more kids, strollers jutting out at every angle, mothers rocking, swinging, standing ready to catch as their charges climbed, watch as they attempted the next bravest thing. It was a whirl of activity, sound, and color—except for the one she was looking for, that broad swath of yellow.

Lark didn't see it when she first walked into the vestibule of her building, but as she unlocked the inner door and was about to enter the lobby, she spotted the rose: one of those long, thick-stemmed ones, with a big healthy bulb of a rose sitting on top. A yellow rose. Just propped up in the corner. Just like that. A yellow piece of wool tied in a bow around its thorny stem. She stopped and let the entry door slam with its own weight as she bent to retrieve the flower. She looked behind her, and out the door to the street. She peeked out onto the sidewalk and up and down the block. Nothing.

Lark held the rose carefully. It had wide, sharp thorns that reminded her of tiny shark fins all along it. Was it meant for her? Whether it was or not, she was taking it as a small consolation for the past couple of afternoons, wandering the neighborhood like a fool.

She rode the elevator, focusing on the flower as though it had some message to deliver that would become evident upon closer inspection. As she walked down the dim hall toward her apartment, she almost missed the second yellow beauty lying across the worn carpet sample her father had placed as a doormat in front of their door.

Yes! That was her first reaction. *Yes, he cares. Yes, he is thinking of me. Yes, I did not make a huge mistake. Yes, yes, yes!* She laughed to herself with relief as the tension of the past two days melted away, and then laughed again at the thought of Jamal finagling his way into the building, figuring out which apartment was hers, and placing the prizes for her to find. The effort he made to do that, made her feel less embarrassed about her own effort to find him, even while pretending she wasn't looking.

Lark slid her backpack off and gently placed her roses alongside her books in the largest compartment. She didn't want to explain them. She tried the door, but it was locked. If someone was home the door was always left open. Could she possibly be this lucky? She rummaged for her keys and let herself in. No radio idiots assaulted her senses. This was good, she thought, locking the door behind her. When her father got home later, she wanted the warning of him struggling with the locks before she had to deal with him.

She walked through the small foyer and peered around the living room, then into the kitchen. All the props were there: the dusty pile of books, the stained coffee mug, the small mountain of cigarette butts atop an old saucer from a long-ago discarded set of dishes. The window was flung all the way open, but no Daddy. Lark stuck her head out the window and looked up and down the empty, narrow alley. An image of her father's broken body lying eight stories below the window flashed across her mind. Lark often fantasized about his death. If he was late for dinner, which happened often, though God knows where he was, Lark would sit by her window and imagine that the sirens she was hearing blocks away meant he'd been plowed down by a bus or unconscious in a burning coffee shop somewhere. She felt guilty about it—normal, good people aren't supposed to think things like this about a parent—but in the end she felt like her only way to get back at him that didn't involve a confrontation.

Anyway, she rationalized, he deserved it. What did his life amount to but the sum of all their suffering? Hers, her mother's, David's. The cumulative effect of all the bullying, the beatings, the bruises—emotional and otherwise—inflicted on them, had fully canceled out any love she'd ever felt for him. So, when she stuck her head out the window and saw only the empty pavement, she sighed, disappointed.

Then she heard an unmistakable whimper coming from her parents' bedroom. She put her backpack safely in her room and tiptoed down the hall toward the sound. The door was closed, but not fully, and Lark leaned her ear toward the narrow opening. She heard soft steady sobs, staccato intakes of air, and moaning, phlegmy exhales. Lark felt a rawness spreading deep in her chest. She gently pushed the door open enough to see into the room. Her mother sat slumped at her small vanity table, crowded with bottles and makeup and the two Styrofoam heads that were home base to her mother's wigs when she wasn't wearing them. What Lark saw shocked her. She hadn't seen her mother bareheaded in a long time. The truth is she'd hardly seen her mother at all in the past year. She'd looked at her, been in the same room with her, even talked to her about this and that, but she hadn't really *seen* her. Now, her face, red and blotchy from crying, came into full focus for Lark. All at once she became aware of the deeply etched lines around her mother's mouth and eyes and the knot of tension that seemed permanently on guard over her face from the spot between her eyebrows.

Lark watched as her mother pulled at the pathetic wisps of her once magnificent mop of hair. The radiant red was plainly being crowded out by an alien gray. Sarah tugged the hair nervously, as if by pulling, pulling hard she could make the chopped hair grow back, all at once, and bring back with it something she possessed when it flowed freely over her shoulders and out into the wind. Lark wanted to scream. The pain in her chest rose to her throat.

"Mommy?"

The sound of her daughter's voice seem to pull the woman apart, dissolving any reserve, any restraint she'd been exercising over her sorrow. She collapsed into herself, hands hiding her sob-contorted face. Lark went to her quickly. On her knees, she covered her mother's shuddering body with her own and held her tightly, repeating only a quiet "shhh" that could have been meant as much for Lark's own rising panic, as for her mother's grief.

After a while her mother became still. Lark sat back on her heels and waited.

"Are you okay?"

"Oh, God," she sighed, wiping the corners of her mouth. "I'm sorry, honey, I'm sorry." She reached for a handful of tissues and swabbed her face, blew her nose loudly.

It was then that Lark saw the envelope at her mother's feet, a photo peeking out of the corner. She picked it up.

"I got a letter from David," her mother said, her voice cracking. David! They hadn't heard from David in over three years. Her father refused to acknowledge him after he went away to school, had destroyed his letters whenever they came. Lark stopped writing after a while, knowing she could never get a reply or know if he'd ever received them.

"He's dead to us," her father declared over and over trying to make it true.

"How? How did you get it?" Rachel flipped over the envelope. She smiled as she saw David's handiwork. Carefully typed were her mother's name, their address, a series of official-looking numbers to one side under the message: "Important Billing Information." The envelope's return address was a printed logo of a bank, with a New York City address. Her father held the only mailbox key; he religiously retrieved the mail and went through it, eliminating materials like catalogues with "inappropriate" clothing or merchandise, but he never looked at the bills. Those he left for his wife, along with the responsibility for getting them paid. David knew that. Even before "the insanity," her father was never the main breadwinner, the responsible one. She loved the thought of David hatching the plan and figuring out a way to get a clean envelope from his bank, carefully typing the official-looking address, sending it off with his hopes.

She pulled out the wrinkled picture and stared at it. There was David. Sweet David, a summer scene from a different lifetime. He stood squinting at the sun, his arm around their mother's waist on one side, his other arm draped over Lark's shoulders on the other. In the background floated the Jersey boardwalk and the blue cloudless sky. It had to be six or seven years ago. Lark only came up to his chest. She remembered that bathing suit.

Unfolding the one-page letter, handwritten, Lark read.

Dear Mom:

I hope my little "bank letter" ruse was successful, and you are reading this in privacy. I've been obsessed lately with trying to get in touch with you again. For a long time I didn't care. I was really angry. I guess I still am, but that's beside the point. I'm graduating in two weeks from Rutgers. All my friends are planning to spend the day with their families. I'm probably not even going to commencement. They can mail me my diploma, it doesn't matter. I'm not trying to send you on a guilt trip, I'm just saying that I suddenly wished I could see you again—you know, share my graduation day with someone who cares. I've had girlfriends, but no one right now. Maybe that's why I've had time to think. That and the fact that I was cleaning out my desk, getting ready to leave this dorm room that's been my home for the past four years, and I came across a bunch of pictures. I found them in an old journal I kept my freshman year. I forgot I'd swiped a few pictures from the album before I left. I'm sending one back to you, now. Maybe you'll think about me and the fact that I am your son, that you loved me once and that I loved you. I still do.

I think a lot about Lark. I hope she's doing okay. Please let her know that I imagine a time when she and I will sit and have a cup of coffee and laugh about everything—that we'll be friends. I miss her.

I'll be in the city for some paperwork I need to take care of at Columbia. I got into the Masters' program there for Journalism. It's all decided, but this meeting is more about the fellowship than anything. Anyway, I was thinking maybe you and Lark could meet up with me while I'm in town. I'll be staying with some friends downtown in the village for the whole summer, until I can get housing near school. I'm listing all the numbers where you can reach me and when. Think about it. You can do this for me, for Lark, for yourself. Love always, your son, David.

Heavy, perfectly formed tears rolled down Lark's face. David. She hardly let herself think about him anymore. Not because she bought into her father's edict about him, but because the longing for him, for their old life together had been entirely too much for her to live with on a daily basis. She could see from her mother's reaction that the letter had unearthed him for her, too, brought him back from the dead, along with the longing itself. And the longing was not one feeling, but a flood of feelings, a torrent of things sorely missed, of selves long ignored.

"We have to meet him." Lark simply stated what hung in the air.

"I know." Her mother fidgeted with the tissues in her hands.

"Do you want me to make the call?"

Lark's mother looked as if she were going to cry again. Sarah looked at her daughter and saw the young woman she'd become and the burden of everything the girl had had to bear over the past few years. Lark had carried the weight of her own weaknesses.

"No. No, I'll call him. I want to."

Lark nodded. "Good." She gathered herself off the floor, feeling a little awkward. Something had shifted between her and her mother—the distance between them narrowing suddenly, but not exactly returning to something familiar.

They both heard it—the fumbling with keys just outside the door, then the buzzer. He never had the patience for all the locks.

"I'll let him in."

Her mother was already busy cleaning up her face. Rummaging for a scarf to cover her hair.

"Wait. You keep this somewhere." She gathered David's letter, the envelope, and photo off the floor where Lark had let it drop.

The buzzer rang again, insistently. Mother and daughter's eyes met and rolled in unison, their mouths turned up in a knowing smile. Lark quickly went to the door, thinking perhaps David wasn't the only one who'd come back from the dead today.

CHAPTER TWELVE

She still wasn't used to opening the door and just seeing him there. This wasn't the first time he'd come to pick her up for a "date" in the three weeks since their engagement, yet each time his presence in the hallway outside their apartment took her by surprise. *Oh, yes, that's right, I'm getting married to you, aren't I?*

"Hi." He carried his large sketchpad, as usual, in a leather-strapped portfolio that hung from his shoulder. He was drawing her; making studies for a portrait he meant to complete but wouldn't let her see any of until he was finished. Rachel was relieved to see that he'd brought it. When he was sketching her, she had every excuse to remain still and quiet, and he did, too. It was a respite from the pressure to dazzle him with her charm, wit, and pious sincerity, all of which she was sure she lacked in substantial measure.

"Rachel, don't let Yakov stand in the doorway! Let him in." Her mother came up behind her.

"That's okay, Mrs. Fine. We are going right out. We're going to ride the ferry."

"To Staten Island? What's there?"

"Nothing. We won't get off there. Just go for the ride there and back. The light is good," he indicated the sketchpad.

135

She looked at him as though he'd said they were going to visit the moon.

"I'll pack you a lunch."

Rachel was about to protest, but he didn't, and her mother seemed so pleased to be able to be involved in their plans somehow. She hurried down the hall toward the kitchen.

"I'll make one tuna, one egg salad, you can split them if you want. I think I only have pumpernickel..." and she was gone around the corner, muttering about pickles and cream soda.

Yakov insisted on shouldering the overstuffed insulated lunch bag even though he had the sketchpad and pencils to manage as well. The two of them headed toward the subway that would take them to Battery Park and the ferry. He hadn't asked her if she wanted to go on a ferry ride, but she found herself pulled along with the tide of things these past few weeks. Like everything from the wedding preparations to where they might live once they were married, the choice of where to go this afternoon was a perfectly nice one. Still, in a small way, she just wished she could have been in on it. And like the sandwiches this morning, people around her seemed to be enjoying taking care of these details so much, it hardly seemed worth complaining about.

The other thing about it was that Rachel wasn't quite sure what she would say if she did have a choice. *No, I don't want to live in the Rebbe's grand home after we get married? No, not such a big diamond ring? No, not that caterer, this one instead, no, not lilac linens, mauve is better? I'd rather not take the ferry, I'd rather...what?* Her preferences weren't strong enough, she realized, to justify making waves. After a lifetime of frustrating her parents and teachers, she found she *liked* making them feel pleased with her. There was a power to it, even in its relinquishing of power. She wondered why she hadn't discovered going along with things sooner. It was a whole lot less stressful, as long as you didn't have someone like Lark around insisting on the contrary.

That's why when she saw Lark coming up the stairs from the subway that rumbled under the neighborhood, walking directly toward them, she tried to get Yakov to cross the street.

"Don't we have to take the other stairway?" She started toward the opposite curb.

"It doesn't matter, they both go down to the same place." Yakov kept on, nearly bumping into Lark.

"Rocky!" She looked genuinely glad to see her. Rachel felt a pang of guilt and a rush of fondness for her friend, and a longing for the bond that seemed to be eroding with each passing day, subject to wave upon wave of the simple but vastly different circumstances of their lives.

She'd seen Lark every day while school was in, but since graduation, they'd seen little of each other. She didn't show up to the traditional all-girls engagement party her mother had thrown, and in some way, Rachel had been grateful. She hadn't had to deal with Lark lurking in the corner, shaking her head with disapproval as all the skirts ooh'ed and aah'ed over her substantial diamond ring and the requisite gold and diamond heart necklace her future mother-in-law had given her. She and Lark had reached a kind of holding pattern—by the last day of school they'd silently agreed not to talk about Yakov, the marriage, or the Rain Man. They stuck to generalities, other summer plans, and the latest who-said-what-about-whom. Stuff, but no substance.

"Oh, Lark!" She feigned surprise. "This is..."

"Yakov. Hello," he took over his own introduction.

"Oh, I know who you are, of course. Nice to meet you. I should say congratulations, shouldn't I, even though I am really mad at you? You *are* stealing my best friend, I hope you know. Already she's too busy to hang out with me." She gave Rachel one of her trademark looks—half mischief, half menace.

"Well, I'm sorry, but I needed a new best friend. I lost mine a few weeks ago, when he got married. So I know how you feel."

"Goody for you, but that doesn't help me, does it?" They both laughed. Rachel stood there confounded by the idea that these two polar opposites of her life could ever meet on common ground.

"Well, don't give up. I can share her." Lark looked closely at Yakov, as if she were trying to gauge if he really meant it. She wasn't used to being so included, especially in the high and holy circle he inhabited. Lark looked at Rachel, who shuffled nervously.

"We're going to ride the ferry to Staten Island. Yakov is making a sketch of me." *Why am I blabbering?* she asked herself as soon as the words spilled out of her mouth.

"Really? Can I see? Please?"

Yakov only hesitated a moment, then said, "Okay, but Rachel can't see. She has to wait until it's done. These are just sketches...the final work will be in oils." He unzipped his portfolio and took out the large pad, flipping pages with his delicate hands for Lark's benefit. Lark took care not to brush up against Yakov or touch him in any way as she leaned in to look—she knew the rules. Rachel watched the pair, unsure why she felt a pang of jealousy—over his attention to Lark or Lark's attention to him? Lark was visibly impressed, almost shaken by what she saw on the pages.

"Wow, these are amazing," she said softly. What Lark saw on the pages awed her. The black, strong strokes and grayish light lines converged across the smudged white to create an image of a serene beauty, a fresh and timeless innocence that was the face of her friend. There was Rachel, in a light she'd failed to see her in, but which this young man caught and captured on sheet after sheet. She knew in an instant that his talent lay not so much in his technical ability, which was considerable, but in what he looked out into the world and saw, what he perceived that was lost to others. *What would I look like if he drew me?* she wondered, then didn't want to think about it.

"We better go," Rachel suggested. "I'll call you later, Lark." She suddenly felt bad about having neglected her old friend.

"Oh, yeah, well, it was really good to meet you, finally. I guess I might have to like you after all," she teased. Yakov favored her with a rare full-mouthed grin. There was that ease with herself, with people, all kinds of people that had made Rachel love and envy Lark to begin with.

Rachel felt a bit of hope. Maybe things could remain the same, even after they changed. She could have Yakov and Lark, too. She could make everyone happy. How that would play out remained to be seen, but she saw a possibility of it standing there on the street, heard the tune of it along with the rhythmic clatter of the trains rushing by below them.

* * *

The salt air hit them as they emerged from the subway at Battery Park where the Hudson River spilled into the sea. Yakov breathed it in deeply, hungrily like a child at a bakeshop counter. He loved that smell. His father taught him to savor it on their many New York Harbor crossings, passing on to him, too, the simple pleasure of just riding the ferry for the fun of it, for the briny tang of the air and the bite of the cold dampness on his face. When his father died they sat shiva for the requisite week. He and his mother, grandfather and uncle were confined to the house, mirrors covered, clothing torn in grief, greeting the hundreds of well-meaning friends, neighbors, and relatives who filed through to daven in the morning or evening, had a cup of tea and extended their sympathies. Every day for the following week Yakov came to the ferry and conducted his own private shiva. He breathed the air he so often delighted in with his father and let the wind whip the endless tears from his eyes. Then suddenly he'd had enough. The salt air had purged and cauterized the gaping wounds of his grief and he wanted them left closed, bloodless from then on. He returned to the rhythm of his life, his studies, his drawing, and Daniel. He hadn't been back here since.

The idea of bringing Rachel here first came to him because of a conversation he'd had with his grandfather earlier in the week. The old man was strong enough now to sit at his desk for a few hours each day and attend to the business of the community, seeing those who sought his council on everything from matrimonial issues to business ethics. One of the newest developments since his engagement to Rachel was that the Rebbe invited him to sit in on these consultations, a privilege extended to no one, except his father, in the year before his death. Yakov's impending marriage signaled to everyone, including the Rebbe, that he was ready to take on the responsibilities of his destiny, to be a leader. Thus, he would learn at the knee of the master.

And there Yakov sat, almost literally at his knee, on a low antique chair behind the Rebbe's enormous desk, leaving it only to help his grandfather get around the desk when, occasionally, he felt the urge to shake a hand or touch a shoulder. A secretary, a recent seminary graduate, let people in and came back to retrieve them when their time was up. Everyone generally accepted Yakov's presence during these meetings as natural, and those that balked at the intrusion on their privacy soon learned they had no choice.

A few days earlier as they prepared to leave the office, after the last appointment had come and gone, the Rebbe gestured for Yakov to take the chair in front of his desk.

"Sit. There is time for one more appointment." He spoke in Yiddish now, as he had most of the afternoon.

Yakov looked around the room.

"No one is coming in. I'm talking about you."

"Oh."

"So, how does it go with the girl? Everything is good? You are meeting with her? Talking? Building a foundation for your life together?"

Yakov told him about their two meetings so far. The coffee shop. The gardens. She seemed nice. A good family.

"I'm making sketches of her." The Rebbe had always encouraged him in his art. The office was virtually a gallery of Yakov's work, a retrospective that included colorful childhood interpretations of simple Torah stories (the Rebbe collected them and had them published as a children's book that was now a staple in all the nursery schools throughout their international outreach network) to more recent charcoal work that was anything but simple.

"She's...very...feminine."

"Feminine? You say that as though you were describing some unusual animal you saw at a zoo! No matter. It is good to be a little in awe of a woman, to understand there is a mystery one can never completely unravel."

Yakov didn't know how to respond. Women were certainly a mystery to him, but to the Rebbe? He thought of his grandmother before she died—small, stout, moving quietly in the background, always there with his grandfather's needs memorized, anticipated at every turn. She'd be there with a scarf as he reached the front door, a pen as the phone rang, a sandwich with the chewy crusts cut away to accommodate his aging teeth and the new bridge work—dozens of caring gestures a day, without complaint. Yakov couldn't think of her as a mystery. His own mother, on the other hand, was an elaborate puzzle he tried to complete, but always came up a few pieces short.

"Ach! I wish your father were here today," the Rebbe sighed. "He would be so proud. Then again, he may have had a hand in orchestrating the whole thing!" The old man clapped his hands and smiled at his little joke, that wasn't really a joke. Yakov knew his grandfather believed and regularly taught that the dead were not dead, just invisible to us without their earthly bodies—that they regularly intervened on our behalf and for our own good, whether we liked it or not. More and more one could catch him having quiet conversations with his departed wife, putting questions out into the ether for her to answer: "What did I do with that book? What was the name of that town in Romania? Where are my reading glasses?" One could only speculate on whether he was getting answers, but one thing was certain: the relationship was intact.

That conversation got Yakov thinking about his father and the ferry rides once again. He'd bring Rachel to the center of the harbor and properly introduce her to his father. Out there where they had shared so much, he could receive his blessing as he certainly would if he were alive. Perhaps on the upper deck of the ferry, out in the wide-open water, a message could reach him, uninterrupted by buildings and traffic and trains and noise. A message from his dear papa loud and clear: *You are doing the right thing, my son. You will be happy. You will be blessed.*

At this time of day, the ferry was largely empty. Rachel and Yakov climbed the clanging metal stairway to the top deck and stood for a while at the railing, the wind pelting their faces and pulling Rachel's hair straight back from her head. They looked down at the hull cutting through the thick greenish-brown water, forcing it behind the bulky boat and flattening it out into the fanning and bubbling white wake that rushed away into the distance. After a few minutes, Rachel said she was getting dizzy watching the water, and they chose a seat toward the middle of the deck, but facing back toward the harbor.

The sun moved in and out from behind heavy gray clouds that seemed to appear out of nowhere. It was too breezy to pull out the sketchpad. Rachel absentmindedly placed her hand on the seat between them. Yakov looked down at her delicate hand, her short but manicured fingernails, and the peachy skin. He placed his own long-fingered, white-as-paper hand down on the seat beside hers, millimeters away from touching it. Rachel turned to him and smiled shyly. They stared down at their hands, and Yakov wondered if she wondered what he wondered, asked the implicit questions that lay in the slice of space between them, that filled part of every moment they were together: *Soon we'll be touching, won't we? How will that be? What will that reveal that all this small talk can't?*

Yakov thought about Daniel and his new bride. Touching, finding each other in the dark. He'd gotten a single postcard from him, from Israel, where he and Gavrielle were spending a month-long wedding trip—sightseeing, visiting family of hers, and beginning their life together. The card showed a picture of the Wailing Wall on the front, hundreds of praying men at its base made to look like miniatures against the backdrop of the holy wall, the only remnant of the Great Temple and the era of myth and miracles. On the back a hastily scrawled three-word message lay suspended in time: *Thinking of you.*

They both felt the drops. Yakov searched the darkening sky.

"There goes the ferry ride, I guess."

"It doesn't matter," Rachel assured him. "We can have lunch down in cabin. It's kind of windy up here anyway." They got up and turned toward the stairway. Manhattan reached to the sky in front of them.

"I used to come here a lot with my father," Yakov began. "This ferry or the one to the Statue of Liberty. He loved being out here. On the way back in he would try to get me to think about what it was like for the immigrants coming from Europe, Russia, to be on a boat for weeks and then suddenly have this city before them, the buildings bigger than they'd ever seen just exploding out of the water like that. He'd say, 'Think of it, Yakov. You know no one, you have left everything behind, you don't even speak the right language and in a few hours you'll be dropped off on that island to make a new life. Can you imagine the courage it took?'"

They stopped to take in the city from that perspective.

"I never looked at it that way. Your father had a great imagination."

"I guess so. I thought he was telling me stories to keep me entertained. Now I think he just had an incredible ability to feel what someone was going through. Not imagination really, but compassion. He was trying to teach me compassion." Yakov hesitated, wondering if he should go on, if he could. "I actually thought I would bring you out here to, uh, well, meet him."

Only a fraction of a moment passed before it became clear to Rachel what Yakov meant. *To meet him.* She looked at Yakov looking out at a place where his father still lived for him, in the swirling air around the city and the womb of the harbor, and she knew that she was going to love him, that she was loving him now. Right now.

She spoke, pushing her voice into the turbulent wind, "It's a pleasure to meet you, Rabbi Rubinstein. A great honor." She did a small, solemn curtsy, and kept her eyes looking outward, steady. It started to rain more heavily, as if on cue. They both turned their faces to the sky, squinting against the downpour.

"I don't think he likes me," Rachel said, holding an upturned palm to the rain.

Yakov looked at Rachel, this girl, so prepared to please him.

"Are you kidding? He loves you." Yakov scanned the dark sky for meaning, the fat drops splashing on his face, getting caught in his sparse beard. "He's just crying from joy, Rachel. Tears of joy." She seemed relieved and let out a small laugh at their little game. He was satisfied to convince her and himself that the bad weather was nothing more than a good omen.

CHAPTER THIRTEEN

Lark ran her fingertips over the expensive paper and raised lettering. In the top right corner was the Hebrew lettering, the ever-present Bet, Yud, Hey that adorned every printed or written communication in the community. It hung like a little lantern atop the page—an abbreviation for Baruch Hashem, translated roughly, Blessed God, or with God's blessing. They had to write it on their homework. Her mother even wrote it on the grocery list! Lark understood that, in principle, all the little gestures like this one—all of the blessings, the rituals, the rules—were meant to infuse daily life with godliness. But while observing the practice of it all, she was left with a feeling that these people she lived alongside (but hardly with) were not so much connected to their God, as they were afraid of Him. To Lark, all the Baruch Hashem-ing and mumbling of blessings amounted to nothing more than superstitious insurance against the potential disaster of God's wrath—the Jewish equivalent of black cats and cracked mirrors and throwing of salt over the shoulder. Their God had to be smoothed over like an unpredictable despot. How exhausting! To Lark it was all too much like the relationship she had with her father—contrived, fear-driven, inauthentic behavior that replaced a once-heartfelt, all-encompassing love that was a part of her ancient history.

She laid out the pieces of the invitation on the bed: "Please join the Fine family in celebrating, with joy and thanks, the marriage of their daughter Rachel to Yakov Rubinstein," *son of blah, blah, blah, grandson of blah, blah, blah, on blah, blah Hebrew day in the blah, blah Hebrew year.* A quick Hebrew to English calculation revealed that the wedding was to be in six weeks, August 19, 1991.

Celebrate with joy? She wasn't sure. Before meeting up with them on the street the other day, she would have said no, definitely not. Big mistake. *The Rachel I know needs to move on, move out beyond the confines of this life, to something broader, freer.* But then she got a glimpse of a Rachel she maybe didn't know, and a Yakov who didn't necessarily fit the narrow view she had of the young men in his narrow world. Lark thought how angry she was when Rachel had so blatantly rejected Jamal as an appropriate possibility for Lark. She had stuffed him and Lark's involvement with him into a little box in her mind and wrapped it with brown paper like a dirty novel. Lark didn't want to react automatically like that. She wanted to be open to her friend's choices, to believe in her happiness and stay connected to her.

After her mother had called David to set up a date for them to meet, he had sent another letter, saying how happy he was about the meeting and how he just knew the great gap, created by the differences of the past few years, would fill up in an instant as soon as they were all together again. He ended the letter with a quote from a book on Zen meditation he was reading: *The mind creates an abyss only the heart can traverse.* Lark read and reread that line. She decided that her relationship to Rachel was not one of the mind. If it had been, the distance between them would have been too great to work out—the disparity in their backgrounds, the stark blackness and whiteness of their temperaments. What allowed them to connect was a matter of the heart, something they felt deeply that linked them. Lark wasn't so sure she knew what it was. Maybe it wasn't meant to be articulated, but it was there and undeniable.

Talk about undeniable feelings: *Where in the hell is that Rain Man?* The yellow roses had wilted along with the sense of well-being they had provided. To her, the flowers had been a talisman, a symbol acknowledging the beauty of their night together, of coming together for those hours after so many months of stolen moments. She felt an involuntary shudder down her back and between her legs with the total instant recall of his touch, his fingers and tongue exploring and tasting every inch of her that night.

They'd danced for a while, long enough to be soaked in sweat, vibrating with the heavy bass in the music. They'd touched and slid their bodies together enough on the dance floor to set them on the sharp edge of desire. Every so often he'd lean over and whisper in her ear, "Look at you, girl," or "You are so sweet, mmm, mmm." Lark had giggled like a schoolgirl, and whipped her thick hair around in a mock-sexy move, which made him smile at her and shake his head. They smoked a little and had a drink, too.

When Jamal got the high sign from someone across the room, he took her hand and led her to a far corner of the dance floor. They stepped through a door into a long corridor ending in narrow stairway that led to a second story above the club. At the top of the stairs were two doors. Jamal disappeared behind one of the doors, leaving her on the landing, but was only gone for a few seconds. When he stepped out again, he pushed the door open wide and said, "Your room awaits you, my lady."

Well, it wasn't exactly the presidential suite, but Lark could see that someone had gone to a lot of trouble to make the untidy club office seem like a love nest. Papers were brushed aside to make room for dozens of little votive candles and others of varying sizes in makeshift holders, all lit and slowly dripping down their sides. A boom box on the floor played slow R&B, strictly old school, just loud enough to block out the music from the club below. A sofa bed at the far end was pulled out and covered in a wildly colored blanket with an African- or Indian-looking design, Lark couldn't tell which. Oranges, bright blues, reds, and yellows shimmered in the flickering candlelight. Similar blankets had been hastily tacked to the wall in an effort to cover the windows that faced the street in front of the club.

Lark was delighted by the room. Her momentary disappointment at not being taken to his house, introduced into his "real" life, evaporated along with the scented wax from the candles. But she had no time to say a word about it. Jamal didn't wait for her reaction to the room. With the door closed and the rest of the world tucked away behind it, it was as if the steel trap that had contained his hunger for her over the past months, that had made him hold back, hold out for the little yeshiva girl, burst at its straining hinges. He pulled Lark to him, held her, and kissed her with an intensity that almost frightened her, but then enveloped her. *This is what I'm here for, after all.*

Within minutes her clothing was on the floor, her shoes kicked aside. He paused only for a moment to take her in, to make her stand there while he backed away and looked. She was luminous, soft pinks and deeper pinks, her thick hair filtering the candlelight through feathery ends. He undressed and posed for her, all strings of muscle, pulled tight like on a finely tuned instrument—shades of brown melting into darker browns.

From then on each breath she took in or let out had a gasp or a moan attached to it. He knew how and where to touch her, and did, how to bring her up and down the roller coaster and up again. He patiently showed her what to do for him. When Jamal finally entered her, the pain of it was almost a relief against the torrent of pleasure that had made her so aware of her senses and so senseless at the same time.

As breathless as remembering that night could make her—even three weeks after the fact—she was tiring of the instant replay, and wanted to see him. Where was he? Should she be angry or worried? Was he dead or just rotten, using her that one night and then dumping her? She had to see him and soon. That night had opened a door in her life, in her being, that wasn't going to just close up. If anything, what she experienced made everything seem that much more unbearable: the clothing, the restrictions, and the platitudes, the pretending.

The only bright spot in the endless stretch of summer was the date she and her mother had made to meet up with David this coming Sunday. Her father had been surprised and pleased when her mother calmly agreed that he should take the opportunity to go on a men's prayer and study retreat to Lakewood, organized by the shul. She almost blew it, Lark thought, by being a little too enthusiastic about him going. Sarah went on and on about the fresh air and how getting out of the city would do him good, until Lark had had to kick her under the table. After all, the last time he mentioned wanting to go, weeks before David's letter, she'd complained about the cost and the fact that he hadn't worked in months. He might have become suspicious of her motives if he wasn't so pleased with himself for having somehow gotten what he wanted from his wife, once again. He'd be gone the whole weekend, leaving early Friday and returning very late Sunday night. Lark and her mom made plans to meet David for brunch on Sunday, and they would have the whole afternoon and evening to be together. She couldn't wait to see him but was nervous, too. What would it be like after all these years? Would the differences just fade as he'd said in his hopeful letter? Would he rescue her at last?

Lark turned her attention back to the pieces of the invitation scattered around her. She took up the reply card and filled in their names: The Shulman Family *will* attend. The Shulman Family: Sarah, Avram, and Lark. And David, she wanted to write, but didn't. And David.

*   *   *

Lark's father left early Friday morning, taking his weekend bag and a snack for the bus ride along with him. The retreat officially began the moment he and the others boarded the chartered bus, with morning prayers taking place as they rolled through Brooklyn and over the Verrazano Bridge towards New Jersey, the bus's bounce adding a reckless dimension to the dipping and swaying in the aisles. Their *tefillin*, little black boxes on leather tethers stuffed with prayer-inscribed parchments, tightly wrapped around their arms and head, had always looked like radio transmitters to Lark, or some sort of mutated antenna that was silently beep, beep, beeping a message out into the atmosphere: *Hello, God, are you out there? Can you hear me?*

Sarah had gotten Lark up to say goodbye to her father. They never slept late. If he was up they all had to be up, listening to W-I-N-S News, "All-News-All-The-Time," reverberating off the kitchen walls. Lark sat sleepily at the small kitchen table, her hands wrapped around the hot teacup placed in front of her, while her father read the itinerary for his big weekend from the flier the shul had prepared.

"Don't forget my cashews. I might need a snack in between for my blood sugar. Did you pack me a bathing suit? There's a pool. And a hot tub!" He was excited, like a child going off for the first time to sleep-away camp—which could be cute, Lark supposed, if it didn't make her sick. She begrudged him his luxuries and his pleasures, because she felt he took them at her expense. She'd never gone to camp, not a real camp.

Their first full summer in Crown Heights they sent her to a so-called camp in the Catskills that was basically an in-the-woods version of her school, with bugs, tons of starchy food, and tiny bungalows that heated up to 100 degrees in the daytime and barely cooled off at night. They had religious study sessions in the early morning, followed by designated girls-only swim times at the murky lake they shared with the ultraorthodox summer resorts that dotted the landscape. In the afternoons, they took turns working in the kitchen, honing their domestic skills to a gleaming sharp edge, learning to whip out braided challahs and other staples of a good Chasidic girl's dietary repertoire. After the first night of rousing Hebrew folk songs and folk dancing around the campfire, Lark had opted to sweat it out in her bunk the rest of the nights, reading the thrift-shop paperbacks she'd had the foresight to smuggle in with her. She refused to go back the following year, even if they were giving her a "generous scholarship" because of their financial situation.

Anyway, it wasn't just the camp. It was everything. She watched her father checking and rechecking his bag, the nuts, the bathing suit, his tefillin. He counted the underwear. *Where is my siddur? Oh, yes, here it is.* It was that everything always had to be his way, according to his needs.

When he was finally out the door, Lark and her mother looked at each other like two jewel thieves reflecting on a big heist, with a sense of wonder at having pulled it off.

"Let's go out for breakfast!" her mother whispered like a secret. So they did. They left the beds unmade and her father's breakfast dishes in the sink. They ordered whatever they wanted without looking at the price. A huge Nova and whitefish platter, thick French toast made from challah with strawberries and whipped cream. Eggs on the side. Blueberry blintzes. Large orange juices. Coffee with half-and-half and lots of sugar. They didn't talk much. Lark watched her mother read the *Daily News* slowly, carefully; savoring the words before her even more than what was on the crowded little table between them. *If you threw a little bacon in next to the eggs, a side of sausage,* Lark thought, *we could be anywhere, not here in Crown Heights living this absurd life, but anywhere else— back in time at a sprawling Jersey diner or forward into the future when the last four years would seem like nothing more than a prolonged bad dream.*

They spent the rest of the weekend in an unspoken agreement to do whatever they felt like. They lit Shabbes candles, of course, but contented themselves with a rotisserie chicken from the kosher butcher, a big salad, and store-bought challah instead of the big production of a meal her mother orchestrated each week, with a fish course, soup, and side dishes. They didn't go to shul, but lay in bed reading.

Lark wondered if Rachel would miss her, but in recent weeks her friend had been surrounded after services anyway. Lark could hardly get to her. Everyone wanted to talk to the girl who was marrying the Rebbe's grandson. Rachel couldn't exactly hang out in the girl's bathroom anymore. She tried not to think about Jamal, about whether he'd show up around shul, smoking in the alley below the bathroom window, just pissing everyone off but not caring as long as Lark could see he was there. But Lark stayed in bed and figured if he did show up and didn't see her, he deserved it. She could play hard-to-get, too, at least for today. And tomorrow, when she'd be busy seeing David.

Lark woke up Sunday morning very early, but could already hear her mother banging around the apartment, talking to herself. She found her in the kitchen, ironing a blouse, wearing nothing but her bra and a slip and two different shoes. Four other already ironed blouses were draped over the chairs, along with two skirts and a dress.

"I don't know what to wear. Why didn't anyone tell me I'm as fat as a cow? David isn't even going to recognize me." She was on the verge of tears.

"You are not fat, Mom. You look fine."

"I don't look fine. I look like an old lady." Now she was crying.

Lark took the hot iron from her mother's hands, pulled the cord out of the wall, and put it on the windowsill to cool. She hugged her.

"You're just nervous. I'm nervous, too. David's probably nervous and crying right now about how fat he looks!" Her mother laughed in spite of herself, with the idea of David, who was always so bone skinny, whining in front of a mirror and trying to pinch an inch of fat on his wiry torso.

"Oh, my God, remember those protein shakes with the raw eggs he kept drinking all through high school? He never gained an ounce!" Lark saw her mother begin to relax, picturing her boy, the familiar face smiling at her from the past. *Okay, it's just David we're meeting. Just David.*

Lark thought her mother looked beautiful as they walked to the subway. They were going to be at least an hour early, but they both couldn't stand waiting around the apartment anymore. Sarah wore the sheitl that most resembled her own hair, the color an almost perfect match, full and wavy. She had it custom-made, paid a fortune for it, and put it on the credit card after she'd declared that she was tired of the cheap, waxy-looking pageboys she'd been wearing for so long. It was a small rebellion in a sea of quiet compliances—one of the many little waves that she seemed to be making ever since David's letter had made its way into their lives.

Even though David was staying somewhere downtown, they'd agreed to meet at a kosher dairy restaurant on the upper west side, where a growing concentration of orthodox and ultraorthodox families had brought with them the inevitable need for butchers and Judaica shops, kosher pizza places and other permissible dining options.

They came up from the train at 72nd Street and walked east on the wide street that dead-ended into the backdrop of green that was Central Park. Lark loved the bigness of Manhattan. Nothing seemed cramped or shoehorned in as it did in Brooklyn, in the six-block-square neighborhood that was their little world. Even with all the tall buildings, there seemed to be more light, more color, more sky. Lark liked watching the people walking by, trying not to be too self-conscious about how she was dressed—so overdressed for the hot summer afternoon—while passing men and women in shorts and sleeveless tops, feathery-light dresses and sandals.

Then she saw him waiting in front of the restaurant, and he saw them.

"Oh, my God..." her mother said under her breath, as he started toward them, to meet them halfway. "Oh, my God..." she said again and turned abruptly around and walked in the opposite direction. Then she stopped dead in her tracks and brought her hands to her face.

"Ma! What are you doing?" Lark called out to her. *She's crying again, that's what she's doing.* Just then David swept by her. As he passed, Lark saw that broader shoulders and the muscular legs of a man had taken over David's scrawny teenage body. He seemed taller, his hair hanging loosely around his shoulders. She watched this new incarnation of her long-lost brother hovering over her mother, trying to get her to put her hands down, to look at him, to let him hug her. And when she finally did, and she rested her head on his chest and fumbled with a tissue he'd produced for her, he looked up at Lark a couple of yards away and gave her the most brilliant smile, the most recognizable David smile. She walked over to them though she had wanted to run. They stood there in a goofy group hug for a minute, then made their way back to the restaurant, holding onto each other and swaying down the sidewalk like happy drunks.

* * *

They reminisced, which is different from just remembering. David, Sarah, and Lark soaked themselves in their shared experiences, the noisy restaurant receding and giving way to the backdrop of their Jersey kitchen, the backseat of their VW van, or the secret hideout in the wooded lot behind their house. Lark could hardly eat or take her eyes off of David, who had become a beautiful man. In her countless imaginings of this meeting, in her long pretend conversations with him, she forgot to take into account the effect the years would have on him or, for that matter, the effect they'd had on her. The first thing he said when they got settled at the table was, "If I knew you were going to be this gorgeous supermodel when you grew up, I might have been nicer to you when you were a kid." They laughed, but she saw in his eyes that he meant it. *Supermodel!*

David talked about school. He might as well have been describing Camelot as far as Lark was concerned, as the stories of lecture halls, dorm parties, and late nights at the school newspaper took on the aura of legend and romance. David was the valiant knight who'd gone off to slay the dragons of ignorance and oppression, to capture the treasures of knowledge and the kind of wisdom that can only come from facing one's complete aloneness in the world. Lark had stayed behind, the captured princess in the tower of the barbarous wizard. Surely her rescue and release were imminent.

They'd avoided the present mostly, until they got the check and their mother went off to find the ladies' room. Then David leaned in and became serious.

"How's the old man?" His jaw tightened.

"Worse than ever."

David just nodded as if that was the answer he'd expected. He knew. *Just seeing us*, thought Lark, *the way we're dressed*. The wig, as nice as it was, was still a wig.

"Mom's kind of a mess," he said gently.

Sarah kept tearing up or downright crying throughout the meal. Her hands shook as she brought coffee to her smudged lips. It was clear that her delight at seeing her son was inextricably linked to the devastating loss of the years in between. His lighthearted presence brought into vivid relief the heavy restraint, the daily, imposed effort of the life she'd been living during his absence. She became unbalanced by the revelation.

Lark folded and refolded her napkin on the tabletop.

"I'm leaving there as soon as I turn eighteen. I want to take *her* out of there, too. Get her away from him, from there. I never thought she could ever leave him, but since your letter things have changed a little...seems like she's not as *into* the whole thing as she used to be. She's not trying to make excuses for him so much, just agreeing with everything all the time. He never works now. He's obsessed with becoming this Torah scholar." She rolled her eyes and shook her head. "Mom's working all the time, doing the home-nursing—up half the night, then trying to be this perfect Chasidic housewife during the day. His drinking is out of control again..." she trailed off as she saw her mother approaching the table, a new layer of lipstick in place, her hair re-fluffed, her skirt straightened. David and Lark exchanged a familiar look. *To Be Continued*, it said, with shades of their old conspiratorial bond reaching across time. They were back.

They strolled through Central Park to the eastside, talking around uncomfortable subjects, keeping it light. Lark could see that David was determined to be smart about it. He wanted what Lark wanted, but it wasn't going to happen if he came on too strong with their mother. She'd freak out if he tried to talk about an abrupt change now, about leaving the fold, leaving her husband. It would be much better to let her get used to him being back, to remember on her own who she used to be, to discover for herself what she'd been missing. David wanted her to reach out to him. And then he'd be there to do whatever it took, including a showdown with the old man, something he'd rehearsed time and again over the years. He wanted badly to play it all out, and more so now that he'd seen them, now that he'd seen Lark—the extraordinary woman she was becoming—but he could wait for the right moment.

They rode a bus to the East Village, where David was staying on a tiny street across from a community center and performance space. Lark scanned the notice board as they walked by: dance classes, yoga, auditions, tai chi, Find The Goddess Within a workshop flier promised, Al-Anon meetings the first Tuesday of every month, the Sacred Circle meeting for a nondenominational spiritual service on Sundays at 11. The world, as contained on that bulletin board, was drawing Lark to it, with all its possibilities for new experiences, for all its unrestricted wonder. The world she was forced to inhabit seemed a smaller, tighter fit than ever.

David wanted them to come up to the apartment and have a cup of tea before they headed back. Only a few flights up turned out to be five, and while it hardly fazed David as he took two stairs at a time, Lark and her mother were sucking wind by the time they reached the landing on the fifth floor. Needless to say, Phys. Ed was not a big part of Lark's education. *This is pathetic*, she thought. *I'm seventeen years old and heaving like an old lady.* Her sore legs, another sore reminder of what it cost her to be a part of her father's experiment with her life. She made a mental note to buy a bike and take up riding again in her new life.

David fumbled with the unfamiliar keys and locks.

"I'm staying with my buddy Doug until the fall, then I get campus housing. He was my roommate at Rutgers, but he's going to law school at NYU, not far from here."

The door was suddenly opened from the inside and a girl in cutoff shorts and a tight NYU T-shirt popped out at them.

"Hi. I'm just leaving. Old Fido is not exactly in the best mood." Her head nodded back toward the apartment. David made introductions.

"Lily, this is my sister, Lark, and my mom, Sarah." They all said hi. Lark took in the pretty girl's long, smooth legs and buoyant bralessness. Oddly, it was Lark who felt overexposed in her modest outfit. She blushed with embarrassment as she felt the girl look her up and down.

"Lily is Doug's sister. She's an undergrad at NYU. Lives a few blocks from here," David explained after she took to the stairs running, and yelled up that it was nice to meet them. "His name is Doug, but we call him Dog, or sometimes Fido, when he's acting like he has rabies." They walked into a dim room that smelled vaguely of beer and dirty socks.

"I've had all my shots. And I don't bite." A voice came from somewhere in the back of the small apartment. The very tall Doug emerged, shirtless and vigorously toweling his closely cropped hair. Lark stood, eyes riveted to his bare and nearly hairless chest, while her mother tried to look everywhere but directly at the young man. David threw a couch pillow at his friend. "Dude, a shirt would be nice. This is my mother, my innocent young sister..."

"So sorry. Dog very sorry." He backed out of the room, bowing elaborately at the waist.

They had their tea, without milk, since the container in Doug's fridge was halfway to cottage cheese, but they didn't mind. The tea gave them an excuse to linger. David brought a box out from his room, filled with photographs he'd taken. He'd majored in journalism, but cultivated a talent in photography along the way, explaining that he liked the way a photo could capture a story in a fraction of a second, tell the essence of it so economically, while he'd have to labor over the written story for hours or days to get the same message across.

"These days the right picture at the right time can be worth a fortune."

It was funny to hear David talking so practically about his future, about money, about making his mark. He was so grown! Lark looked at the photos he'd snapped— Guatemalan villagers during a work-study trip last summer, inner-city kids in the spray of a sprung hydrant, a homeless shelter in Manhattan, bleak with hopelessness, a sleeping woman sprawled on a sun-drenched bed. His woman? His bed? The world he'd witnessed, that had witnessed him since he'd left home, had etched into him something more than he used to be. It gave Lark the idea that wanting to escape wasn't enough. Having a destination, somewhere you wanted to end up, became important.

They rose to leave. Doug, who turned out to be a goofy puppy more than a dog, offered to walk with them to the subway, so the four of them headed toward 14th Street together, stopping to browse through a vintage-clothing display and read headlines at the newsstand along the way. When they reached the entrance to the train, Sarah began to cry again and David huddled with her, reassuring her that they would talk soon, that nothing would come between them again. Lark, feeling a bit awkward, stood waiting with Doug.

"You live in Brooklyn?" he asked.

"Yeah, Brooklyn." She didn't want to offer details.

"Well, uh, we're gonna throw a party on the roof next Saturday night. I do one every summer for Bastille Day. I supposedly have some relatives that go back to the French Revolution. Anyway, it's a good reason to party. Did David tell you?

"I don't know if..."

"You should come. I know at least twenty guys who would love to meet you. If they want to fight me first, that is." He broke into an aw-shucks grin.

"Well, I'll talk to David..." Lark stared at the ground, then up at Doug, then down again. She felt David's arm slip around her waist.

"Is this guy bothering you?"

"I'm just telling her that if she comes to our roof party, I will person-ally protect her from all the animals in the zoo."

David looked at Lark, remembering she wasn't fourteen anymore, then said, "Can you get away?"

Lark wanted to be there more than anything she could think of. "I'll figure it out."

"Great! You can stay over. And I'll protect you from the animals. All of them." David gave Doug a mock-serious look for her benefit, and then gave her a pager number where she could reach him anytime, day or night. Lark hugged David hard, and when she turned to go, Doug was there with a bear hug for her and her mother.

"It was really good to meet you guys." He didn't know about not touching them because they were women and because their sages had decided that was what their God wanted.

Not my God, thought Lark. *Not mine.*

CHAPTER FOURTEEN

Daniel was home from the wedding trip. Gavrielle and he were installed in their new apartment, not far from where her parents lived.

"Come to us for Shabbes dinner. Bring Rachel, of course," he shouted above the roar of a passing bus, pouring quarters into a pay phone in Manhattan. He was on a break from his new job. It was his third day working in the diamond district at his father-in-law's store, situated just a few blocks from Radio City Music Hall, but worlds away just the same.

He'd made the decision to leave studying, leave the seminary, while they were traveling. "I'm not the scholar type. That's you my friend. I'll be the big diamond maven, make a lot of money, and give to whatever holy cause you tell me to. We'll argue over Talmud now and then to make me happy," he'd told Yakov. Gavrielle's family had hopes from the beginning that Daniel would work in the family business, though they would have deferred to his wishes had he insisted on a scholarly career. Her father was not entirely well and her three brothers were all under the age of seven and hardly ready to take over the lucrative business that supported Gavrielle's family of thirteen children, as well as relatives overseas and other worthy causes. Daniel had resisted the notion initially, hanging onto the idea of being linked with Yakov as he had always

161

been, in study, in plans for some gloriously idealized future, but it seemed as though his wedding trip had turned him toward a more mundane reality.

"I am of mere flesh; you are of the soul," he teased Yakov when he tried to question his friend's decision. Daniel was underplaying his ability as a scholar. He'd more than kept up his end of their study partnership; he alone, among their class, was a match for Yakov in intellect and insight. "Anyway, I really enjoyed the traveling, seeing the world outside of our little neighborhood. I think I am going to like going into the city every day. I'm a Chasid, apart from the world—yes—but I like to be in it, too."

Yakov couldn't help but wonder about the forces at play. Had marital intimacy, the kind of blessed intimacy that they are taught is one of man's rare chances on the material plane to be in the presence of the divine, shown Daniel a truth about himself that was powerfully and irrevocably transforming? Perhaps in the arms of his wife he saw the face of God and, in seeing it, found that surrendering to His will—whether it be diamonds or domestic life—was not a burden at all, but rather like taking sweet instruction from a cherished lover. Yakov wanted to believe it for Daniel, for himself and for Rachel, too. Believing it fit into the kind of faith he was supposed to have, fit neatly into the decisions he and Daniel had already made about themselves and that others made for them each day, as well as centuries ago.

What didn't fit was the wave of animal pleasure that nearly knocked him off his feet when a hearty handshake turned into a two-fisted hug on the sidewalk outside of shul that Friday evening just after sundown. It was their first meeting in over five weeks. So much had occurred to change everything between them in that time—Daniel's wedding, more than a month of married life, his career decisions, Yakov's engagement to Rachel—but in the space of a moment's embrace Yakov's body sent him this bulletin: *Nothing has changed. Nothing.* A passerby would have seen nothing out of the ordinary; they were an affectionate and gregarious community of men. Except, on closer examination, they would notice one man had his face nearly buried in the curve of the other's neck, instead of the usual air kiss or the hammerlock quality of hugs between men. And from the color staining Daniel's face as he pulled away from the slightly too-long embrace, Yakov knew that the feeling was more than mutual. A flicker of a glance between them before they turned with the tide of men pouring into the shul acknowledged the moment then, just as quickly, let it go. Shabbes was waiting to be welcomed.

*   *   *

Rachel arranged the two braided challahs on the brightly colored platter. They posed there for her, puffed up with self-satisfied pride. *Look how beautiful we are,* they seemed to pronounce, homemade and gleaming with a patina of egg yolk baked onto them. *We are made golden from the eggs in our dough, but also from the mitzvah performed in our making.* She quickly draped the gold and white embroidered cloth over them, caught between admiration and frustration. Gavrielle's apparent skill with challah making only highlighted for Rachel her own lack of talent in the kitchen. Third in a line of girls, in a household that regularly employed kitchen help, she had been able to avoid the details and the drudgery of domestic duty. Her own mother would rather work a twelve-hour day in the store than an hour in the kitchen. But making challah was a principal commandment of the preparations for Sabbath. As a young bride, Rachel would have to attempt the task. There were specific instructions for making and blessing the dough: a piece of the sticky mass had to be separated from the whole and burned in the oven to commemorate the sacrifices once made at the Great Temple in the great ancient era of Judaism. The rest of the dough would rise to become the golden loaves, sweet and moist, except, of course, if it was Rachel who was making them. Hers, no matter the recipe or her diligent attention to the various women in her life who had tried to pass this skill on to her, were dry bricks or stiff footballs, better used as projectile weapons than the opening of the week's most important meal.

Rachel looked at Gavrielle's beautifully laid table. She'd arrived early to help her get ready before the men returned from shul. Though it was a gesture that was somewhat expected of her, Rachel really wanted to help. Gavrielle was married to Yakov's closest friend, and though she'd never been that friendly with her over the years, especially after Lark arrived on the scene, she felt it was wise to get to know the girl better now.

When she first entered the small apartment, she remembered what had always annoyed her about Gavrielle. The place was already a model of perfection, just like Gavrielle's fifth-grade diorama of the Jews' exodus from Egypt with its elaborately detailed plaster of Paris pyramids, or her report last year on the Warsaw ghetto, complete with a scale model that took up the entire surface of a folding-card table that her father carried in for the occasion. The girl had returned from her honeymoon only twelve days ago and there wasn't an unpacked box in sight or a fork out of alignment.

In the summer, Shabbes started late, after eight o'clock and, in the fading light, the beautifully dressed table and new furnishings, crisp rugs and fresh paint, looked like an artfully lit photograph, a thoughtfully set stage. Rachel became acutely aware of the standards for homemaking that she would somehow have to compete with. Her mother had the demands of the family business as her excuse. What would Rachel have? As the rebitzen to the Rebbe's grandson, the future Rebbe himself, every eye in the community would be on her, not to mention those of the household she would become a part of. She and Yakov would have their own apartment in the big residence, but they would still be under the Rebbe's roof. Would she have help? What exactly would her domestic duties be as she became a member of the Rebbe's family? Where would she fit in with Yakov's mother, clearly a woman who liked being in control? These are issues they hadn't discussed. She doubted that Yakov had even given them a thought, but she was thinking about it now and getting the beginnings of a headache behind her eyes. She pinched them shut and pulled her fingers over her closed lids toward her nose several times. Her fingers came away smeared with the black mascara she forgot she was now wearing at her mother's insistence.

"What's wrong with a little makeup? You're engaged now; you should always look your best. You are going to be in a position of setting an example for people, Rachel. You can't live in your head anymore, inside you little world. Whether you like it or not, people are going to look at you, so why not look good? Eh?" She thought of her mother pumping the little mascara brush up and down in its tube, scraping the chalky excess off on the lip and showing Rachel the best way to coat and separate her long lashes with the stuff. Rachel could hardly stop herself from laughing when her mother opened her mouth wide and pulled her face and eyes into a long, distorted version of itself as she applied the mascara to Rachel's batting eyes, like a young mother who can't help opening her mouth each time she feeds a spoon of food to her baby. It was comical and endearing.

"It's ti-ime, it's ti-ime!" Gavrielle came sing-songing into the dining room, shaking the little silver box that held matches. *Even her matches are perfect*, thought Rachel, as she hastily ran her fingers under her smeared lashes and wiped them on the back of her dark skirt.

They each lit two candles to usher in the Sabbath. As they recited the bracha, the women swept their hands over the flames, once, twice, a third time, gathering toward them the blessed air that now hovered there, gathering it toward a place over their hearts, near to where their souls might reside. With the third sweep, their hands came to rest over their eyes and Rachel and Gavrielle took the moment, this moment when there is a direct line open to God, created by this lighting of the candles, this performing of a mitzvah, through which their prayers could be especially heard and answered. It was a chance for a woman to ask for special blessings for her loved ones, for the healing of ills and strengthening of weaknesses.

Rachel heard Gavrielle's quiet murmuring to her right. *Of course, she knows what to ask for,* Rachel thought as she blankly struggled to use the moment before it passed. *Help. Help.* The word raced around her head. *Help!*

"Gooooood Shaaaaabbes!" Gavrielle warbled at least an octave above her normal speaking voice, turning to Rachel with a quick double air kiss. Rachel felt herself doing an internal eyeball roll, the kind she might share with Lark if she'd been there. *Is she going to sing every thought all night? Yes, I am going to need help to get through the evening, a lot of help!*

As if in answer to her prayers, Yakov and Daniel could be heard in the foyer, the heavy door slamming behind them.

"Goooood Shaaaabes!" Gavrielle sang out for them.

"Good Shabbes," the two men said simultaneously as they entered the living room.

"Good Shabbes," Rachel greeted them and heard herself adding a bit of singsong to her voice, too.

"And this is Rachel, of course," boomed Daniel. "I feel as if I already know you. My friend never stops talking about you...but then again he is well known for his tendency to ramble. In this case, I can understand why, so I forgive him."

Yakov observed his dramatic companion with a raised eyebrow. *I hardly know what to say about Rachel, much less ramble.* Embarrassed, he offered a sheepish smile to Rachel, pretending what Daniel said was true.

"It's nearly nine o'clock. Can we sit?" Gavrielle entered the adjacent dining area, waving her arms at the expectant table.

There was so much food, but Rachel hardly ate beyond the soup. She felt on display, and eating seemed too dangerous. She might have splattered the beet-infused horseradish on her white blouse, spoken with parsley plastered across a tooth, laughed with a mouthful of the honeyed carrots. She didn't want to embarrass herself or Yakov, whom she felt, instinctively, wanted so much for Daniel to approve of her, of them as a couple. She watched him with his friend and suddenly missed Lark.

The men seemed enclosed in a circle of their own making, Daniel at the head of the table, Yakov to his right. Daniel leaned in, one forearm serving as ballast laid flat on the table, the other arm waving to reiterate his points, punctuating his wisecracks, pounding out the rhythm of an ancient *niggun,* or landing lightly on Yakov's arm or shoulder every so often and linger there. Gavrielle sat to Daniel's left, but was hardly in her chair. Rachel sat next to her, and was up and down constantly as well. They waited on the men, who expected such attendance to their appetites, who presided over the Shabbes table, a little like boys playing house, but in charge, nonetheless.

In the small kitchen, Rachel spooned the nondairy whipped cream into yet another beautiful serving bowl. Gavrielle positioned the homemade fruit tart on a matching platter, making little swoops along the bare edges with a sauce made from raspberries. Suddenly Gavrielle dropped her spoon, mid-swoop and grabbed Rachel's arm.

"I have to tell someone, Rachel. I'm going to burst! But you have to be able to keep a secret; I haven't even whispered a word of it to my mother."

Rachel wiped at the glob of topping that had backfired into the crook of her elbow when Gavrielle grabbed her.

"A secret? Sure." What could she say?

"I'm positive that I'm pregnant!" she windily whispered near Rachel's ear so that it almost hurt. "Baruch Hashem! I'm going to the doctor Monday, but I already did the little kit, you know, from the pharmacy, this morning. Positive! *Kehnynah Hora,*" she quickly added to ward off the jealous evil eye, who might want to rob her of her bull's-eye of a blessing.

Rachel's reaction was letter-perfect, despite the feeling that what little dinner she'd eaten had just jumped from her stomach and lodged in her throat.

"Oh, Gavrielle, that's such a blessing. Mazel Tov!"

She hugged the happy girl who, she felt certain, could float away at any moment. But Rachel suddenly felt like a creaky old chair about to bust, the weight of everything that encompassed married life sitting down on her. Babies! She hadn't let herself think about babies.

Next week, just as all the engaged girls before her, she was going to begin her private "consultations" with Rebitzen Adler, who specialized in the teachings of Jewish "family law." These are not things a girl discusses openly, even with one's own mother who may find it embarrassing to instruct a daughter in these matters and therefore not be thorough. These details are too intimate, considered too private, and modesty precludes talking about them openly. So it is left to teachers, like the Rebitzen, to shed light on the rituals practiced by observant married women in the privacy of their homes, or in the mikvah, the ritual bath that is taken each month to prepare and sanctify a woman so she can be intimate with her husband. These laws laid the ground rules and context for sexuality: the when, where, and how between married couples. The laws of *niddah*, or separation, which governed the time during and just after menstruation, when a woman is considered unclean for her husband to touch, were an integral part of the complicated and highly orchestrated relationship between a man and woman living the Chasidic way. She would learn it all and practice it to the letter of the law, but she hadn't focused on "it" until this moment, until Gavrielle's joy translated into her own absolute terror.

Rachel let go of the girl suddenly, as if what she had might be contagious then recovered quickly with, "You must be so happy!"

"Well, after all, we were in the land of miracles, Rachel. Yerushalyim! The old city takes your breath away. I'm telling you, we went to the Kotel, the wall, our first day, even with the jetlag, we had to go. I asked

Daniel to put a note for me in the cracks. 'Don't read it!' I said, 'just deliver it to Hashem!' It's exactly what I asked for! It's amazing, Baruch Hashem!"

Miracles. God providing his blessings, his bounty. Rachel wondered what hers would be, what gift from the heavens she would ask for at this very moment. *Help.* The word surfaced for the second time that evening. *Help!*

CHAPTER FIFTEEN

She almost didn't recognize him without the yellow coat on, almost brushed passed him, head down, rushing to the store for the few items her mother needed before Shabbes, wondering why this idiot was blocking the middle of the sidewalk. She felt a jolt to her chest as she realized who it was.

"Where's your slicker, slick man?"

"What? Oh my coat, well, it's too hot for that now. In the winter I'm Rain Man, in the summer I'm Tropical Rain Man." He grinned at her and pulled at the lapels of the garish Hawaiian-style shirt he wore.

Lark kept her head down. After two weeks of agonizing over where he was, she had little patience for his clowning now. She started walking away.

"Whoa, Bird, slow down. I know you been looking for me, and here I am." There was no apology in his broad smile, just the confidence of a bad son who knows he is his mother's favorite.

It was still daylight, a good forty-five minutes before candle-lighting, the streets crowded with any number of people who knew her, could observe her, as they hurried home for Shabbes.

"Not now!" she pressed through her clenched teeth, sidestepping his long legs as he tried to block her path and moved toward the market at the end of the block. He followed her, a few feet behind.

"Did you get the roses?" he said to her tightly hunched back.

She threw a glare over her shoulder. "That was two weeks ago, Romeo." Lark disappeared into the grocery store before he could answer. A few minutes later she emerged into the fading light and saw him waiting for her across the street. He was performing an elaborate mime of a parent scolding a child, finger wagging, head shaking, then repeatedly slapping his own wrist. "Bad boy, you're a baaaad boy!" she heard him say out loud for her benefit. The entire tableau, including the Chasidim, who walked a wide berth around the obviously crazy, young black man, muttering to themselves as they passed, had its intended effect on her. She laughed and felt the tension evaporate from her face and shoulders. Crossing to his side of the street, Lark held his gaze for a moment, then kept on toward home. It was all the encouragement he needed to follow quickly and more closely than before.

"I'm sorry, baby. Pee Cee was supposed to get word to you for me. Didn't you ever get the message from him?"

Lark checked around her to see who might be eavesdropping and saw that, for the moment, she and the Rain Man had a small window of privacy. "No, I never heard from Pee Cee. And I never heard from you!"

"Listen, baby, maybe I should have called your house and had a nice long conversation with your mama." He flipped an imaginary phone to his cocked ear. "'Yo, Mrs. Bird, yeah, this is Jamal, yeah, your daughter's black boyfriend...uh-huh...could you please tell her that I won't be able to see her until I finish my two-week GED course. You see I'm a high-school dropout and..."

"What?" Lark stopped short and spun on her heel. He collided with her and her tightly held groceries, ripping the flimsy paper bag and spilling its contents to the sidewalk. A box of Shabbes candles upended, sending the waxy white cylinders rolling to the curb and plopping one by one into the gutter. "You're telling me you were in school for two weeks? Are you kidding?"

He wasn't. "Every day for two weeks. Then I had to go straight to work."

"You never finished high school?"

His eyes narrowed at her tone. "I was busy at the time." He spoke to the top of her head as she scuttled along the sidewalk to retrieve the candles, the now-leaking milk container, and the bruised bananas.

"Why don't you watch where you're going, schmuck?" A tall and wide Chasidic man barreled into Jamal and sent him stumbling off the curb. "Or if you can't manage that, at least you could help the girl with the mess." It was her father.

"Fuck you, man..." Jamal punched the air in the Chasid's direction. "Fuck yourself you black-hat-black-coat muthafucka!"

"Daddy!" Lark sprang to her feet, fists full of candles, and positioned herself between the two men. "I'm okay. It was an accident."

Jamal's face registered momentary confusion, then he understood. "Yeah, Big Daddy Bird, nothin' but an accident. It's cool." He bent to pick up a few stray candles at his feet.

"Don't touch them! Leave them. They're better off in the gutter than for you to touch them." Her father lunged off the curb to grab the candles himself. Jamal backed away from the man's frenzy and looked at Lark, who fidgeted with the torn grocery bag, trying to make it whole again, rolling and pressing the ragged end of it. He shook his head, twisting his mouth in disgust. "Later, Bird, much later." He turned and quickly entered the flow of pedestrians on the other side of the street.

"What is this 'bird'? Is he calling you a bird? What does it mean? Do you know that *schvartze*?"

"I don't know. I mean, no, I don't know that person, if that's what you mean. I told you. It was an accident."

"Nothing is an accident. What are you doing out shopping so close to Shabbes? And look at that blouse, it's too thin—I can see everything. You insist on wearing that in the street and you wonder why the *persons* are following you and bumping into you for a little feel."

"What? What's wrong with this blouse? It's a normal blouse." Her father shoved his big mitt full of candles at her chest. He looked about to explode, then looking around him, thought better of it. Instead, he turned away from her.

"Go home," he shouted over his shoulder. He headed in the direction of the shul, taking long, determined strides down the sidewalk. Just then, a piercing siren erupted. It was the neighborhood candle lighting alarm, warning everyone that it was fifteen minutes to sundown. Its whooping, circular waves of sound set the very air around her to vibrating, pushing whoever was still on the streets toward their Shabbes destinations that much faster. *Boooop, boooop, boooop,* blurted the electronic taskmaster. Don't be late! Don't be late! Lark left the few candles that remained in the gutter and hurried toward home.

* * *

"I *hate* him, I *hate* him!" Lark screamed as she slammed the door to the apartment. The sob she held in her throat the entire walk home rode out of her on the heels of her words. "He goes off to that stupid retreat and comes back even more brainwashed than ever. He's insane!"

"What happened?" her mother called from the kitchen then came quickly into the narrow foyer where Lark lost hold of the groceries and crumpled to the floor amid the errant candles.

"Lark, honey, what is it? What's wrong? Come, move away from the door, come on." They both knew that every word said in the foyer would be heard distinctly in the hall and even spill over to the two apartments closest to theirs. They'd heard their share of their neighbors' petty arguments and complaints. Her mother helped Lark to her feet and they walked to the front of the apartment to Lark's bedroom. She pulled the curtains together, but left the window open, it was so hot. Lark flopped on the bed. She stared at the ceiling, her face smeared with tears and dirt from the gutter.

"Tell me what happened!" Her mother's voice had a touch of panic to it.

"It doesn't matter what happened. It's *been* happening. It's been happening for years and it's getting worse. If you don't care if your life is totally ruined, if you don't care that he's keeping us a prisoner of the fucking dark ages here, then fine, but I am losing my mind and I am getting the fuck out of here as soon as possible. *Do you understand me?*"

"What happened, Lark?" He mother measured out the words. She wore the look of a woman who had just been struck, a look Lark had seen there before, but it wasn't usually she who put it there. Lark guiltily capitulated and told her what happened, eliminating, of course, the tiny detail that she actually knew the young man that had bumped into her and that they collided because of her total shock at finding out that he, her lover, her obsession over the past eight months, had been neglecting her because he was in school!

"Someone bumps into me and all of a sudden I am some kind of a tease, flaunting my boobs on the street and deserving to be molested! I mean I've had this blouse for two years. It's practically a strait jacket. What is he talking about? It's sick. I'm sick of it!"

Her mother stood with her face in her hands. This time short staccato bursts from the siren outside signaled three minutes to candle lighting.

"Why can't we leave? Don't you want to leave with me?" Lark asked, trying to be gentle.

Her mother's hands fluttered to her wig, checking it. "Let's talk about this again after Shabbes. Okay? You are upset. It's my fault. I shouldn't have sent you out in such a rush before Shabbes."

"It's not your fault, it's him!" her anger erupting again. "When are you going to get that? And after Shabbes I'm going to meet David, remember? His party? I'm talking to David about this, that's for sure."

"Help me pick up the mess at the door. We've got to light the candles." Her mother drifted out of the room and down the hall.

Lark raked her fingers over her scalp once or twice, pulling hard at the tangles there. She got up from the bed and followed her mother, thinking there was nothing to do now but light the goddamn candles. God rested on the Sabbath. Maybe her father would too.

*   *   *

They felt momentarily relieved when he entered the apartment and sang out "Good Shabbes" in an almost lighthearted fashion. But when he lumbered into the kitchen, glaring at them both and hissing, "It might be a good <u>Shabbes</u> if my daughter wasn't running around like a whore on the street five minutes before sundown," she knew the saccharin greeting was for the neighbors' benefit, not theirs. Her mother said nothing, just turned her attention to the table, straightening forks that were perfectly straight, smoothing a wrinkle in the tablecloth that wasn't wrinkled. Lark had a choice in these situations: to keep the peace or sometimes just to mess with his head, she would stay silent, avoid his eyes, pretend that what he was saying was right, challenge nothing. His ugly mood would blow over with no resistance or the copious wine he'd consume at dinner would put him to sleep before he could really blow up. The other choice became her default when her emotions took her beyond choices, when all she could do was strike back, try to hurt him as much as he hurt her—let it rip and take her chances with how crazy it might get. This was one of those times.

"That's right! I'm a famous whore in this neighborhood! My busiest time is right before Shabbes. All the *schvartzes*," she twisted her mouth on the word, mimicking her father's way of spitting it out like a bad taste in his mouth, "just get their paychecks cashed, and they are really horny for a nice Chasidic girl." She grabbed her long skirt with both hands and lifted it to mid-thigh, doing a mock-sexy shimmy to punctuate her story. Too bad she looked down.

The blow to her head sent her into a collision course with the chairs and table behind her. She'd heard his animal grunt as he swung his heavy arm with all his weight behind it, but not soon enough to duck. He got her right above the ear and it rung now with a thin metallic ping. Her mother screamed and lunged toward Lark, but had to immediately turn her attention to the lit candles that had tipped over onto the table, spilling wax and scorching the "good" tablecloth. Lark extricated herself from among the chairs and from behind her mother and ran for her room. Her father bellowed behind her.

"You can't talk to me like that!"

"Oh, but you can call me a whore and accuse me of anything and I'm supposed to just take it!"

Lark slammed the door to her room in his face, but she knew it wasn't over. There was no lock. He burst in, his face a mask of rage, bubbles of spit dotting the corners of his mouth.

Her mother whimpered from behind, "Avram, stop. Stop this. I'm calling the police. I'm picking up the phone on Shabbes and calling the police!"

"Shut up! It's because of you she's like this. I told you we should send her away to camp or to that school in Wisconsin...at least until she can be married properly, but no!"

Lark backed away from him, toward the corner of the room and her bed. She fell back onto it, shouting, "You got rid of David, now you want to get rid of me. Don't worry, because I am leaving, but it is not going to be to some brainwashing, stupid fucking assembly-line school that turns women into baby machines and slaves!"

He was on her in an instant. Lark was on her back, her legs in the air, her shoes pinned against his wide chest, keeping him, at least, from reaching her face with his blows. The best he could do was pound the sides of her legs, his broad, thick hands smacking open against her exposed thighs and hips.

Lark kicked at him and locked her eyes on his distorted face. "I hate you. I hate your guts!" she repeated like a menacing mantra. At one point his eyes met hers, and the steam just seemed to go out of him. It is no small thing to look at the face of a once-cherished child and see nothing but monstrous contempt. It shook him.

He backed away from her, looking as though he barely recognized her or the room he was in. In the silence that fell between them they could hear the crying and murmuring of her mother on the other side of the apartment. He turned toward her voice. "Sarah! Sarah, put down the phone! It's Shabbes!" He hurried down the hallway.

Lark knew her mother was not on the phone. She always threatened but never actually did it. Not now and not the dozens of other times when she should have. She was back there, talking to the walls, praying to whomever, for God-knows-what. She also knew that he'd be back in a while, blubbering about how much he loved her and only wanted the best for her, the best life that God had to offer a girl, a clean, pure life devoted to Hashem. In the days following these incidents he would be elevated to a near-martyr status in his mind, sure that though his actions had been harsh, they were righteous; though his family may not understand him, he followed a hallowed path. *I just can't listen to all that right now,* Lark thought. Not again. She couldn't face his watery, bloodshot eyes and his unapologetic backpedaling. Sorry? No, he was never sorry about what he'd done, never aware of the damage he'd inflicted on body and soul, only about how it all made *him* feel. He was sorry they'd all made him so mad and made him feel so bad, was what it came down to.

Lark rolled into an upright position and sat at the edge of her bed. She almost laughed when she saw her legs. Bright red welts in the shape of her father's thick hands rose on the surface of her otherwise pale thighs. She stood up and let her skirt fall. As she walked mechanically down the hall toward the front door, the starchy fabric brushed against her pulsing bruises. She heard her parents arguing in their bedroom. *I just can't listen to all that right now,* she thought once again, as she quietly closed the front door behind her.

CHAPTER SIXTEEN

Lark took the stairs down to the street, one step at a time instead of her usual two or three. The sound of the creaky old elevator running on a Friday night would have brought too many people out snooping in the hallway, including the super, a cranky gossip whose ground-floor apartment gave him a particular vantage point on the comings and goings in their building. When she reached the lobby she tiptoed past his half-open door. A broomstick wedged in the doorjamb kept it that way practically all summer long for "Crossink ventee-layshun," as Mr. Putnik described the tepid channel of air that crossed from the front of the building to the back alley that his tiny apartment faced. Lark peeked in and saw the blue light flickering from the old man's living room TV. What she wouldn't give to curl up in front of a TV all night and watch Hollywood's idea of a family get into the darndest situations! She heard canned laughter and remembered it like an old friend. She smelled something spicy—ribs maybe, or Chinese takeout—and felt her empty stomach grumble.

Once she hit the street outside her building she walked quickly then broke into a run for three full blocks until her lungs and already shaky legs gave out. She didn't want to take any chances on being stopped, on

181

having to go back up there. She had no idea where she was going, but she knew she just had to get out.

The streets were fairly deserted but not quiet. Flung-open windows on the warm night spilled the sounds of Shabbes into the air. Singing and the pounding of rhythms on sturdy tables, laughter, conversation, hearty l'chaims and rich smells swept around her and swept her forward toward the edge of the neighborhood, the six square blocks of Crown Heights.

Lark had been told over and over that Crown Heights was like a heaven on earth, the name being an English translation of *Keter Elyon*, a spiritual realm described in the Kabbalah, the ancient mystical texts. To her father, her teachers and peers, the place was magical, with street names that held prophetic messages. Lark heard her share of them. Wasn't the Rebbe's house, after all, on the corner of *King*ston Street, alluding to his obvious divinely-appointed role of spiritual sovereign for their community and all the unaffiliated Jews in America? And the mikvah, the place where women go to fulfill one of the most important of the mitzvahs regarding family, wasn't that on Albany Street...*al beni,* in Hebrew meaning, "concerning my children"; didn't the very house numbers tally up to have enlightening meanings according to their *gematria,* a complex code that assigns numerical value to Hebrew letters, so that the Rebbe's address wasn't just a number but translated into a word that held great mystical potential? People she knew spoke of such things as though they were definitive messages from God, signposts along their spiritual paths that validated their beliefs. Lark thought they were desperate contrivances—just a bunch of insecure, frightened people trying to make sense of the world, trying to order it and number it, assign it a meaning, control it and explain their place in it. She was sick of people, mostly men, telling her what they were sure God meant by this or that, and what that now meant she had to do, think, eat, drink, or wear. They were a community of experts, all of them, so absolutely sure that God's intention was imprinted in their Torah and that their copious interpretations and ruminations were all dead-on to His will.

And what happens to people when they get so goddamn confident that they know God and they know what he wants? Do they suddenly find themselves in love with the world and life and celebrating all living things and the miracle of each individual and all that crap? No. Not at all. They think they do, but they don't. Lark hashed out these bitter thoughts as she walked. She remembered something that the young rabbi from Monsey, the one that got the whole ball rolling for her parents in the first place, told them during one of those long Shabbes nights at his cramped table. He was trying to make some point about the sanctity of the Sabbath. Lark couldn't quite remember how it came up, but she remembered that David grabbed her knee under the table and squeezed hard when they'd heard it. The rabbi had said that *halachah*, the law, dictates that if a Jew comes upon a dying man on the road during the Sabbath, a man who needs help or could benefit from your lifting him or dragging him or otherwise "working" on the Sabbath, that a Jew could only help the dying man if he was also a Jew. If he was a gentile, you had to just pass him by. Let him die. Better to keep the Sabbath than help a gentile was what he was basically saying. When David finally let go of her knee they exchanged horrified glances. They knew better than to say anything. They'd only get hell later for "embarrassing" their father with their challenges or questions, so why bother? Still, in David's eyes she saw his contempt for this kind of religion, this utter disregard for life, this withholding of simple human kindness and delivering sheer cruelty, all in the name of pious reverence for some God.

So as Lark wandered the streets, she didn't feel like she was in any heaven on earth, some reflection of a divine world. She felt like she was in a ghetto, a dark place walled off from other places, populated by people who refused to join the world because they were convinced they were destined to be apart from it, above it in some way. She knew it wasn't just Chasids who acted this way. And it wasn't all Chasids. But she knew that whenever people or governments went to a place where they started believing and preaching that they knew exactly what God wanted, or Allah wanted, or Jesus wanted, or Zeus wanted, then there were going to be people suffering. Mostly women, because whenever a group of men decide they know what God wants, it usually turns out that God wants women to be controlled and covered up and tied to bed and birthing. Also, expect wars and the senseless killing of other groups of people who are also certain what their God wants, because guaranteed, it's much different from what yours wants.

Lark realized she was nervously clenching and unclenching a fistful of coins that remained in her skirt pocket from her run to the store. The sound of the jangling coins brought her out of her major analysis of world religions in time to see the dirty look a passing Chasid shot her when he'd heard the jangling, too. Carrying money on Shabbes...shame!

"Mind your own business!" she yelled in response to his wordless rebuke.

"And who is minding yours?" he threw back, dismissing and scolding her all at once.

What am I doing? What do I care what he thinks? Pulling the coins and crumpled bills from her pocket, she counted three dollars and eighty-five cents. She wished she hadn't impulsively grabbed the bananas on the way to the register, thinking it would be nice to have them on her morning cereal. She'd have more money now, could get something to eat maybe or...*what? Who was she kidding? Where was she going with three bucks and change?*

Lark heard the rumble of an approaching train and realized she'd wandered as far as the subway, the entrance just across the street from where she stood. Why hadn't she thought of it before? She could go to David's! She planned to go tomorrow for the party, but why not just go now? If she disappeared for a couple of days, wouldn't that just serve her parents right? They could drive themselves crazy thinking she was dead or kidnapped or something. Maybe it would wake her mother up, raise the stakes on finally taking some sort of stand against her father.

Racing down the stairs to the station, she bought a token from the bored and sleepy attendant and bumped her bruised hips through the turnstile. She went straight to the pay phone tucked into a steel girder halfway down the platform. *I'll just call David and make sure he'll be home to meet me.* She dialed the pager number she'd memorized the day he gave it to her and entered the number of the pay phone so he could call her back. He would, too. Last week when she'd called him, just to hear his voice, just to make sure that they actually saw him and he was really back in her life, he'd called back in a matter of minutes. "What's wrong?" he said as soon as her heard her voice. It gave her goose bumps to hear his concern.

Now that she had a plan, Lark felt exhilarated. She paced back and forth, waiting for the phone to ring and for the next train to Manhattan to come in. She hovered near the phone, but walked to the edge of the platform every now and then to peer down the track expectantly. She was the only person down there, aside from an old heavyset black woman who took over most of the only bench, spreading out her ample self and her many overstuffed shopping bags, checking and rechecking them, as she sat waiting for the train.

A breeze stirred through the tunnel down below the hot streets and it felt good. Lark's legs were sweaty under her skirt and they stung. A distant horn sounded, signaling that a train was approaching, but it was only the train coming in from Manhattan on the opposite track. It roared into the station, whipping pungent air and dust around it. She pressed her ear to the cool steel casing of the pay phone to make sure she wouldn't miss the call with all the noise. Still nothing. *Maybe he's out with his friends...needs a minute to find a phone, get some change. He'll call.*

When the train pulled away, Lark saw a group of kids—they looked to be about her age—had gotten off the train and headed toward the exit. One carried a boom box that blasted some heavy rhythmic rap, the others walked in a bounce to the rhythm, talking loudly and amiably with each other. She watched them with a vague sense of longing. She'd become a loner these past few years, aside from her unlikely friendship with Rachel, and her connection to Jamal. As intense as these relationships could be, she remained an outsider in the lives of both these people. Accepted, perhaps even loved by them, but not wholly welcomed into their larger lives or the groups they ultimately belonged to. As the kids disappeared down the stairs to the street and their music became fainter, she thought how nice it would be to just be a part of something, to find something, some "gang" of her own that she felt at home with.

She thought of David somewhere with his gang, his group of bright and beautiful college kids. She pictured Dog and his leggy sister, David and some others sitting around, sipping strong coffee or beer, laughing, talking in the din of some incredibly cool East Village cafe. Then she walks in, the runaway sister, disheveled, bleary-eyed, dressed in old lady clothes, with a pathetic story of being beaten up by her ex-hippie-turned-religious-zealot father. She shuddered to think of them feeling sorry for her, clucking over her black and blue marks, exchanging pitying looks behind her back. *Forget it!* She knew in that instant that she couldn't go. Not tonight. She'd go tomorrow as planned, walk in to the party on her terms, an invited guest, one of the crowd. No drama, no history, just a bright future.

She let the heavy steel exit gate to the train platform slam behind her. A distant rumble told her the train to Manhattan was finally coming through and, as she headed up the stairs that led back to the street, a metallic ringing sounded from below, letting her know that David was coming through, too.

* * *

It was moments like this that made Lark believe in divine forces, believe that there could be a swarm of angels beating their wings about her, stirring a breeze that brought with it the answer to her most pressing prayers. So when she recognized his unmistakable silhouette against the backdrop of the brightly lit donut shop across from the subway stairs, she murmured a breathless "thank you" to her winged guardians. When she left the platform below she'd closed the door on one option for escape. And here, bathed in the light of a neon donut and steaming cup of coffee, was another one.

"Jamal!" she shouted but her voice and the panic in it were drowned out by the Manhattan-bound train rumbling and squealing away on the tracks just beneath the street. He began to walk down the block, away from her, moving on to whatever transaction was next for him on this balmy summer night. Little did he know it would be with her. Lark ran to catch up to him, and should have known better than to startle a black man at night in a rough part of the neighborhood. She came up behind him and pulled at his billowing shirt, but was nearly knocked down as he spun around to face his would-be assailant, jaw set, arms extended in front of him, a small knife appearing in his right hand, poised to strike.

"What the...?" he began.

"It's me, it's me!" she stumbled back, tripping over her feet, her ass heading for the sidewalk, skirt flying up over her knees. Her hands, breaking the fall behind her, got good and scraped in the process.

"Shit!" they barked at each other at exactly the same moment.

"What are you doing, girl? You gonna get hurt jumping behind someone like that. What's the matter with you?"

The fall hadn't really hurt her, the scrapes on her hands, superficial. A few beads of blood on the fleshiest part of her palm bubbled up, but someone would have thought she'd severed a major artery the way she sat there staring at them. She began crying in that pitiful, totally chest-heaving, snot-dripping way. One more injury in a night of opened wounds, old and new, put her over the top.

"Come on, get up." He moved in behind her to help her to her feet and that's when the dark shadows on her splayed legs turned into bruises before his eyes. He knew all at once what his little bird was doing flying around on a Friday night.

"Can you walk, Bird? Are you okay?" The care in his voice got her slobbering worse than ever. Any remaining bravado cracked with the sound of his kindness, the press of his hand on the small of her back.

She kept crying quietly and he said little to her, letting loose an occasional string of foul expletives directed at her father. He'd heard enough about him over the past months and seen him in action just hours earlier, so there was no doubting who was responsible for what had happened between their little meeting on the street and now.

Lark had no idea where they were going, but just allowed herself to be led. She would have to go home eventually, but she didn't have to think about that now, did she?

They turned off the storefront-lit main thoroughfare and continued down a narrower side street. She looked down at her feet mostly, her hand fluttering at her mouth, stifling her whimpering as best she could. Lark felt embarrassed about the state she was in, but not uncomfortably so. That's not why she was crying. The crying was a relief. Something she felt safe to do now. The Rain Man had become her home, her safe haven in the absence of one where she lived. Though she tried not to dwell on her "real" life when she was with him, he knew enough. Neither of them was living some all-American dream, springing as they did from their diametric corners of the Crown Heights ghetto. Opposite ends of the same cloth, they were set apart from each other and from the mainstream, but had common ground along the fringes to cling to.

Jamal took Lark down an alley behind a nondescript apartment building and halfway past a row of ground-level windows covered with bars. He took a stairway that led below the ground to a heavy metal screened door.

"Watch your step."

He took his time with her on the narrow concrete steps. On the landing, he searched for a key on a ring that was hooked to his belt loop. The ring was on a retractable steel cord that zipped back into its chrome container when he was done unlocking the door.

The air inside was heavy with spices she didn't recognize and stale smoke. The apartment opened directly into a small living room. A boy, eight, maybe nine years old sat on a worn sofa across from a TV, which threw off the only light in the room. His small hands were tight around a control of some sort, hooked to a box on the floor that was connected to the set by a jumble of wires. On the screen a midget-like man, with a mustache and a cap clamped down on his head, leaped over various obstacles that sailed at him. With flicks and jabs of the boy's skinny fingers, the little man threw fireballs and other weapons that seemed to come from nowhere as he negotiated the two-dimensional world. All the while a simple, nickelodeon-type melody accompanied him on his way.

"Where is she?" Jamal asked the boy.

The boy turned to look their way and a broad smile spread across his face.

"Hello Jamal." The smile faded as he saw Lark and he abruptly turned his focus back to the TV.

"Oh no, oh no" he said quietly over and over as he watched his little man crash and implode into a dainty puff of smoke at the bottom of a long pit. In an instant the screen dissolved into a new image with the tiny hero back intact and ready to go another round.

"New game. New game." The boy repeated, then fell silent, intent on the screen.

Jamal took her hand and led her through the room behind the boy, to a hallway with several doorways. They quickly passed a small kitchen, the source of the foreign, spicy smells and, as they got closer, the sourness of rotting trash. He reached to close the wide-open door they next passed, but not before Lark could see a woman lying across a bed that took up most of the small room. She looked like she'd just fallen there face-first atop the crumpled bedspread, one arm half buried beneath her, her head twisted to one side, her mouth dropped open, one foot hanging off the side, one scuffed slipper on, the other dropped to the floor.

They entered the last room off the hall, a dark, narrow rectangle with two high windows that looked out onto the alley floor through tightly spaced bars. The space was jammed with stuff: a bunk bed, two lopsided dressers belching out clothes from overstuffed drawers, a bicycle with a missing front wheel. A small closet at one end overflowed against a half-open door that could never close with all that was draped over it. The walls were almost completely covered with dated military recruitment posters and magazine cutouts of fighter planes and helicopters. "You can be Black and Navy" one poster declared, a young man with a foot-high Afro wearing a Black Power t-shirt stood looking earnest below the headline. The shiny brim of an officer's cap pulled low over strong black eyes looking proudly into the distance filled another poster that promised "We'll take you as far as you want to go. Army." Lark tried to take in all in. A faded camouflage jacket was somehow tacked to the ceiling above the top bunk. The alley light streaming in from the windows let her read an embroidered slogan on the jacket: "Black and Proud 1969" on one side; the name "R. Whitmore" on the other. He led her to sit on the bottom bunk then closed the door.

"Who's the kid?" Lark already thought she knew.

"My brother. Half-brother. He's not right." And then as if to save her the trouble of asking, "That was my junkie mother on the bed."

Lark took a deep breath and took in the whole story packed into these few words. She realized that while he knew what her home life was about, she'd been told little of his life beyond the reason for his ink-rimmed fingernails, and she hadn't really asked. The Rain Man was to her as he appeared on the street corner, a cocky and confident genie in a bottle. He materialized in the park or behind the shul or outside the neighborhood store to help make her wishes come true, transforming her prison into a playground for a few pick-pocketed hours here and there. In an instant she knew he was not just her genie. He was making things happen on this side of town, too—like groceries and bikes, video games and rent payments.

"And all the soldier stuff?" Lark thought she knew this too.

Jamal pulled at the chain around his neck—a tarnished rope of little chrome beads that she'd noticed before, but never examined closely. At the end of the chain dangled the metal rectangles she recognized from movies she'd seen as dog tags.

"R. Whitmore," he read off the tags. "He came home on leave from Nam long enough to get married to my mother. Then he went and reported for another tour. He came back in a big black bag in '72, a few months after I was born."

Jamal climbed up to the top bunk and flopped on his back on the thin mattress. The bed creaked and swayed under his weight. He reached up to the jacket suspended on the ceiling and slipped his long fingers into one of the breast pockets, pulling out what was hidden there. He jumped down to the floor, landing lightly and sat next to her on the lower bed.

"This is him." He handed Lark a picture. It was pressed between sheets of laminate, but under the protective plastic she could see the old photo had been much handled, crisscrossed as it was with creases and stained with ink along the dog-eared edges.

In the picture Lark could pick out R. Whitmore among the group of six black soldiers who posed in front of a weather-beaten barrack wall. A makeshift sign above their heads read "Brothers 459" She recognized him. He had his shirt off and his lean body assumed a stance she knew intimately. If it wasn't for the shaved head on R. Whitmore, she'd have sworn it was a photo of Jamal, one of those trick carnival photos, in which you'd be dressed up in a fake vintage costume, and end up with a strategically faded print of yourself locked in some other era. There was no mistaking that this was his father.

"And these. I have these." Jamal dropped the medals in her hand and took back the photo.

Lark held them out in front of her to get a better look. There were five of them—different shapes. Some of the ribbons were shredded, others looked less worn. She could read some of the words in on the medallions, "Viet Nam Service", "National Defense," "Merit," "Valor, Honor, Fidelity." She didn't know what the medals meant, but she knew instantly what they meant to Jamal.

"Looks like he was some kind of hero."

Jamal stood up slowly. He took the metals from her, stretched up and buried them and the photos under the pillow on the upper bed.

"Yeah."

Then, he knelt down in front of Lark and gently lifted her skirt. She sat in the shadow of the bed above her but could see his face in the light coming from the high windows. He looked solemn, as though he knelt not at her feet but in front of an altar at which he was about to pray. He passed his fingers lightly over her welts, then began to gently kiss her legs starting at the knees. Lark tried to stop him, tried to pull his bowed head upward, but he took her hands and held them at her sides while he continued anointing each of her bruises with his breathy kisses. By the time he reached the softest part of her upper thigh, and had gently pulled her legs apart so that he could reach what waited for him beyond the bruises, she had eased herself backward onto the bed and let whatever reason she may have had for stopping him slip away. She let her father and mother slip away and her life in another world six blocks across town slip upward and out the cracked-open window, through the bars and into the night.

CHAPTER SEVENTEEN

The day dawned hot. By ten in the morning it was nearly 85 degrees, and the motionless trees that lined the block ahead gave Rachel advance notice that there would be no breeze to mitigate the rising heat. She had on her lightest linen, another new dress that had materialized in her closet over the last month. Her mother was hard at work assembling Rachel's "married lady" wardrobe. A week before she'd been forced to stand for two and half hours at Mandel's while the seamstress pulled and pinned and chalked half a dozen suits, another dozen dresses, and who knows how many skirts, while her mother barked out directions.

"Shorter on the sleeves, Rivka. A suit that costs this much shouldn't look like a hand-me-down, no? Can we have a waist? Pull it in a little here and there. A little waist wouldn't hurt anyone. After all, how long will she even have one, after all the *kinder* come, Baruch Hashem?"

Rachel had never paid much attention to clothes, but as the number of days until her wedding became fewer, the number of things she had to pay attention to, care about, and worry about multiplied—clothes, makeup, her posture, her skills in the kitchen, and her hair. Her hair! The appointment with the wig maker was quite possibly the most unsettling thing she'd endured thus far. As uninterested in fashion as she may have been, she realized she had a kind of pride about her hair. It was long and thick and captured the light among its chocolate-colored strands. Her hair had a weight and width she could feel when she twisted it upward into a ponytail or divided it and slipped it over and under into a hefty rope of a braid. She was glad her mother had not come with her that day as she sat in the swivel chair, facing herself and the chatty attendant in the mirror, who explained how her hair would be cropped very short just before the wedding to accommodate the wigs that would become a part of her daily routine. Rachel was sure her mother had expressly avoided this particular fashion errand on purpose and not because she was suddenly needed at the store. Miriam didn't want to see the tears she knew would come, that had probably streamed down her sisters' faces—except perhaps for Ahuva who, relished exchanging her own frizz-prone hair for the lacquer-y, humidity resistant coiffures—or be reminded of her own tears, when she'd had to face the reality years ago, of losing her hair and the feeling of the sun streaming through it forever after. The fact that her father insisted on the highest quality sheitls for her—real human hair, not the cheaper synthetic helmets that separated unnaturally and had no movement—was of little comfort to Rachel that afternoon. Nor was the idea that her hair, once shorn, would be donated to an organization that made wigs for chemotherapy patients. The irony that someone else could wear her hair in public while she covered hers was not lost on her.

Rachel took her time walking toward shul, enjoying the chance to be alone and think. Once she got there, there would be no end to the small talk, the polite questions posed: Are you excited? How many more weeks? Are you taking a wedding trip? Where? Where will you be living? Who's catering? Her carefully composed answers belied no worries, no fears, no second thoughts, and no complaints. To convey anything but absolute serenity and assurance about her marriage would be, at its highest level, flying in the face of God's will, and at a more mundane level, just plain confusing for the well-wishing women who chatted her up, eyes twinkling. They all, young and old, envied her.

She was making an exceptional shidduch, a match made in heaven. What on earth would there be to complain about? New dresses by the dozens? The highest-quality wigs? No expense spared for a wedding that would be attended by over a thousand people with dancing in the streets and police kept on overtime to close down the block? That's why when she felt like crying at the sheitl place, she didn't, so the old matron wig-maker who took and retook the measurements of her head could go on thinking that what made Rachel's eyes shine so brightly was the excite-ment and pride she'd seen in other countless young brides who sat in her chair over the years.

Rachel found herself facing the park at the corner of Lark's street, having automatically followed the route she'd taken every Saturday morning for the last few years, though not in the last few weeks. Since her engagement, a lot of her routines slipped away from her, but stand-ing there that morning she felt a particular loss over this one. Within weeks of meeting Lark, she'd begun meeting her for the walk to shul. They met on the corner or out in front of the building or across the street in the park. Lark didn't want Rachel coming up if she didn't have to; the cramped apartment was nothing like the rambling family brown-stone that housed Rachel's family, but Rachel sensed that Lark's discom-fort had little to do with the messy apartment and more to do with who lived there. Lark shrank inside her own home. She wasn't the girl Rachel knew, around her father who tried too hard to get Rachel to sit for a snack or stay for dinner, or her perpetually exhausted-looking mother who seemed always on the verge of tears. Lark didn't actually ask Rachel not to come up, but after the first few times they just met on the street and it seemed right.

Then, as if on cue, the door to Lark's building swept open and out popped her friend, one hand shielding her eyes from the sun, the other clutching a hat she probably didn't want to wear. She quickly stuffed the thing over her head—one couldn't carry it around the streets on Shabbes.

Rachel felt rewarded by this happy coincidence and was about to call to Lark when she saw that she held the door open, waiting. In seconds her father came through the door and headed down the street toward shul without a passing look toward his "doorman." A few more seconds passed and her mother followed, her face almost completely hidden by a large hat whose brim nearly touched her rounded shoulders. It was odd. They never walked to shul together.

The men traditionally left earlier. In a small shul, every man would be needed to make a minion, the essential ten men required for prayer in which the Torah could be read. In a larger shul, where a minion was not an issue, it was just a matter of being there from the beginning of the davening, to be a presence in the community and fulfill a man's obligation of daily prayer. The women were not even required to be at shul; they could simply daven at home, or not at all if their domestic duties were pressing. Rachel had been taught at school and by example that a woman's spiritual life was a given, that women were naturally closer to God in their role as co-creators, nurturers of life. This, the rabbis explained, was why it was not a requirement for women to daven at the pace and schedule laid out for men. Men were more of the earthly plane, more of the body than the soul and therefore needed the discipline of prayer throughout their day to keep them on track. They must rise with prayer and lay down at night in prayer, stopping to complete other prayers during the day on top of it. Women could if they wanted or had the time, but if the babies cried and the kitchen called, they were allowed to forego. On Shabbes if they had the luxury of attending shul it was a blessing, but better not to go until lunch was on the table for the men when they returned. In all this was a double-edged sword Rachel innately felt stabbing at her. Something about it wasn't completely right with her. She understood what it was only after she'd had the benefit of her rogue friend's insight, during one of her many ladies' room harangues.

"That's what they want you to believe now. It's like a politically correct version of what basically amounts to good old-fashioned discrimination and repression. These ancient guys decide women don't have to pray, that they can't touch the Torah because they might be having their period and are therefore unclean, and therefore shouldn't come to shul; they don't need to study, to be educated. Why? Is it because they really believe the spiritual superiority of women? I doubt it. If that's the case, why aren't the women the priests and the rabbis and the teachers of men? No. No sir. These guys set it up right. Right for them! *'We'll do all the communing with God and leading and all; we'll be all self-important and sacred and everything and we'll just make sure the ladies are freed-up to attend to our every need, have our children, and basically stay so busy twenty-four hours a day, seven days a week that they can't even worry about spirituality or personal growth or anything that might lead them to ask the question, 'Why am I this guy's personal maid? What's in it for me?'* And they get them to do it by convincing them that it's some spiritual high road! And they fall for it. They all fall for it!"

Rachel wasn't as convinced as Lark was that it was all so bad, that it was all a big lie concocted to keep women suppressed, barefoot, and pregnant. In many ways, women were honored, propped up on domestic pedestals in their world. Her own mother was like a queen bee, presiding over their lives, her father a mild-mannered worker. He treated her mother like a partner in business, in life, but nonetheless, it was always his word that was final on any subject. They were financially well off, able to hire help, and her mother had been unable to have any more children beyond the three girls, so she wasn't tied down with a large brood. With all this, Rachel also knew that other women in the community and throughout the ultraorthodox world struggled with one baby after another into the double digits, along with poverty due to husbands who preferred Torah learning over labor. The Israeli welfare system was glutted with families who received barely livable government compensation because their heads of household were declared scholars and were enrolled in one *Kollel* or another. The women in these situations were held in place by the wedge of these beliefs, the beliefs that this was their esteemed role, that this was their only option, their sole destiny, their one chance to do God's will in this world. Their men were even exempt from serving in the army, but the women were sentenced to serve and serve for their entire lives.

Rachel saw Lark's mother taking quick little heel-toe steps in her floppy flats to try and catch up with her husband, who barreled along a half block ahead. She turned, her arm scooping the air to hurry Lark along and saw Rachel standing there, observing them from the corner.

"Look who it is!" She nearly shrieked with delight. "Look who's come to meet you!"

Rachel began walking toward them and Lark turned to look. She met Rachel's smile with one so unguarded it made Lark seem changed in some way.

"Hey! Rocky!" Lark nearly ran to meet her.

"You girls take your time. Have a nice walk. I'll see you at shul later!" Lark's mother turned and flitted down the street, hand on head, holding hat and wig in place as she tried to match her husband's pace.

Lark looked terrible. The hat clamped down over her eyebrows framed bleary, red-rimmed eyes, with the skin below them puffy and dark. Her lips were dry and cracked as though it were January not July. Rachel tried not to stare as Lark approached her, and they gave each other a quick hug.

"I know I look terrible. I could use a gallon of Chapstick."

"Well..."

"It's okay. I know. I didn't get much sleep. Big night at the Shulman place."

"What do you mean?"

"Oh, just them. My parents. Going at each other. Again. My father going at me. Again. Just the usual Shabbes evening. Isn't that how it is at your place?"

"Lark, what happened?"

"He went nuts on me again. I guess I'm just not the good little maidela he so desperately wants me to be. Not that I ever gave him one reason to believe that I would be, but every once and a while it hits him. He realizes I am not going along with his master plan. Then he freaks." Lark pounded her chest and did a little mock Tarzan yodel, then threw her hands up in disgust.

"After that, I just left."

"What do you mean you left? What did you do? Where did you go?" Rachel thought of her own evening at Gavrielle and Daniel's where the most dramatic thing that happened was her intercepting some flying whipped topping with her elbow.

"I wandered around. First I thought I'd go see David, but I couldn't. Not in the shape I was in. Then luckily I ran into Jamal. He took me to his house for a while. After that...uh...I felt better...I mean, I felt like I could go back home."

"You went to his house?" Rachel wished she hadn't sounded so shocked. She had decided after the last time she saw Lark, after she and Yakov had run into her on the street, that she was not going to be negative about Lark's relationship with Jamal. She'd acted badly about the whole thing to begin with and decided she didn't want to lose Lark over it. She was losing hold of so much in the wake of this engagement, moving into so much that was unknown, she wanted to hold on to whatever familiar ground she could, even if it meant accepting Lark in a relationship she didn't understand.

"Yes, I went to his house," Lark shot back, then grabbed hold of Rachel's arm and pulled her toward the entrance of her building. "Come here." She opened the door to the vestibule and dragged Rachel in.

"You think I was in danger going over Jamal's? This is where I am in danger, Rocky. Right here in this building, in my own house." Lark looked around to make sure no one was in the lobby or directly outside the door. Then she lifted her skirt so Rachel could see the bruises that had turned from the almost comical hand-shaped welts into deep purple and yellow bruises all along her legs. Rachel shut her eyes against the sight.

"Where was I supposed to go? To your house? How happy would your parents be to see me in the middle of Shabbes dinner, telling my little sob story? How weird would that be? I was lucky to run into Jamal. He gave me a place to go; he took care of me while I waited for my father to get drunk enough to fall asleep so I could go home."

Until now, Lark had more or less protected Rachel from the gorier details of her home life. Or maybe she had been protecting herself. Exposing her legs, bringing the dark truth of it into the light left Lark not relieved, but further burdened with shame. It didn't help that Rachel looked like she was going to throw up when she saw the bruises. She could only imagine how her parents would react. The worst things you could say about Rachel's *haimish* parents were that that they were constant, reliably boring, predictable. What was happening to Lark, what had been happening to her and around her for years, would be so outside of their cozy world that it could only serve to push Lark further outside the perimeter they allowed her to inhabit now.

"Oh, Lark, I didn't know. You never told me it was...like that." Lark let her skirt fall.

"I know. Who wants to talk about it? Now you know why I have to get away from here. Why I have been thinking about nothing else since you've known me. Since before that, even. Since David left." Lark opened the door and held it for Rachel. They walked out in to the light and toward shul.

"How soon would you leave?" Rachel asked tentatively. She had just made up her mind to hold on to her friend and now she found herself trying to prepare to let her go.

"I'm not going anywhere until my birthday, unless something crazy happens. I'm not going to take off, just to be dragged back here by the police. When I leave, I don't want them to be able to do anything about it, because there is no way I can come back."

"Where are going to go?

"I thought I'd move in with you and Yakov and the Rebbe." They needed a laugh and that was it.

"Can you imagine?" Rachel mused and they exchanged a few hilarious scenarios that could play out under that ludicrous living arrangement. But Rachel wanted to change the subject because the joke was getting too close, making her feel too close to thinking it was ludicrous for her, too.

"What's happening with David? Is he going to help you? Will you go live with him in the city?" The city wasn't so far.

"Well, that's what I'm hoping. I'm supposed to see him tonight. I've only really seen him once remember? And talked to him one other time? I think he wants to help, but I don't know how much. He wants to get my mother out, too, but I don't know. I don't know if she's ready for that. Anyway, I'm not waiting for her. When November 5th comes, I'm blowing out my birthday candles and you know what my wish is going to be—'get me out of here!'"

Their conversation had delivered them to the door of the shul. Climbing the stairs to the women's gallery, Rachel asked, "What, no ladies' room?"

"Well, after last night, I have to make my appearance. I've had enough insanity for one weekend. Gotta keep the wild animals subdued. For now."

They scanned the packed gallery for seats. Lark's mother waved at the girls, pointing to two seats she'd saved beside her toward the back. In the front row, overlooking the sanctuary below, Rachel's mother sat tête-à-tête with Yakov's mother. A lone empty seat was waiting beside them.

"Go ahead." Lark solved her friend's dilemma for her. "Ya gotta do what'cha gotta do. I'll catch up with you at the kiddish. Save me two brownies, no nuts."

"Sure, no nuts."

Just then all of the ladies rose to their feet in deference to the Torah scrolls that were being taken from their hiding place, behind the closed doors of the Ark at the front of the sanctuary. The scrolls were paraded down the aisles below. Men crowded each other to steal kisses, with the tips of their prayer shawls, from the scrolls as they passed on their way to the bima, where one would be unraveled and read. Above, women reached out their bare fingers in the direction of the scrolls, then brought these 'air kisses" to their lips. Try as they might, from where they sat, they could never reach them.

* * *

The service was over soon enough. Maybe it flew by because Lark spent the rest of it in a half-doze, which her mother insisted on interrupting every so often by jabbing her in the arm with her elbow. Lark knew she wasn't just trying to keep her awake. Sarah was trying to get her daughter to look at her, to show some sign of remorse, forgiveness, anything but the hardness she'd been telegraphing from her eyes since she came home the night before.

Lark made her way home from Jamal's a little after midnight. He'd walked with her until they got near her neighborhood, then a half block behind her until she got to her building. He tried to convince her not to go back, but they both realized that staying there with him was not exactly an option. Staying out all night would only ruin her chances for going to David's tomorrow. If she went home, she'd have a chance. He'd be passed out. There were good odds that by morning a hangover and guilt would make her father manageable, if not altogether agreeable.

When she tested the front door to the apartment it was open. Her mother was waiting up, but they said little to each other. Neither of them wanted to wake her father who lay splayed out along the couch, a dead arm and the strings of his tzitses reaching to the carpet. And after all, what was there to say? Lark was in no mood to hear her mother make excuses for him, to say how upset he was after she left, how sorry he was, how worried they were when it got later and later and she still wasn't home. Lark headed for the bathroom and locked the door behind her before her mother could follow her in. Even as she ran the water and washed her face and hands, the soap and suds turning gray with the city soot and sweat of the long evening, she felt her mother's presence just outside the door.

"Mom, I'm okay. Go to bed," she whispered into the door.

"I...I thought you might not come back. I...," her voice trailed off as if any further effort was out of the question.

"It's okay. I'm back. I just walked around. I lost track of time." Lark opened the door an inch and startled her mother, who had been leaning her forehead into it. Lark met her eyes through the narrow opening for the first time since she'd entered the apartment.

"But I *am* leaving. It just wasn't tonight. You understand?"

Her mother nodded as though she took in the information, but remained stranded there in the hallway, swaying just slightly from leg to leg, as though she wasn't sure what her next move should be.

"Mom, go to bed. You look really tired. I'm okay." Lark peered down the hallway and watched her mother pad away, her stocking feet barely gripping the wood floors with their thick, yellowed layers of shellac. As she crossed under the archway at the threshold to the living room, all the lamps suddenly went out. The Shabbes timer had kicked in, rigged so they wouldn't *manually* turn lights on or off during the holy day, and the darkness swallowed her mother up in an instant.

In the morning, things were tense but controlled. A headache and a hot night spent hanging off the sloping sofa made her father grumpy but subdued. They silently agreed to ignore the entire episode and each other for the most part. His only concession to the whole incident was that he got his own cold cereal, even offered to get Lark hers instead of waiting to be served, and he said to no one in particular that it was good to spend breakfast together on Shabbes instead of rushing off to shul. Even so, when it was time to leave, he seemed agitated that he was getting such a late start, and bounded down the street anyway, leaving his wife and Lark far behind.

* * *

After the service, Lark filed out of the gallery and down the stairs along with the throng of women headed either toward the ladies' room, or the basement for the kiddish—the spread of challah and sweets sponsored by one family or another in honor of some auspicious occasion. Isaac's bar mitzvah, little Tamar's birthday, Rachel's engagement. The kiddish last month to honor the latter had featured much more than the brownie squares, mini Danish, and grape juice on display today. The Rubinsteins and the Fines catered a dairy spread extraordinaire: lox and bagels, three types of cream cheese, whitefish salad, baba ghanoush, tabouli, tuna salad, egg salad, rings and rings of neat, miniature rye bread laid out like dominoes, piles of Tam-Tam crackers, mountains of challah. There was even hot *cholent*, the savory Shabbes bean and potato stew, prepared before candle lighting and ready to eat after a night spent stewing in a slow cooker—the perfect Shabbes trick for a hot meal on a day when cooking is banned. In the days before electricity and the convenience of slow cookers, Jewish women in the shtetls of Europe would, on a Friday afternoon, bring their prepared cholents to the local baker, whose ovens were stoked to last through the night. The next day they'd be picked up and, courtesy of the eruv that surrounded their neighborhoods, carried home for a hot after-shul meal.

Lark found Rachel at the far end of the room, balancing brownies on her upturned palms, waiting for her.

"No nuts? Good." she popped a moist, dark square into her mouth. Rachel wouldn't be alone for long, so Lark wasted no time informing her friend of the role she was to play in tonight's plans for meeting up with David.

"Listen, Rock, I need your help...for tonight." Rachel slowly chewed her brownie, her lips pressed tightly together. She arched her brow in response, but said nothing.

"You know I made plans to see David tonight. I'm supposed to go to his place...he's having this party. I'll get a chance to, you know, just really hang out with him and get to know his friends," the thought of the burly and bashful Dog, David's roommate, brought an unexpected flutter in her gut.

"Of course, I need a cover, especially after last night. My father is not letting me out of his sight unless I have a totally irresistible excuse for being out all night—like an invitation from his favorite, yours truly, to have me all to herself for a sleepover." Lark observed her friend's face darken at the prospect of this charade, but barreled on. "You could just say that...uh...what with the engagement and all, we've had such little time together, and with the wedding coming up so soon, who knows when we'll ever be able to hang out like this again, you know, just us girls..." She ran out of steam when the truth of what she was saying hit her and her eyes began to sting with the rising emotion. Rachel handed her the last brownie and from the look on her face, and her suddenly reddening nose, Lark knew she was feeling it, too.

She waited until they were both done chewing, swallowing the brownie and the lumps in their throats.

"Will you do it?"

"I'll do it only if you promise we can have that sleepover, for real, sometime before the wedding. I'll sleep over at your house, I don't care, but that's the deal."

"Deal."

Rachel found Lark's parents in the crowd, while Lark stood back across the room and watched them react to the request. Her mother looked out over Rachel's shoulder and found Lark's eyes. *So this is your plan. I hope you get away with it,* her tired, worried face telegraphed. Her father soaked it up, turning on the charm for Rachel, whose continued association with his daughter held promise for a better position for himself in the community one day—if she didn't blow it! He waved Lark over.

"What a nice invitation Rachel has made. Are you up for it...uh, you didn't sleep well last night? Probably, the heat..." he looked cautiously at his daughter's unreadable face, then smiled broadly at Rachel, cheese Danish imbedded in the cracks of his teeth.

"No, I'm okay. I really want to go, if it's okay with you. I'll go home with Rachel after shul so we'll have the rest of the afternoon, too," she chirped, in her best good-girl voice.

Rachel followed her lead. "Sure, don't even worry about pajamas, I can lend you something; it's no big deal."

That accomplished, the girls slipped out of the crowded hall. Rachel walked Lark to the edge of their neighborhood, where the neat rows of grand and well-kept houses with their yawning bay windows ended, and the featureless, rundown apartment buildings and graffiti-scratched walls began. They stopped at Lefferts Avenue, the essential dividing line between the two worlds. Lark would continue on for several blocks so she could catch a subway into Manhattan, where no one would notice one way or the other that a Chasidic girl was riding the train on Shabbes.

"Thanks." Lark rocked on her heels and pulled some nonexistent lint off of Rachel's shoulder.

"Have fun. I hope it all works out."

Lark wondered if Rachel's hope was for them both, for the life that lay before them on either side of that street.

"Hey, it's in God's hands, right?" quipped Lark as she gave Rachel a quick hug and kiss and stepped off the curb. She reached the other side of the street and turned, expecting to see Rachel standing there waving, but her friend had already turned and begun the walk back toward home.

CHAPTER EIGHTEEN

Yakov flipped through the keys on the bulging ring, each bearing a small strip of smudged and curling white tape as a label, each one corresponding to a lock in the enormous complex that was the Rebbe's residence and office—BMNT, BLR RM, LNDRY, PNTRY, LIB, STRG. He stopped at the brass Medco labeled DOV APT and took a moment before he opened the heavy door to the rooms where he'd last seen his father alive. During *shiva* Yakov and his mother received the crowds of well-wishers down in the main house. Exhausted and still in shock at the end of these days of mourning, walking the stairs to the apartment seemed impossible for them, as was the idea of inhabiting the apartment without husband and father there to make it a home. The Rebbe ordered that guest rooms be made up in the main house, and they never really went back. One morning Yakov saw that all his clothes had been moved into the guest room closet and his art supplies were stacked neatly in the corner. It was a signal that the transition was complete, that life was forever changed with no effort on his part, and even less discussion.

The lock offered little resistance, though the tumblers had not been tumbled for well over a year. As he pushed open the door he was met with more than just the stale air of the overheated rooms on the other side. Emotions and memories floated in the air along with the dust particles suspended in the sunlight that poured into the space. He moved quickly across the room to throw open a window. A warm breeze sent the dust to churning in spirals around him and whatever else was churning inside him sent him from window to window—unlocking stiff latches, straining against dry paint and time, not stopping until everyone was open. Then he sat finally on the edge of a sill and caught his breath, pulling his shirt in and out from his chest to create a little breeze for his dampened skin.

His mother and uncle were joining him there in a matter of minutes, along with Rachel and her mother. Decisions would be made about decorating and outfitting the place for the newlyweds, who would occupy the apartment in a matter of weeks. Vendors with fabric samples and carpet books and furniture catalogs would descend. Most of what he saw before him now would be replaced, refurbished. A new life would begin here. But as he sat there, he could not for the life of him remember agreeing to let go of the old one. He'd had to, been forced to the day his father died, but had anyone asked his opinion, his permission? He hadn't been looking for a change; he'd been perfectly content in the well-worn orbit of his father's influence, in the routines of his education and art, and the unbroken circle of intimacy with his fellow students, with Daniel. The tripped domino of his father's death set in motion a series of changes that left him far from the life he had experienced in these sunlit rooms.

Yakov heard a creaking on the landing outside the door and the labored breathing that was a dead giveaway for his uncle Yossi, who, seconds later, loomed in the doorway. Yakov kept his exchanges with the man down to a minimum if he could; he had little to say to him and his uncle had little to say back that wasn't derisive or derogatory. He was not prepared for the look that crossed his uncle's face as he took in the room and his nephew perched on the windowsill—a look of undisguised despair.

"A *shonda*," he said, a Yiddish word for something that is a shame, a black mark. "A total mistake," he continued softly, shaking his bulky head. Yakov gave a small nod and felt a momentary connection, a shared outrage.

"Hashem took him and left us," he said, his tone flat, dull. "Ha!" he suddenly barked out. "What a joke, what a bad joke!" The familiar menace returned to his voice—the recognizable Yossi was back after a moment's reprieve. Still, it left Yakov wondering what joke the uncle was alluding to and how they were somehow lumped together in his twisted mind as better candidates for a cold grave than his father.

Before Yakov could say anything in answer (as if any answer would matter to the bitter man, or make any difference in their relationship), they both heard his mother's voice rising up the stairwell, chatting at lightning speed, as she often did when she was nervous, to Rachel and her mother.

"Of course, no one's been living there, so at least it's in good order, I think. Anyway, no matter, we'll have the place totally cleaned and freshened up and the floors done, with some new furniture; I was meaning to replace the sofa soon anyway, and some nice curtains...and you'll have your own dishes, of course...I think, definitely a new dishwasher—the old one was on the way out, all those little dots left over on the glasses, totally unacceptable...Oy, these stairs, you can tell I haven't walked them in a while..."

Yossi stepped aside to let the women by—his mother, Rachel's mother, and then Rachel, who looked as though she'd been dressed by someone else for the occasion, in a linen suit that had yet to hold so much as a wrinkle, a matching purse, pristine shoes. Yakov could see her struggling with her presentation. Would the life they were entering together always seem so ill fitting?

"Oh, Yossi, thank you for opening the windows...I sent him up to open the windows because I knew it would be stuffy...there will be air conditioners, one in here, and in the bedrooms, they just took them out during the winter, after Dovid..." her voice trailed off.

"Yakov opened them. He was up here already when I got here...."

"Oh, really, well...." She threw a worried look toward her son, which Yakov met with as big a smile as he could manage. He knew she was imagining him sitting in the apartment, brooding for hours before her arrival, and he didn't want her to think he was sliding back toward the inconsolable place he'd occupied for so long. His mother was not the most nurturing person, as focused as she was on her own general malaise. If and when she worried about her son, it often resulted in Yakov having to take care of her, reassure her. While Yakov was not totally convinced the decision he'd made for his future would result in his happiness, just deciding, just being in forward motion had given him a degree of momentum and nervous energy, if not authentic contentment. His mother seemed convinced of it and he wanted to keep it that way.

There was an awkward moment. They all stood there, present to the history of the place, and no one wanted to be the first to talk about its future.

"It's really bright and sunny up here...look, there's even a view."

Rachel joined Yakov at the window that overlooked the back of the house, a small courtyard, and dozens of other patches of grass and asphalt that made up the city yards of the houses that surrounded them.

"It's a blessing to be facing the back." Rachel's mother followed her daughter's lead. "It's so quiet up here you don't even feel like you are in Brooklyn."

"Except on garbage day, then you know exactly where you are!" Yakov's mother shot back with a smile. The moment passed on the wings of the small joke. The meeting could begin in earnest.

"Yossi, we'll make a list of everything that should be moved into storage or over to the thrift shop..." The two mothers moved toward the back of the apartment to begin the inventory. Yossi followed them, pulling a small pad and pen from his pocket.

"Are you okay?" Rachel asked.

Yakov turned his gaze from the rooftops. "I'm fine. Actually, it's nice to be up here again. I missed it."

"So, maybe you'll like living up here again. Or do you think it's a mistake?"

"What, getting married?"

"Well, no! No, that's not what I meant...I meant..."

"I was kidding, but it wasn't funny. I'm sorry. I know what you meant. I don't think it's a mistake. I need to be nearby for my grandfather, and now that I am up here after so long, I think it's perfect. It's just what my father would have wanted." He could see in her face that his answer was exactly what she needed to hear. That was easy. Maybe being married would be easy.

"Hey, I came to rescue you." It was Daniel. He held his broad hat aloft and mopped his reddened and sweat-streaked neck and brow with an already damp handkerchief. "You better have an elevator put in immediately...those stairs!"

"Looks like you need to be rescued, not me. Since when do a few stairs bother you so much?" Yakov teased his friend, though glad to see him. He was aware of a feeling in his stomach, a jolt he might have felt when Rachel walked in the room, but didn't. A jolt he felt now.

"Since it's 10 a.m. and 90 degrees already and I am an old married guy now...anyway, you'll see! I heard from my wife that you were going to be trapped up here with three women talking about decorating, and I thought I would rescue you. They'll ask you your advice for two hours on things you know nothing about and then they will do whatever they want to do anyway, so you might as well go have some breakfast with me. A big Sunday breakfast."

Yakov glanced at Rachel. She was smiling at Daniel. "Go. He's probably right about the decorating. Though, I doubt I'll have much to say about it either, between my mother and yours...so, really, you should go!" She walked back toward the voices of the women, gave a little wave, and disappeared down the hall leading to the bedrooms.

*   *   *

That the two men ended up back at Daniel's apartment, sitting shoulder to shoulder at the edge of one of the two single beds in his marital bedroom, was, oddly not surprising to Yakov in the least. The moment they hit the sidewalk outside the Rebbe's house and Daniel broadly feigned forgetting something at his apartment, patting down his pockets and hitting his head with the heel of his palm announcing, "I can't believe it; I left it right on the dresser so I would remember it...something I have to show you, from Israel," Yakov knew there would be no big breakfast. He also knew that Gavrielle was away for a month, having joined her mother at the Catskills bungalow her family occupied every summer at this time. Daniel was meant to join them on the weekends but hadn't this week. They would go to the apartment where they would be alone for the first time in months. Something would happen. Something, Yakov had decided in an instant, he would not stop this time.

They walked to Daniel's, saying little, their pace hurried for a lazy, hot Sunday morning, their breaths a bit shorter than the exercise demanded. Daniel, always a stride or two ahead, his muscular legs eating up more sidewalk then Yakov's thin stilts ever could, looked back at his friend, surprised to find an enigmatic curve of the lips, not so much a smile as a suppression of one. A look that said, *I know what you're up to.*

So, they sat at the edge of the bed, the long line of their legs barely touching. Yakov had followed him to the bedroom to retrieve whatever it was he was supposed to have forgotten. Why pretend? That was the thought that pulsed through him along with the blood that pressed a rhythm against his temple and rippled through his stomach on its sweep toward his groin. It pushed him toward whatever would happen between them now. But why? Of all the inevitabilities that took shape in his life over the last few weeks, this moment seemed to weigh in as the most necessary to his survival, the most inevitable.

The single beds were pushed together, set in the position they normally occupied half of the month, during the nearly two weeks when Daniel's wife was accessible to him, according to their laws. The other two weeks of the month the beds would be pushed apart. However, since she was pregnant, there was no need to fulfill the rituals of family purity, of *niddah,* when a woman was deemed untouchable, unclean. During this "unpure" time she was off-limits even to Daniel's casual touch, and then for five to seven days thereafter or until all bleeding could be guaranteed to be over. They were prohibited from so much as passing the salt between them, lest they touch during this time. On the last day, if no sign of blood resulted from her careful inspection, she'd visit the community ritual bath, the mikvah, and then return home. She'd move the small night table that separated the beds during this time to the opposite wall as a signal to her husband that they may once again inhabit their conjugal bed.

Yakov and Daniel sat on Daniel's side of the bed. Daniel handed him an envelope, the blue and white border of an airmail missive. It was addressed to Yakov. An unsent letter.

"I wrote to you when I was in Israel. It never made it to a mailbox."

Yakov carefully opened the unsealed envelope and unfolded the letter inside. It looked like it had been folded and refolded many times, crumpled, then smoothed out again. Daniel's familiar handwriting floated over the onionskin texture of the page. Yakov felt a wave of nostalgia for their yeshiva days, his friend's scrawl reminding him of the scraps of paper passed back and forth between them, scribbled with urgent insights, gossip, inside jokes that could never wait for a break in the lesson—they had had to be sent *now,* under the desk, their fingers brushing in the delivery. An excuse to touch.

He read:

Yakov,

Only one thought passes over me like a memorized prayer each moment of this trip... "I wish you were here." This cliché of all travelers who send messages homeward, this one line scrawled on the back of dime-a-dozen postcards, is a kind of lifeline to me. A line from my new life, back to my old one. A line from the lie I now lead with my words, deeds, and my body, back to the truth of you....my feelings for you. I have always loved you with my heart, my mind, but now that I have felt with my body what a man should feel, I know I love you with that part of me, too. I suppose I knew it before...that ridiculously awkward time in my room...but I was easily distracted from that feeling by your fear, by what I believed was holiness. I didn't want to feel what I felt that night if I had to feel it alone...if we couldn't share it. If you didn't feel as I did, then I was going to kill that part of me off forever.

Look at me writing a love letter! I am no Solomon, that's for sure. But what am I? A freak of nature? Someone doomed to this eternal struggle? I am a newlywed. I am a groom who last night shared intimacy with a trusting, nervous wife, exploring pleasures of the body for the first time, and could have only one thought: "I wish you were here."

And soon you will be married, too. Will your wedding night be the exercise in imagination mine was? Will you touch your wife; caress her, whisper psalms in her ear as I have, as I have been told to, all the while holding the image of another in your mind's eye? The secret to my trick? On the pillow underneath my unsuspecting bride's head I have spread my handkerchief. A handkerchief I lent to you at my wedding, soaked in your sweat, stained from the oils on your face, the spit from your beard. Never washed, it wreaks of you. With you in my lungs, your face in my mind, I become the husband I am supposed to be. In a month, Baruch Hashem, I'll learn that I will be a father as a result of this charade. Can I continue this farce for the next 50 years? For the next ten children?

I know that magicians should never reveal how a trick works, but one day soon, my friend, you may need some tricks of your own. I gladly share mine with you. This trick may be the only way we shall ever share intimacy.

Through sheer will, through the power of the imagination, and a string of dirty handkerchiefs, we will have our love affair.

Tomorrow I have an appointment to see the Rebbe Yehuda Avlam, of whose wisdom and compassion we have heard so much over the years. His father was my grandfather's Rebbe in the shtetl back in Russia, which is the only reason I even got an appointment. He lives not far from here in Yerushalyim. I go alone, of course and I will consult with him on these feelings...I can hardly consult anyone in Brooklyn! I will ask him to guide me. I cannot believe that Hashem has made me this way only to face a lifetime of deceit, a lifetime of longing. I feel you and I are so much of one soul that our being together in every way can only be in harmony with Hashem, not against him. Though I believe this, I do not have much hope for the Rebbe's response...we'll see what happens.

My wife is waiting for me to finish. She writes postcards in the other room. We have sights to see and a distant relative to meet later this afternoon. Gavrielle can show off her perfect new husband. No one will know what bubbles under the surface. I will not give her this letter to mail. I'll mail it myself later, or maybe not at all. Maybe it will offend you. Perhaps you are not like me, and that night so many months ago you were not afraid, but truly disgusted. So, I'll give her a postcard to mail to you—The Wailing Wall. We went yesterday. I davened there and placed a note in the cracks, begging Hashem for a way to happiness for us both. As I write the postcard, know that I am "Thinking of you."

Daniel

Yakov rose abruptly from the bed and went into the bathroom just off the bedroom.

"Get me a match," he said over his shoulder.

"Why?" Daniel followed him.

"I said get me a match. Now!"

Daniel went to the dining room hutch, where he knew Gavrielle kept matches and candles for Shabbes. His eyes stung. His stomach was a pit of shame, his worst fears about to materialize.

He brought the matches to Yakov and watched him burn his letter over the sink, holding on to it too long, his fingertips licked by the flames that climbed the delicate pages quickly.

"Ouch!" He drew his hand to his lips and blew on them. Then he turned toward Daniel, whose face registered such bleak pain that Yakov realized what he must be thinking.

"No one can ever read that letter," he explained.

"Of course," Daniel acquiesced. He waited for his death sentence—the death of his friendship with Yakov, the death of his hope for something between them, something that could sustain him through the charade that would constitute the rest of his life.

A haze of smoke and sulfur floated in the air between them. Yakov stepped toward Daniel, who stepped aside to let him through the narrow doorway of the bathroom. His bony friend could have passed easily in the space, but instead he pressed close to Daniel and as he passed, leaned in to whisper, "There can never be any evidence, you know." Yakov's words, his breath, then his lips fell lightly on Daniel's ear, and he kept them there.

"It will be our secret," Daniel replied, pulling him closer still.

CHAPTER NINETEEN

Shorts. That's all Lark could think about in between reading the sub-way ads on the long ride into Manhattan. I want to wear shorts. She shuddered to think how ghostly white her legs were after over four years beneath thick stockings and long skirts. The only color on her legs right now were the blue, green and purple-stained bruises she'd accrued the night before, but they were high up enough on her legs that she might be able to get away with a pair of not-too-short shorts. I want to feel the sun on my knees.

Lark mentally tallied the money she had hidden in her left shoe, knowing it would be dumb to take it out and count it right there on the train. Retrieving her stash from between her mattress and box spring that morning before shul, she'd hoped it would be enough to buy a pair of shorts and a real summer top at one of those tiny boutiques that lined the narrow streets of the Village, with metal racks and folding tables heavy with merchandise sprawling out to the sidewalk. Summer was half over, she reasoned, so there was no reason she couldn't find what she needed on sale, too.

Then she remembered shoes. Lark looked at the clunky "shul shoes" she was wearing and wanted to flip them out of the subway doors as they slid open at Canal Street. She tried to remember from the week before where the thrift shop was, the one with the enormous barrel of used shoes out on the sidewalk, chained to the front door. They'd seen it on the way back to the subway from David's apartment. Sarah stopped to rummage through it for a moment. They all laughed as she pulled one pair after another of women's shoes, size 10 or larger, from the heap. She surprised everyone by blurting out, "This must be the Drag Queen exchange!" Sarah Shulman in her sheitl, joking about drag queens?

That day had been full of surprises, not the least of which was the feeling that stole over Lark when David's roommate "Dog" had given her a too-tight hug as they said their good-byes at the 14th Street entrance to the subway. A reprise of that feeling was worming around her gut at the moment, just thinking about it. If she was going to see Dog again today, and hang out with David's crowd, Lark knew she had to have something to wear besides her current matronly getup. She'd spend whatever she had, saving just enough for the subway ride back tomorrow morning.

By the time she got through browsing at the third shop, Lark realized she had a problem. She had no idea what would be "cool." The clothes at these shops ran the gamut from leather to lace, shredded denim to vintage 40's. The last thing she wanted was to waste her money on something that was going to make her self-conscious—she could stay in her shul clothes for that! She remembered the long-legged blonde, Dog's sister Lily, who ran by them on the stairs. She had that squeaky-clean, all-American look: T-shirt, cut-off jeans, sneakers, and the smoothest golden-tanned skin. Lark understood that her subway mantra of *shorts, shorts, shorts* had sprung from that moment on the landing, and that their brief meeting with the girl existed like a snapshot she'd been holding and admiring since that day, *I want to be this girl!* written across its back.

So, Lark almost fell into the rack of skirts she'd been flipping through when someone behind her said, "Hey...aren't you David's sister?" and she turned to see Miss America herself standing there, grinning. "Do you remember me? I'm Lily. We met for like a minute? My brother, Dog, is David's roommate."

"Oh, yeah, of course. I'm Lark. I can't believe you would recognize me, we met for about thirty seconds," all the while thinking, *Of course you recognized me. I'm the only teenager in the East Village dressed in clothes that would suit the average grandmother.*

"Well, I remember that hair...it's incredible with all those curls. I am so jealous." She held her own straight-as-a-board yellow-gold strands up for inspection, making a face as though it was so much cold spaghetti. "Is that really your color? It has to be; no one could ever make that color up."

Lark turned her back to the girl, to gain a moment's composure. She shoved a skirt she held back into the rack and caught a glimpse of herself in a mirror just behind it. *Nice hair!* Now she was grinning. She turned back.

"Oh, yeah...I guess red hair runs in my family from way back in Russia or someplace."

"Well, at least you got something good from your ancestors. Everything I got from mine, I'm trying to get rid of in therapy! Ha!" She laughed loudly at her own joke and fully expected Lark to be wise to the huge burden it obviously was to be descendant from pedigree white Anglo-Saxon stock and be perfectly beautiful. Lark laughed with her, not at the joke, but at the thought of this girl's view of her upbringing as intolerable...*if she only knew!*

"Hey, don't waste your time in here...there's nothing left that's worth anything after all the July fourth sales. Why don't I lend you something to wear for tonight? You must be dying to get out of those heavy clothes. It is so hot." *Maybe she did know.* Lark felt suddenly caught. *So much for showing up looking all normal and impressing everyone.*

"My place isn't far from here and it's on the way to David's. We'll call him from there and tell him you're with me. You can even take a shower if you want. If you get there too early they'll just make you lug beer and stuff up to the roof for the party. Anyway, I have this green dress I'm thinking would look amazing on you..."

"Is it short?" Lark wanted to know.

"Oh, yeah. Definitely."

"Let's go."

* * *

Over the phone, David sounded mostly relieved that Lark wasn't coming over until later.

"We're in the middle of trying to figure out how to string lights on the roof. Dog went to the hardware store and came back with broomsticks and duct tape. We've borrowed an extension cord from every single apartment in this building and the one next door. The roof will be lit but we may burn down the neighborhood doing it. I think it is so funny that you ran into *Lily*...Dog!" he shouted into the room, "My sister ran into your sister on the street and she got kidnapped."

"Oh, no, that's the end of Lark being a decent chick...tell her to run while she can," Dog shouted back with mock panic in his voice.

"They're saying I should run, that you are going to ruin me," Lark told Lily, who was getting some Diet Cokes from the refrigerator for them. She whirled around and grabbed the phone.

"Just for that you can forget about us showing up to help. We have so much to do...hair, nails, a beauty nap... we couldn't possibly get there before eight. Bye!"

Lark and Lily sat at the impossibly small table that she insisted made the room a true eat-in kitchen, even though one person had to get up and move into the foyer in order to open the fridge.

"Try this, it's my favorite thing." Lily grabbed a thick, salty pretzel from the bag she'd plopped down on the table between them and put it in her mouth, then drowned it with a big swig of the soda. "I love the sweet and salt all mixed together."

Lark tried it. *Why does this taste like the best thing I have ever had?* thought Lark, as she crunched away. She'd had Diet Coke before. And pretzels. But not like this.

It reminded her of a story she'd heard Rachel's grandmother on her mother's side tell during one holiday meal. The bird-thin old woman with the high-pitched voice spoke about the day the Americans marched into Paris and liberated it from the Germans during WWII. She had been hiding under a false identity in the city, working as a cook for a gentile family, who suspected her true story but maintained a merciful eyes-closed attitude. Standing in the kitchen, she was washing a dish when she heard the news on the radio that Paris was finally free from Nazi control. Rachel's grandmother, about 25 at the time, dropped her dish and ran from the house, apron and all, tearing through the crowded neighborhood with no destination in mind. She wasn't alone. People everywhere had left their houses—they just wanted to be on the newly free streets. Finally, out of breath, cheeks rosy, she found herself in front of a bakery where she fished some coins out of her pocket and bought a hot, fresh baguette along with a sliver of ripe brie. Directly outside the bakery she plopped down on the curb and, crossing her legs in front of her in the gutter, she tore at the bread and cheese as if it were her first meal in months. The old woman had ended the story by declaring in that fluttery voice with the heavy accent, "For me nothing will ever have as much *tam,* as much flavor, as that bread and cheese did on that day." Between the concentration camp she'd escaped from and the dozen or so hiding places that followed, she'd been a prisoner for nearly eight years until that day. The *tam* she tasted in that moment on the curb was the flavor of freedom. That was the obvious point of the story that everyone understood, but Lark really *got it* now, as she felt that Diet Coke bubble in her mouth like it was expensive champagne. She could taste her own freedom. This day would whet her appetite for what life could serve up for her once she found her way out of Crown Heights for good.

She looked across at Lily, who pulled a basket filled with nail polish and related paraphernalia out from under the sink and offered to do Lark's nails. *Is this what my new best friend looks like?* She felt a little disloyal, thinking of Rachel, of the ease with which she could leave her old friend behind, and then pushed the thought from her mind. *She's made her choices. I have to make mine.*

"What color do you want?" Lily held up a bouquet of polishes.

"This coppery one is really nice."

"You read my mind. Green dress, red hair, copper nails. Perfecto! The only problem is that no one is going to pay any attention to me with you there!" She cracked herself up again. Her laugh was loud and easy, without a hint of restraint. Lark took another sip of the ice-cold soda. The bubbles burned deliciously on the way down, then reversed direction and came right back up as a nasty burp.

"Oops!" Lark quickly covered her mouth and stifled a hiccup.

"Lovely, just lovely, my dear. Maybe I will have a shot at the party, after all. But I can see you already speak my brother's language, so you are guaranteed his attention."

Lark giggled—and held her left hand out at arm's length to get a good look at her newly polished nails. "Perfecto, absolutely perfecto!"

* * *

She last saw him only a week ago. Still, when she recognized David across the already crowded roof, making some last-minute adjustments to an errant string of lights, she felt the shock once again of how much he had changed in the four years since he'd left home. She crept up behind him and jabbed into the part his back that was once a bit doughy, but now nearly hurt her fingertip with its muscled hardness.

"Hey, Bro."

"Hey!" He twirled to face her, wrapping himself in tiny white bulbs that flashed on and off. Lark could tell he was wondering what happened to her baby fat, too. From the direction his eyes were taking, she saw that he guessed it had all moved upward and toward the center of her chest.

"You look stunning! Hey, did you call me last night? I got a page from some Brooklyn number but no one picked up. It took me a while to get to a phone..."

"No, wasn't me—it's tough to get to a phone on Friday night, if you know what I mean." *He doesn't need to hear the details of last night*, she thought. The present and future were so intoxicating, who needed to be sobered up by the past? The green dress, though short enough to get her knees into the moonlight, fell just below the bruises on her thighs.

"Right...Shabbes...well, I thought you were calling to say you couldn't come after all. So, I'm glad you could. Where are you supposed to be?"

"At my friend Rachel's. Sleepover. In Pop's eyes, she and her parents would be saints if Jews had them. So it's cool."

"Good...good. I wouldn't want you to get in any trouble over this. The old man would freak if he knew."

"He's freaked over less. Anyway, I don't want to talk about him. He's not going to find out...and if he does, I don't care. The worst that could happen is the same shit that's happened before." She smoothed her skirt over her thighs. "Right now I just want to live one night of my life as though he does not exist and see what that feels like. You've done it for four years and you look like you survived."

"Not bad for a black sheep." He smiled at her but a dark thought passed behind his eyes as he turned his attention back to the lights. Lark saw it, but if something about walking away from the family, from their father had left a mark of regret on David, had made these past years less than the giddy spree Lark imagined it to be, she didn't want to know right now.

She gave him a hand, securing the last of the jerry-rigged broomsticks that held the lights aloft around the roof. Music started blasting from speakers nearby and some of the crowd gravitated toward the middle of the roof to dance, while others hung at the edges, drinking beer that came from kegs set up at the far end. Near the kegs, two big garbage cans filled with ice held mini bottles of vodka, tequila, cans of soda, and wine coolers. The only food consisted of huge plastic bowls filled with tortilla and potato chips, pretzels and nuclear-orange cheese puffs. A lonely bowl of salsa attracted a few high-flying yellow jackets. Lark surveyed the store-bought, meager food spread with satisfaction. It was a decidedly un-Jewish affair.

"I'm going to walk around," she told David. "You don't have to watch over me or anything. I just want to blend. Okay?"

"Sure. But I don't think you have to worry about me watching you...it's every other guy here you should worry about. Whatever experience you've had with yeshiva boys in the last couple of years, I don't think it's going to be anything like what you are going to encounter tonight. I'm no chaperone, but don't mind me if I keep an eye out to make sure you're okay. Okay?"

A shiver shot through her as her body recalled Jamal's touch the night before. There was no way she could tell David that she was way beyond yeshiva boys.

"I'll be fine. I didn't spend my whole life in Crown Heights, you know. I do have some memory of normal, even if it was back when I was fourteen."

"Yeah, big brother, lighten up! She's a big girl. She can take care of herself."

Dog came up behind them. He wore cut-off jeans, flip-flops, and a Hawaiian shirt with a bright but odd pattern of Eiffel towers, wine glasses, and fashionable French poodles.

"Happy Bastille Day! A day for the underdogs! Those who profess to be in power may face the guillotine!" He wagged his finger at David and then pointed toward the far end of the roof where Lily was working an actual mini-guillotine, chopping up fruit for tequila concoctions someone else was making in a blender. "Besides, Dave, I'm going to keep an eye on Lark myself. I already promised, remember?"

"Uh-huh, that's what I'm worried about."

They all knew he was kidding, but Lark liked being back under her brother's protection. David had always been that way. More like a sober parent than their mom or dad ever was during their stoned-out hippie phase, more of a role model and spiritual guide during their "finding God" phase. ("They are always looking for God, as if they think he's is hiding," he told her once.) He helped her shape a personal sense of faith in a "universal power" that she could relate to and tap into, even while her parents tried to get her to swallow whole the dogma and doctrine of whatever religion-of-the month-club they were hooked into. Even in his absence, it was David's memory, not anything her parents did or said to her, that served as the holy grail of her life: *He got out; I'm getting out.*

"You have to try one of these Bastille Bombs." Dog took her arm, wrapped it around his, and led her toward the syncopating chop and whir of the guillotine and the blender. "It's a secret family recipe...a little fruit, a lot of alcohol, tons of ice. It's my family description, actually! No, seriously, it's like nothing you have ever experienced."

Just what I'm here for, Lark thought. He handed her a frosty plastic cup overflowing with a rosy slush. It was delicious.

CHAPTER TWENTY

Technically they did nothing against *halachah*. This is what Daniel was babbling about as they dressed. Yakov could barely button his shirt, his bony hands trembling, let alone make sense of what his lover was trying to convince him of. *His lover.* Yakov had to sit down as the idea of such a thing passed through him. *I'll button my shirt later. Maybe I can get my shoes on for now.* Sweat seemed to pour from him; even the soles of his feet were clammy, so getting his socks back on proved more daunting than the buttons. He lay back on the bed and threw a damp arm over his eyes.

Daniel continued pacing the room as spoke. He was already dressed. "Remember? I wrote in the letter, I was going to meet with Reb Avlam in *Yerushalyim?* In hindsight, I see how the man handled me brilliantly. I thought he would throw me out of his office when I started to talk, you know, about...everything. But he listened, and asked me a lot of questions. I mean, he didn't actually say it was 'okay' or anything, but he *didn't* say what everyone else told me. He *didn't* say I should get help to get cured. And he *didn't* say that being married would help me grow out of it. Of course, he said that men with men is strictly forbidden, an abomination, all that—but at the very end it was as if he was giving me a clue, you know. At the very end he looked at me for, like, three whole minutes without saying a word, thinking, thinking—I was going crazy—then he simply quoted the text, but with a little different twist. 'Leviticus: A man shall not lay with a man *as he would a woman*.' Then he stops for a fraction of a second and adds, 'For procreation, for intercourse.' Then he shakes my hand and basically dismisses me. At first I was completely devastated; it seemed like he was telling me there was *no way*, no way to live *Chasidishly* and to, well, you know..."

Yakov tried to tune in to what Daniel was saying. Was he saying that somehow what they'd just done, the intimate boundary they had crossed, was somehow acceptable in Jewish law? Was this some fairytale story Daniel was telling that would end with the cliché and comfort of a "happily ever after"? Yakov tried to back that particular ending onto a story that featured two homosexual Chasid's and their wives. He mopped more sweat off his forehead with his sleeve.

"Are you listening, Yakov? Later that week I met some...uh...people, a group of ex-*kollel* students, that...uh...someone had told me about, who were sort of living the life, you know, in *Yerushalyim*. Not really openly, of course, but sort of."

Yakov paid attention now. *Someone* told Daniel about a group who were *living the life?* What was going on while Yakov lived cloistered within the Rebbe's walls, training to be a future *tzaddik*, a holy man, making his wedding plans and sketching a portrait of his bride-to-be for their mantel? Daniel was roaming the world from Crown Heights to Israel, consulting rebbes, and swapping information and whatever else with ex-Chasids who were living it up, or *living the life,* whatever that meant! And now he found himself lying on his friend's marital bed, trying to recover from his first consensual sexual encounter with a man, or anyone, for that matter.

"Who's this *someone* who told you about this group? Who else have you been talking to?" *So this was how jealousy felt.*

"It doesn't matter. There are people out there, even in Brooklyn. They don't want to be known. But there are people, believe me. Anyway, let me finish! These guys in Israel told me that Reb Avlam was hinting to me what they already figured out...that one *svora*, one interpretation was that as long as there wasn't, you know, *intercourse*," Daniel made a school-boy gesture with his hands—the classic finger in the hole—in answer to which Yakov rolled his eyes—"then you could possibly say that *everything else* wasn't really forbidden." Daniel sank heavily down on the bed next to Yakov, as if the whole speech and its far-fetched conclusion had taken all the wind out of him.

Whatever joy and pleasure they had shared between them in the last hour was being sucked out of the room by the insinuating need to somehow reconcile it all with their God. Yakov wondered if it couldn't have waited just a bit longer. If he could have only held the feeling to himself for a while, made it last a few days, memorized that sensation of being so completely hungry and at the same time so absolutely sated. As it was now, he could hardly recall what it felt like just fifteen minutes ago to be uniquely, utterly, and wildly unselfconscious. So un-Yakov, but yet, really, really Yakov. He finished dressing. Daniel lay on the bed, wiped impatiently at tears rolling down from his eyes into his ears.

"I'm an idiot," he said softly.

"For what?"

"For crying. For everything. For trying to think there is a way that it could be okay. For trying to have everything."

Yakov didn't know what to say. He covered Daniel's hand, clenching and unclenching the bedspread below him, with his own. Yakov was being groomed by the Rebbe to be able to look people in the eye and tell them how to live their lives. His razor-sharp mind could summon up thousands of Talmudic and mystical references that could be brought to bear on the most mundane or life-threatening situations. At this moment, no words, no references came to mind save one from the *Shir HaShirim*, the Song of Solomon: *Ani ledodi ve dodi li. My beloved is mine and I am his.*

Yakov leaned over to Daniel and whispered the phrase from the ancient love song into his friend's ear to console him. The words seemed to comfort Daniel, who threw his arm around Yakov and pulled him close. But Yakov was only reminded that in a few weeks his bride would utter these same words to him under the *chupah* as they became man and wife.

CHAPTER TWENTY-ONE

Lark stepped over more than a few sleeping bodies on the way to the bathroom. It occurred to her, the night before, that she might want to slip out early and not disturb anyone, so she stashed her Crown Heights clothes under the sink. She'd abandoned the green dress about two in the morning for a T-shirt and sweatpants belonging to David. She stepped with care, not so worried that she'd disturb anyone, but rather determined to not being seen departing in her Crown Heights costume.

Lounging around the apartment's cramped living room after the roof party wound down, she, Dog, David, and Lily, along with a few others, talked until dawn. The T-shirt she wore said "Rutgers" and a small logo at hip level on the sweatpants spelled out the Greek letters of David's fraternity there. Lark must have fallen asleep on the couch for an hour or two, her legs splayed across Dog's lap, where he'd arranged them after massaging both her feet as they all talked.

At first, the massage was kind of embarrassing, especially since he'd made a big deal about getting this special oil from his room, and everyone teased him about trying to use his "oily" tactics to hit on Lark. Even so, Lark enjoyed the attention, not to mention his strong hands kneading her aching feet. The dainty high heels that Lily lent her were nothing like the clunky "wap" shoes she was used to wearing. David had nicknamed the "sensible," heavy shoes her father insisted she wear by the sound he said they made when she walked in them: *Wap, wap, wap!* Lily's designer shoes made a *click, click, click* sound, but by the end of the night the balls of her feet burned and her calves felt drawn up into a ball somewhere behind her knees. The massage, she told herself, was purely therapeutic, but Lark couldn't help noticing how other, completely un-related parts of her tingled as he dug his strong fingers into her tired feet.

When she woke up, she was alone on the couch with a blanket tucked neatly around her. Dog and David had retreated to their rooms. She had to get going, even though she wasn't sure what time it was. In the bathroom, Lark looked at herself in the mirror and hated to give up her comfy, college girl identity. By the end of the evening she had felt completely at home with the David's friends, even though some of the conversation flew slightly above her head when it turned to the latest movies or music. She was surprised that she was able to hold her own with politics and current events, thanks to her father's addiction to news and talk radio.

Seeing herself back in the long skirt, baggy blouse, and *wap* shoes, Lark wanted to cry, but instead grabbed what she hoped was David's toothbrush and brushed her teeth. She could just stay, couldn't she? Why even go back? She'd be eighteen in a few months and by the time they figured out where she was and tried to bring her back, it would be too late.

It sounded like a great plan to her until she remembered that her mother knew exactly where she was and couldn't be trusted at this point. With a little pressure she'd crack and lead her father right to Lark and an ugly confrontation with David. Lark couldn't do that to him.

Also, there was Rachel, who would be caught in the middle for hav-ing lied to cover for her. The whole incident, once it got out—in Crown Heights, very little remained private—it could even ruin her engagement to Mr. Holy. Lark enjoyed the thought of it: releasing Rachel from her set-in-stone destiny, and how maybe ruining it for her wouldn't be such a bad thing. Ultimately, Lark gave up the whole "instant freedom" plan when she realized that she and David hadn't actually talked about her leaving Crown Heights and coming to stay with him. What if he didn't exactly want her there? This wasn't even really his place, since he was just crashing there with Dog for the summer; and just because Dog had rubbed her feet last night didn't mean he was ready for her to move in either.

"Don't tell me you are about to sneak out of here without saying good-bye."

She was so surprised by Dog standing right outside the bathroom door as she opened it, that she stumbled back into the bathroom, toppled over into the tub, bringing the plastic shower curtain and spring-loaded rod down around her head. There she was, a vague molehill of moldy vinyl with just her dreaded sensible shoes and heavy tights sticking out and over the side of the tub. Her mind flashed on the scene in the Wizard of Oz where the wicked witch of the East is crushed by Dorothy's house and her legs. Once relieved of their Ruby slippers, the legs shriveled up and rolled away underneath it. She wished she could pull off a similar disappearing act this very moment.

"Oh, jeez, I am sorry. Are you okay?"

Lark just hid her face in her hands and refused to look up at him even when he managed to get the curtain off of her and extend a hand to help her up.

"I am so sorry." He tried to sound sincere but a giggle was creeping into his voice.

"I can tell." She feigned anger but really thought she might laugh, too, or cry. She held up her arms for him to grab on to. He either overestimated her weight or underestimated his strength, because with one tug he managed to get her nearly airborne. Her feet hit the bathroom tiles but her body kept going and slammed into him, throwing him back against the door and her against his chest. Only a shabby terrycloth bathrobe hanging from a nail on the back of the door softened their trajectory.

He kissed her then. It was a deep, slow kiss, a kiss that felt as though he had all the time in the world to deliver it—pulling away from her lips like they were sweet taffy and biting them a little and then just kissing the corner of her mouth or a spot above her upper lip as he cradled her face in his big hands. He kept his eyes open and he looked like he was almost laughing at her. It was not a kiss that demanded, "I need you; I have to have you." It was more like, "Isn't this fun?"

Then he stopped.

"I guess you gotta go, huh?" He smoothed back the dampened hair around her face. The rest of her hair was buzzing wildly around her head, beyond frizz. A few hours on the couch were hardly beauty sleep and a minute or two under the shower curtain hadn't helped either.

"You are so beautiful."

You lie as good as you kiss, Lark thought, but couldn't bring herself to say.

"I better go."

"Hello?" David rapped on the bathroom door. Lark almost fell back into the tub as she backed up to let Dog open the door. She felt giddy from the kiss and found it impossible to suppress a silly grin, even when David, eyebrows raised, peered in at them and asked "Plumbing problems?"

Before either of them could explain (sorry, we were kissing!), David threw up a hand and said, "Never mind, I don't want to know!" and turned around and headed back to his bedroom. From there he shouted that he'd be ready in a minute to walk her to the subway.

Lark squeezed past Dog and made her way back through the little living room, past the kitchen and out onto the landing that led to the stairs. He followed her.

She could feel the heat of the day already, covered as she was. He stood there in just jeans, nothing else, cool as the drink of water she was craving.

"If David doesn't kill me later, maybe we could get together sometime, you know. Have a date?"

"A date?"

"You know, a movie, a bite to eat. More kissing."

She laughed. "Sounds good," then added darkly, "if my life were normal."

"Hey, you got away last night, maybe you can again. Or we can meet for lunch. They show movies in the daytime, you know. Very decadent. In fact, I like the idea of that even better. Lunch, a matinee, kissing."

"Can you stop mentioning the kissing?" She was blushing. And still grinning.

"I can't call you, so you'll have to call me." He reached into his pocket and pulled out a small square of folded paper. "I wrote down my number, see. I knew I wanted to see you again, even before the kissing."

"You are mentioning it again."

"Sorry. Can't help it." He'd begun to move toward her, just as David opened the door.

"Big brother to the rescue." He threw a disapproving look at Dog and started down the stairs. "Lark, it's after noon. You want back before anyone starts looking for you."

Lark stuffed the slip of paper with Dog's number in her skirt pocket, gave him a quick hug, and her version of a meaningful look. He held an imaginary phone to his ear and mouthed the words, "Call me," as she followed David down the stairs.

"Hungry?" David asked when they hit the sidewalk. They found a bagel place within a block and sat at a table set out on the sidewalk in front. Lark couldn't quite tell if David was angry or amused by the thought of her and Dog making out in the bathroom. She wasn't sure how she felt about it either, for that matter, now that her brain was getting some oxygen again and her body was getting some caffeine.

"I'm not upset, if that's what you're thinking," he said over the rim of his cup. It was coming back to her now. It used to be scary how David could always figure out what was going on in her head. Not in an annoying, finish-all-your-sentences kind of way, but he just knew her. And still did, after all this time.

The bagel was hot and perfect and the warmed cream cheese was attractively accumulating at the corners of her mouth as she chewed. David pushed a napkin toward her.

"Sorry."

"Nothing to be sorry about. I'm not your papa. Doug is my friend. He's a good guy and you are not a baby anymore. I figured it was going to happen anyway...how could he not fall for you? You're like the ultimate challenge."

"What do you mean?"

"Forget it. Let's just say that you are a breath of fresh air to him."

"You mean a virgin? How can you be so sure?" Lark said with mock innocence.

David did a classic spit take, but luckily he was facing out instead of toward her and the mouthful of coffee sprayed over his own sneakers. Now she pushed a napkin toward him.

"I don't think I'm ready for those details." He wiped coffee from his chin. "How about those Yankees?"

The subject was officially changed and Lark was glad. She was just as uneasy about filling David in on the details of her love life as he was of hearing them. Anyway, now they would finally have a chance to discuss her future, the one that would begin the minute she could come down from the Heights and live among the peasants.

The night before, on the roof, she'd asked Dog why he had the Bastille Day parties every year. He said he started celebrating the French Independence Day in high school the summer after they'd studied the

French Revolution in history, just to irk his parents. "They are the worst snobs...my dad's a local politician by default since he practically owns the county I grew up in. You know, horse country, whole country club thing." Lark didn't know. "I told them Bastille Day should become a family tradition to remind them that if there were ever a blue-collar revolution, they'd be among those who would have their heads rolling into a basket. They were not amused. They told their friends I was having the parties because I was a budding history buff...the perfect major for a future lawyer or senator. The real reason was that I identified with the peasants."

Lark could hardly relate to his privileged upbringing. Or, could she? The rich, old money parents didn't fit for her, but there was something about Crown Heights, and the people who populated that six-block-by-six-block area, that made her feel she was in some parallel universe with her new friend Dog. After all, the Heights might as well be some gated country club community, as closed off from the world as it was; and there was a kind of elitism that pervaded day to day life there, an unspoken or sometimes shouted belief that those who walked the ultraorthodox walk and talked their talk were better than the rest of the world, and would be better off in the great beyond, or when the day came for the Messiah to appear and bring heaven to earth. It wasn't just the whole Jews-as-The-Chosen thing—it was more like, we are the *chosen of the chosen*...the aristocracy among the rabble. Lark felt that discrimination all the time in the Heights and in some ways that was one of the most shocking things she had to reconcile when she first moved there.

All her previous experience with Judaism—Israeli Day Parades along Fifth Avenue, Purim festivals at the local reform Jewish Center, bar mitzvahs, Holocaust remembrance events and the like—had left her with a feeling that, if nothing else, being Jewish was like being in some club you automatically got to be a member of the minute you were born. Anywhere you went, Jews would kind of recognize each other in a tribal wink-wink sort of way, through a joke or a well-placed Yiddish-ism.

Even watching comedians on TV, 90% of whom were Jewish, you felt as if you not only got the joke everyone else got, but got the "inside joke," too—that being Jewish meant you were smart and funny and special, no matter what government was trying to kill you at the time. Being Jewish was a kind of home base, even if you weren't religious, or maybe especially if you weren't. But in the Heights, she soon found out that Jews were not created equal. As a transplant from the secular world, a bali teshuva's daughter, she sat on a low rung on the ladder to heaven.

She learned this in the first Shabbes she spent there, a kind of pre-flight Shabbes she was sent to spend with a random family a few weeks before her parents actually made the move. They thought the experience, doing Shabbes with a family who had a daughter the same age as her, would convince Lark that the impending move was going to be just swell, everything a girl could hope for. The enduring memory of that weekend, in fact, the only thing Lark could really remember about it, was a moment that passed in the alley behind the family's apartment building. They stood back there, she and the Melnitz family—the father, the mother, two of the boys, and the girl that Lark was supposed to be bonding to, Chaiki Melnitz. They were there because Chaiki forgot to "wear" the house key around her neck like she always did when they went to shul on Friday nights.

So, there they were in the alley because one of the boys remembered that he might have left the window of his bedroom open and, if he did, he could just climb in and unlock the front door from the inside. As the wiry boy, lost in the billowing suit that was handed down to him a good year too early, approached the window, it was clear that it was too high for him to simply climb in. He would need something to step up on or someone to give him a leg up. Then, once in reach of the window, it would have to be pushed wide open, not an easy task with an over-painted, sticky-with-soot city window. The younger boy, a seven-year-old, spotted a milk carton a few yards away by the trashcans, and ran to drag it over for his brother to stand on. A panicked, "NO!" stopped him in his tracks. His father glared at him and called his sons over. He conferred with the boys in Yiddish, throwing sidelong glances Lark's way.

"Maybe the girl could do it?" he said finally. They all turned to Lark. She didn't understand a word of Yiddish beyond some standards like "schlep" or "tuches" "schmuck" or "schvitz," but she understood exactly what was being asked of her that night. She knew that she was being asked to take the fall for moving a milk crate across an alley on Shabbes, asked to take the mark against her soul for breaking the rules of no carrying, no working in that sacred 24 hours between sunset on Friday and sunset on Saturday. Why would they ask her? Because, what would it matter to her, a secular Jew, whose life was an overcrowded junkyard of broken rules anyway? For their pristine, aristocratic souls, the transgression would have more weight, more meaning in God's imagined book of life. But for her, what could it matter? They made the decision to use her like a "Shabbes goy," a gentile who is hired to do tasks forbidden to Jews on holy days. Only, she wasn't a goy. And it was the first time a fellow Jew made Lark feel like an outsider— the only "dirty Jew" moment of her short life.

She was a little stunned as she dragged the crate across the alley and lined it up against the wall. When no one rushed to step up on it, she knew they meant her to execute the entire tainted deed. The window took more than a few minutes to slide open enough for a person to fit through, but no one made a move to help her. Chaiki stared at her shoes. The rest of them watched the entrance of the alley to make sure no one could see and misunderstand what was going on or think that it was their daughter dragging milk cartons around and climbing in windows.

Lark hoisted herself up and over the grimy sill, soiling her dress. Once inside, she stood framed in the window, looking out at them. She wanted them to know that she knew, that she understood how they had used her.

"Hey, no wonder you forgot your key," she shouted out at them. "How could you find anything in here, it's so dark!" She leaned over to a lamp by the boy's bed and switched it on.

"Don't!" she heard more than one of them scream from the alley. The father sprinted to the window, panicked. "Don't touch the lights. They are on a timer."

Lark stepped back from the sill and began brushing the soot from her dress with broad, deliberate strokes. She looked at the frantic Chasid out in the alley and said, "Makes no difference to me anyway, right?"

Lark turned and walked through the bedroom out to the hall to the front door to let them all in, and switched on every light in the apartment along the way.

CHAPTER TWENTY-TWO

S *o this is how Cinderella felt the morning after.* Lark squinted into the sunlight as she emerged from the subway onto the streets of Crown Heights. She laughed out loud when she thought: *Chasid-erella!* That was a bit more accurate for her this morning. She'd gone to the castle, danced with a prince, forced to return to an unenchanted reality, involving evil relatives and a bad wardrobe.

She took her last quarter and dropped it into the slot and held her breath to dial, since every pay phone in New York City and the five boroughs usually smelled like bad breath and/or urine. But the reconnaissance call was necessary. She had to know if she was walking into an ambush or if her evening's cover story still held.

A breathless Rachel picked up the phone on the eighth ring, just as Lark began to worry.

"Hello!"

"Rocky, it's me...were you out?"

"Yes, I just walked in. I had no idea, but my mother set up this meeting with Yakov's mother at the apartment to go over stuff, decorating, furniture...I had to go."

"Did anyone see you?"

"I saw people, but not your parents. I just walked two blocks to the Rebbe's house and back."

"I thought you were going to the apartment?"

"I did...the apartment we are taking is Yakov's parents' old apartment above the Rebbe's house."

"You are going to live in the Rebbe's house?"

"What? I can't hear you."

"Nothing."

Just then a recording told her to deposit an additional fifteen cents to continue a conversation that could take a while if Lark really said how she felt about Rachel entering not only a traditional Chasidic marriage, but one in which she'd live under the roof of a man who controlled an entire community's life, let alone the day-to-day actions of her friend. What would be left of the girl whose mind and heart had opened up to Lark and the kind of questions she had brought with her...questions that couldn't be asked under the Rebbe's roof?

"I gotta go home," Lark shouted over the recording.

"No, why don't you come over? My parents are going to be out all afternoon. We can talk," she shouted back just before the line went dead.

Lark was in no rush to get home, and being at Rachel's for a while could extend her fairytale just a little longer. She loved being at Rachel's house, especially when her parents weren't there to make her feel like she was from another planet. Everything about the house, and its furnishings, was so solid and polished. Gleaming wood floors interrupted by well-padded rugs that seemed to hold whole worlds in their color-saturated designs. Heavy "real" furniture that couldn't be carried on her father's back to yet another of their shabby dwellings or tied atop a station wagon, wrapped in a blanket on the way home from a garage sale. Creamy china shone in a lighted breakfront in the dining room, along with a collection of small porcelain figures whose sole purpose was to bring delight and beauty to their owner. Everything in Lark's house had always been cheap and functional, nothing more. At the Fines', artwork and books in leather bindings arranged artfully on mahogany shelves, sculptures, albeit all with Jewish themes, added to the richness of the house, to the "home-ness" of the home, in Lark's mind. And it was all so well kept. Clean. Orderly. It made her ache.

Lark had always yearned for a home that looked like Rachel's, even if she rejected the ultraorthodox dogma of those who lived there. Sometimes when she was visiting she felt the most overwhelming urge to take something, to pocket some *chachke*, one of the dozens of knickknacks reflecting on smooth side tables and dust-free shelves, or a wrapped soap, put out for show in the guest bathroom. She never did—it was too crazy to steal from her friend—but she was aware of the longing to take a piece of that kind of existence back home with her when she left.

Her family's house, no matter where they lived, no matter the size of the place they lived in, always seems slightly soiled. Her mother worked and slept odd hours, could never afford to hire help, and wasn't much of a housekeeper besides. A little dirt here and there didn't bother her, or she was too exhausted to care. This had turned Lark into a stickler for scrubbed toilets and wiped-down counters, and had the same effect on David, too. By the time he was ten, he would never use a glass in the house without inspecting it first. Whether he had his own room or shared one with her, he always kept his things meticulously ordered and dusted. *Well, at least we'll make great roommates again,* Lark thought happily.

When David walked her to the subway after breakfast he had all but promised that if she wanted to leave home when she turned eighteen, he'd take her in.

"What about Mom?" she'd asked but knew the answer.

"Lark, she's had my phone number now for a few weeks—since my letter. She called to set up our meeting. That was great, but she's not exactly making me a part of her life again or planning her escape with me. After four years, I show up back in her life, I offer to help her out of there if she wants it, and she's not really biting. It's like she's seen a ghost...maybe she heard Pop say kaddish over me one too many times and doesn't realize I am really alive and trying to have a relationship with her."

"I know. I thought she'd see you and snap out of it, but she's not dealing with it. I want to save her, too. But she's got to want it."

"Exactly. Well, what do *you* want to do?" He searched her eyes and she didn't look away. She wanted to drink in what his eyes were offering her: a chance to live as herself with nothing held back, hidden, pushed down, or bullied.

"Me? I have been waiting to leave there since the day you left, and you said to me 'only four years to go!' I'm dying to get out of there!"

Part of it was bravado. It was hard to imagine leaving without her mother. The leaving fantasy had always involved liberating her mother as well. Lark had saving Sarah as her agenda from her earliest memories. Her mother had always had a way of making her feel like they "were in this together," that they were going to suffer through the whole ordeal and come up laughing someday. It was just lately that Lark realized her mother had made a similar pact with her father, that she'd always had a pact with him that superseded anything else. It made her feel disappointed and betrayed.

"I'm being offered student housing for September, but if you are serious, I'll start looking for an apartment we can both live in. You are going to have to work. I'm not going to be able to swing the rent alone, going to school and everything."

A job! An apartment! He could have been saying "your kingdom, my lady" for how incredibly exotic and exciting it sounded to her.

"Once you get on your feet, we can look into school, maybe City College or something you could do part-time."

It was all going to happen exactly as she planned for the past four years. She would work and live and go to school and pass neatly from her messy childhood into a promising and well-planned future.

When Rachel answered the door, Lark had to admit that whatever she felt about the impending marriage, it certainly agreed with her friend. Rachel looked beautiful. The attention she was getting from her parents and all the sudden admiration from the community had lent her a sort of confidence in her appearance she'd never seen in Rachel before. She seemed to stand straighter, occupy her full height. *Maybe it's the heels and that over-starched linen,* thought Lark meanly. But Rachel's tight hug and purposefully planted kiss on her cheek reassured her that the friend she loved still lived and breathed under the married-lady outfit. No air kisses and patronizing back pats just yet.

"You look great," Lark told her.

"Thanks!" She did a little self-deprecating swirl, letting Lark know she was in on the joke of how strange it all was. Still, Lark could see the grace with which her formerly awkward companion had learned to take a compliment, something that would have reduced her to a blushing, shuffling puddle just a few months ago. It was a wonder what eight weeks, an engagement ring, and a gold Rolex could do to a girl's poise. Lark grabbed Rachel's wrist to take a better look at the watch that had somehow become a must-have common gift to the bride among those whose families could afford the exchange. It was another way to signal that along with the match came money. Rachel's parents had presented one to Yakov as well.

"With diamonds of course," Lark teased.

"If not me, who?" Rachel teased back. She was right. The most prestigious match to happen to this community in decades would, of course, come with all the trappings.

"So, how was the party? Was it good to see David with all his friends? Tell me what it was like."

Lark didn't know if she could. Would Rachel get judgmental on her like she did when she found out about Jamal? She made a decision to just tell it like it was. After all, if there were any hope of their friendship continuing they would have to be able to share everything. She remembered that Rachel hadn't been so outraged about Jamal as much as she was hurt that Lark had kept it all from her.

Lark told her the whole story: her serendipitous meeting with Lily, the glittering roof-top, the drinks, Dog's flirting and foot massage and his wanting to see her again. She arrived breathless at the climax of her story: David's reassurance that her future would be guaranteed, that Lark was invited full-time into his world as soon as she was ready to enter.

Rachel remained mostly quiet during the re-telling, with an occasional jaw-dropping reaction around the foot massage and falling asleep on the couch with David's friend, who couldn't seem to stop talking about kissing. She seemed genuinely excited for Lark that David was going to come through for her in the long run. When she first got off the subway, Lark made a fairytale connection to her night in the city, but she was clear from the ache in her back and the butterflies in her stomach while recounting it that what had happened was real, very real. She thought that Rachel's reaction to her experience was like one of a child's upon hearing some fantastic tome read aloud on a rainy night; it stimulated, excited, and even frightened her a little, but Rachel could be reassured that it was just a story that took place in some far-off land and that such things would never, ever befall her.

In turn, Rachel told Lark about her dates with Yakov. They strolled the Metropolitan Museum and didn't avoid the sculpture and other "immodest" exhibits as most young Chasidic couples would. Yakov raced her from exhibit to exhibit, sharing his appreciation and understanding for what they were looking at, sometimes without words. In her world, art had been mostly another vehicle for expressing Judaic themes, but what she saw that day at the Met through and in her future husband's eyes was a revelation.

"The more time I spend with him, the more I realize he is not at all what you'd think."

THE FAITHFUL | 249

Is that a good thing? —Lark wanted to say, but held her tongue. "Well, who is? I mean, we all have ways we judge people and never take the time to actually get to know them." She faked a loud cough and looked pointedly at Rachel when she said it.

"Okay, okay...point taken. I was a jerk, I guess, about..."

"Jamal? Well, forget it. I was, too, about not telling you, so we're even." Lark felt a twinge of guilt when she thought of Jamal now. Two days ago she thought the angels had answered her prayers when she ran into him; today she was knee-deep in her story about Dog and her future with David in the city. Where did Jamal fit in? She didn't want to think about that now, or give Rachel a chance to ask her that question either.

"So, what else have you guys done on these hot dates besides looking at a bunch of naked statues?"

Rachel told her that they rode the ferry again, this time to visit the Statue of Liberty and then Liberty State Park, where there was a science museum they went to. They played absentmindedly with the interactive exhibits and avoided the eyes of other young Chasidic couples, who used the museum as a neutral place to get to know each other, too. It seemed as though certain destinations, like the science museum or the Waldorf Astoria Lobby, or certain restaurants on the upper west side, were "regular" rendezvous points for these couples trying to escape the prying eyes of their close-knit community. These were safe, open, public places where they could spend a total of 30 to 40 or so hours together, talking, walking, eating, and flirting before they got married. None of that time would involve foot massages or kissing.

"Hey, I better go." Lark rose from the cushiony sofa that threatened to lull her into the deep sleep she was suddenly craving. A lot of things happened over the weekend. Any kind of real sleep was not one of them. She wasn't exactly looking forward to going home, but could think of nothing she'd rather do than crawl into her own lumpy bed and go unconscious for at least twelve hours.

"Wait, can I show you my dress?"

"Sure, I'd love to see it if it's not bad luck or evil eye or anything."

"Well, not if *you* see it. C'mon." She bounded up the steps with her stiff skirt slipping up over her knees as Lark took one slow step after another behind her.

"Where'd you go?" She stood at the top of the stairs and tried to pick out which of the three doors on the second floor her friend was behind.

"Behind door number one is a fabulous trip to the Caribbean; behind door number two is a new washer and dryer...."

"...And behind door number three is the lovely bride, the amazing Princess of Crown Heights," Rachel mocked herself as she swung open the spare bedroom's door and moved into the hallway, holding the gown up against her and posing like a game-show model.

Lark chuckled, then said quietly, "You do look like a princess. A real princess."

She gave Rachel a tight hug, gown and all, and a firm kiss on her cheek.

"I've got to get some sleep." Lark turned and walked down the stairs and out of the house. She'd had enough of fairytales for one weekend.

CHAPTER TWENTY-THREE

Yakov rose earlier than usual. He needed to get to the mikvah before
the crowd of men who practiced this daily ritual started arriving.
He wanted the water over him today. Yakov didn't want to face anyone
this morning, feeling as he did, self-conscious that his transgressions of
the day before lay like a map across his face—a map that showed how
lost he was. Yakov had been avoiding the mikvah as often as someone in
his position could, avoiding the feelings that arose in him in the company of so many naked men, who's only thought or desire was to do what
they came to do—connect to God, fulfill a commitment, then rush off to
davening and get on with their day. Yakov had those thoughts, too, but
it was the other thoughts that frightened him—seeds of desire that until
today had been controllable, suppressible, kept in the cold shadow of his
intellect. Given the light of day, those seeds had erupted over night into
something lush and terrible. He felt taken over by it, his body awake and
hungry the moment he opened his eyes.

Even though the Torah did not command a man to immerse himself
each day—most mikvah requirements fell officially by the wayside once
the Great Temple, the *Bait Ha Mikdash,* in Yerushalyim was destroyed
and the Jewish people dispersed into exile—the tzaddiks taught the merits of such non-mandatory devotion. Chasidic thought abounded in such

251

extremes of observance. Not only should we do what is required, but also we should do what is not required, do it daily, and use the discipline of it to deepen our connection to Hashem.

The Rebbe's discourse on the subject many years back sealed the practice in the heart of his followers by uncovering for them the hidden meaning and beauty of the simple emersion, or *tevilah*. It seems tevilah in the Hebrew has the same letters as another word *bittul*, meaning humility and subservience. Such semantic musical chairs were the essence of the bottomless, horizon-less study of Torah; that each word was not just itself, but a Jumble puzzle's opportunity for myriad meanings. The idea with *bittul*, the Rebbe had said, was that as one immerses in the waters of the mikvah, one is willing to dedicate oneself to Hashem, to submit to His almighty will. Just as a man is willing to be completely covered by the waters, so, he is willing and ready to, without any reservation, give himself completely to the fulfillment of Hashem's will.

As Yakov dressed to go to the mikvah, another portion of his grandfather's discourse came back to him, and he began to feel hopeful. He hadn't even been born when the Rebbe had spoken these words to a *fabrehgen* crowd nearly 40 years earlier, but like all students, he had studied the transcript of that and thousands of other discourses. In it, the Rebbe mentioned visiting the mikvah daily as a specific cure for a certain spiritual ailment, *Timtum HaMoach,* which can only be described as a cluttering or muddying of the mind, a sort of inability of the intellect to understand and relate to God and his word, even if there is emotional willingness. He went on to teach that upon immersion one not only makes the transition from a place of impurity to a place of purity but there is the potential to be transformed thoroughly. By *tunken zich in mikvah,* by "sinking" his old essence in the holy waters, a new essence devoid of ego and arrogance could emerge. The waters, Yakov hoped, could remake him.

The day before, lying on the bed with Daniel, Yakov felt light and lightheaded, the building pressure of contained sexual energy had finally been allowed to escape. The container felt gloriously empty and, in the vacuum, rushed in the realization of how much he loved Daniel. He knew he loved Daniel as one loves a friend from before memory, as one would love such a constant companion and cohort. He loved him, he was certain, from within his *neshamah*, his godly soul. In the past year he'd had to acknowledge that for more than half of his life he'd been wrestling with the idea that he loved Daniel with his *nefesh habahmish*, his animal soul, as well. To actually feel the physical expression of that love, to touch him and be touched with the almost brutal intensity of these feelings (he ran his fingers over his bruised mouth, felt the ache of a body used in a totally unfamiliar way) was a revelation.

Afterwards, they'd left the apartment and headed for their original destination, the dairy restaurant on Kingston. They ordered as though they hadn't eaten in a week. They hardly spoke, but their eyes met every so often and Yakov was surprised to see a hunger reflected in Daniel's eyes, a hunger stoked and burning, not sated.

Yakov felt giddy—a thick, heavy something pulsed in his chest, a smile plastered to his face, even as he stuffed it with food. He longed to touch Daniel across the table, but felt grateful for the occasional knock of their knees underneath, as they had done so many times during their years of study together. Only now they knew more of each other than just knocking of knees. They *knew* each other. *I am in love,* thought Yakov, and understood immediately the danger of it. Love obscured every rational thought in his brain. This love made him forget or want to forget who he was or what was expected of him. He fantasized about some seamless escape that could take place, some domestic serenity that could be shared in a remote place where two men in love could live in peace with each other and with God. Love Conquers All. All You Need is Love. Love Knows No Bounds. These secular ideas bounced around his head. He wanted to apply them to his life.

As he drained his last cup of coffee, Daniel revealed that he harbored no such delusions. His delusions took on a practical tone, though Yakov would lie tossing in his bed later that night, realizing they were delusions nonetheless. Daniel postured as the voice of reason within the unreasonable mess they found themselves in. He proposed order in what could only be described as chaos—the chaos of what they faced now that the floodgates had been opened. He had been thinking, and this was his big plan.

"We must look at ourselves as 'doubly blessed' my friend," he said as they walked out onto the hot street. He had picked up the phrase from his acquaintances in Israel, those nameless people he'd met, "living the life."

"Doubly blessed because we can love both a man and a woman." Yakov felt a knife to his full belly. *He loves Gavrielle? The same as he loves me?* Daniel quickly explained himself, as though sensing Yakov's thoughts. "I don't have for Gavrielle what I have for you, my friend." He stopped and faced him when he said it. "I will never feel that way, but," he continued to barrel down the sidewalk, "I know that it is unthinkable to not have what Hashem can bless me with through her. A *hamish* home, children, a place in the community, a good livelihood. This is what Hashem wants for us!"

Yakov reached the entrance to the mikvah but it was still locked. He was already sweating from the early heat and from remembering Daniel's elaborate and certainly unrealistic plan for their future. He rang the bell and within a minute the morning attendant unlocked the door, surprised to see Yakov standing there.

"I'm sorry, we don't really open for fifteen minutes, Yakov," he said apologetically. "Come in, come in, but I'll lock the door behind you. I don't want any more early birds. You can have the place to yourself until I'm ready to open."

Yakov was grateful for the privacy as he tried to prepare himself spiritually for his immersion. His only hope was to be reborn as of this morning, to bring a veil of faith and forgetfulness down over what had occurred between him and Daniel the day before. To return to, or to really have for the first time, some normalcy, some sanity with regard to his most personal desires. The idea of living out Daniel's plan was impossible. The duplicity of it, the blatant disregard for what was clearly against Torah and God, the lies and utter denial of the truth that it would require, made the whole fantasy not only unworkable but totally unacceptable to Yakov. And then there was Rachel. Was she, as Daniel proposed, just a component of the fine and fulfilling life the Rebbe's grandson was meant to lead, a jewel on the crown of his embarrassment of riches? Did Hashem mean for him to have everything at her expense?

No, he didn't feel for her what he felt for Daniel, but he'd spent time with her over the past few months, stared for hours at a time at her extraordinary face, sketching and painting. She was beautiful. His aesthetic self appreciated this. He saw her love for him growing, warming her eyes. She was smart, a deep thinker, and his scholar self admired her for that. She was his friend now, if nothing else. He cared enough about her to chafe under the notion of a lifetime of betraying her. With all of this, what could he give her? What would he be able to give her, honestly? Would he be able to love her, touch her with the desire he'd felt in Daniel's arms, and would he be able to give her pleasure as he had been taught was his duty to ensure, even before his own, as a good Chasidic husband? His sect of Chasidim was not one of ascetics who believed devotion to God and sexual enjoyment were mutually exclusive. Within the confines and in accordance with the laws governing the marriage bed, pleasure was a divine right, elevated even to the level of mitzvah. Would he be able to fulfill this mitzvah with Rachel? Yakov didn't know the answer, but he was certain there would be no chance of it if he took his pleasure first with Daniel.

He walked to the edge of the pool, where the attendant waited for him to witness his immersion and make sure it was kosher—that every square inch of him was covered with the water while he recited the bracha, and that no part of him touched the sides of the pool or the bottom.

Yakov thought again of Daniel and hoped the water could wash away his desire for him.

Yakov walked down the steps into the water until it was waist high. His arms crossed over his chest, he said the required prayer. He took the last step into the deep water and pulled his legs upward to keep them from hitting the bottom. The water covered his head. As he floated there he pictured himself a child in the womb and prayed to be reborn with his next breath.

* * *

Daniel liked Mondays. The workweek was new; all was possible. The subway sped him back to the city and the wide world. He thrived on being busy, and the business world was suiting him more than he ever imagined it would. Something about closing a big sale, negotiating a better price with the wholesalers, even going to the bank to make the deposits, made him feel good and productive. He was, he knew, a small cog in the wheel, but he felt part of what made the world tick. It was exciting. Not that being a student hadn't been a challenge, but now he knew that the excitement he felt as a student was more about parrying and partnering with Yakov, than any intellectual or spiritual calling. After all, you debated for hours or days to settle on an interpretation of a phrase in Torah, a word, or even the occurrence of a single letter, and for what? To find out that Rambam, Rashi, the Bal Shem Tov, or some other scholar who lived hundreds of years ago had thought of it first, or explained it better? Whatever your interpretation was or whatever conclusion you had come to, it mattered little. Nothing was going to change the way anyone did things as a result of your conclusions.

This was new thinking for Daniel. He hadn't leaned toward rebellion or questioning for most of his student life. However, in the last year, the well-handled and well-hidden copies of the *Village Voice* had begun to change all of that for him. Some distance from that sheltered life, both in time and in experience, made him look back on a lot of his toiling over Torah as futile tail chasing. *If nothing new could come of it,* he thought, *if in the end all the old interpretations were simply held in place, how was that serving the world as it continued to spin and change?* How would it help him as his own life spun recklessly away from the core of all known interpretations and all known accepted behavior? How were the certainties of the ancient scholars helping him now? If he were to live his life by their cautious interpretations or by the black and white of the text, he would be facing an existence filled with misery, deprivations and limitations he was not sure he could live with. When a man, and he was a man now, after all, leaves the "what if" world of yeshiva and enters the real world, decisions have to be made; one's own modern circumstances have to be considered.

As he walked up the street toward his father-in-law's store, passing one "Fine Jewelry" and "Diamonds, Diamonds" storefront after another, he saw his face reflected in the mirrors that lined the back of the empty showcase windows. *I look the same,* he marveled, even as he knew that after everything he'd been through in the last few months, culminating with yesterday's turn of events with Yakov, he was not the same man and never would be again.

To begin with, marriage had changed him. He went into it with a blind righteousness, believing that it would fill every hole in his life, as it seemed to for everyone else. God would be on his side and make it so. The ugly wound that was his sexual depravity would dry up and heal. Except that being with his wife only opened everything up again. The truth of what his body was telling him was undeniable. He had no desire for her. Even with the wonder of such allowed intimacy, it was only with his eyes tightly shut and the image of Yakov or his various *Village Voice* favorites (he didn't tell Yakov that part), that he was able to do what was expected of him. On his wedding trip he realized with finality what his undeniable nature was.

Daniel continued down the block toward the store. Parked toward the end was the "Mitzvah Tank," the RV sent by the Rebbe to "work" the various New York neighborhoods. The big "shul-on-wheels" was manned by groups of students who were trained to approach strangers on the street and ask them, "Are you Jewish?" If they said yes, then they would be asked if they'd like to put on tefillin and pray. Or on Fridays the Mitzvah Tank would be staffed with girls who would stop women and give them Shabbes candles and handouts on how to light them, with the candle lighting time, and the bracha, both in Hebrew and in phonetic transliterations for those who couldn't read the ancient language.

Daniel remembered his days on the Tank. The street work could be brutal, depending on the neighborhood, with all the name-calling and rejection. Daniel and most of the boys were pretty armored against it. They had the strength of their conviction that, as the Rebbe taught, each Jew they could bring back from the periphery, from non-observance, each mitzvah they could convince these secular Jews to do, brought them all closer to the day that the Messiah would come and God would live among them. The dead would rise. Peace on earth. No more suffering, persecution, or separation from the truth of the Divine. If you were a Chasid from Crown Heights, this was the ultimate in motivation.

As Daniel approached the Tank, he saw a few familiar faces, younger boys from the yeshiva, and some new ones, boys from various outreach cities around the world whose parents sent them to Brooklyn during the summer for study close to the Rebbe, and to do this kind of field work, to learn how to talk to anyone, anytime about mitzvahs, Judaism, and Torah.

Daniel passed, nodding hello to those few boys he recognized, but was distracted by a banging from the inside of the mitzvah tank window. Someone inside, with tefillin half hanging from his arm, was trying to get his attention. The tinted window didn't help. Daniel had no idea who it was until the young man dashed for the door of the tank and came out onto the sidewalk to greet him.

"Daniel! This is incredible. It's Barry, you know, Baruch, from Tel Aviv? I met you at the meeting at Sandi's, while you were in Jerusalem."

"Barry, yes, yes, of course. I remember. Sandi's house." Daniel looked nervously around as he returned the young man's enthusiastic handshake. "You look different," Daniel offered.

It was in Jerusalem, on his wedding trip, on an evening when his wife was attending a women's dance group with her cousin who lived there, that he met the most unholy assortment of men by ducking into a doorway marked with a sign that read, to his astonishment, "GAFA, the Gay and Frum Alliance. Meeting Tonight!" The headquarters of GAFA turned out to be a small dimly lit apartment up four flights of stairs, belonging to a warm and gregarious rabbi in his late 30's by the name of Sandi Sandberg. That night Daniel sat dumbstruck as Sandi talked openly about his struggle with being *homosexual and deeply devoted to Judaism!*

In turn, one man after another spoke of his own life with a candor that was unlike anything Daniel had ever heard. He could hardly bear to listen to their stories and felt embarrassed at the utter vulnerability of it all. Yet after a while he found he couldn't help telling his own story to the group as they gently urged him along. Of course, he kept Yakov's identity a secret—would anyone believe it anyway? The Rebbes grandson! The meeting that evening was combined with a quasi-celebration/going away party for one long-time participant, a fair-haired Chasid in his late 20's named Baruch. Baruch had managed to avoid marriage by moving to Israel after high school and telling his family he was devoting himself to study. Baruch looked like any other young man Daniel might see at shul in Crown Heights—the garb, the beard—but when he spoke it was as though he'd landed there from a different planet, as far as Daniel was concerned. He entertained the group with a wry take on his nearly ten-year process of "becoming who I really am." The group congratulated him, applauding and patting his back when he spoke of how he was going back to the States, facing his family, and "coming out" for good.

Daniel learned the word "out" and that where he was, was "in the closet." Some people came "out to themselves and God" or within the safety of these meetings, but stayed "in the closet" or just plain "in" to their wives, community, and families. Others were "out-out" and lived openly gay lives in big cities that had thriving gay communities: New York, San Francisco, Tel Aviv, Amsterdam, Paris—not Crown Heights. Married two weeks by then, Daniel felt that God had slammed a door shut in his face and trapped him, just when he thought it should be opening and rewarding him for "doing the right thing." The marriage covenant and the marriage bed had not brought him the salvation and relief he'd sought. Now, in this back street of Jerusalem, in the small living room lit with candles and swirling with sweet incense, in the company of eight men he didn't know, a new door indeed was being opened for him, that offered, if not total comfort and freedom, then at least a context for his despair.

Barry, he remembered now, tried out the secular version of his name Baruch for the first time that night of his farewell party, but still sported an untrimmed blond beard and the common uniform of the Chasid. Today, his beard was trimmed tightly around his angular face. His hair, a dirtier blond than his beard, hung longer, the loose curls beginning to cover his ears. Barry now wore jeans and a bright T-shirt that advertised a music festival in San Francisco. The tzitses strings still poked out from under the T-shirt and a small knit yarmulke lay buried amongst his curls at the top of his head, but there were no other outward signs of the ultraorthodox man he had met in Jerusalem.

It was awkward for Daniel. He was known on 46th Street. The students around him from the tank knew his family.

"Barry, I would love to talk, but I am late to open the store...my father-in-law..." Daniel gestured vaguely toward the east end of the block.

Barry was oblivious. "Let me get rid of this," he said, lifting his arm with the unraveling tefillin still on it, "and I'll walk up the block with you. I'm headed to Fifth."

Before Daniel could reply, Barry had turned to one of the students on the sidewalk and said, "Can you take this for me?" and handed off the tefillin. They walked.

"So how is married life going, my friend?" Daniel thought Barry must be making fun of him, but then he saw the real concern on his face.

"It's going. Gavrielle is already expecting."

"You were very busy in Jerusalem then, besides the meeting?"

"Yes, I guess so."

Barry clucked his tongue at Daniel and said, "Honey, you are a mess. There are meetings in New York, you know. I've even started one myself. You should come."

Daniel started to protest. He didn't need meetings. He had everything handled. He and Yakov were going to have the best of both worlds, and wouldn't have to give up anything, like Barry had.

"Let's get together. You can come to my place for lunch or dinner sometime. I live here now. Straight down 46th between 9th and 10th— Hell's Kitchen. Appropriate, don't you think? Anyway, think about it. You are going to need to talk to someone, my friend. Trust me."

Barry pulled a business card from his wallet and a pen from his backpack. He scribbled something on the back of the card and handed it to Daniel.

"Sure. Sure. We'll get together. I'll call you." Daniel stuffed the card in his pocket and turned to unlock the big roll-down gate that covered the entrance to the store.

Barry stopped him by holding on to his wrist.

"If you throw away my number, like I know you are thinking of doing before your wife cleans out your pockets and finds it, you can always find me at the Midtown Public Library on Fifth. You know the one with the big lions out front. I work there: Judaic Reference Room." Barry let go of him and started to walk away but turned to wave at Daniel, who stood outside his father-in-law's store and fumbled with his keys.

CHAPTER TWENTY-FOUR

These are the *bedeka* cloths." Rivki Eisenblatt looked discretely away as she slid the flat, unadorned package across the wide dining table toward Rachel. "You can keep those. It's my little gift. To get you started."

Rachel peeled her sweaty forearms from the thick plastic that showed off but protected Mrs. Eisenblatt's prized lace tablecloth—"my grandmothers, from before the war." She reached for the little box. The cover, printed plainly in red Hebrew letters, spelled out the rabbinical supervision and stamp of approval required to make the cloths kosher. White, blemish-free squares, manufactured solely to capture blemishes, the tiny smears of blood that are the last vestige of each month's flow. Mrs. Eisenblatt explained that Rachel would begin using these at the end of the fifth day of her cycle.

"Wrap the cloth around a finger, maybe two after the babies come," she joked. Rachel stared at her unsmiling, uncomprehending.

"With each swipe, a new cloth, until the cloth comes up clean, really clean, without-a-doubt-clean." If there is a doubt, the cloth could be put in a baggie, inside a plain envelope, and dropped off to her husband, Reb Eisenblatt, who made judgment calls on these matters. He would decide: Yes, clean, or no, wait another day, check again.

"Then start the counting. Use a little calendar and keep it in your pocketbook. Count seven days from the day of the clean cloth, and on the evening of the seventh day you go to the mikvah."

Rachel would have her first visit to the mikvah right before her wedding, with the wedding day itself planned around the timing of her cycle and the business with the bedeka cloths. Starting with that first visit, just weeks away, and for every month thereafter during her childbearing years, she would take the same non-negotiable steps to prepare herself for her husband.

"Before you go to the mikvah, you take a good long bath at home. Scrub with a washcloth wherever you can reach. Cut your fingernails short, really short. Toenails, too. Cut back the cuticles, or any hangnails. Remove any Band-Aids or scabs even. Wash your hair. Twice." The waters of the mikvah must be able to touch and flow unimpeded around every surface, nook and cranny of her body.

Once bathed, she would dress and slip out to walk the few blocks to the mikvah. There, she would shower and wash again, be checked carefully by an attendant for stray hairs or dirt imbedded in fingernails, then be allowed to immerse in the mikvah waters and say the prayer that would sanctify the act, cleanse her bodily physically and spiritually, and insure the health and well-being of her future children. She would no longer be impure, would have passed the time of month where each woman carried a little bit of death in her—the egg that had never sparked to life that month, that would never house a Jewish *neshamah*.

"Let me give you some advice. Have you ever heard your mother announce, 'I'm going to the mikvah, I'll be back in an hour!'? Of course not!"

Rachel didn't want to be thinking about her mother taking part of in any aspect of what Rebitzen Eisenblatt was teaching her.

"So, you should be discreet, understand? Your husband might realize where you are going. Believe me, he might be counting the days in his head or keeping a little calendar himself—if you know what I mean—but he's not going to say anything if you suddenly have to run out after dinner one night a month. He'll know and you'll know and that's enough, and you certainly don't want to make a big deal of it around the children, Baruch Hashem, when they come along. You can think of a signal of some sort. Something that tells him the waiting is over."

The stout middle-aged woman suddenly blushed, her ample cheeks taking back some of the youthful aura she'd surrendered to the years gone by, the bearing and responsibility for eight children, and life in general in Brooklyn, New York, where sun and sky and fresh air was doled out in rations between shoe-horned buildings and parked cars.

"You don't need to hit them over the head with a hammer, believe you me. You come home, put your hand on his arm, casual-like, stand close enough for him to smell the chlorine from the mikvah in your hair. After two weeks of no touching he'll get the message."

The Rebitzen blushed again and fidgeted with her snood, tucking in escaping gray and black hairs here and there. Rachel was more than ready to leave.

Mercifully, the Rebitzen Eisenblatt seemed to have enough excitement for one afternoon herself.

"*Gahnoocht!* Enough, Rochella. Come back on Thursday, same time. We'll talk some more." She handed her two of the hard buttery candies with the gold wrapper that she kept in a bowl by the front door, and patted her hand as she showed her out.

CHAPTER TWENTY-FIVE

Lark had not seen him in over two weeks. That wasn't exactly true, since she had seen him sitting across the street in the park, his eyes trained on her window more than once during that time. She watched him move impatiently between the swings in the glaring sun and the benches under a lacey canopy of trees. Instead of the trademark slicker, he wore what they called in New Jersey a "Guinea-T," under an over-sized Hawaiian-type shirt that caught what little air there was in Brooklyn on that July day, and billowed behind him like a proud sail. The shirt's tropical print made her think *Rain Man turns Rainforest Man!* Then she felt bad for making fun of him, even if it wasn't out loud. The last few times she saw him out there, she stood back from the window to watch him so he wouldn't be able to see her, then she got busy cleaning her room again or reading or making her father lunch when he was around, until she'd look out the window again to see that he was finally gone.

Lark wasn't really sure why she was avoiding him, but admitted to herself that she was. She stayed in a lot during that time—it did rain for about six days in a row, and then it was pretty hot outside when it wasn't raining. When she did venture out to meet Rachel for an afternoon of waiting for furniture deliveries at her and Yakov's future apartment or to call David at a payphone, she took the long way around Jamal's most common hangout spots. *I just want a break. What's wrong with that?* The weekend before last and its duplicitous itinerary had exhausted her, she justified. Lying and sneaking around and worrying about getting caught were hard work! She'd been doing all that to see Jamal for nearly a year at this point. She was tired.

And confused. Her mother, instead of being anxious to hear about David's party, her conversations with David, or her experience there, was basically avoiding *her*. Sarah stayed uncharacteristically close to her husband, lingering over dinner, sitting with him in the living room to read instead of retreating to her room as she usually did. Lark couldn't catch her alone to talk to her openly about anything. Feeling abandoned by her mother was nothing new, but each demonstration of it wounded her nonetheless.

It was no coincidence then that Lark found herself walking to shul alone on Saturday morning, her mother having rushed out early to walk with her father. And it was no coincidence that the Rain Man's cousin, the surly Pee Cee, who never disguised his distaste for Lark or his disgust for Jamal's association with her, came barreling into her at the corner, knocking her flat on her ass.

He made an unconvincing show of being sorry.

"Oh, I am so sorry, girl. Are you okay? Oh, let me help you up. I am so sorry..." He extended a limp hand to help her up, and when she took it reluctantly, she found he'd passed her a tightly folded piece of paper.

"The man wants to see his dirty little pigeon," he spat out at her and turned away. She stuffed the note into her skirt pocket and concentrated on brushing off the gravel and dust imbedded in her palms. *I'm ending up with my butt on the ground a lot lately!* She put off looking at the note until she was safely hidden in her usual stall of the ladies' room at shul.

DD 9 p.m. —RM

Dunkin' Donuts. *How utterly romantic!* It would be easy enough to get out after Shabbes ended. After the lighting of the braided Havdallah candles, a ritual that ushered out the Sabbath with a bittersweet good-bye-sorry-to-see-you-go prayer and a sniff of spices, people poured out of their hot apartments and onto the streets. Saturday night was a late night in Crown Heights, especially in the summer when Shabbes ended after 8 p.m. It would be easy to get out, but would it be easy to be with Jamal in her current state of mind?

Lark laughed as she crumpled the note and tossed it between her legs into the toilet. *How much time do I spend trying to figure out stuff in my life while sitting on the toilet in this place? Hey, Shul, is a place where people are supposed to commune with the heavens and figure out what life is all about. Why should the bathroom be exempt from that energy?* Lark decided that the ladies' lounge *was* the best place to find enlightenment and truth because the "energy" was more powerful there— all the mirrors reflecting back and forth, creating some kind of spiritual vortex or something. And lo and behold the toilet seat had barely made its dent on her rear end before the truth behind what she'd been avoiding all week hit her.

Before last weekend she'd been obsessed with Jamal. But being with David and his friends opened up something for her. It was one thing to have a fantasy for four years of escaping, of going back to some kind of normalcy and gaining her independence, but she had taken the virtual tour of it at David's and felt like it rearranged her reality completely. Was she exchanging one obsession for another, Jamal for Dog, or was it all part of the same obsession: freedom?

Jamal, the adrenaline of the clandestine meetings with him, the smoking, and the sex were all about transporting her out of her life somehow. While she was with him she was not confined or defined by Crown Heights. It was the Bird flipping the bird at everyone who was out to control her: her father, the rabbis at school and practically every other gossiping, judging member of their small community. A train ride to Manhattan was nothing new to her, but the last one opened her eyes to what else was available for her, possible for her. Suddenly, Jamal didn't feel like her freedom anymore. He was a part of the Heights she needed to leave behind. Lark was not going to be happy with her round-trip moments of escape for much longer—she wanted the one-way fare out of there.

And Dog kissing her the way he did had nothing to do with it, she mentally insisted, as she came out of the stall, but the mirrors caught her blushing as she remembered those kisses and everyone knows the vortex doesn't lie.

CHAPTER TWENTY-SIX

The bitch is not coming. Let's get the fuck out of here." Pee Cee blew air into the empty Dunkin' Donuts bag. He twisted the top closed then held it tightly in one hand while he smashed the bottom with the other. The pop sounded like a gunshot, but no one even looked up from their coffee.

"She's only ten minutes late. And I didn't ask you to come with me. In fact, when she gets here I want you to disappear." Jamal threw the last bite of his donut at his cousin and hit him squarely in the forehead.

"Fuck you, man. Fuck you!" He swiped at the grains of sugar that stuck to his eyebrows. "You are taking this shit too far. This girl is taking over your brain, man. And one day you are going to find yourself in deep shit over this bitch. One day her big, black-coat daddy is gonna find out about you—he got close enough once—and you think he's gonna sit around and let you fuck with his baby girl whenever? He's gonna run to his big 'ole Rebbe, askin' for help. You know that muthafucka got cops escorting him 'round the city and shit, like he's the fuckin' president...the cops are practically his own army, and the politicians 'round here are all Jew-kissin', money-hungry muthafuckas that would throw any nigger in a jail cell to make the Rebbe and his tribe happy."

"You don't know anything. You don't know her. You don't even know me and you been around me my whole life."

"I know you! I know you. I know you have lost your mind. Since when you wait around, rippin' up napkins over some late ass?" The table between them was littered with shreds of paper, twisted or balled up, and mutilated plastic stirrers. Pee Cee stretched his bulky, tattooed forearm across the tabletop and wiped the debris to the sticky tiled floor, disgusted.

Jamal wasn't listening. He was turned toward the door.

"Sheeee-it!" leaked out from between Pee Cee's clenched teeth as he recognized just by the look on his cousin's face that Lark had finally walked in the door. "Later," he spat out as he bolted for the door, knocking into Lark on the way out.

"What's the matter with him besides the fact that he hates my guts for no reason?"

Lark bent down to pick up the chair Pee Cee had knocked over when he stood up, and sat down across from the Rain Man. He looked at her but didn't say anything for what seemed like a long time.

"What?" She couldn't take it.

"Nothing," he said finally, chewing on another coffee stirrer he produced from somewhere.

"You're looking at me funny." Lark looped her fingers over her ears, tucking her hair back.

"I'm just trying to get used to you. I haven't seen you in a while."

"What, it's only been a week?"

"More like two."

"Well, I've been busy. I went into the city, went to a party at my brother's house. I met a lot of his friends from college, his roommate."

"Oh, yeah. You gonna trade me in for some college boy?"

Lark did not want to deal with how close to the truth he was hitting.

"Look, I've been tired. And busy. And it rained all those days...."

"Tired of what?"

Jamal's head cocked at an angle and his hazel eyes stared out at her from behind his half-closed lids, the gnarled stirrer tucked in the side of his mouth was momentarily still. He was giving her that "look"—the one she had tried to avoid thinking about these past weeks while planning her new life. It was that look that made her start breathing funny. Lark suddenly wished she hadn't come. *What was I thinking?* Before she could give him a reasonable excuse to leave, Jamal stood up and leaned over the table toward her. He whispered in her hair, "I miss you," then quickly walked out of the place.

She knew she'd find him down the long alley that snaked behind Dunkin' Donuts, a dead end they'd spent time in before. Or she could just go home. She heard and felt the subway rumbling beneath her feet, the train speeding toward the East River. Manhattan seemed far off all of a sudden as she followed the sweet scent of smoke down the alley and took hold of the fat joint he held out to her.

*   *   *

Rachel sat as still as she could even though she felt on display, like a mannequin in Macy's window. At least a mannequin was oblivious to its audience, while she was acutely aware of the eyes that assessed her at that moment. Yakov, who stood partially hidden by his easel, not so much looked at her as dissected her with his eyes. He took in little bits of her at a time and pinned them onto the canvas stroke by stroke.

Today it seemed she was simply hair, his gazed locked somewhere on the top of her head or occasionally to the sides of her face. Last week he looked at her only from the neck down. Then, there was the intermittent "other" audience that drifted by to watch him put her back together. The Rebbe even pulled up a chair behind Yakov to watch. He seemed to approve of it. Not the painting, but the way the young man transcended his awkward body and self-conscious manner and acted with confidence while approaching the canvas. The old, wise eyes moved not from Rachel's face to the canvas, as it would if he were checking the progress of the work, but moved from his grandson's face to her face, from her eyes to his eyes. He was painting his own mental picture, but of what, Rachel could only guess.

Rachel spent almost every Saturday night after the end of Shabbes in this way since they'd gotten engaged. The painting was meant to be finished in time for the wedding and that was less than three weeks away. She wasn't allowed to see it until he presented it to her after the ceremony, in the *yichud* room, during the time the bride and groom are sequestered off by themselves to spend their first moments together as husband and wife. There, she'd see herself as he saw her. Would it all become clear to her then? Would she see the painting and know exactly how he interpreted their life together, how he felt about her? Rachel knew what was expected of her to a certain degree. Her mother, her sisters, every girl in the community lived out the expectations of her gender, so that was not in question. She knew what she would be required *to do*. What she wouldn't know, and couldn't know until after it was done, was how it would feel.

One certainty, among others that her ultraorthodox world gave her was that on their wedding night, husband and wife would be on equal ground—equally inexperienced and scared out of their minds.

"Where's the beard?" smirked Uncle Yossi as he passed through the room and leaned closely over Yakov's shoulder, observing the unfinished portrait. His little "joke" froze Yakov in his tracks. Rachel mustered a chuckle to be polite, but was uncomfortable whenever the strange man was around—not only because she could sense Yakov's stiffness around him, but because Yossi was just plain scary. He looked at Rachel in the eyes just a little longer than was normal or proper, and stood just a little too close. His breath was always stale. Yakov seemed to shrink in his presence.

"What did you mean by that, Yossi?" Yakov's mother appeared in the doorway. She stared at him icily. Now it was he who froze.

"A joke. Just a little joke. Has everyone lost their sense of humor with this wedding?"

"A joke? I guess I just don't get it. Maybe we should ask the Rebbe to come in and interpret it for us. I'm not so smart that I get such jokes."

"Forget it!" He stamped out of the room, using the door at the opposite end of the parlor. Rachel was confused about what had just happened. Her future mother-in-law was a formidable force, to say the least. Rachel hoped she wouldn't have the power over her that she'd just seen her use on Yossi. Nevertheless, whatever force she employed with him, Rachel was glad to be rid of the oddly dangerous man. Once he left the room the three of them acted as if he had never been there. There was no discussion of it, no further reference to the joke or the man. Rachel tried not to think about the relationship between Yakov and Yossi and Yossi and his mother-in-law or why it was funny that a portrait of Yakov's wife should include a beard. She accepted the delicate little cordial glass Yakov's mother offered her and sipped the sweet sherry she was suddenly eligible to have.

"L'chaim." Yakov lifted his glass over the canvas toward her. Yes, "to life," Rachel repeated back to him, then resumed her pose.

*　*　*

Daniel smiled to himself as he pressed one of the little pink and white antihistamine capsules out of its little foil compartment. For once his allergies were proving to be a convenience, not a curse. Because pollen and mold aggravated his sinuses, he was able to stay in the city most weekends while his wife and in-laws took off for the rustic and rotting little bungalow colony they loved in the Catskills. It confirmed for Daniel his theory that God was complicit in his plan to live a double life.

Why else would he have blessed him with allergies and a wife that loved the country, if not to give him these glorious weekends to arrange his meetings with Yakov? The fly in the ointment that he couldn't explain was why Yakov was not equally available. They'd managed to be together only two other times in the past few weeks since their first intimate encounter, and that had been hurried in between Yakov's other Sunday obligations with the Rebbe, his future in-laws or with Rachel. Even now, at the close of Shabbes, he wasn't sure if Yakov could get away tomorrow to come over, and just thinking about wasting the day waiting around for him was turning his mood black.

Daniel tried to reel in his irritation by telling himself it wasn't easy for Yakov either. After all, Yakov had to endure his marriage to Gavrielle. Hadn't he come to him on his wedding day and tried to talk him out of it? Hadn't he tried to get him to face his true nature, even when he was barely admitting to it himself? Now, it was Daniel's turn to stand by mutely and watch as Yakov constructed the public, "normal" part of his life that would make the hidden part of it possible. Yet, the idea of having to be the last person on the list that Yakov could turn his attention to was making him feel like a child on the brink of throwing a tantrum. Too much time alone and his mind drifted to impossible topics, for example: What would life be like if he and Yakov could live without all these complications, could just be free of all the guilt and the lying and the hiding?

A few days earlier, Daniel was in the store. It wasn't that busy, but his father-in-law was standing next to him when he answered the phone.

"Daniel. Is that you?"

He knew who it was immediately: Baruch aka Barry from the group in Jerusalem, the "out-out" ex-Chasid who he had run into on the street a couple of weeks before.

"Can I help you?" Daniel tried to sound like it was any other customer calling.

"Yes, you can help me. Meet me for lunch. I need a little Yiddishkeit connection, if you know what I mean, and you could probably use someone to talk to at this point."

Daniel stood there. What should he do? Hang up, that's what he should do.

"Daniel, are you there or did you spontaneously combust because the big, bad *feigella* called you."

"Yes, we purchase estate jewelry. I can look at what you have and give you an estimated value."

"What are you talking about...oh, I see! Yes, let's play that game. *Yes!* Can you come over right away and look at my family jewels, you slut!"

"What is your address? I can be there by 1:30. Is that good for you?"

"Oh, I think it is going to be very good for me. And for you, too. You sound like you are losing your mind, honey." He gave him the address of his apartment.

"I'll see you then." Daniel hung up and wiped his sweaty palms on his pants, took the Post-it note he'd written Barry's address on and jammed it into his pocket.

Daniel passed his father-in-law in the doorway as the older man was returning from lunch.

"I'm grabbing a quick lunch then going to look at some estate stuff from an old lady on the Upper East Side. I'll be back in a couple of hours."

The older man nodded and waved him off then turned his attention to the couple pointing at settings in a case.

Daniel set himself on an automatic course west down 46th, past the Broadway theaters he had never entered and the row of restaurants he had never eaten in. He knew if he thought about what he was doing he would turn around, grab a Glatt kosher falafel at a stand on 47th, and go back to work.

Standing in front of the building that matched the address he had, he cursed himself for obviously writing the number down wrong. Daniel stood staring up the long stairs that led to the bold red door and brick façade of St. Clements Church. Maybe this was Barry's idea of a joke? He was about to turn away when he heard his name from above and almost fell backward looking up to see who was talking to him from the sky.

"Daniel!"

Daniel would not have been surprised to see a fireball heading toward him from the heavens. Instead, he saw Barry's face sticking out of a high window of the church.

"I'm up here. Wait right there. I'll come down and get you."

When Barry emerged from behind the big red door he was laughing.

"I was watching for you from up there because I wanted to see your reaction when you got here."

Daniel just looked at him, still not in on the joke.

"I live here. In a church. Isn't it hysterically fabulous? And wildly ironic?"

Daniel's first thought was that Barry seemed more "gay" then he did even just a few weeks ago, even though he still wore a yarmulke on his head and had the long strings of his tzitses dangling from underneath his T-shirt.

"It's not totally a church. I mean, they have services here on Sundays, but the rest of the time it functions as a theater, or sometimes an art gallery, and they have all kinds of meetings here, like AA and different support groups. I started one just like the meeting you came to in Jerusalem. At first I didn't know if I could get any observant Jews to walk into a church...they all think they're going to be struck by lightning or be brainwashed into being Jews for Jesus, or something, if they do."

Daniel felt nervous entering the building, but followed Barry up the four flights of stairs as the chatty man explained what his job was at the church.

"I'm basically the caretaker-slash-janitor. I unlock the doors, sweep up, make sure there is toilet paper in the bathrooms—that kind of thing—before I go to my regular job at the library."

For that service he earned a room under the eaves of the eclectic Hell's Kitchen haven. Daniel wondered where Barry would be living, what kind of work he would be doing if he had stayed "in." What life had he forfeited for this one?

The room was down a long hall past a common bathroom.

"It's no penthouse, but it's all mine."

The tiny room seemed crowded though it only held a double bed, a chair, a thrift-store dresser, a mirror, and a small table overflowing with a large spread for lunch. Two windows crowned by stained glass panels, depicting angels with trumpets, dominated the small space. It was warm up there, but the window angels had captured a breeze that smelled of the Hudson River just a few blocks away.

"I'm not going to bite you." Barry had accurately sensed his anxiety. "Unless you bite me first. Listen, I wouldn't want you to feel guilty about cheating on your boyfriend. You have enough guilt already."

They ate kosher sandwiches and potato salad that Barry had gone out of his way to get for the occasion. Daniel recognized the name of the deli on the bags as a place he would be allowed to eat from, and relaxed about that, too. Barry sat on the bed, Daniel on the rickety chair that his big frame comically dwarfed.

Barry, for all his affectations and cynicism, proved to be an attentive listener, and Daniel found he couldn't stop talking. He told Barry about his wife. They talked about Yakov and the roller coaster of elation and frustration Daniel rode. Barry kept his face neutral and his opinions about Daniel's predicament, though he had many, to himself.

"I miss the life sometimes," Barry said, standing up, stretching his long wiry frame, and took the few steps between the bed and the window. He picked up Daniel's big black fedora from the dresser where he'd placed it and put it on. It was ridiculously big for him, but looking at himself in the mirror, he didn't smile.

"But I could never go back now. I guess it's the old Genesis thing. Once you taste the fruit, you can't really hang out in the garden anymore. I wonder if Adam and Eve really got thrown out, or if they decided, once their eyes were opened, that Paradise was way too quaint. Do you ever wonder why God set it up as an either/or kind of a thing?"

"Who knows?" Daniel lifted his skullcap nervously and smoothed the damp hair underneath. "Who knows what God really wants?"

Daniel was uncomfortable with such blasphemous statements, but around Barry he felt his guard come down.

"That's exactly my point!" Barry flipped the hat at Daniel and it floated the short distance like a Frisbee, landing lopsided on his head. "No one really knows. I think no one has a clue what God is, what form he or she takes or what 'it' wants from us...if anything! But that doesn't seem to stop people from making up all this crap, all these stories, to make themselves feel like they have some control over their lives."

Barry started stuffing the trash from the lunch into the plastic bag it came in. "I don't see this working out for Jews that well. For instance, Nazis? Hello! And every other form of persecution and shit-end-of-the-stick for the last 5000 years?"

Barry crushed the empty cream soda cans and tossed them in the bag. Daniel had no explanation for Barry or himself. He handed Barry his paper plate to throw away. Barry snorted a laugh at the look on Daniel's face.

"Don't mean to burst your bubble, *bubbella*. Next lunch we'll talk about something neutral."

Sitting in his apartment, thinking back on the meeting with Barry, Daniel felt a peculiar satisfaction. It was his secret. Something for him and him alone, something he did for no important reason, no special universal significance, with no longstanding precedent.

Daniel picked up the braided Havdallah candle in front of him. *If I don't light this, like I've done at the end of every Shabbes for my entire life, will my life get any worse? I've done everything by the rules and still God has cursed me, thwarted me from having true happiness.* Each night, before sinking into the oblivion of sleep, as he murmured the last prayers of the day,

Daniel wondered what The Almighty had intended by creating him as he was, giving him a lifetime of struggle to contend with. He prayed for answers, hanging on to the belief they could come from this same God.

Daniel lit the Havdallah candle and said the prayer: *Blessed is the Almighty God who creates the illumination of fire.* He knew the Chasidic tale claiming that this was the first prayer uttered by Adam, who spoke it when God showed him how to make fire from two flints to alleviate the cold darkness of his exile from the Garden. Daniel stared past his fingertips into the double-flamed candle that tradition required to show the strengthening of Jewish souls when they unite. He lifted the silver spice container to his nose, inhaling. *Blessed is the Almighty God who gave us spices.* The aroma of the cloves was meant to comfort him, as he left behind the holy Sabbath, returning to the mundane workweek. Daniel then doused the candle in a waiting cup of wine, but could not for the life of him remember the reason why it had to be done that way.

CHAPTER TWENTY-SEVEN

Rachel would not see Yakov for the full week leading up to the wedding, as was the custom before. The portrait was finished as far as she knew and sent to the framer. Her dress was picked out and the alterations complete. Her wigs had arrived by messenger. The furniture for the apartment had been delivered and placed. The catering, the flowers, the hundreds of other details of the ceremony and reception were poised to unfold. Rachel felt as though she had awakened into the eye of a hurricane, the temporary calm that swept away the chaos and confusion of the past few months, yet belied the whirlwind that would be her married life.

The Rebbe's growing reliance on Yakov would not allow them to take a post-wedding excursion like the one Daniel took with Gabrielle. Yakov told her about a conversation he'd had with the Rebbe about a trip.

"This idea of a trip after the wedding is not for us," the old man had told him. Yakov didn't have to explain to her that when the Rebbe said "us" he didn't mean it in a personal way. He didn't mean "you and me." He meant their whole community.

According to the Rebbe, honeymoons were a modern convention, attached to secular marriages, based on something called romance that guided the rest of the world's choices for a spouse—a strategy that was hardly working for the world, given the number of divorces among those who employed it.

"The time after a wedding is not a time for trip," the Rebbe reasoned. "This time is for setting up a Jewish home."

Rachel was reminded often enough by family, or by just about any-one in the community, that Yakov was not just any new husband. He was going to be setting an example and a standard with his marriage. Rachel could see how everything about her life from now on would have this double edge to it. Nothing would be just about her, or her and Yakov. It would be about everyone. She expected that the Rebbe wanted to make this point clear to her, so he asked to meet with her privately. His assistant had called a few days earlier to set the appointment. Rachel had been worrying about the meeting day and night since then.

"Don't worry so much, Rachel. He is just wanting to set the tone, most likely," her mother told her, looking a bit worried herself and thinking again that her Rachel was not exactly the most poised or obedi-ent of her daughters. What if she insulted the Rebbe?

"Set the tone? What does that mean?"

"I don't know exactly." Miriam waved her hand in the air, as if trying to catch the answer, "but whatever it is, you shouldn't worry because it will be just as it should be. He's the Rebbe! Think how blessed you are to be meeting with him privately and to have him guiding you in your marriage! Most people are lucky to get five minutes privately with him in a lifetime. You, he's asking to see." Rachel's mother looked pleased with her response and calmed by the idea of passing the responsibility for molding this troublesome young girl into a good wife over to the formidable leader.

Lark had a different take on the meeting when Rachel shared her nervousness with her over a quick lunch. "He probably just wants to get to know you better. And then drop the big bomb on you about how you have to be this big role model for the whole community now and that everyone will be watching you and judging your every move. Stuff like that...no big deal."

Rachel threw a French fry at her smirking friend. "Thanks. That really relaxes me."

"Look, there is still time for you to back out. You can go home, pack a bag and, meet me at the subway. We'll run away to Manhattan together. I've got connections."

"Very funny." Rachel was not laughing. She knew that she'd forfeited her escape option when she said yes to Yakov that moment at Daniel's wedding.

Lark offered to walk Rachel over to the Rebbe's residence—soon to be Rachel's new home—and even wait for her until the meeting was over.

"You don't have to. I'll be fine."

"It's no problem. I want to hear what he says. I mean, he is *the* Rebbe. Maybe he'll say something so incredible it will make me want to go off and marry one of those losers my father keeps trying to set me up with."

"You are not helping me," Rachel complained, but was glad she had Lark to keep her laughing on the way there.

"Well, good luck. I don't think I'll hang out right here and wait."

Lark tilted her head and indicated the always-lingering group of young men who congregated in front of the sprawling building that housed the Rebbe's residence, Rachel's future apartment, administrative offices, and the main shul of the community. "I'll wait for you down at the bakery."

When Rachel was led into the Rebbe's office a few minutes later, she wished she had worn lighter clothing. The room was kept warm for the aging leader, and she was already sweating from sheer nerves and rushing over to be on time. The old man sat, with a dark sweater on, in a stream of sunlight.

When the assistant who led her in left the room and closed the door behind him, the Rebbe looked up from a thick volume that covered a good portion of his desk, and read her mind. "You look like you could use an iced tea." He spoke to her in Yiddish, the old-world language that most of their community was fluent in. The leader encouraged his followers to keep the *mama loschen,* the mother tongue, alive amongst them. To Rachel, speaking Yiddish and the slight accent and rhythmic change it seemed to give their English, was another way to keep their people apart from the rest of America. She understood it fairly fluently but had resisted speaking it all these years. She answered him in a mixture of halting Yiddish and English.

"I'm an old man, so I sit in the sun even in August. I like the way it feels on my back. Believe it or not, it's cooler in the kitchen at this time of day. The sun is not hitting that side of the house. Let's go sit there and have tea. You want a cold tea, yes? I'll have a hot one."

Already this was not happening the way Rachel had expected. Sit in the kitchen? With the Rebbe? The two women who worked in the kitchen, preparing meals for two or 20, depending on the need for the day, did not seemed phased when she and the carefully stepping old man walked through the swinging door.

"A cold tea for Rachel. Sugar?"

"Yes, please."

The women hardly looked up from their work. One was busy stirring a bubbling pot on the stove, the other pushing dough around on a well-worn marble-topped table in the center of the room. Rachel and the Rebbe took seats across from one another at the old kitchen table that looked like something out of the 1950's—chrome and faded yellow Formica.

Without a further word exchanged, a glass of iced tea was placed in front of Rachel, with nearly an inch of sugar resting on the bottom, and a pot of hot tea and a matching cup in front of the Rebbe. A plate of fresh rugelach was placed down between them; the little pastries always looked to Rachel like little rolled-up rugs. The Rebbe pushed them toward Rachel, smiling, urging her to have one. He fixed his tea with a little milk then plucked a sugar cube from the brimming bowl of them on the table. He placed the cube between his teeth then quietly sipped the hot tea through the cube until it melted away.

"Ahhhhh," his delight in the tea came out like the hiss of hot radiator. "There is nothing like the first *schluk* of a hot tea. You feel it go all the way down."

He pulled the plate of pastries back toward him and chose one. Dunking it in his tea, he finished it in two quick bites. Rachel sipped cautiously at her icy tea, holding it with both hands. She tended to get clumsy when she was nervous, so even though her hands were getting numb, she held on to the glass.

"Rachel," the Rebbe finally spoke after taking his time wiping his mouth and the surrounding white beard, "can you imagine a young girl waiting seven years to marry the man she knows is destined to be her husband, then giving him up for the sake of someone else?" *Oh, brother,* thought Rachel, *here we go.* Rachel knew the story. How could she not know it? It was taught every year when that portion of the Torah reading came up—the story of Rachel, *Imeinu,* the biblical matriarch, and her namesake. The story of how the patriarch Yakov thought he was laboring for seven years for the hand of one daughter, Rachel, only to have the older daughter, Leah, substituted at the last minute. Yakov had suspected something like this might happen, so he and Rachel devised a secret signal they would exchange under the chupah so he could be certain he was marrying the right daughter. When Rachel realized her father meant for Leah to marry first, she gave Leah the secret signal, to save her from the embarrassment of being rejected in front of everyone during the ceremony.

"Hashem forgave Rachel for deceiving Yakov because her motives were unselfish. She made a sacrifice of her own interests for the sake of her sister. She gave up her own good, her own desires at that moment." The Rebbe explained as though he was teaching it for the first time.

"Yes, I know," Rachel answered.

"How good are you at waiting, Rachel?"

Rachel knew how to answer this. Rachel *Imeinu* was the mother of all Jewish women. They all supposedly descended directly from her line, all hopefully inherited her trait of selflessness genetically, some more latently than others. The right answer was, *Of course, I am like Rachel, my mother. I put all others before me.*

Instead, Rachel heard herself say, "I don't know."

"Ha! You don't know? That is the right answer!" He pointed a rugelach at her. "How could you know? Have you ever been asked to do such a thing? No, I don't think so. You are a privileged girl from a good family. What sacrifices could be asked of you...take out the garbage? Wash a dish? Ha!"

The Rebbe gave her a mischievous smile and crooked his head, please with his joke.

"Our mother, Rachel, didn't know who she was really was, didn't know her own greatness, until she was in the situation with Leah. In that moment she understood that it was better to postpone her own dream for a while than to allow someone she loved to face such public embarrassment."

The Rebbe's pale hands, with their bas-relief of blue veins, dove around in front of him as though he were conducting music. Rachel thought she could hear the melody; it lulled her, made her drift off, seeing the old story played out newly like a dream.

"And she could have decided differently," the Rebbe continued. "She could have said 'They are tricking me, they lied to me, this is not the way it is supposed to be,' and anyone would have said she was right, had a right to stand up for herself, after all. Up until that moment she was just another girl. But after that decision, that sacrifice, she was a *tzaddikeh*, a holy woman with a destiny to always be totally committed and devoted to the future of the Jewish people."

Rachel felt the enormous charisma of the Rebbe wash over her. This is what everyone was talking about when they said being with the Rebbe was like experiencing a piece of heaven coming down to earth. It wasn't just his passion for what he was saying, for what he believed; it was more like a goose bump feeling; a feeling that would make her sign up for walking through a parted sea or for wandering a desert for 40 years behind this man. This was the feeling that connected her to emotions, decisions, and sacrifices made by her ancestors for 5,000 years. They were having tea and cookies in a hot kitchen in Brooklyn, she and this old rabbi, but they might as well have been at the summit of Mt. Sinai, witnessing a burning bush that spoke, for the awe that she began to feel.

Rachel looked down into her tea as she gripped her glass. She swore she could see the ice cubes shrinking with the heat she was generating just thinking about what all this meant in relation to her. What was it exactly that the Rebbe was trying to prepare her for—what ultimate sacrifice? What would she be asked to wait for? Who would she have to share Yakov with?

The Rebbe had stopped talking and just looked at her for a moment, his hands folded in front of him on the table. Again, he read her like one of the hundreds of books he'd pored over in his scholarly life, understanding at a level beyond what others would see.

"It is not for us to know in advance how we will be tested, Rachel. One thing we can be certain of in marriage, in a marriage to my grandson, who is…" he searched the ceiling for a word, sighing, "…a …complicated and…sensitive young man…with many facets…many expectations to fulfill…there will be tests."

He rose from his chair slowly, using the table for leverage. He looked around the kitchen and inhaled deeply, briefly closing his eyes. "I come here to this room when I want to feel the presence of my wife, when I want her help with something. She was…" he searched again but found what he wanted to say quickly, "…a good wife. So, now you know where you can find her, yes?"

Rachel nodded in answer, but the Rebbe had already turned to go, leaving Rachel in the kitchen, surrounded by the aroma of spices and the whispering of the spirits.

CHAPTER TWENTY-EIGHT

L ark stopped the waitress with the doily-lined tray.
"I'll have a couple of those. What do you call these things? It's Greek for spinachy-cheesy triangles. 'Spank-a-cop,' something like that."

The server stared at her blankly. Lark grabbed two by the mini-swords that stuck up from their plump middles and turned away quickly as though she just saw someone she needed to talk to across the room.

Lark had an impressive collection of these little swords in her pocket by now, keeping herself busy with the seemingly endless assortment of appetizers being offered up at the pre-ceremony reception Rachel was hosting. Lark's only real ally there was Rachel, and she was being monopolized by the "suits," and the matrons in their expensive, chic but modest ensembles during this girls-only gathering. They hovered around her, oohing and ahhing over her dress, her watch, wanting to know the details of the new furniture, the china. *Blah, blah, blah,* thought Lark as she tossed a half-eaten triangle onto a nearby tray.

She'd had enough of this food and the gushing girls. She was bored. Rachel looked beautiful, of course, but Lark thought she also looked like she could easily throw up any minute if it weren't for the fact that her stomach was empty from the daylong fasting required by brides before the ceremony. Today, according to the "hype," mused Lark, Rachel would be absolved of all sins committed up until this day. The fasting, certain prayers she'd say today, prayers that were normally reserved for Yom Kippur only, would give her a clean slate to start her marriage sin-free. The idea of sin was another one of Lark's pet peeves about religion. It bugged her how no one was ever good enough, ever pious enough for God's total love. Lark couldn't understand why no one else could see what to her was obvious: that sin was just every religion's attempt to explain away the inexplicable cruelty, tragedy and loss that was a part of their inexplicable time on this planet. *It's not God. No, God is all good. It's us. Yeah, that's the ticket. We must deserve to suffer! So just toe the line, do this, don't do that and you'll live a calamity free life! Maybe.* How this made people feel better about life, feel safer, she had yet to figure out.

Lark saw Rachel head toward the bathroom. With her tiny feet hidden below her dress, it seemed like she was gliding her way there, as if on ice, instead of the dull carpet of the shul's lower level. She knew this might be her only chance to talk to Rachel before they headed outside for the ceremony where she would be watched by a couple of thousand onlookers from the community and beyond. After the ceremony, her friend would be whisked away to the *yichud* room to be alone with her husband and then at the dinner afterward she'd be swamped by all the well-wishers pressing envelopes into her satin bag.

Rachel's eyes met Lark's across the small, crowed room and they silently agreed to meet, once again, perhaps for the last time, in the bathroom. Lark caught up to Rachel and grabbed her lace-covered arm and directed her away from the main ladies' room toward the one-person handicap bathroom a few feet down the hall, where they'd be able to lock the door behind them.

"You've got to help me hold up this dress," Rachel pleaded the moment she heard the door lock click.

Lark helped Rachel gather the edges of the gown and the layers of fabric underneath that gave the dress its Cinderella-at-the-ball shape, and swept them up and away from the toilet where her friend proceeded to take the world's longest pee.

"I thought you were fasting. Shouldn't you be all dehydrated or something?"

"I am fasting. But I haven't been able to get to a bathroom since this morning and, of course, I ate and drank everything in sight last night, thinking it would hold me over today. It never works. I'm bloated but starving."

"Want me to sneak you in something? A mint? You could use one."

"Tell me about it. Yom Kippur breath! No, I don't want to spoil the fast at this point. It's almost over and I need all the help I can get. What time is it?

"If they start on time, you've got about another half hour till blast off."

"I'm exhausted already." Rachel struggled with her panty hose, while Lark continued to keep the dress out of her way. Lark let the folds of the skirt drop and Rachel ran her hands along the fabric, smoothing it back into place intently. When the bride lifted her face from the task and looked at Lark, a tear was traveling down her face to the corner of her mouth. Her tongue peeked out to catch it.

"Uh, oh. What's going on?"

Rachel took a few moments to stabilize her quivering chin. "I don't know. I don't know. I wish it were over. I just want to be on the other side of tonight. I want this part to be over."

"What part? The wedding?" Lark had a feeling it wasn't the wedding.

Rachel was over-washing her hands, then focused on over-drying them. Finally, she looked at Lark, who had plopped down on the toilet, while waiting for her friend to get to what she needed to say.

"Have you, you know...?" Rachel gave Lark a look she hoped would finish her sentence.

"Have I what?"

"You know." Rachel made a face. *Don't make me say it.*

"Have I what?" Lark made a face back. *How can you do it if you can't even say it?* "Had sex?"

Lark took the two steps that separated them in the small bathroom and put her arms around her friend, who was trembling even though it was warm in there. In her heels, Rachel was still not as tall as Lark, but her head was at the perfect height to fall comfortably onto Lark's broad shoulder. Rachel felt she could just stay there, just like that, and maybe everyone would go home and forget she was there, and she could go home and take up her life back before any of this got started. She'd wake up, go to school, or cut classes and sneak into the city with Lark like they had those couple of times. They could see another movie with gangsters shooting each other up or teenagers that could travel through time, and eat a huge bucket of the popcorn that Rachel loved the smell and taste of it even if it did give her a guilty stomachache. Then they'd rush back to Crown Heights in time to make it seem like they'd been in school all day like good girls. *Everything would be back to normal, if I could just stay here like this and not move for a while.*

"Sex..." Lark began slowly, almost whispering, "...is a good thing. It feels great, don't worry." She thought about her own first time with the Rain Man leading her through that uncharted territory. Lark knew Rachel wouldn't have the benefit of such a savvy guide.

"I don't know...they don't tell you much."

"You'll figure it out. You'll figure it out together, right?"

Rachel guessed they would. She shrugged.

"Then you'll come over and give me the play-by-play and I'll tell you what you or Yakov did right or wrong. I'll write up a little instruction list for him if you want...you know...I'm sure he'll totally appreciate me getting involved."

"Right."

Rachel's slow chuckle at the thought of this kind of absurd meeting between the three of them seemed to re-inflate her. She lifted her head and smeared her errant tears into her hairline. "I'm a mess."

She turned to the mirror and began doctoring the smudge of mascara under her eyes. Lark watched, a hand absently over her heart, which felt achy, like it was actually breaking apart inside her chest—breaking for her friend, for herself.

"Look. It's gonna be okay. You like this guy, right?"

Rachel looked up into the small mirror and saw Lark's face reflected there.

"I think I love him."

"Well, then, that's good, that helps. And that's why you're probably freaking out. It's normal...in fact, you're not even really nervous. What you are is excited; you're excited now. You're just confused about it. Okay? Get it? Don't think of yourself as nervous. Think of yourself as incredibly horny."

Lark loved it when she could shock Rachel like that. Her reward was her friend's belly laugh and balled-up, mascara-smeared paper towel to the nose.

*   *   *

Daniel lifted the wide brim of his black hat and passed his handkerchief over his sweating brow and neck once again. He wiped his palms then folded the handkerchief in half and then in half again until it was a small, damp square. With his hands slightly trembling, he carefully placed it in the inside pocket of the traditional knee-length black satin coat. He fussed with the sash that was wrapped around his waist several times and tied in the front, as though it was cutting him in half. Gavrielle, who stood beside him, glanced up at her husband.

"Are you okay?"

He was sweating more than the August evening warranted. This evening there was a very un-Brooklyn-like dry breeze moving the air around. You could feel September knocking on the door.

"I'll be fine. I think it's the scotch I had before."

Daniel looked over his shoulder at the densely packed crowd covering the barricaded street in front of the Rebbe's residence for as far as the eye could see. He and Gavrielle stood on the raised platform built for the chupah to stand on. Yakov insisted that Daniel and Gavrielle be two of the four witnesses required for the ceremony. They waited in position for the main event to begin, for the Rebbe and the bride and groom to be escorted through the crowd and take the stage. On chairs set up near the far edge of the platform was the immediate family: Rachel's parents, her sisters and their husbands, who'd flown in a few days ago, and Yakov's mother, who occupied her folding chair as though it was a throne, and looked, unlike Daniel, perfectly at home on a raised platform in front of thousands. Police cars parked along the perimeter of the crowd spun their blue and white lights, making it look to Daniel as if the scene—already feeling a bit surreal—was blinking on and off, on and off. Out of the corner of his eye he saw that the Rebbe was slowly making his way up the stairs to the platform with the help of his son Yossi on one side and his assistant on the other.

The buzzing of the crowd suddenly hushed to total stillness in deference to the Rebbe's presence above them on the stage. The old man walked to the edge and faced his community, those who came to bask in his aura, to share this important celebration, to witness a wedding ceremony conducted by the man—something he rarely did—and especially to benefit from the benediction he now offered them. With his weak arms raised, his palms facing the crowd, he mouthed a near-silent prayer and sent it out to them. Strength, unity, holiness, the coming of the Messiah, whatever he had intervened with God for on their behalf, they would gratefully accept.

The crowd erupted as Yakov, the *chassen*, made his way along the velvet-roped path from the residence to the platform. Yakov walked alone. Had his father been alive, he would have walked by his side, beaming with pride. He could have had Rachel's father accompany him, but asked to be allowed to publicly honor his father's memory in this small way. Privately, Yakov felt his father would be right there with him, that all of this was in some way *for him*—a playing out of what he would have wanted for Yakov—so holding the space open for his spirit to fill seemed fitting. Dressed completely in white, Yakov floated, a buoy of light in the sea of black-coated brethren. The crowd roared their love at him. Beloved grandson, handpicked for succession, he was their future. Their hearts ached for his solitary walk to the chupah; they had gotten the message he had wanted to convey: a devoted son who still mourned. Yakov tried not to think about what his father's hovering spirit might make of his activities of the night before with Daniel, and pressed on toward the stage and his future.

Not far behind him was the bride. Rachel, blinded by the heavy veil that was placed over her face by Yakov in a short ceremony before they came outside, was being led down the path by Lark, who hoped that blood would eventually return to her nearly numb hand. Rachel was currently holding a vice-like grip on Lark for whatever strength she needed to walk this last fifty feet to the platform in order to take her place under the chupah. Rachel's mother had argued that Lark was not the most appropriate choice of person to escort her to the stage, but Rachel had thrown her only tantrum of the entire betrothal and wedding process by insisting that her closest friend was her only choice for the honor. She would compromise and let her mother escort her from the edge of the stage to the chupah, but she wanted Lark to get her from the residence to the stage. Her parents, who had felt both bewildered and blessed at the rebellion-free few months they'd gotten out of their daughter thus far, quickly agreed to this one concession.

Lark took Rachel to the stairs leading to the stage where she nearly lifted the bride off the ground with the force of a parting hug. She tried to whisper in her ear, but needed to shout over the buzzing of the crowd.

"I love you!"

Rachel shouted something back, but Lark never got what she said. Between the veil, the crowd and her mother who was pulling on her to turn around and head toward the canopy, it was lost. Lark could have followed them up to the stage and taken a seat amongst the family, but at the last moment, decided not to. She turned around and headed back down the path. The blaring music was abruptly cut off. After a few seconds of silence from the speakers followed by the scratchy sound of a microphone being moved around, she heard the Rebbe's voice. The ceremony had begun.

Lark lifted the velvet rope and pushed her way into the women's side of the crowd. She wanted to watch from here, where she could imagine it was just another wedding. From out this far, with people stepping on her toes, with the sweat and smells of the crowd, with murmured comments, whining children, she thought she could forget for a little while that it was Rachel up there. She kept a detached play-by-play going on in her head to try and make it so. *The bride is walking the seven circles around the groom now; he's putting the plain, but flawless gold band on her pointer finger, which she will later move to her ring finger. He is lifting her veil.* Lark couldn't see the bride's face from where she stood, but she imagined it radiant, almost cocky with the accomplishment of such a good marriage, such a beautiful night, so much approval.

A sudden cracking "pop" sound seemed to Lark to be the loudest she'd ever heard of the smashing of the wine glass under the groom's foot, the symbolic gesture that ended the ceremony. Several more of these cracking "pops" put the sound at the edges of the crowd, not the stage, and the panicked screams that followed meant it was not exploding wine glasses they were hearing, but gunshots.

Lark, like everyone else, was craning her neck to see what was going on. The edges of the crowd erupted in all directions, men concentrating toward the center, women and children fleeing in opposite directions. Sirens blared as the police cars, stationed like a circle of wagons around them, tried to move through the frantic crowd toward the disturbance, but could get nowhere near it. Growing hysteria, with women falling to the ground, covering their heads, wailing prayers, surrounded Lark. Others pushing, shoving, aggressively trying to take ground and escape whatever it was that was happening across the wide expanse of Eastern Parkway.

When more shots rang out, a new wave of panic moved through the crowd, pulling Lark along with it. One shoe already gone, her ankles kicked bloody, desperate hands pulled on her, tearing her dress at the armholes, elbows finding her ribs, demanding that she move out of the way. Unable to control where she was going, she stumbled along with the horrible momentum. People shouted their panicked guesses about what was going on. *Someone's trying to kill the Rebbe, it's a terrorist attack, it's the schvartzes, the blacks, making trouble, it's the coming of the Messiah, finally, it's the end of the world!*

On stage, the screams and cries of the wedding party were broadcasted to the crowd over the speakers, creating real fear for the Rebbe's life. Uniformed police, positioned around the scaffolding, sprang onto the platform shouting for everyone to get down. The path back to the residence was overrun by the crowd, blocking anyone from taking refuge at that moment. Everyone huddled close to the ground around the Rebbe. Metal folding chairs became shields.

Just then, a blinding ball of light was catapulted into the sky. Flames instantly consumed an exploding parked car, at the edge of the crowd where the gunshot had sounded. Black smoke poured from between white hot and blue licks of fire. The smell of gasoline filled the air.

Around Lark the pressure from the crowd began to ease up as people were quickly scattering toward the side streets. Free to finally move on her own, she decided to turn around and head, like a salmon swimming against the current, toward the wide steps that led to the front door of the residence. Lark figured that on this higher ground she might be able to see what was happening. She flipped off her remaining shoe as the heel snapped off. Her bare and bleeding toes peeked through her shredded hose. The hem of her dress was splattered with blood, her own or someone else's—she'd never know. She limped—a big bruise was rising around a nasty cut from a high heel that had used her instep as a launching point.

Reaching the stairs, by now crowded with others who had had the same idea, Lark was still able to get high enough to see above the crowd to the far end of the broad avenue with its park-like median separating eastbound and westbound traffic. There to the right, the burning car was still belching smoke. The scream of a fire siren in the near distance meant a truck would arrive on the scene soon, but too late to save what was already a charred skeleton. Lark could see a mob of young blacks yelling and throwing things into to the crowd of mostly Chasidic men— the women and kids had scattered by now. Though some of the Chasid's were still moving away, a growing front of them were turning to answer the mob, shouting, bending to pick up the debris aimed at them and sending it back. On every side the orange sawhorses and traffic cones that had blocked off the street were lying prone and useless like casualties on a battlefield. Another enraged mob, armed with all kinds of trash, a few two-by-fours, crowbars and bats, rounded the corner at Kingston and nearly tripled the existing one already there.

"What do they want from us? Has anyone been shot?"

A woman behind Lark asked the question everyone was wondering. No one could answer her.

From above the crowd, apartment windows that had been open to the festivities, giving those who were lucky enough to live across from the Rebbe's residence a bird's-eye view, now framed outraged spectators, some raining debris down upon the angry mob below. Lark saw soda cans flying down, pots, plants, and a dish tub of water being spilled out by an old lady with a kerchief tied tightly around her head.

Lark heard herself scream, along with those around her when a fire erupted at the base of the scaffolding holding up the chupah platform and the huddled wedding party. Several men, who had been part of a group that remained close to the platform, perhaps out of concern for the Rebbe's welfare, now frantically ran in circles, their clothing on fire, their beards singeing away in an instant, leaving them yelping and clutching at their faces. The men disappeared from her sight as they hit the ground rolling, and the surrounding Chasids jumped on them to help smother the flames with a blanket of bodies and black coats.

"They are throwing Molotov's!" someone shouted, creating more fear. Behind Lark the quick clicking of heels on the stone steps ended with a crying woman slipping and slamming down headfirst at Lark's feet. She was out cold in an instant. When Lark bent over her to try and keep her from rolling down the stone steps, she saw the woman was at least seven months pregnant.

The police were now working quickly to get everyone off the platform, starting with the fragile Rebbe who, Lark saw, was sandwiched between two uniformed and vested cops that carried him like a tightly folded bundle, each clutching a leg and an arm.

As they moved quickly through the parting crowd, the Rebbe's stiff-brimmed hat flew off his head and got lost behind him, exposing a closely-cropped shock of white hair, and a black *kipah* that began to flap around as though it was going to blow away, too. Just then, one of the officers flanking the Rebbe reached around with his free hand and clamped the skullcap down on the old man's head.

Yakov, Daniel, Yossi, Rachel's father, and the other men from the wedding party followed, forming a tight circle around the women, including Rachel, who clutched the long skirt of her dress to her chest so she could run. Two other policemen, plainclothes, with weapons drawn, moved ahead to clear the way for them across Eastern Parkway to the sidewalk and up the stairs to the front entrance of the residence.

As the party swept past Lark, she yelled out Rachel's name, but Rachel's head remained buried in the center of the group. Yakov's head popped up and he made eye contact with Lark. He then turned to one of the officers escorting them and pointed at her just as they reached the huge residence's doors and disappeared inside. Less than a minute later, one of the plainclothes policemen came out and made a beeline for Lark.

"They want you in there, Miss. Come with me, please."

"This woman needs help, she fell...she's pregnant."

"We can't move her." He released a walkie-talkie from his belt and began calling for paramedics. Lark knew no one was going to get over there anytime soon.

"Well, fuck it, I'm moving her. She's going to get trampled."

Lark stooped down and hooked her arms under the unconscious woman's shoulders and began dragging her slowly up the few stairs toward the door.

"Shit!" The cop spat out, exasperated, and knew he had no choice but to lift the woman's lifeless legs and help Lark get her inside.

CHAPTER TWENTY-NINE

T he Jews get everything they want."
A spray of spittle punctuated the young man's words, delivered while standing on the hood of a parked car in front of the high school. His growing audience was black students and others from the surrounding community who were spilling out onto the sidewalk after a blues concert that had just been held there.

"We can't take this anymore! We get no respect, we get no justice."

The story circulated quickly. A mother, a black Jamaican woman over on Utica near Lennox called 911 and reported that someone was breaking into her apartment and she was alone with her young, autistic son. When police arrived more than 25 minutes later, the woman was found beaten to death and the young boy strangled by a cord from a videogame controller.

"Why does it take 25 minutes for the goddamn cops to get to Utica and Lennox? Why are they in no hurry to save a black mother and her black child from a horrible crime? Because they are busy at a fucking wedding...they got all the cops in Crown Heights making sure the goddamn Rebbe got the protection he needs, making sure his relatives and all the blackcoats and wigs got their fuckin' street blocked off for their mother-fuckin' party. Cops can't even get through with all the streets blocked off, blocked off to keep *us, the black man, away from them.*"

The speaker grabbed his tie and swung it upward, rolling his eyes in his head and letting his tongue drop from his mouth, miming for the crowd the ugly vision of a lynched victim.

Jamal, with Pee Cee tagging along, filtered out of the school along with the crowd, whose rhythm-and-blues mood was quickly transformed into shock and outrage. Jamal's blood ran cold as he heard the details of the story. Pee Cee was close behind him as his cousin took off sprinting toward home, toward Utica, then south toward Lennox.

"Let's go up Kingston and pay the motherfuckers back!" Another speaker incited from the roof of a minivan. Someone muscled a nearby city trashcan over his head and smashed it down into the windshield of the van, its "Moshiach Now!" bumper sticker identifying its owner as a Chasid.

A good part of the crowd, mostly young men, answered the call to action and moved north up Kingston toward the main Jewish shopping area, scouring trashcans for bottles or anything else that would serve as a weapon to be wielded or thrown. Others were already armed with pocketknives or even small guns, not uncommon possessions for this neighborhood. The mob got larger as it traveled toward its target—the line where the black neighborhood gave way to the Jewish one, spreading the story and the blame for its tragic ending along the way.

* * *

He ran, making bargains in his head with some God he didn't know if he believed in.

Jesus, please, Jesus, please, Jesus, please.

Jamal ran as if his running could somehow save them, as if he still had time to get there and stop it all, as if he was on a treadmill that, when spun fast enough, would turn back time. His chest burned and bile rose in his throat, but he did not slow down until he saw what he knew he would see, what his rising panic had told him would reveal itself as he came within a block of his apartment building. The police cars wedged headfirst at different angles around the alley that led to the back basement apartment, his apartment, where his mother and brother now lay dead.

The Rain Man stumbled toward the curb and vomited. He felt a hand on his back and spun around, ready to fight. It was Pee Cee.

"Sweet Jesus, cousin. It's not going to be them. I swear to you, it cannot be your mama."

Jamal let out a sound that was somewhere between a moan and cry and pushed past his cousin and his thin optimism. He swung his shoulder around, wiping his foul mouth and running nose on his shirt, and stumbled toward the whipping police lights and the morbid mob that filled the sidewalk in front of his building.

Someone in the group who lived in the building spotted him. "Here comes the other son!"

The crowd turned as one toward him and the cacophony of chants and taunts they were directing toward the police stationed outside the building gave way to an expectant silence.

Jamal kept placing one foot in front of the other, and the building was getting closer and closer, but he felt as though he moved through gelatin, slowly, with the sounds around him strangely muffled.

"Jamal, honey, Lord have Mercy, Lord have Mercy!"

He heard the building superintendent's wife wailing at him and felt her patting his back as he passed by, but he kept walking. He stopped only at the yellow-tape barrier that blocked off the alley and the entrance to the basement apartment back there. Pee Cee followed a few paces behind him.

When one of the policemen started aggressively toward Jamal, the crowd started up their abuse again. After establishing who Jamal and Pee

Cee were, he radioed the detective in charge in the apartment and got someone to come out front and escort Jamal back to the "crime scene," as the writing on the yellow tape reminded him they were entering. Jamal wondered if that wasn't just the way you could have described what went on in that apartment not just today, but every day. *It was a crime his mother was a junkie and no matter what he did, how many miserable shifts he worked, how much money he brought home, how well he tried to take care of her, she would never clean up and stay clean. And it was a crime that he had a brother whose daddy could have been one of a dozen drug dealers or other motherfuckers his mother found herself in the company of back in the day when she could still get a man to look at her. And it was a crime that that little brother sat in that dark hole most of his life, playing video games, his head all messed up from his mama being on drugs when he was a baby in her belly, a crime he couldn't even go to a normal school or have a normal life, whatever the fuck that was. Fucking crime scene.*

When he saw the apartment he knew what had happened. Every drawer was ripped out and overturned, every surface swiped of its contents, every cushion, mattress, pillow slashed open. When he'd left earlier that day he'd sealed her fate.

"I need something, sweetie." She had asked him a few hours ago like she'd asked him thousands of times before. Jamal just didn't feel like it. He just allowed himself to think, to hope one more time that she could just do without it if she really wanted to, if she wasn't so weak. *Why couldn't she just make up her mind and make her life something? Why couldn't he make his life something, quit taking care of a junkie mother and broken brother and be someone else?*

He had thought about Lark and her Manhattan college boys that were everything he wasn't and could never be while he was stuck in this dark hole, feeding this always-hungry monster.

"Take a day off, Mama," he told her, as he got ready to meet Pee Cee and go to the blues concert.

"Sweetie, you know I'm gonna. I'm planning to. My sister is coming up from Haiti soon and she gonna help me, too."

He didn't want to hear about the sister again. He was not in the mood for that game.

"Mama, your sister is not coming. You don't even know if your sister is alive, with all that's happening on that island. You haven't heard from her in how long?"

"Don't say that! You don't know that! I heard from her. I just don't tell you everything. I don't have to tell you everything. Who are you, my daddy? Just go do what you supposed to do and get me my something."

"I'm busy today, Mama."

"Oh, you so busy. You such a big man. You wearing Hawaii shirts when you never been to Hawaii, and you wearing that big-ass raincoat when it don't even rain, like some kinda cowboy. You fucking some little white girl makes you feel like some big American cowboy. You think I don't know? You just like all men, just a big dick, that's all you are. Nothing else."

He left her, throwing things and shouting out the window as he passed through the alley to the street. His brother had remained in front of the TV, rocking just a little, back and forth, back and forth while he kept control of the reality on the little screen.

Pee Cee lingered just outside the "crime-scene" door, keeping his eyes trained on the ground. He didn't want to see anything he wouldn't be able to get out of his mind later. The detective in charge looked, to Jamal, like he was a character from a TV show, a rumpled trench coat and pen stuck in his ear. He asked Jamal to identify the bodies, which had not been moved yet, and Jamal began to feel as though he might be part of the TV show, too. *Maybe this whole thing's some Hollywood version of what happens almost any night on the streets of Brooklyn, New York, and we are going to break for a commercial real soon. Or I'm inside one of my brother's games and all I have to do is find the right little chimney chute to jump down to take me to some higher level.*

Standing no closer than the threshold of her tiny bedroom, Jamal numbly thought that his mother looked no worse than she did on any given night he'd come across her strung out on the bed, except for the congealed blood-filled dent in her skull just above her right eye, and the contrast of the white of her skull showing through against her dark skin. And he'd seen his brother curled up next to her in the bed before, just not with a video game controller cord wrapped tightly around his skinny neck, his lips so dark blue, his eyes popped open as though surprised to see his brother home so early.

"Do you have any idea who could be responsible for this?" The rumpled detective stood poised with his pad, plucking the pen that sprouted from the dark curly hair that almost hid his ear. He droned on about how forensics had already recovered the needle and the cooker, determined that she had had time to inject herself before she was killed. She probably hadn't felt a thing—if that was any consolation.

"Did she do business with anyone in particular, anyone on a regular basis?"

No one Jamal knew on the streets would do business with his mother anymore, or if they did they wanted their money up front, so they dealt with Jamal only. Whoever it was had to be new to the area. His mother had made too many promises on the streets that she didn't keep. For all he knew she'd been running up a bill behind his back, cranking up a habit he thought he was easing down to a manageable pace. Whoever it was, they decided they wanted to get paid tonight and were either going to get their money or get even. It was a good way for a dealer, especially the new guy on the block, to show a neighborhood how not to fuck with him.

"When did she make the call?"

Jamal felt the need to reconstruct the scene in his mind, suffer each detail along with her. When did she get the chance to make the 911 call? Later he would hear her familiar slur on the tapes and realize she was already high when she made the call and whoever was there was probably already in the process of ransacking the apartment, looking for money or anything else worth taking. He could practically hear his mother putting on her sweetie-pie voice to get what she wanted from the dealer first, and face the consequences later.

The detective looked over the concert ticket stubs Jamal had offered up when asked where he'd been the last few hours, pulling a pair of reading glasses down from on top of his head to examine the fine print as though it might reveal something profound about what happened that night.

"My cousin was with me the whole time." Jamal tipped his head in the direction of the propped-open alley door where Pee Cee was chain-smoking and examining the doorjamb with the tip of his boot.

"And he'd say he was even if he wasn't, right? Don't think I don't know the deal. Anyhoo, you just stick around for the next week or two. We may need you to fill in some details."

"I'm not going anywhere."

They had him sign releases.

"They're gonna have to do an autopsy, you know, criminal investigation, etcetera, etcetera."

Jamal tried to focus on the detective's mouth as he spoke, concentrating on reading his lips because someone seemed to be turning down the volume on the man's voice as he discussed the details of dealing with *the bodies*.

"You can call the coroner's office in four or five days to check the status."

The cop checked all his coat pockets before he pulled a business card out of the last pants pocket he got to, and wrote the coroner's number on the back of it.

"You call me direct if you got anything I should know. Otherwise, here's the number you call to make, ya know, arrangements."

He'd been taking care of his mother since he was ten years old, making money on the streets any which way, until he was old enough to get a real job. He'd been taking care of basic details like food on the table, running down and paying the electric bill, the rent, straightening up the apartment, and cleaning the toilet for years. He could take care of the "arrangements," too: talking to the funeral home, calling the few relatives, letting the cleaning service his mother sometimes worked for or the special school his brother sometimes attended know that they wouldn't be coming in anymore. He could keep being the good son until that was all done.

But right now he had to get out of there.

Jamal found Pee Cee in the alley, kicking the wall and cursing to himself. When he saw Jamal he exploded with rage.

"Those muthafuckas killed her! Maybe she coulda been saved if those fuckin' Jews didn't have every cop in the neighborhood at that wedding. They havin' a fuckin' party over there while your mama is dying."

Jamal looked down the alley and saw the angry crowd gathered there. He stared into his cousin's eyes, brimmed with tears that did little to extinguish the rage burning there. He wondered when his own hot tears would come and hoped the answer was *never*. He didn't want to think or feel. If he could assign the blame, perhaps he would never have to take it himself. He did not want to stop and think about the fact that his mother's brutal death was the simple sum of an equation that had been calculated long ago—an adding up of years of abuse, neglect, denial.

He wanted to act, to take action in the face of so much helplessness, produce some tangible result when the result he'd been scrambling to get to—that he would save her, somehow save her from her past, from herself and, by proxy, save himself—was now forever out of his grasp. Inflicting pain might be better than feeling it. Jamal bounded down the alley to the street toward the crowd, who welcomed him, swallowed him up as their cause, their ready reason to finally act outside the margins so neatly drawn for them by everyday restraint. Pee Cee trotted close behind, excited to see something in his cousin's face that he recognized for a change.

CHAPTER THIRTY

I still have ten fingers, ten toes, and a wedding to finish, so enough!" The Rebbe set the tone by insisting he was "in one piece" and shooing away the EMT sent in to attend to his injuries, as well as his frantic, hovering housekeeper of 25 years. In rapid-fire Yiddish he gave instructions for the caterers, the household staff, and the frightened wedding party.

A quick inventory proved that no one was really hurt beyond some scratches, blooming bruises, lost hats, and tilted wigs. The unconscious pregnant woman was soon revived and, despite the circumstances that got her there, was delighted to find herself inside the Rebbe's private quarters with an ice pack on her now lumpy forehead.

With the Rebbe taking charge, the group began to be lulled into a sense of security, the sirens and sounds from the streets muffled by the thick, brick walls of the complex. Uniformed police stationed at the door and house staff running around pulling heavy drapes closed, checking the many entrances to make sure they were all locked, made them feel further insulated. Yakov's mother brushed vigorously at her hopelessly soiled silk suit and paced. "It's a terrible omen. Last year, I lost my husband out of the blue, now this! Why is this happening to me?"

The Rebbe addressed his daughter-in-law impatiently. "Whatever this is, it is certainly not happening to you alone, my dear. With time, all will become illuminated." His words did little to visibly calm her, but sufficiently chastened her into sitting and accepting a cup of tea.

The old rabbi was determined that the remaining wedding rituals be summarily carried out and that the disturbance, whatever it turned out to be, would not interfere with this important milestone in his and his grandson's life. It was a milestone for the community as well, and would be the final detail that allowed the Rebbe to put his intended successor in place.

It was bad enough that the planned reception—the food, the music, the customary dancing to all hours—was not going take place with all the Chasids of Crown Heights and other guests now scattered and fleeing for their homes. So, the Rebbe directed that the bride and groom be escorted by their parents to the already prepared yichud room, where they would be alone together for the first time as husband and wife. The marriage could not be questioned or postponed. The Rebbe had no illusions about his immortality, even if there were those among his followers who thought he'd live forever, become the Messiah they were all waiting for. Only he lived with and laboriously breathed through his fragile state of health, and while everyone hoped he was getting better, regaining his former strength, he feared it was not the case. When all the formalities were complete, when the marriage was indisputable, he would turn his attention to the chaos of outside world, but not until then.

"I can't believe he's going ahead like nothing is happening," Lark leaned in to whisper to Rachel before she stood to follow through with the Rebbe's instructions and join her parents and Yakov as they headed toward the yichud room. Though Rachel thought it upsetting to keep barreling ahead, she looked at Lark and shrugged her shoulders. This was the Rebbe's wish and they were used to following him without question. Rachel found some comfort in numbly acquiescing, silently agreeing like everyone else to be confidently led from one thing to the next.

The bride kissed her parents outside the door to the Rebbe's study, and prepared to step over the knife, fork, and spoon set in the threshold—another symbol, another tradition carried out for hundreds of years, another hedge against disaster, a small ransom paid for a hoped-for outcome. Rachel found herself thinking that with her ruined wedding, this small gesture was too little, too late. But, Yakov was close behind her, and their parents behind him, so she just stepped over the offending utensils and moved a few steps into the room. She wasn't sure what was supposed to happen next.

Yakov entered the room without making any eye contact with her. He closed the door behind him and walked over to the settee at the far end of the room and sat down. On a coffee table were some snacks for them, some vodka on ice, and a pitcher of water in a basin they could use to wash their hands before eating. Another ritual, one they'd both performed thousands of times, he dispensed with quickly, wiping his hands on a small towel that had a large "R" embroidered on it, flanked by a small "Y" on the left and a small "R" on the right. Monogrammed towels. One of the small details someone had arranged for, Rachel noticed with some satisfaction. Yakov spread something, chopped liver or hummus, she couldn't tell, on a cracker, mumbled a bracha, and popped it into his mouth, making it disappear in two chews and a swallow. Then with the intensity of someone who'd forgotten something important, he prepared another cracker and held it out to her, looking directly at her for the first time since they'd escaped the chaos outside.

"Are you as hungry as I am?"

They'd both been fasting for nearly 24 hours by then. With his question, Rachel realized she was starving. She quickly washed her hands, said the requisite prayers and then devoured his offering. She sat on the settee with him, but not close enough to be touching. Yakov poured himself an inch of vodka in one of two small cut crystal tumblers set out for this purpose and half as much in the other for her. He handed her the glass. "L'chaim." He lifted his vodka briefly toward her, shot back the thick-with-cold liquid, then began pouring another one before he finished swallowing. Rachel swallowed hers quickly, too, knowing enough about vodka to understand that she didn't want to sip it or have it sit in her mouth long enough for the bitter burn to register on her tongue. They busied themselves for the next few minutes with crackers and spreads, the carrot sticks and olives, until the sharp edge of their hunger and nerves were dulled. She was not used to drinking, but thought it could only help her adjust to everything else that was going on that she was not used to, so she had two more little shots while he had two larger ones. Then Yakov rose, slapping his hands together to wipe off any crumbs, and positioned himself, next to the draped portrait propped on an easel near the fireplace. Rachel hadn't even noticed it until that moment.

"Are you ready?" Without waiting for her reply, Yakov faced the portrait and, using both hands, carefully removed the cloth that had been tucked behind the ornate frame. He stepped aside, turning toward her, and waved the cloth like a matador. Rachel faced his image of her for the first time. As much as she had tried to prepare for this moment, to have some praise at the ready, to have some gracious reaction that would disguise any disappointment she might have in seeing herself translated to canvas or express approval if she loved it, she could not have predicted her actual impulse at that moment. She wanted to cry with relief.

He loves me.

It could have been the vodka, this feeling of her shoulders relaxing and the knot in her stomach untying and her breath now able to fill some deeper compartment of her lungs. But this revelation, this knowing how he had to feel about her to paint her this way, to make her so alive on the canvas, so solemnly beautiful, held its own power to intoxicate her.

He loves me.

The thought made her feel as though she'd gotten away with something, something everyone had told her would not be a part of an arranged marriage: romance. They said their love would grow over time, they'd be partners in a mission that was bigger than fantasies of storybook love, they'd respect each other, honor each other in accordance with Chasidic tradition. But the painting proved to her that her new husband was a romantic, by the story he'd layered into her eyes, a story that began with, *Once upon a time there was a beautiful maiden named Rachel who adored her husband.*

"It's amazing." Rachel spoke finally, knowing she couldn't say what she really felt—that she knew now that everything was going to be all right, that she'd made the right decision, and life was going to unfold not as a mystery, but as a lovely tale of requited love and righteous action being rewarded with all good things. Walking to where Yakov still stood by the easel, Rachel faced him and took his two hands in hers as though it was the most natural thing in the world to be touching him, to warm his cool fingers against her hot cheeks and to brush them with her lips.

CHAPTER THIRTY-ONE

Sarah Shulman recognized her husband's gait from a block and a half away. When he was in a hurry he had this kind of half-walk, half-run thing he did—one leg kept almost straight and the other leg bent and loping, propelling him forward. Seeing him now racing down the street reminded her of watching a younger, nimbler version of him so many years ago on the basketball court. They were in college, a small liberal arts school for chronic underachievers in New Jersey. He wasn't a star player on the team—the team itself was a bit lackluster—but her eyes always gravitated to him during games. He had great legs is what it came down to—perfectly formed calves and this halo of reddish-blond hair that lightly insulated them. When he pivoted around the floor, high-tops squeaking on the thick varnish, wearing the tight little shorts they wore back then, she could see the lines in his thighs where one muscle sloped and gave way to another, or see a tendon pull tight then release when he jumped in the air to block a pass or dunk a ball. He had grace.

"He's groovy." She remembered leaning over and whispering that to her roommate during one particular home game. She had to smile remembering that word and how sincerely they used it then, a fleeting time when using the term meant you were quite groovy yourself and hadn't yet passed into quaint obsolescence like the word later would. His long hair used to be pulled back in a ponytail that swooshed around behind him on the court. When they actually met through a friend of a friend who got her invited to his fraternity's after-game party, it didn't take long to confirm that he was, indeed, very groovy. He'd been to a rally in Washington, protesting the war, and gotten arrested. And what made being arrested so cool was that having a record now for "inciting to riot" made him ineligible to serve, even if he was drafted. They talked in a corner of the kitchen in the frat house.

"You've never been to a demonstration?" He'd seen the awestruck co-ed look before, and challenged her.

"No. My parents would kill me."

"You've got to grow up, little girl. Our parents are letting our young brothers die, man. It's up to us to turn over the system. Look at me...fucking little Abie the Baby Shulman, from Bayonne, New Jersey. I'm living proof that you can 'fuck the system.' I'm not going to Nam because I showed up at a demonstration and went nuts on them...I got to use the system to screw it!" He ranted and preened for her and a few other girls that gravitated into his magnetic field, and he liberally quoted his hero, Abby Hoffman, who wrote a book that was his Bible du jour.

Sarah remembered the offhanded flattery she gave him that changed her life. "Hey, you should change your name. You know...from Abie to Abby, like Hoffman. Abie's too Jewish, too establishment for you, man." He paid attention to her after that. She wasn't just another co-ed anymore. She saw him the way he imagined himself. That night, they talked for hours with all the seriousness that being that young and that high in 1968 made them. All the pot they smoked could have been a contributing factor to the chemistry between them, or the fact that she called him Abby for the rest of the night and whispered the name in his ear while they made love later. Whatever it was, they'd been together ever since.

But here he was now, no longer her Abby, really. When they moved to Crown Heights, he insisted that everyone call him Avram, the Hebrew pronunciation of his given name, Abraham. He no longer wanted to be the voice of rebellion—just another in the long line of Abrahams who lived their lives with an ear cocked for the voice of God. He was Avram now, his golden calves hidden by his Crown Heights uniform. His rushing walk was a dead giveaway, but otherwise he looked now like every other Chasid on the street, a narrow black totem from behind.

Sarah hoped she'd find her daughter with him. She knew, from the vantage she'd had of the ceremony, that Lark wasn't on the platform with the rest of the wedding party, that she never made it up there for some reason, even though that's where she was expected to sit. Once the shots had rung out and the chaos started, Sarah could think of nothing but finding either Lark or her husband. And here he was, just a block ahead of her, but no Lark.

"Avram!" She called out to him, but he kept up his loping, oblivious. Careening sirens heading into the area filled the airspace across the block that separated them. Her voice, scratchy now from the smoke, could hardly compete. More than one car had been turned into a bonfire and the result was a low-lying fog permeating the streets. *Where is he going?* A right turn at the corner would have made sense—he'd cross the street and head toward their apartment—but instead, he rounded the corner to the left and slipped out of sight.

"Abby! Abby!" Sarah suddenly felt desperate to get her husband and get off the streets, to find Lark, to be somewhere safe and all together. She thought of David. They would never be "all together" until he was with them, too, until her husband opened his heart and home to their son again. She made a silent pledge to work on that, to have the courage to bring it up again, to open that possibility with "Avram" and not let him slam the door shut on it. She would talk to the part of him that was still Abby, the young man who would have approved of his future son's rebellion, not the man she lived with now—old and rigid at 45, who had shrunken his world to a series of do's and don'ts, black and white and nothing in between. At the very least she would insist that she was going to have a relationship with her son, even if her husband didn't want to. Yes, she would insist on that. David deserved that much from her. She deserved it.

Sarah allowed the danger around her to crystallize her priorities—the prospect of harm or even death bringing into hard focus what was left undone, what life's ultimate fragility demanded she recognize. David popped up for her as something she needed to attend to, to wake up about. *I want to remember this.* She willed herself to be present. She looked around her, trying to memorize the elements that were catalyzing a certain truth in her mind, one that fear and the shouts from a gang of black youths charging up the street toward her husband conspired to snatch away even as she barely glimpsed it. *I've lost myself somewhere along the way.* Maybe it was as long ago as that night after a basketball game in a dark frat-house bedroom smelling of discarded fast-food and dirty socks, a night when other elements made it easy for her to be altered forever. Perhaps it was then that she began to transform from a whole being into half of a whole or, more to the point, to be absorbed by another, groovier whole, and fully disappear.

"Abby!" She screamed it this time and he finally turned and saw her just as the violent circle closed in around him, some of them chanting, "Kill the Jew!" in rhythm with their swinging fists and kicking feet. She could hear him screaming, too, "Run, Sarah, run!" and she did. She ran for her life.

* * *

In the vortex of that circle of raging men, really just boys most of them, puffed up to a state of uncontrolled aggression they mistook for manhood, Jamal suddenly stopped himself from delivering blows to the shrieking Chasid. The guy was shrieking first for someone at the other end of the block to run, then without skipping a beat, he was hurling insults at his attackers. "You black beasts, you shit of the world, you cowards!" The crazy Jew, blood from his split lips mixing with the foaming phlegm that spewed from his twisted mouth, refused to look away from them or curl into a ball to protect his face. Instead, he challenged them. "Kill me, go ahead, fucking kill me, you filthy pigs...then rot in hell!" He wouldn't stop. "Throw me in the gutter to die. I'd rather die in the gutter than have your filthy hands on me."

Jamal stopped when he realized he recognized the man, had taken a similar insult from him some other time on the sidewalk a few blocks from where they were. This was Bird's daddy. "Leave him, leave him in the gutter like he wants. Let's get out of here!"

But no one was listening to Jamal. He wasn't their leader or their reason anymore; it had gone beyond that. From behind him, he felt an arm shoot in toward the center, passing his ribs. The muscular hand at the end of that arm clutched a long knife and before Jamal could react, it pushed the wide blade into the screaming man's gut, twisting it, pulling it out then burying it deeper still in another spot. "That will shut you up, you motherfucker!"

Jamal didn't recognize the voice at the other end of that arm, except for the raw hatred in it, and when he turned to see who it was, who had wielded the knife, he saw more than one of the boys backing away from the group, their faces a mixture of fear and triumph. Before he could figure anything out, the three boys were halfway down the block.

"Let's get the fuck out of here." Jamal felt Pee Cee pulling at his arm.

"Wait!" Jamal turned back to Lark's father who looked more confused now than anything, as if puzzling what could possibly be the cause of this sudden sharp pain in his middle, the quick damp warmth spreading from the center of that pain, and the vague pulling feeling down there that was making it hard to breathe. Just as the stabber had predicted, the Chasid did stop yelling finally, his mouth filling with blood. One by one, the others in the group began to scatter, too.

"Come on, let's go! We got to get out of here." Pee Cee pulled at his cousin again who still knelt in front of the Chasid. Jamal shrugged him off and inched closer to the bleeding man.

"What are you doing? Pee Cee screamed.

"Go, man. Just go. I'll catch up to you."

Jamal looked across at Lark's father. The man's hands clutching his belly were covered in blood. "I'm killed." He said it as a simple fact, like the time of day, except for the gurgle at the back of his throat.

"Hey man, I'm going to get you an ambulance, okay?" Jamal met the man's dimming eyes.

"Fuck you!" Avram spat blood at Jamal and his offer.

Jamal stood up and could see flashing lights four or five blocks down the street heading his way. An ambulance. Maybe Bird's daddy would be lucky, and it was on its way to get him. He turned away from the Chasid who had slumped down, his upper body sloping into the gutter between two parked cars, his screams replaced by incoherent murmurings now.

Jamal walked slowly away, almost strolling, as though he had all the time in the world on this unseasonably cool summer night. Perhaps, he reasoned, if he didn't run it meant that there was nothing to run from. If there was nothing to run from, then it meant a man had not just been killed. If a man had not been killed then maybe this was just an ordinary night in Crown Heights, and if it was an ordinary night, he could go home and surprise his mother and brother with a big bag of Chinese takeout, and they could fight over the fortune cookies. And if they could fight over the fortune cookies that meant they all had a future to look forward to.

CHAPTER THIRTY-TWO

What's wrong?"

Is there any other response to a phone call received at three o'clock in the morning? Lark thought as she leaned her hot forehead against the cool metal face of the payphone in the emergency room waiting area. The receiver smelled of the stale breath of countless others who had waited around the frigid and antiseptic anteroom, pacing or staring blankly at the TV hanging down from the yellowed acoustic panels. Set to the distraction of the Home Shopping Network, the screen reflected the glare of the long dashes of fluorescent light that punctuated the ceiling, creating the shadowless flat light that contributed to the disorientation of those whose bad luck had led them there. Like her, they'd held their breath for someone to push through the heavy double doors that sealed in the emergent, and give them some news—what they were hoping for, or praying never to hear. And they'd used that phone to deliver that news to the blissfully unaware, waking them from their innocent sleep. Those loved ones who went to bed with the world in order would grope in the dark toward the tearing ring, heart already beating in their throat, pulse going zero-to-60 in the time it took to answer, and ask what, while they slept, had gone terribly, terribly wrong.

"David, it's about Pop."

"What did he do now? Lark, this is it. You are moving in with me now!"

"No, wait...it's nothing like that. David, listen. There's a riot going on in Crown Heights."

"A what?"

"There are mobs of black guys all over the streets, setting cars on fire, shooting, throwing things...it happened in the middle of my friend's wedding. I don't really know the details, but it's like a war zone around here. Looting and cars on fire and shit. Something about some woman and a kid dying and they think it's because of the Jews blocking off the street for the wedding...I don't know. Everyone was running in the streets, you know, trying to get away. Pop was attacked by a gang. Beat up bad. Stabbed."

"Oh, my God. Is he...?

"I don't know yet. I'm at the hospital. Mom is in with him, I think. There are news trucks everywhere, maybe you should turn on your TV."

"Hold on." She heard the phone crash to the floor and pictured David in his bedroom, scrambling around in the dark to turn on the little TV that sat on his thrift-store dresser, dragging the phone off the milk crate alongside his bed that doubled as a bookshelf and nightstand. It was only a matter of weeks since she'd been there for the party, since David caught her with Dog in the bathroom after a clumsy but spectacular first kiss. Dog had sent a message to her through David that he would be traveling most of the rest of the summer, but really wanted to get together with her in the fall, that he was looking forward to her joining the normal world and "hanging out." If he thought the world she lived in wasn't normal before, how would he categorize the surreal events unfolding on this particular evening? David got back on the line; his voice pitched a bit higher now.

"I'm looking at it now. This is insane!"

"Turn it up, I want to hear."

David blasted the volume and Lark could hear the studied, somber tone of a reporter: "... reports of a victim of brutal violence in the Jewish community, a Chasidic man, was allegedly attacked and stabbed just a few blocks from here. An ambulance rushed to the scene after a 911 call from the man's wife, who witnessed the attack and ran for help. He is currently at King's County Hospital and officials there say only that the victim is in critical condition. This attack is just one incident in an explosion of incidents here in the Crown Heights section of Brooklyn that are a reaction to, or retribution for, the deaths last night of a mother and her son who, initial reports from the black community allege, could have been saved if it weren't for police in the area being tied up and a large area of the neighborhood being blocked off for the wedding of the grandson of the prominent leader of the Chasidic community, 'The Rebbe'..."

Lark heard another voice in the background. "Hey, man, what's going on?" It was Dog. He was back?

"See for yourself. Riots in Brooklyn. I got my sister on the phone."

David came back on the line. "Lark, I'm coming out there."

"Holy mother of god," Lark could hear Doug's reaction to the broadcast, "...it's like a friggin' war zone. I'm coming with you. You are going to need an assistant."

"For what?"

"Your cameras. There are pictures happening all over the place, look at this!"

David switched the TV off abruptly. "Dude, my father's in the hospital, maybe dead, okay? Shut up for a minute, I gotta talk to Lark." He turned his attention back to the phone. "Like I said, I'm coming out there. Wait for me at the hospital. I'll look for you in the emergency room area. If they let you in to see him or if you go somewhere else, leave word for me at the desk where you'll be."

"Okay." She hung up the phone and wiped her sweaty palms on her already blood-and-soot-stained dress. She was sweating despite the air-conditioning. What she wouldn't give for a pair of comfortable shorts and a T-shirt right now. She'd run the entire way to the hospital from the Rebbe's residence, insisting she be allowed to leave once she heard the news. Shortly after they reached the safety of the residence, the Rebbe asked the officers at the house to keep him informed. He wanted to know if the violence was escalating or if any community members were killed or hurt.

Once Rachel and Yakov went into the yichud room together, the rest of them—Daniel, Gavrielle, Rachel's parents, along with Rachel's sisters and their husbands, were sitting around the big main parlor of the residence in a kind of daze, waiting for word that it would be safe to go home. They drank the tea provided and distractedly picked at platters brought up to them by the caterers, who were happy to have even this small portion of the grand meal, planned and now ruined, enjoyed by someone. The officer whose radio suddenly came alive with the crackling report no one but he could really decipher, walked over to the Rebbe, tucked back in a corner of the room, praying and swaying with a single-minded concentration, and gently tapped him on the shoulder. He was the same cop who had saved the Rebbe's yarmulke from flying off his head, and he looked sorry to have to interrupt the old man's prayers.

"S'cuse me Rabbi..." and leaned in to tell him what he'd heard.

As the cop talked, the Rebbe closed his prayer book, kissed the binding, and placed it down on a nearby table. He nodded every few seconds, his big square beard flattening out on his chest, then lifting. Then, as though someone pulled a plug from somewhere on his body, his already fragile frame deflated, his shoulders rounding and his head falling, shaking back and forth as if to say, "No, no" to whatever he was hearing.

Everyone had stopped what they were doing, fixing their attention on the Rebbe and his reaction to what was obviously bad news. Lark stiffened with fear as it became clear the Rebbe was walking directly toward her, clutching the sturdy officer's arm for support. He stopped a foot or so in front of her and studied her for a moment before speaking. "Tell me, you are a Shulman, yes?"

She nodded, her eyes questioning.

"Your father, is he Avram Shulman?" he asked in Yiddish, pronouncing it "Shoolmahn." She was not fluent by any means, but she'd been around the community long enough to understand this much. She answered him in English, just the same.

"Yes, that's my father, Abraham. Why, what's wrong?"

The Rebbe looked at the cop and tilted his head toward Lark, deferring to the careful public servant to deliver the life-changing news. She was at the door and out before anyone could figure out how to stop her. The Chasidic men weren't going to hold her back physically, she knew, and the cop's concern for her safety did not constitute a legal reason to restrain her. Lark took off, sprinting the eight or nine long blocks to Kings County Hospital.

Crossing the neighborhood, she felt as though she was traveling in a bubble, invisible to those engaged in what she witnessed along the way. No one seemed to notice the tall, barefooted redhead in the tattered dress racing toward something. They kept up with smashing storefronts and windshields and throwing trash and swinging bats, dumping over trashcans and denting hoods. Things flew through the air but missed her, epitaphs were hurled past her but she imagined herself leaping over them, pivoting around them, ducking under their trajectory. She ran mostly down the middle of the street where the surface was smooth with warm tar and there was less broken glass. Because of the still-standing barricades on some of the side streets and the late hour, there was little car traffic. Her eyes burned and teared from the smoke, or was she crying?

When Lark got to the hospital, the woman at the ER desk could not tell her much. With no ID on her she couldn't prove to this gatekeeper that she was related to the patient. "Look, you don't have to tell me anything, okay, but my mother might be back there with him—my mother,

Sarah Shulman—and maybe you can tell her I'm here, that I'm out here. She could come out and tell me what's happening."

Lark pleaded with the woman, but saw in her eyes that she would get to seeing if Lark's mother was back there in her own good time. It was just another night in a long line of disaster-filled nights for the woman, and she could only do so much, even if her colorful scrubs did have little angels wearing nurses' caps printed all over them. She directed Lark to the waiting area and told her where the payphone was near the vending machines.

She warned her, "I don't give change here. You want change, you have to go down to the cafeteria," she warned.

Lark was relieved that David made the decision to come out without her having to ask. She knew from the minute she dialed his number, calling collect, that she wanted him to come, that he had to come, that somehow the evening's events themselves conspired to bring him to her—to break up the distance between them and wipe from the record the very reason for their long separation. *This is all happening for a reason.* She hung on to that idea, treading water. A flood of emotions threatened to drown her. Guilt: *Hadn't she wished her father would die?* Fear: *What if he does die?* Anger: *He deserves a beating, the bully.* Remorse: *A beating maybe, but not murder.* And more guilt: *This is my fault somehow.*

"Oh, God, *please.*" Lark said it under her breath even though she didn't really believe in that kind of prayer. She'd said to Rachel over and over that God, whatever He/She/It was, did not get involved in the minutia of our individual lives. If he did, then he was an unfair brute, busily arranging good luck for some and ignoring the horrible tragedy befalling others, whole countries of others. She despised it when she heard people say they were so "blessed" with this thing or that, implying that others weren't for some reason of their own doing. Sibling rivalry on a huge scale: Daddy/God loves me best!

Still, she wished she could ask for an outcome and make it so. She remembered a time, lifetimes ago, when the family was camping on the beach out near Montauk Point, at a state park there. She couldn't have been more than seven or eight. They lay on their sleeping bags and stared at the sky intently. Her father was instructing them on the heavens as he saw them then: "August is a good month for shooting stars. The first one to see one gets their wish-come-true."

She liked the idea of wishing on a star, when she thought about it now. Somehow putting out a request to a neutral celestial object whose sole function was to turn air into fire, producing heat, energy, and light, was a comforting notion. No judgment, no good, no evil. You could send a star your energy in the form of a wish, and it would just send it right back, warmed up and bright. When David saw the first shooter that night, it hadn't made her jealous. The sky was so generously populated with points of light, she felt it would be her turn soon enough. Lark didn't really have that kind of faith in the generosity of God—He went missing-in-action on the world way too much, as far as she was concerned—but she was not beyond hedging her bets and beliefs with a quiet prayer.

As a girl long disappointed by her father, she had the tiniest active hope somewhere in her being that there could be this Big Daddy deity in charge who would come through for her in her time of real need. And when that happens, she told herself, she'd be happy to say like she'd heard others say, *what a blessing it turned out to be after all; it changed us, brought us together! God works in mysterious ways, but always for the best.*

More than an hour passed and by that time almost every seat in the waiting room was filled. The casualties of this war on the streets were streaming in. Confused and contorted with anger, bleeding, burned and hobbling, they sat waiting their turn. The unconscious and ambulance-borne pushed to the head of the queue. The room had a natural dividing line—a narrow, low table piled up with dog-eared magazines and public health brochures. The white injured congregated to the right of the table and nearer to the windows, the black to the left and nearer to the door. Someone had changed the channel on the TV to local news and turned up the volume. Lark hadn't been paying much attention to the screen. She was too busy hovering around the front desk area, hoping to be a physical reminder to the bitch behind the desk that she wanted to get to her mother, needed to have some information, some update, some something to keep her sane at this point. She wanted to be right there by the door if her mother came out, didn't want to miss her. *If I sit down, I'll fall asleep or fall apart.*

The noise in the waiting room drew her back in. People were shouting and pointing at the TV screen like it was the Super Bowl.

Lark didn't really recognize him at first. *You don't expect to see someone you know running from reporters on TV. It's just some young black guy, pushing his way past a crowd of people, shading his eyes from camera lights, camera flashes, pushing microphones out of his face.* "Jamal!" one of the photographers on the scene shouted as a series of flashes washed over the Rain Man's distorted features, twisted with pain and something else, something that made her see it was him, a reckless defiance in his eyes. "Jamal, over here! Give us a minute!"

The floor beneath Lark became liquid and a wave pushed her back against the nearby wall. She slid slowly down and sat, stunned. To no one she said aloud, "I know him." A chill ran through her and she gathered her skirt and hugged her legs.

On the screen, Jamal broke into a run, his cousin appearing in the frame, following close behind. Then as an afterthought her Rain Man turned and flipped the bird at the camera and crew trying to capture his grief and anger for the entertainment of millions.

Without their subject there to speak for himself, or any new developments in the story, reporters recounted what they knew of it, over and over. They played the tape of Jamal running away and flipping them off and speculated on his state of mind and everything else they could think of in the absence of any real information. The stiff TV journalists used the building she recognized as a backdrop to their segments. They stood near the alley she had walked down with Jamal the night just two

months ago that she ran out of her house bruised and battered and ended up at his house, cared for and caressed. The talking heads put on their
most sincere and serious faces and droned on about the little brother
she'd seen that night and the mother Lark really hadn't seen but felt the
presence of, not only in that apartment but in the eyes of her tough and
tender lover. They were the mother and son whose death, just hours
earlier, and the blame for it afterward had plunged the neighborhood
into hell.

Finally, the shouting and confrontations in the waiting room began
to get out of hand, and a security guard was sent to preside over them.
The TV was changed back to the drone of home shopping. New fashion
for fall, available in "plus" sizes was safer ground.

"Lark." When she looked up and saw David towering over her, she
realized she had somehow ended up on the floor, but couldn't remember
how she'd gotten there. There he was, with bed head and bleary eyes,
helping her to her feet, so she finally let go. He pulled her in and held
her. It was a relief to let it out, to not be alone now that everything had
gotten even more surreal. Dog, strapped up with camera bags, moved in,
making it a group hug. Over David's shoulder Lark saw her mother appear from behind a door that swung open as if by magic.

"Mom!" Lark broke away and ran to Sarah, searching her eyes for
what she knew. Somewhere Sarah had lost her wig, and her short red
hair, streaked with gray at the temples, was damp and pressed to her
scalp. The front of her pale summer suit, from her breasts to her hips,
was stained brown with dried blood. An image passed through Lark's
head of her mother, kneeling on the street, holding her bleeding father,
using the weight of her body, the iron thread of her will, to pull him
back from the brink of death.

"He's alive," she said out loud for her benefit as well her children's.
Sarah Shulman cupped a rough hand to Lark's wet cheek, something she
hadn't done in a long time, something Lark didn't even know she'd
missed until the feel of it started her crying all over again. She looked at

David as though it was perfectly normal for him to be standing there. "For now. He's alive, for now."

CHAPTER THIRTY-THREE

The room looks beautiful, don't you think?" Rachel stood in the doorway to the bathroom and calmed herself by taking an inventory of their new bedroom. The heavy brocade curtains pooled luxuriously on the refinished wood floor sealed them in from the world outside the window. The imported rug, whose price tag Rachel could hardly believe when her mother picked it out, was as she had predicted, perfect. The spectacular weave of jewel tones had provided them with the palette for all the other fabrics in the room—the skirts on the bedside tables, the accent pillows that contrasted so nicely with the newly upholstered easy chair fitting so neatly in the corner, sitting in a warm shower of light from a thoughtfully placed reading lamp.

The bedspread, draped over the two twin beds pushed together, was made from the same fabric as the curtains, except that it had been quilted with a layer of batting to give it weight, softness, and depth. Her husband lay curled up on one edge, taking up as little of the expanse of bed as possible. Yakov was fully clothed, shoes and all, creased into a tight zigzag, holding a handkerchief in a loose fist partially jammed under his cheek.

"Yakov?" When he didn't respond, Rachel tiptoed toward him. "Are you asleep?"

She leaned in toward him for closer inspection and heard him snore lightly to prove it. Rachel could smell a hint of vodka in the air, and then saw the crystal tumbler half full of it sitting neglected on the night table nearest to him.

Had she spent too long in the bathroom? Rachel couldn't tell. What time was it, anyway? Her mother had urged her to head up to the apartment, when she and Yakov emerged from the yichud room weaving from the many l'chaims they'd obviously consumed.

"I'll walk you up." Miriam Fine looked a little alarmed by her daughter's condition, despite or maybe because of the ear-to-ear grin she couldn't seem to wipe off her face.

"It's okay. I can go by myself," Rachel protested.

"And how much vodka did you have?" Her mother looked over the top of her glasses at the grinning bride, her plucked eyebrows so raised they almost disappeared into her hairline.

"All right. Walk me up."

The plan was that Yakov would follow after a while. When Rachel left them all in the parlor, her mother nudging her along, steadying her with a hand on the small of her back, Yakov had gravitated to a corner with Daniel, who was hunkered over his drunk friend. The big man had one hand over Yakov's shoulder, his free hand poking him gently in the chest as he spoke with quiet intensity. Yakov sat there, his eyes almost closed, nodding intently. The rest of the women were given rooms to rest in; the men were assigned various couches or portions of the floor to catch some sleep. Everyone agreed they would not head home until daylight, when they could figure out what the situation on the streets was.

At the top of the many stairs leading to their apartment, Rachel and her mother paused to catch their breath. "Oy, you are going to have to visit me, Rochella. I don't know how many times I can survive these stairs. Or call me when the Rebbe decides to install an elevator."

Mother and daughter smiled at the little joke. They looked at each other and held their gaze in a kind of awkward intimacy. Rachel could see her mother's eyes were shiny with tears. Miriam reached out and pinched her daughter's quivering chin between her French-manicured fingers. "You might want to take a little shower."

Rachel burst out laughing. And Miriam laughed, too. Of all the ways to tell a daughter you loved her on her wedding night, this was her way. All the annoying inspections over the years, the toilet checks, the breath checks, the underwear monitoring, the fruit and vegetable intake charts were Miriam Fine's wordless love notes to her children. Rachel understood that deeply for the first time on that landing. The two women hugged tightly and parted. Miriam took the stairs slowly on the way down. Her heels made a "clopping" sound on the creaky stairs, which was punctuated by an occasional sighed "Oy!" on the way down.

It actually seemed like a great idea to take a shower once Rachel entered the quiet apartment. She was sweaty, sooty, and drunk. The hot water felt delicious. Maybe she did sit in the tub and let the water drizzle down on her for an extra-long while, inhaling the soft mist to clear her nostrils of the smoke and dust she'd inhaled earlier that night. Still a bit drunk after the shower, Rachel moved in that slowed down, exacting way the drunk do, purposefully trying to defy their body's temporary loss of motor skills. She had to comb out her hair and put lotion on her skin and put on the new stiff nightgown and robe that she had left hanging on the door so it would be waiting for her, waiting for her wedding night appearance in the doorway of her new bedroom. Of all the possible scenarios she'd imagined for this moment, his being sound asleep and oblivious to her charms was not one of them.

"You're totally asleep," Rachel said out loud to her snoozing bridegroom. "Hmmm."

Rachel kneeled on the floor beside the bed and looked at Yakov, his eyes tightly shut. He seemed tense even as he slept—like a dog dreaming of chasing rabbits—but what did she know of men or dogs since she'd spent little time with either species? She'd never watched a man sleep before, except for her father, who occasionally nodded off in an over-stuffed chair on a Shabbes afternoon, his mouth hanging open.

Now what? She couldn't decide if she should wake him, reach over and shake him back into the room. Would he be upset if she did, or would he be upset tomorrow that she hadn't? Was it important to "be together" tonight because of some mitzvah or law associated with the wedding night? She couldn't remember anyone mentioning anything about that. She sat on her heels and tried to will him awake with her thoughts. Finally, her calves fell asleep and the pins and needles progressed from mildly irritating to unbearable. She stood up too fast and then became temporarily immobilized as the blood rushed painfully back into her legs. Biting her lip and leaning against the nightstand, Rachel waited for her legs to stop throbbing. She limped over to the window where she pulled aside one panel of the heavy curtain and was surprised to see the sky lit with streaks of pink and gold. It was already morning. If it weren't for the spirals of black smoke that spun upward here and there, she could almost believe that everything about the night had been a bad dream, some nightmarish projection of her fears of marriage that she could wake up and shake off. Since the window didn't face the street, but only an expanse of backyards behind the residence, she could almost believe it was going to be another fine summer day with nothing to be worried about except perhaps sharing her first breakfast with her mother-in-law or being embarrassed by the idea that they all thought they knew what had happened in the privacy of her bedroom the night before, hoping the outcome would be a "blessed event" nine months hence.

Rachel let the curtain drop. She was suddenly very tired and walked around the big bed toward the empty side. As she passed Yakov's feet at the end of the bed she stopped, hesitating for only a moment, then bent over and gently began undoing the stiff new laces on his polished but scuffed new shoes. She pulled off the right shoe and let it drop to the floor. She began working on the other shoe when he stirred, pulling his feet up closer to him, contracting away, then stretching his legs out again. Rachel froze. She thought she saw his eyes flutter open, but couldn't tell in the dim light. She moved back around the side of the bed to get a better angle.

"Yakov?" She waited.

After a minute or so, when he didn't move again, she turned her attention back toward the remaining shoe. She managed to get it off without further incident, then took his shoes and lined them up neatly on the floor of their closet next to the other shoes placed there, waiting, like she was, for their life together to begin. Rachel went to the bed, pulled back the stiff spread, and slipped in between the cool, expensive sheets. She worked at smoothing out the long nightgown—she was used to sleeping in an old camp T-shirt—but then decided she was most comfortable with it pulled up above her knees so she could move without getting twisted up in it. Turning on her side, she faced the black lump that was Yakov's back. She had to laugh, and turned her face into her puffy goose-down pillow to muffle it—so new, it still smelled like Macy's. So! This was the big-deal wedding night she had spent the last few weeks worrying about? For a moment she tried to be horrified, terribly disappointed, but couldn't muster it. Maybe she felt just a little relieved after all they'd been through in one night. No one would have to know that nothing happened. And certainly no one would dare ask her, so her secret would be safe. There was no rush. After all, they had the rest of their lives together to be intimate in that way. Rachel thought of the portrait and felt reassured that his affection for her was real. Earlier she'd overheard her sisters whispering to each other about how the evening's events could be a bad omen for Rachel's marriage. She refused to believe it. Her marriage, she thought, as she drifted off to sleep to the rhythm of her husband's breathing, was simply going to be full of surprises.

CHAPTER THIRTY-FOUR

Good morning." Yakov mumbled to the group, but was mostly ignored. Someone had brought a television into the house, a rarity in any Chasidic home, let alone the Rebbe's, but there it was, materialized on a side table in the parlor, blaring out the local news from its tinny speakers. His uncle Yossi hovered over it, adjusting the antenna, molding and remolding the aluminum foil around the tips. Yakov thought Yossi looked like he knew what he was doing with the thing. He'd heard that some people in Crown Heights kept televisions in their apartments, hidden in a closet somewhere, that they watched with curtains drawn, late at night, the sound turned way down. Was his uncle one of them? Here under the Rebbe's roof, in his room at the back of the house, did he spend his late nights lit up by the blue light of this forbidden box, trespassing in the world the Rebbe warned against, a world of flat images that could nonetheless reach out from the screen and change you, harm you, set you adrift?

Like some powerful magnet, the TV drew everyone's attention. Even when they spoke to each other they did not take their eyes off the screen and the images of smashed storefronts, walls spray-painted with anti-Semitic slurs, the interviews with city officials whose rhetoric rang hollow: *Bridge Building. Dialoguing. Reaching Out. Reaching In.* In the meantime the chaos on the streets continued.

"That was our store! Dovid, did you see, they showed the store. It looks fine, a little graffiti, but that's it! Fine's looks fine!" Rachel's mother beamed, relieved. "Nobody wanted those ugly roll down gates on the store, remember? They were so expensive, but now look. Thank God I insisted on them."

Yakov helped himself to some coffee from a small buffet of pastries and breads that had been set up—more leftovers from the wedding feast that never was. *The dinner is not the only thing that didn't happen,* Yakov thought bitterly. He scanned the offering on the table but found that his hangover and the sick feeling he had about having to face Rachel about what didn't happen on their wedding night left him with no appetite.

"You slept late." Daniel appeared beside him, helping himself to a clean plate from the stack and systematically filling it with the little cakes. Yakov checked behind Daniel, and then behind his own shoulder to make sure no one was within earshot.

"This is not going to work, Daniel."

Daniel put his loaded plate down. "What do you mean? What happened?"

"Nothing happened. With Rachel."

"Nothing? Well, that can happen. You were nervous."

"I wasn't nervous. I was horrified." Yakov checked around his shoulder again. Behind Daniel, across the room, Gavrielle stood, her arms folded above her stomach, which was beginning to bulge with the efforts of Daniel's own post-wedding nights.

"What are you talking about, horrified?"

"Maybe you didn't notice that my wedding was interrupted by gunshots, a riot? People being burned, trampled, attacked..."

"I know, I know, you told me last night, it's a sign from Hashem, just for you! He arranged the whole thing to let you know what a bad boy you are. Come on, Yakov, I know you are a big *macher* now, but the world is not revolving around you and your pecker just yet. I thought we talked this all out last night."

Yakov wondered what was more painful, his belief that God was punishing him now for everything or the way the love of his life was now mocking him for feeling this way, for being so afraid, so confused, so determined to try and do the right thing. Or maybe Daniel's impatience was all part of the unraveling, part of the sentence he would have to live out for his attempted crime.

"Yes, we talked. You gave me the big pep talk, and after that I went up there. She was in the bathroom. I heard her humming in the shower. She sounded, I don't know...so happy."

"Why shouldn't she be happy? She just made the best match in our entire community." Daniel said the words with contempt, which pleased Yakov, who recognized it as jealousy. All the passion he couldn't muster the night before flooded his body as he inched closer to Daniel and touched his bare forearm just under the crumpled rolled-up sleeve of his white shirt.

"I can't be with her. I only want you." He spoke with his jaw clenched, the words escaping like trapped steam.

Now Daniel looked over his shoulder, then picked up his plate as if to put something, anything in the charged air between them. "I told you, it's not going to be easy, but it's the only way for us. Can't you think of it as just another mitzvah out of the 613 mitzvahs we are supposed to perform? Are they always easy? Don't we struggle to keep the Shabbes, to pray three times a day, put on teffillin, to do everything we have to do to be a good Chasid? What isn't hard? Answer me that question? What isn't hard about it *all?*"

"Daniel, it's not a question of hard or easy. It's not right. It's a lie. I know it. You know it," he leaned in over the pile of cakes between them, "and my body knows it."

"Ah, here comes the bride." Daniel's tone changed abruptly as he looked over Yakov's head and popped a mini cheese Danish in his mouth. Yakov turned and saw Rachel in the doorway to the parlor. She looked like a girl dressed for the first day of school, her clothes starchy-new and her face sleepy. Only the too-smooth hair of her new wig gave her away as a wife, not a schoolgirl.

"Be a good husband, Yakov. Get your wife a cup of coffee," Daniel said loudly and nodded to Rachel as she approached them.

"I prefer tea, but thanks," she reached for her own cup and unfolded a teabag.

"You see, my friend, it will take time to get to know each other. Who knew she liked tea and not coffee in the morning? Excuse me, I'll leave you newlyweds alone." Daniel turned and walked back toward Gavrielle and the others, still intent on the local news.

Rachel hoped she was successfully hiding her complete embarrassment from Yakov. What had he and Daniel been discussing? What did he mean, "It will take time to get to know each other?" Did he tell Daniel about last night's "non-event"?

"Listen, Rachel, uh…about last night…I'm sorry. I must have had a little too much to drink…"

Rachel looked at him, struggling to keep his coffee cup steady on its saucer. He stared down into the black liquid as if the words he needed were forming there. She felt sorry for him, then protective. *He's just a nervous wreck*, she thought. *It's cute!*

"Don't mention it. I was tired, too." She was more forgiving than Daniel had been, thought Yakov gratefully.

Rachel looked around the room. She wanted to look anywhere but into his apologetic blue eyes, or she might start trembling, too. She looked at the group gathered around the TV and nodded in their direction. "Where did that television come from?"

Yakov shrugged, not wanting to share his suspicions about his uncle.

"It sounds like the mess outside is not over yet."

She pulled the teabag out of her cup of hot water, squeezed it dry against her spoon, and tossed it into the small trashcan under the table.

"You take milk, right?" Yakov poised the creamer over her cup.

"Yes, thanks." He poured just the right amount.

Rachel took a sip of tea and their eyes finally met over the rim of her cup. She survived the moment. It was going to be fine. There were other things to focus on.

Yakov gravitated toward the television and the footage of rock and bottle-throwing mobs facing off across familiar streets. The housekeeper came in and dropped a pile of newspapers on the coffee table at the other end of the room. Rachel was feeling like she could really use a seat at this point, her head aching from the vodka and her legs sore from last night's crouching under the chupah and sprinting for safety. She was anxious to know what had happened to Lark's father overnight, so she headed for the newspapers and the overstuffed, vacant sofa.

Rachel had only met him that one time in the park with Lark, but she knew who he was the minute she saw his face under the explosive block letters on the cover of the *Daily News*: MURDERED WAITING FOR 911. The sofa caught her as she fell back stunned from what she was seeing, reading. She kept her mouth pressed shut so she wouldn't say out loud what she was thinking, what she knew about this young man who was at the center of the day's turmoil. Rachel took her eyes off the words only to check and recheck the accompanying pictures. Was it really *him?* She had to make sure she wasn't mistaken, hadn't confused Lark's Jamal with this tabloid Jamal whose grainy black and white image was distorted with anger and grief.

Could what she was reading be true—that her wedding, the blocked off streets, the police coverage, or lack of it, was the cause of this tragedy? The question gnawed at her as she read on, flipping the pages to find the article that continued toward the back of the paper amongst automobile dealership ads.

It startled her when her father sat down on the sofa next to her. He looked like he hadn't slept all night, his eyes a little too wide and bleary. He took his glasses off and rubbed his face roughly.

"Can you believe this?" He put his glasses back on, picked up the *New York Post* with one hand and smacked the front page with the back of the other one.

"This *schvartze...*"

"Poppa...please."

"Okay, excuse me, Miss United Nations, I'm so sorry. But this woman, this person invites a drug dealer into her apartment, with her young son there," his index finger whirling up to the ceiling for emphasis, "shoots up drugs, ends up getting herself and her son killed, and it's not her fault! No, it's the Jews' fault!" He hit the page again to punctuate his point.

"There was a drug dealer?" Rachel hadn't gotten to that part of the story.

"That's what they think. They know she was doing the drugs right before she was killed and there was drug...uh...tools or paraphernalia or whatever you call it right there next to her."

"But do you think she died because of the wedding? Do you think it's true?" Dovid Fine turned and looked at his daughter, then turned back to all the newspapers covering the coffee table. He picked up the *Daily News* and started flipping through the pages, avoiding her question, looking for answers.

"Did you read the story about Mrs. Mendel? I don't know if you know her. She always came into the store every few weeks for those coffee candies we have—the ones from Austria. She was a little German lady, a Holocaust survivor, had to be at least 75, 80. Every time she bought a pound of the candies and then immediately put one or two in her mouth in the store, like she couldn't wait to have one. She told me she used to have them when she was a girl, before the war. Well, her neighbor found her dead in her apartment this morning with her head in the oven. She left a note saying '*ich habba ganoocht.*'"

Rachel knew it meant "I've had enough" in Yiddish.

"That's terrible."

"Her window looked over Eastern Parkway. She had a good look at what was going on last night and thought, 'Not again'."

"But this isn't like that; it's not like the Holocaust."

"God forbid! But you think the Holocaust started with concentration camps and ovens? No. It starts maybe one night with madmen on the streets who decide it's a good idea to take out their frustrations, to blame their circumstances on the Jew, to smash their storefronts, to hurt a few or kill a few. So what! No Big Deal. A small group acts out what a lot of the people are secretly thinking or not thinking up until they hear it... then suddenly because someone is doing it, someone is saying it's OK to do it, they feel like they have permission to do it, too. Five years later you have the camps. Five years later."

"Daddy, what are you saying? You are scaring me."

"I'm not saying this is going to end up a holocaust! I'm not saying that—even though it doesn't seem to be letting up, it's worse today, what's going on out there—but even so, we can't just lie down and take the blame for things. We can't just be sheep like we were in Europe. Poor Mrs. Mendel."

Rachel had heard her father rant on the subject before. She wanted to get back to her question, the one she couldn't stop wondering. "But do you think that this woman, this mother and her son, could have been saved if it weren't for the wedding?"

Dovid looked at his daughter and felt moved. He wanted to spare her, but knew she was too smart for easy answers. He'd fielded her pointed questions since she was in kindergarten.

"I don't know, Rochella. We'll never know the answer to that. But the wedding isn't even the point. This is just an excuse to explode over things. Things that build up over a long time and eat away at people, things that everyone ignores."

"But why does it have to happen? Why does Hashem let it happen?" She felt like a four-year-old asking the question, but that's what it came down to for her. *Why now, why this, why me?* Rachel wanted to know.

"If I knew the real answer to that question, they could declare me 'Moshiach' and start celebrating. Right?"

Rachel knew it was a joke but he said it wearily, and she didn't laugh. "I could use a coffee, I think," he said, changing the subject.

"I'll get it for you, *Aba*."

"No, I have to get up. My back is better when I stand. Sit, sit, *tattella*."

Rachel's father tossed the newspaper down on top of the others scattered in front of him. He pulled himself up slowly, using the heavy table for leverage, groaning a little from the stiffness in his back or the weight of the subject matter, or both. When he walked over to the buffet table, Rachel thought her father had become an old man overnight, and wondered what other indelible changes would result from her wedding, which things would continue, but never be the same.

CHAPTER THIRTY-FIVE

It was three more days before the streets settled down enough for the members of the wedding party to head back to their homes and their lives. Rachel hoped that she'd be allowed out, too, since she desperately wanted to connect with Lark. She wondered how her friend was handling it all. Lark would need someone to talk to, someone who she could confide in. Rachel was fairly certain that she was the only person who knew that Lark was at the intersection of two lines of tragedy, not just the one drawn by her father's fight for his life, but another, cruelly etched by her feelings for Jamal and his loss. Rachel thought about the way the riots slashed across her own life—her grand wedding plans laid to ruin—the event meant to celebrate her marriage before God forever tainted by the accusations that the festivities were responsible for the death of a mother and child. In the wake of all this, four days on, another event meant to celebrate and consummate her union with Yakov, had still not taken place.

For those four days, Rachel, like everyone, sat glued to the television news that highlighted how the city officials, from the mayor's office to the police commissioner, were fumbling the whole ordeal, unable to agree on what should be done. Police were ordered to the area, but not in the numbers that were needed to quell the violence sooner. Battalions of uniformed

347

and vested cops were told to be there, but stand down. The city's mayor, a black man, took photo opportunities in the neighborhood where the mother and child had died and posed with his arm around the tight-jawed and glazed-over Jamal, as news cameras rolled and a gospel choir sang in the background.

The Rebbe made no public statement as to allegations of responsibility for the deaths, nor did he extend any words of sympathy. He did little to acknowledge the events publicly, but privately met with prominent members of the Chasidic community to debate what should be said or done, if anything, and how these events should be officially interpreted by them and by proxy for the community. These deliberations droned on all day and into the night, interrupted only for sandwiches, coffee, and fervent prayer. Yakov was by the Rebbe's side throughout, sometimes representing him when the old man's need to rest superseded his mandate to preside. Rachel hardly saw Yakov during the day, and at night he did not come up to the apartment where she lay awake waiting for him until she couldn't keep her eyes open. He brushed off his absence explaining that by the time he was finished with the Rebbe, he decided not to disturb her and caught a few hours of sleep his old room downstairs.

When the television coverage became too repetitious, when Rachel felt she couldn't see the same clips again, or the hypothetical, theoretical ponderings of the pundits assembled to fill in for the absence of any real news, she turned to the papers. The inky pages showed pictures that looked like they were from a war zone in some other part of the world: a Chasidic boy crouched, crying by the unconscious body of his father, knocked out by a hurled brick; on a debris-covered street, a row of helmeted police, their dark visors pulled down, reflecting the flames of a dumpster on fire; a narrow, plain casket, buoyed by a procession of black hats and bearded faces, that held the body of an old woman, the Holocaust survivor who would not, could not live through what looked like another *Kristallnacht*; two other caskets, white and polished, laden with flowers, one smaller than the other, raised up and carried to their graves by straining black arms, while an incensed speaker addressed the mourning crowd. The photographer credit for this series was given in a small sidebar feature alongside the photos:

CROWN HEIGHTS — With riots raging just blocks from the hospital where his father lay in critical condition, David Shulman took to the streets with the only weapon he knew how to wield: his camera.

A Columbia University graduate student in Journalism, Shulman said he wanted to "document the pain going on outside the hospital," because he "felt helpless to do anything inside, except wait." His father, Abraham Shulman, the victim of the brutal stabbing that took place during the first hours of the Crown Heights rioting, lay in critical condition in Kingston Hospital's ICU.

Douglas Spencer, Mr. Shulman's Columbia roommate and self-appointed "assistant," who carried camera cases and helped load film, said, "It was like being in a movie about some third world uprising or something...not New York."

Shulman said he hoped to "not only capture a historical catalogue of these events, but a visual catalyst for this community and for the country to address the divides that exist between Americans, divides created by religion, race, and ignorance."

The photos were devastatingly bleak; Rachel couldn't take her eyes off of them. She felt like a snoopy bystander, with the rubbernecking smugness of someone safely tucked inside a car while passing an accident by the side of the road. The photos impressed her with their stark honesty— the horrible beauty of them held nothing back. The images analyzed nothing, just told the story for what it was. The photos made her think she wanted to meet David Shulman someday, meet someone who could see and record life without adding any explanation. Maybe she would meet him, if she could get to Lark.

Rachel wanted to be there for her friend, but she had her own selfish reasons for wanting to see Lark too. Who else could she confide in about what was going on or *not* going on between her and Yakov? The rioting certainly dwarfed any domestic concerns she might be having at this point, but should she be worried? She knew she could count on Lark to think it through with her, to help her blow it off as insignificant, or blow off steam if it wasn't.

So Rachel was disappointed to learn that she would be going to the hospital only as a part of a group, including the Rebbe, Yakov, and others in the Rebbe's inner circle who thought they needed to finally be seen by the press, consoling the family of the victim, to be recorded praying at his bedside, captured at the doors to the hospital expressing their outrage for the fact that the perpetrator of such a heinous crime was not yet in custody.

Rachel chose her outfit carefully, now that she was going to be part of an official visit to the hospital, one of the entourage trailing the Rebbe on his mission. She was slowly smoothing on a second pair of opaque ivory hose, having pulled a huge run in the first, trying too hard to get them on in a hurry over her still-damp legs. Her drawer held at least twenty pair of the same neutral, not-too-sheer hose, just as other drawers had been filled by her mother with multiples of other essentials, all brand-new.

"Mom, this is enough underwear for a small country," she'd said as she helped her mother put things away a few days before the wedding.

"Very funny. Maybe I'll just leave you with one pair you can wash out every night, like some peasant from a shtetl. This is your what-a-ya-call-it? Your 'trousseau'."

"What's that?"

"It's French. Its means your things that you bring with you when you get married. The exact translation is 'enough underwear for a small country.'"

Her mother had taken so much pleasure in preparing for Rachel's marriage. Rachel was going to be the only one of her daughters who would remain near home. The other two had chosen to be *schlichim*, far-flung "missionaries," bringing the Rebbe's brand of *Chasidus* to wherever it was deemed needed—Denmark, Des Moines, Dubrovnik, or anywhere else there were Jews who could be brought back to mitzvahs and faith. It was all very noble, thought Miriam, whose store profits helped to finance a great deal of this outreach, but with Rachel she could be involved in all the details she missed with her other daughters. Miriam enjoyed every minute of it, even as she pretended she "needed more to do like a hole in the head."

Rachel wondered what her mother would say about the small detail of her marriage to Yakov that was still not in place. The closest they'd ever come to discussing sex was when Rachel came back from her first visit to the mikvah, the day before the wedding. Her mother came into Rachel's room to say goodnight, something she didn't ordinarily do.

"So, everything went okay?"

Miriam was dying to know how her daughter's first experience was, but it was immodest to refer to the mikvah directly.

"Oh. Fine. Everything went fine. My nails were short enough. I was fine."

"Good."

"Thanks for your help."

"My pleasure."

"Mom...?"

"What happened?"

"Nothing. Nothing happened. I told you it went fine. I just had a question."

"Oh. A question."

"Can I ask you something, you know, personal?"

"Oh. Personal? Of course." Her mother sat on the edge of the bed and grabbed a pillow to hold on to. She smiled a kind of forced smile that Rachel had seen her put on at the store with complaining customers.

"Go ahead with your question," Miriam chirped.

"Well, I know that after the mikvah, for the next two weeks a husband and wife are free, you know, to...well..."

"Be together. They can be together." Miriam fluffed the pillow vigorously.

"Right! They can 'be together.' I know that, but what I'm wondering is, do they *have to*...you know, be together *every night* during that time?"

"Well..." Her mother's head rocked from side to side as though it was a lever on a scale weighing all the possible answers to such a question posed by a daughter the day before her wedding. Finally finding the answer, she looked Rachel in the eye for the first time in the conversation. "Look, my dear. By the time you go to the mikvah, your husband has been waiting almost two weeks. Such waiting is not easy for a man. So, after the mikvah, you shouldn't be having any "headaches" or excuses. Just be a good girl, you know?"

She stood, smoothing her robe. She looked satisfied to have handled the question well.

"Any other questions?" she asked at the doorway, hoping there weren't.

That night Rachel turned her light off and lay in bed, thinking about the answer her mother had so confidently given her: *Be a good girl. No excuses.* She didn't know what sex would be like but, if she understood what her mother was telling her, then *when* it was going to happen was not really going to be up to *her*...if she was being "good." The laws of family purity dictated her abstinence for two weeks out of the month, and now she was being told in no uncertain terms that her husband's insistent desires would dictate the terms of the other two weeks. The Rebitzen Eisenstatt, with whom she had her family purity "lessons," told her the laws "are really there to protect women from having to do 'it' all the time. "They give us a break, you know...privacy. It's set up to honor the woman." Rachel was new to all of this, but she couldn't help the question that kept nagging at her. All this "protection" and enforced "privacy" was all well and good, but what about when *she* might want "it" or *not* want "it"? Was it about honoring her as a woman, or was it about her being clean or unclean, "out of order" or "open for business"?

Never in a million years would she have thought that less than a week later, just four days into their marriage, she'd be wondering if and when "it" was ever going to happen. The fear she had back on that wakeful night before her wedding, that she would feel as though she had little or no control over this aspect of her married life, was becoming a reality sooner than she had imagined.

CHAPTER THIRTY-SIX

Nothing about the world felt familiar during the first weeks after the riots, those days where Lark's life consisted of going to the hospital to sit with her mother, who sat with her father who lay in a coma, and coming back to the apartment to rest or get something to eat. Except for that one evening, at the tail end of dusk, when it was just dark enough to notice that the street lights were on, and Lark saw the Rain Man sitting on the swing in the nearly empty playground, and felt for a moment, like life had rewound to another less complicated time. Lark crossed the street and entered the park.

She'd thought about Jamal often these past weeks, even after his face stopped showing up on the evening news. After his fifteen minutes of fame, after his role expired as the focal point of the racial conflict Crown Heights had yet to fully resolve, after the neighbors stopped showing up with covered dishes, their faces pouting with pity, he was left alone with his loss. Lark knew how he felt. For a week or so the camera crews kept a vigil at the hospital, trying to get interviews with her and her mother or comments from doctors involved in her father's case. David spoke to them mostly, but they even lost interest in him and his fantastic photos when her father fell into a coma and there was not much further drama to report.

The Yankees were in the playoffs, so New Yorkers turned their attention away from the messy loose ends in Brooklyn. Once the riots had died down, some people from the community came by to visit. There was the Rebbe and his entourage with Rachel in tow (they hadn't had much of a chance to talk that day) and a few of the men from her father's on-and-off-again study group. The shul's women's group sent over three well-meaning representatives who didn't quite know how to react to Sarah's nurse's scrubs and bare head, so they didn't return. David had to get back to the city; his new semester was starting.

Now, it was only Lark and her mother taking shifts, keeping watch. They sat or paced, tracking the movement of the red lines and the flashing of the digital numbers on the tall stack of monitors near her father's bed. They listened to the incessant bleating and buzzing, the signaling for someone who invariably took their time getting there as you panicked. They'd arrive to change the bags of fluid, clear or red or yellow and reset the machines and end the noise for a while. Soon Lark memorized what her mother already knew, what each monitor meant and in what direction the numbers had to go to show progress, to suggest recovery was possible. By watching closely, it felt as if they could somehow influence those numbers, intimidate those beeping boxes into complying with their hopes.

In the fading light that late afternoon, the Rain Man looked small to her. Shrunken. Maybe he'd lost weight or was dwarfed by the oversized hooded sweatshirt he wore—she couldn't put her finger on it. Maybe he had just seemed larger than life on TV, with the camera always in his face. Jamal saw her approaching but didn't wave or stand up to greet her, he just sat there on the swing, waiting, rocking on his heels. Lark took the swing next to him and without a word started pumping and moving through the cool evening air, back and forth. He watched her for a moment then pushed himself off from the pavement and began pumping his swing, too, until they both cut through the air in a synchronized swoop and bend, swoop and bend. There was no joy in it. They didn't laugh with exhilaration. They looked ahead and fought with tight arms and heaving backs to throw the swings and their bodies higher and higher. Then, after a few minutes of this, Lark slipped her arms through, letting herself fly forward through the air as the swing flew backward. She hit the pavement hard on her feet but used the momentum to keep running toward the park's exit.

"C'mon," she yelled backward at him and saw him take his own flying leap off the buckling swing. He ran after her. Lark let them both in her building then headed for the stairs instead of the elevator—Shabbes was about to begin, if it hadn't already. She didn't care at this point what the neighbors thought—it seemed like her family was more on the fringes of the community than ever—but there was no point in drawing more attention to herself than necessary. *The last thing my mother needs right now is some nosy yenta telling her they saw her daughter riding the elevator up to the apartment with her black boyfriend on Shabbes.*

Lark wasn't sure that her mother would even care at this point—at least not about the Shabbes part of the equation. Something about what had happened to her father made her mother throw off the most basic conventions of orthodox life practically overnight. Lark was still wearing the skirts and modest blouses, but that was more a function of not having anything else to wear than a desire to keep it all up. Maybe, thought Lark, her mom had been doing the religious bit only because her father wanted it that way, was convinced it was how they should live, and now that he was no longer in control, there was no reason to keep pretending. Or maybe Sarah felt like all the rituals and the prayers and the sacrifices had bought her nothing, as far God was concerned. They hadn't protected her from tragedy or loss, so what was the point? One of the women from the shul who visited them in the ICU had told Sarah it was a test, a test of her faith.

Sarah told Lark after the women left, "Well, I guess I'm flunking the goddamn test. Or maybe it's God that's flunking out. Maybe I was testing

Him, lighting all those candles week after week, for years, waiting for life to get better. Maybe he's the one that's failed me."

It was the kind of thing Lark herself could have said, but it surprised her, coming from her mother. She'd wished for this kind of rebellion for years now, but when it came, so immediately and fully as it did, Lark felt a little disoriented. It wasn't like her mother went back to being her *old* self. The Sarah that was emerging from underneath the bad wig and long skirts was someone Lark did not quite know. The alchemy of disappointment and loss had distilled another more concentrated and bitter Sarah.

Jamal kept a good distance behind her as they climbed the stairs and walked the hallway to her apartment. If anyone peeked out and saw them, it couldn't be said they were together. Once she unlocked the apartment and stepped into the foyer, he was there, suddenly on her, wrapping his arms around her, lifting her off the ground, pressing her against the slamming door, burying his face in her hair, kissing her, almost choking her with the force of his tongue in her mouth.

"Wait!" Lark could barely breathe. She wanted a minute to think before her body took over the decision-making.

"Wait for what? I been waiting, Bird. Please." Jamal's face was fighting against the force of emotion rising there, his lips now clamped against it. He crossed his arms and grabbed at the hem of his sweatshirt, pulling it over his head, the T-shirt underneath coming off with it. His body had always been lean, but what Lark saw now was a shredded version of it. His hipbones jutted out. The torso rising above them was a network of tensely drawn opposing lines, etched by the sinew and muscle just beneath his paper-thin brown skin. A tattoo that wasn't there the last time she was with him, now took up all the space over his breastbone, reaching up almost to his collarbone. It was a bloated and beating red heart torn in two, blood dripping from the tear onto the date inscribed below it: August 19, 1991. In one side of the heart the word "Mama," in the other the initials "DW."

"Oh, baby," Lark said, even though she'd never called him that before. She came back toward him and placed her open hand over the tattoo as if that was the exact location of his emotional wound and her touch could somehow heal it. And maybe it could, because as she held her hand there and wrapped her other arm around his waist he let out the most mournful sound she'd ever heard, an unearthly moan that dissolved into the sobs he'd been holding in check for weeks.

Lark led him down the dusty hall to her bedroom. She pulled the crumpled covers off the bed and made him lie down. She quickly undressed, tossing her clothes on the floor with the other piles that had accumulated there, then opened his jeans and pulled them off, throwing his sneakers to the floor with them. She lay down on top of him and pressed herself against him, her breasts over that terrible tattoo, her hips hard against his jutting bones, holding his head in her hands, kissing his salty face. His racking breaths dissolved into a shallow, quick rhythm as he met her kisses, signaling that he was leaving his sorrow for now, was being called away by the force of the pleasure she was offering him instead.

They made love just as they had pumped the swings, pulling and pushing each other, with more violence than joy, tightly drawing themselves to and fro, arms taut. Lark felt her own anger and sorrow rising in her chest as they raced toward the explosive release they both needed. When it happened she too cried, finally. She shed the tears for her father she didn't know she had anymore. She cried, realizing that she'd loved him once, so much, and that they'd been lost to each other much longer than these past few weeks.

And Lark cried too for Jamal, because she knew even as she lay there with him, vibrating from the intensity of it all, that he was not part of the future she was planning—especially these past weeks being around David again. She'd spent time with Dog, too, who'd stuck around for days, keeping David company on his photographic forays into the heart of the riots. Camped out in the windowless ICU waiting room, not sure of the time of day, they had rambling conversations about what her future might be, knowing somehow that it would help her get her mind off of the present. Student, actress, model, waitress—anything beyond yeshiva girl excited and distracted her. The conversations made Lark realize she didn't know what she wanted to be when she grew up. Life was suddenly unfolding now as a multiple-choice question: the answer could be A, B, C, or all of the above. Dog talked about his own future: law school, public defending for a while for the experience, then joining the international law firm that generations of men in his family had built as a fortress of fortune. He'd been raised knowing that good things would happen to him and for him, and Lark liked how he spoke of her future with that same confidence: *You'll figure it out. It'll be fine. We'll help you.*

Even if it was a borrowed bravado, it still made her feel that now there was a chance she could live out some of her dreams. And she spent some time in the stairwell near the hospital cafeteria trading kisses with Dog, too. They were supposed to be on a coffee and bagel run for her mom and a few of the relatives who heard it on the news and drove all the way from New Jersey to visit. With her father in a medically complicated limbo, her future and the future of her family was on hold. But one thing was certain: things would never be as they were just a month ago. That life was over. Lark knew this, but she also knew that Jamal might be thinking of her as all he had left, clinging to her as the one thing that hadn't changed. He was wrong.

Jamal held her while she spilled her tears on his chest. She ran her fingers along the outline of the heart tattoo, so new, its edges were still swollen.

"I'm so sorry about your mom and your brother," she said quietly. "It's unbelievable..."

She felt him stiffen. "I don't want to talk about it."

"I'm sorry."

"I'm talked out, you know?"

"Yeah, I know what you mean."

"It's all I think about...how I wasn't there, how I could have stopped it from happening, how I'm going to kill the motherfucker who did it as soon as I figure out who it was."

The truth was that Jamal didn't trust himself to talk about it with Lark. He was too afraid he'd reveal something about what went on that night, how he was not only a witness to what happened to her father, but a perpetrator. He would have loved to let her know that he stopped the beating, that he came to his senses, that he tried to help her father after all, but he couldn't risk her knowing he or his cousin were involved.

"Okay. Okay, let's not talk about anything...shhhh." Lark smoothed Jamal's brow until it unfolded, releasing the thoughts that seemed to congregate directly behind it.

They lay there quietly until Jamal's gently jerking hand let her know he had fallen into a merciful sleep. She pulled herself gently from underneath the arm and the leg he'd thrown over her to draw her close, and got up to open a window. She was hot and tired and too agitated to sleep. Lark stood in the window and let the cool air wash over her damp body. There were no lights on in the now dark room, so she could not be seen from the largely Shabbes-empty streets, and the rare Brooklyn breeze felt too good to move away from anyway.

The playground across from the window, where it had all begun between her and the Rain Man, was in darkness too, a few circles of light from streetlamps around its edges. In that darkened playground she'd found so much freedom over the past year. Jamal had opened up new worlds for her, but he couldn't take her any farther on the road she wanted to travel. If anything, his being in her apartment, lying there sleeping on her bed, his having left the playground and entered her "real" life felt wrong somehow, oppressive, thwarting. After a few minutes she felt chilled. She wanted a shower and took a long one, washing her hair, shaving her legs, leaving the conditioner on for the full recommended 10 minutes, using the shriveled loaf of a loofah someone had given her mother a few birthdays ago, to rub her skin red and squeaky clean. Lark thought, *how can you want him so badly in one moment then want to wash him away so badly in the next?* She felt in turns disloyal and smart, betraying the unsuspecting Jamal with her thoughts and yet honoring her own truth.

Coming out of the steamy bathroom, wearing her mother's old terry-cloth robe, she saw a light in the kitchen and found Jamal sitting at the table, his jeans and t-shirt thrown on, the tattoo and his emotions duly re-covered. The coffee maker was hissing and popping, the smell of the fresh brew effectively masking the stale, days-old garbage smell.

"Hi."

"Hello. No trouble finding the coffee then?"

"No. I hope you don't mind."

"No. I could use some coffee. I have to go back to the hospital, soon—give my mother a break."

"How is your old man doing?"

"Out of it, basically. He was out of it by the time they brought him in. They didn't think he was going to make it since he lost so much blood, but he hung on."

Lark moved around the kitchen, getting out the milk for coffee, a loaf of bread, the peanut butter and some jelly, and started making sandwiches. She cut off the crusts and made neat triangles out of the soft white bread, something she would have never done around her father, who would have complained it was wasteful. Maybe Jamal thought it was, too, since he grabbed the narrow castoffs as she cut them and popped them in his mouth.

Lark continued the report of her father's condition, sounding as though she'd recited it many times already. "Then he had a lot of internal bleeding, and fluid in his lungs. He ended up having a respiratory arrest; his lungs couldn't handle it, and then a heart attack because of that and then he just went into the coma." Lark piled the triangles on a paper plate and brought them to the table. Jamal pulled two coffee mugs out of the pile of dirty dishes in the sink and rinsed them out. He poured them coffee.

"It's so weird, because they cut off most of his beard when they put in the breathing hole in his neck and then my mother went ahead and shaved the rest of it off. It was kind of a shock. I hadn't seen his whole naked face in like four years. He looks so much younger without it. He looks like my old dad, you know? It's so strange because I really hated the guy with the beard, but this guy, the guy without the beard...that's my daddy lying there. You know what I mean?"

"But shaving off a beard doesn't mean he's changed, Bird. He didn't shave off his beard and say 'fuck it all, I'm going back to normal.'" Jamal remembered the savage rantings of the man as he lay in the gutter, beaten. "They shaved him when he was unconscious."

"I know. I'm just saying...it's weird for me. And you never know. Maybe when he does wake up, maybe the whole experience will change him, you know. It's already changed my mom. It's changed me."

"Oh, yeah? How has it changed you?"

"I don't know, exactly. Stuff like this just changes you. You, of all people, should understand that. Tell me you don't feel like all this has changed you."

He put two heaping teaspoons of sugar in his coffee and stirred it noisily. "Yeah, I'm changed. I used to give a fuck. Now I don't. I guess that's a big fucking change."

Lark decided not to challenge his pessimism. She wasn't so sure she had anything encouraging to say.

"So..." Jamal changed the subject back to her Dad, away from his feelings. "...he hasn't been awake since he got to the hospital? He's never been able to talk to the police or anything?" Jamal let his eyes wander around the room as he asked the question, as if the answer was of no real consequence to him.

"No. Why?"

"Just wondering if they knew who did it."

"Some people came forward as witnesses, but mainly they said it was a group, you know, a mob of kids, not enough specifics to make a case. Never found a weapon, nothing. The police are on to the next thing anyway. I don't know if they'll ever figure it out. Have you heard anything about it, I mean, who might have done it?"

"No! No, I didn't hear anything! There was a lot of shit going on that night for me, remember."

"Of course, I didn't mean..."

"Including your friend's wedding."

"What are you saying?"

"Nothing. I'm just saying some people had a wedding. Some people died."

"Oh, I see. So you believe the bullshit that the wedding is the reason..."

"I guess we'll never know if it's bullshit, will we?"

"I guess *you'll* never know. I know what I know."

"What the fuck does that mean?" He slammed down his coffee mug, sending a burst of the black liquid up and onto the table.

Lark new she didn't want to get into this argument with him. She was supposed to be consoling him, and making herself feel less guilty about her plans for the future, Dog, everything. The look on Jamal's face was scaring her, too.

"Nothing!" Lark backpedaled fast. "Look, all I meant was I know that horrible things happened that night—to your family and to my family—and that blaming the wedding or the Jews or yourself doesn't change anything or make it better. No matter what, nobody deserved what happened. Not your mother and brother and not my father. Nobody deserved this nightmare, not even my friend Rachel, who was just trying to get married. That's all I'm saying."

Jamal just looked at her, his jaw set against any answer he may have wanted to give. Lark watched him muscle up the restraint he needed to keep from alienating her. It made her feel bad all over again, seeing how hard he was trying, how much he needed to stay connected to her, despite her hokey whitewashing of the subject. She grabbed a paper towel and wiped up the spill, topping off their cups with more from the pot. Then they sat without speaking for a long time, washing down the sticky peanut butter with fresh, hot coffee.

CHAPTER THIRTY-SEVEN

D aniel fingered the business card in his pocket. He took the soiled and much-folded rectangle out again and reread the faded type and handwritten note in Barry's hurried scrawl. *Call me when you need to talk to someone sane.* Daniel noticed that the "out" ex-Chasid, he'd first met in Jerusalem, hadn't written "*if* you need someone to talk to," he wrote *when*, as a kind of premonition of Daniel's future need to unburden himself. Though that time had come, he couldn't bring himself to make the call. It wasn't that he feared Barry's cynical "I knew you'd call," as much as he hesitated letting Barry and what he represented deeper into his life. On some level he understood the kind of advice Barry might give him and he didn't know if he was prepared to follow the path Barry walked: complete openness about sexuality and severed ties with his community.

But Daniel could hardly reveal his dilemma to anyone in the community whose advice most people seek. Their advice would be too extreme in the opposite direction for him to consider. Still, he had to talk to someone, and his options right now were Barry or no one.

Daniel's plan for "having it all" was unraveling into an unmanageable and unsatisfying mess less than two months after Yakov's wedding. Barry had laughed at Daniel during their lunch together months before, for his enthusiastic "twice-blessed" theory of how his life would turn out.

"Oh, that's a good one. I hope it all works out for you, dearie, but I doubt it. Too many things could go wrong, or drive you crazy. You'll end up like one of those guys trolling around in limos picking up little Dominican boys."

"What are you talking about? What limos?"

"You don't know about the limos? The Chasids out for their weekly blowjobs and God knows what else in the backseat. I'll take you there sometime. You'll see them."

Daniel was stunned by the existence of the "limo" men, but certain that he had nothing in common with such monsters of perversity. He had a relationship with Yakov: they deeply loved each other and they deeply loved God. There had to be a certain morality in that, he insisted. He wrote off Barry's comments as cynicism or jealousy. After all, Daniel was going to preserve for himself everything that Barry had lost by coming "out"; and even though nothing sexual had happened between them, Barry flirted with Daniel in a way that telegraphed a green light for more than friendship if Daniel wanted it.

New York was having an unseasonal streak of Indian summer, so Daniel began taking a lunch over to the park behind the big library on 5th Avenue—the library where Barry worked. He was hoping to run into the one person who might be able to give him perspective, albeit a biased one.

On the fourth day of lunch behind the library, Daniel tossed his half-eaten sandwich in the trash, disgusted. He'd lost 20 pounds since Yakov's wedding—his hearty appetite replaced by a gnawing, nervous gut. He was still a towering man, but had a decidedly less boyish look now with his hollowed-out cheeks and flat belly. His clothes hung on him, making him look even thinner.

As he was about to leave the park, Daniel saw Barry standing on line at a cafe kiosk near the entrance. *Well, here we go,* thought Daniel, his wildly beating heart acting like he was about to ride a roller coaster instead of greet a friend.

"Daniel! You look great. That's a wonderful color on you, all that black and white! You should wear it more often!"

"Very funny. Such a comedian for a librarian." Daniel took his suit coat off and folded it over his arm. "It's warm for this time of year, but you look like the heat isn't bothering you." Barry had knee-length shorts on, sandals, and a bright yellow T-shirt advertising the merits of a Mexican beer.

"Hey, let me buy you a mocha-licious frozen thing-a-majig. It's almost better than sex." Daniel hesitated. "Oh, please, don't tell me you are worried about whether the milk is kosher. Honey, kosher milk is the least of your worries."

Barry seemed genuinely glad to see him, which made Daniel feel less self-conscious. They got their drinks and found a bench to sit on toward the center of the park. Daniel noticed some small but significant changes in Barry—the absence of a yarmulke, as well as the dangling strings of tzitses.

Barry read his mind. "You are looking at my naked head, no doubt wondering where my *kipah* is. It's obvious a fedora wouldn't exactly go with my current outfit, would it? No, and no strings attached either, figuratively and literally. What can I say? My descent into Hell is now complete."

"Jews don't believe in Hell."

"Oh, right. I guess I have my fundamentalists mixed up! Excuse me."

Daniel countered, "Who am I to judge?" Daniel meant it. If anything, he was fascinated by and attracted to Barry's transformation in the months since he first met him. He saw him get lighter and lighter, in his clothing and in his outlook, as he threw off one obligation of ultraorthodox observance after another. While Daniel felt more than a little afraid of Barry's blatant blasphemy, he was also envious of how his transformation seemed to translate into more and more freedom for the man.

"So, enough about me, what's new with you, you big teddy bear? I'm glad to see you survived the riots intact."

Barry held a chocolate croissant daintily between the fingers on one hand, while unraveling a flaky section of it and stuffing it in his mouth with the other. "So, what's new?"

"Well, my wife is expecting. Almost six months now." Daniel offered this as small talk, and then regretted it. He knew how Barry felt about his trying to live a double life, and braced himself for a lecture.

"Well, Mazel Tov...I guess." Barry gave him "a look" over the top of his little oval eyeglasses that felt like a slap on the wrist and said more than an entire lecture on the subject could have.

"And did your boyfriend get married?" Barry asked, still looking over the rim of his glasses.

"Yes. I was at his wedding when the riots broke out." Daniel knew by admitting this that Barry would instantly realize Yakov's identity. The wedding and its relationship to the riots had been all over the news. Daniel knew it was a risky thing to do, but for that moment he didn't care. He wanted to have one person in the wide world know his story, the whole story.

"No way! *The* wedding the night of the riots? The Rebbe's grandson is your boyfriend? This is incredible. No, it's absolutely perfect."

"It's not perfect. There is nothing perfect about it."

"I mean it's perfect in an ironic, iconic sort of way. Talk about 'a God thing'! If the Rebbe's own grandson turns out to be gay, then they won't be able to say it's someone's *black sheep* child, or some misfit they can say Kaddish over and pretend never existed, going on with their twelve other kids like nothing happened. No, this time it will be Yakov, the Golden Child, raised perfectly in the ultimate *haimish* home, and still gay! *I love it!*"

"You can't tell anyone about this, Barry. I am serious. This is strictly confidential...like the support group, remember? Anyway, you think we're just going to go up to the bima on Shabbes and announce to whole shul that Yakov is, *you-know-what*...and then they are going to welcome us as some opportunity to face the issue with an open mind?"

Barry chuckled, his mouth full of the last hunk of his croissant. "Good point. Don't get your tzitses in a tizzy, honey, your secret is safe with me. True, I was being delusional for a moment, running my little 'perfect world' scenario."

Barry wiped the corners of his mouth with a napkin, erasing the traces of chocolate there. He patted Daniel's hand. "Look, you can trust me. Let's pretend you never told me his identity. So, you were saying..."

Daniel didn't know if he could trust Barry, but risk seemed to be a staple of his life at this point and he was willing to take on more of it in exchange for the chance to talk it out right now.

"Well. It's difficult." Daniel churned his straw up and down into the domed cover of his sweating drink, chopping the soft pyramid of whipped cream down into the layer of icy coffee below it. He took a long sip of his drink, and a deep breath. "Yakov, he's crazy since the wedding. He can't seem to, you know, 'be together' with his wife. He says he can't because he doesn't have any sexual feelings for her, that he respects her and genuinely likes her and it wouldn't be fair to her. I don't know what is going on in her head by now! It's been over two months and they still haven't—you know—and on top of that, he's calling me constantly, crazy to get together and then when we get together, he's crazy, too."

"What do you mean, crazy? Don't tell me, I think I understand. He is all hot and bothered to be with you but when he gets there he won't do anything."

"He starts out okay, but then he stops himself from having any pleasure or if he does, it only lasts a minute before he is miserable again."

"*Oy Vey*. You know what? I feel sorry for him. I used to get spooked by just seeing the Rebbe's portraits everywhere you turned, in the classrooms, the shul, my parents dining room, everywhere, just staring at you! Can you imagine living with him day in and day out? Living up to his standard? No wonder the poor schmuck is so tortured."

Daniel felt like weeping when he heard Barry's take on Yakov's dilemma. He thought of how impatient he had been with his friend lately.

"I guess I'm being an idiot. I'm only thinking of myself."

"What? Daniel, you misunderstand me. I feel sorry for Yakov, but you don't need to be a sacrificial lamb here, honey. You don't need to start thinking about your needs less, at this point. You have to start thinking, I mean really thinking, about this in terms of *what you want*, and need. Not what *they* all want from you."

"What about Gavrielle? What about Yakov? I care about these people. I'm just supposed to say, never mind about you? I'm more important, what I want is more important?"

"Why not?"

"That would be selfish."

"Oh, really? And the way you are handling things now, is that so good for everyone involved? Is it so altruistic?"

"Well..."

"Come on Daniel. Think. Your boyfriend is on the right track actually; that's what's driving him crazy. He, at least, understands that what you are attempting to do is not only insane and will never work, it is selfish and hurting everyone involved."

Daniel felt his jaw clenching as he bit down on his straw. This conversation was not going the way he wanted it to. "Well, no one gets *everything* they want! I don't. I'm making compromises, sacrifices to give Gavrielle, most of what she wants. It's Yakov who is being selfish. He is holding back with Rachel and with me. What's so noble about that, what is so fucking noble about it, you tell me! I'm the one who is being unselfish. Making sacrifices, *that's love.*"

"It's so incredibly sad, but you really believe what you just said, don't you? Look, my friend," Barry continued, "let's face facts, all this talk about the welfare of others is just that: talk. You aren't doing your wife a favor right now. You married her, got her pregnant, all the time planning how you were going to get together with your male lover on the side. What's so nice about that? So either take care of your needs, I mean really figure out what you want and build your life around that or don't, but this halfway crap is hurting these people you care about more than helping them and it's getting to be hell for you, so who's winning here?"

Daniel slipped farther and farther down on the bench as Barry spoke, his back bowing with the weight of it all, his head becoming heavy. His clothes were nearly soaked through, despite the cool drink. He felt tired, even while the shots of espresso in it set his nerves on edge. The argument he'd been having with Yakov over the past two months, the one he attempted to have with Barry about having it all, was draining out of him. Daniel couldn't, for the life of him, think what could possibly replace it and fit. He cradled his hot head in his hands and stared at his feet.

"Are you okay?" Barry crouched down next to him, placing a hand on Daniel's shoulder.

Daniel looked up at Barry and saw real compassion in his eyes. They were green, outlined by light eyelashes. He noticed light freckles on his face for the first time.

"So, now what?" Barry cocked his head at Daniel, not sure what he was asking. Daniel continued, talking at the ground. "If I listen to you, if I believe that it's all wrong and everyone involved is getting hurt, then what's next?

"What do you want to be next, Daniel?"

"I don't know. I can't picture any situation that would make me completely happy."

"Well, that's because your frame of reference is way too narrow. You have only imagined two scenarios—*all* or *nothing*—and you've only tried to live out one of them. What if your "all" could be different? What if your 'all' had more to do with what you want, what you were born to want, not what everyone thinks you should have?"

"Go on." Daniel lifted his head.

"What if you could have a boyfriend that didn't have Yakov's hang-ups, or larger-than-life grandpa, no tragic, betrayed wife? What if you could someday have a relationship with a man and with God that didn't involve hating yourself, punishing yourself, or waiting to be punished?" Barry tightened his grip on Daniel's shoulder to physically emphasize his offer, to show him a scenario that could offer him options for happiness. He made it clear to Daniel that whatever was going on with Yakov, he, Barry, was more than happy to light up his Shabbes candle anytime.

Daniel felt Barry's strong fingers digging into him and the definite stirring of desire. For over two months his meetings with Yakov had mostly ended in frustration. He'd avoided, for the most part, being with Gavrielle during her pregnancy and, though he managed to perform with her, it was hardly what he needed. Barry's touch was reminding him how lonely he was, how hungry. Suddenly nothing seemed more important than satisfying that appetite. Daniel looked at his watch.

"What are you doing right now?" Daniel asked Barry, meeting his eyes for a moment.

Barry tried to keep a grin from taking over his entire face.

"Whatever you want, Teddy Bear. Whatever you want."

The two men left the park and walked west toward Barry's apartment at a hurried pace, stopping only to use pay phones and make their excuses for not returning to work for the rest of the afternoon.

CHAPTER THIRTY-EIGHT

Cursing the hospital lasagna she'd eaten the night before while on her shift with her father, Lark clutched her stomach and wretched the remnants of it into the toilet.

With her bare knees dug into the small white hexagons of ancient tile on the bathroom floor, she could see the dust balls and errant hairs accumulated in the corners and crannies of the cramped space. The odor from the toilet, which hadn't been really cleaned well in months, wafted up toward her and made her retch again. The wastebasket tucked in the corner in front of her overflowed with used tissues, cotton balls, and tampon wrappers. Lark was used to the fact that her mother was no great housekeeper, but the state of the apartment after these months of hospital vigils was out of control. Lark, feeling superior, thought that when she had her period she took great care to bury any traces of her "feminine hygiene" products at the bottom of the trash, or to tie them up in grocery store bags and take them out to the incinerator immediately. The idea of her father seeing them, or everyone in the house knowing she had her period, made her feel too weird. Apparently her mother had no such qualms. Ripping off a good length of toilet paper to wipe her mouth, she stopped dead mid-wipe as a startling question crossed her mind. *When is the last time I had my period?*

Lark scrambled to her feet, her stomach still cramping. She flushed the toilet, gargled a swig of mouthwash, then headed to her bed where, instead of lying down to relieve the cramping, she lifted the mattress and pulled out the journal she'd erratically kept over the last year, but more regularly in the last few months since the riots. Sitting on the floor near the bed she frantically leafed backward over the entries and scanned her messy cursive for any clues about where she was in her cycle. Finally, she found what she remembered writing. *Ate four packets of those neon-orange peanut butter crackers from the vending machine at the hospital and two bags of M&Ms. Cried over this animal shelter thing I watched on Oprah in my father's room. Either I am getting my period or am finally losing my mind for good.* The date was September 1. Then the entry for September 2 began, *I knew it. Well, at least I know I'm not crazy. Yet. Asked the nurse on duty for some tampons. They had none — had to use industrial size pads they gave me until I got home. Gross.*

With one day blurring into the other, Lark wasn't sure of the date. She ran to the calendar that hung on a nail inside the door of the kitchen broom closet to check the date and do the math. The colorful Jewish calendar put out by the shul informed her it was the ninth day of Adar, the year 5768 or October 28. She should have had her period about three and a half weeks ago, toward the beginning of the month. Lark went back to the journal she left on the floor of her room to check the entries for the rest of September and for the first weeks of October.

She read through the pages from mid-month, describing the meeting with Jamal in the apartment, then those that followed a few days later about her conflicting feelings for him, her growing feelings for Dog—he called her regularly now and came out with David to see her on the weekends. There were pages filled with her anger and frustration about the situation with her father. *How long is this going to go on? I hate the endless waiting. Sometimes I wish it would just end already...I want him to wake up and be normal, really normal. I think of him opening his eyes and saying, 'What are we doing in Crown Heights?' and wanting to go back to our old life. I don't want him to die, but I know that if he wakes up and wants to go on living here...he'll treat me like I'm dead for wanting to go.* Seeing her ambivalence on paper made her wince, but what worried her more was that nowhere in that week's entries was there any reference to her getting her period. Not there, or anywhere in the rest of the month's entries either.

It could still be food poisoning, she rationalized. She'd heard that people under stress sometimes stopped having their periods, but also knew that women in the same household often had synchronized cycles. From the looks of the overflowing wastebasket in the bathroom, her mother, who was pretty stressed, was nonetheless having her period right now, and Lark clearly wasn't. Add the fact she was puking her brains out this morning to the fact that she hadn't felt that great (come to think of it) for more than a week or so, and the obvious conclusion was enough to send her back to hugging the bowl.

"I'm an idiot!" Lark shouted to the empty apartment, and wrote the same phrase in big bold letters on a blank page in the journal, before shoving it back between the mattress and box spring. Jamal had used condoms in the past when they'd been together, making jokes about "little rain man needs a rain coat, too" that embarrassed her but made her giggle and turn away while he took care of business. This last time, when he'd come to the apartment, he had other things on his mind beside silly penis jokes or birth control. Lark, swept up in the emotion of their meeting, just hadn't thought about it. She lay on the floor near her bed and allowed self-pity to take over—O*kay, so my father dying in the hospital is not enough, I have to be pregnant, too?* —which was replaced by fear—*what the hell am I going to do?*—which gradually gave way to denial—*maybe I'm not pregnant! Go get a test and prove it.*

She grabbed a twenty-dollar bill from her mother's stash in her underwear drawer and walked to the drug store over by the hospital where no one would recognize her, or be shocked that she was buying a pregnancy test kit.

She knew every ladies' room in the hospital by now, which were cleaner, less populated, had more toilet paper, smelled better—she'd even found one with a shower, meant for resident doctors, that she'd used more than once during her shifts there to help her freshen up and stay awake. She went to that one now and locked the door behind her.

Lark ripped open the narrow box containing the little pink kit. *This is it? This little plastic toy thermometer thingy is going give me the most important news of my life so far?* She read and reread the directions. *Just pee on the thing and that's it? Just pee on it and wait for the little circle to turn blue?* She didn't believe it could be so simple, but did it anyway, urinating all over her fingers in the process. She placed the kit on the edge of the sink, checked her watch. Three minutes. She washed her hands. Twice. She checked her teeth in the mirror then glanced at the kit, panicking. Was it turning blue? Was that a blue tint she was seeing? She checked her watch again. Only a minute had gone by in what felt like ten. She sat on the toilet and covered her eyes with her damp hands. She counted to a hundred and twenty, using Mississippi's: "one-Mississippi, two-Mississippi," like a calming mantra.

When she finished counting she added another 20 for good measure and to postpone looking. When she did, the powder blue circle was there, plain as day against a white background, announcing her big stupid mistake.

Shit. Now what?

She thought about leaving the bathroom, going down to the ICU and telling her mother. It would be a relief to finally confide in her about Jamal, about everything. Three months ago she could have never imagined telling her, but things had changed. The tragedy, the vigils, the shared grief, the us-against-the-world quality of their lives at this time had brought them closer than they'd been in years. Her mother would understand. She would tell her what to do next.

Outside the ICU, Lark picked up the phone and dialed the extension for the nurses' station to ask permission to enter. Sometimes the staff would be busy with a patient and didn't want visitors at that moment. She recognized the voice of a Jamaican nurse who was there most mornings.

"Mary, it's Lark Shulman to see my dad, David Shulman."

"Oh, hello, Miss Lark. You wait out there, your mother coming out."

Sarah came through the ICU double doors a few minutes later, looking beat up. Her face was swollen, eyes rubbed red, her growing hair damp and flattened against one side of her head, dry and sticking out on the other. She greeted her daughter with a lingering squeeze and a cracking voice. "Let's go to the waiting room and get some coffee." Lark normally loved coffee but the thought of it now sent a cold wave of nausea through her.

"Mom, what's wrong?"

"It was not a good night."

The waiting room was strewn with newspapers, take-out containers, and piles of bedding left by other ICU families who routinely spend the nights and days there, commiserating with their extended families and hanging on every development of their loved ones on the brink. There was a Hispanic family whose eighteen-year-old honor student son was hit in the head with a stray bullet during a drive-by shooting meant for a gang-member neighbor; congregants of a church who led gospel sessions in the windowless room for their reverend, in a coma six weeks from complications that arose during a gastric bypass operation; two daughters who took shifts watching their 86-year-old mother slowly die because her aging body couldn't bounce back from injuries sustained in a car accident. Every scenario was unbearable, but made just a little easier by the exchange of knowing, compassionate looks between the families as they kept their vigils.

This morning the room was empty. Lark's mother poured herself a coffee, swirled some powdered creamer in it and offered to make one for Lark.

"Mom, forget the coffee. What is going on? Is Daddy okay?"

"Well, he's not okay. He hasn't been okay since he got here."

"Are you going to tell me what is going on?"

Sarah tasted the hours-old coffee and grimaced. She tossed the full cup in the trash, but kept the plastic stirrer to chew on. "He had another heart attack."

"What? What is going on? He never had any heart problems."

"Well, he's stable for now. There's so much fluid around his lungs and chest cavity from the internal injuries, and the longer he lies here the more fluid builds up. Anyway, all the fluid, it's making his lungs work very hard and, in turn, his heart is getting overtaxed, worn-out. Yes, he didn't have a heart problem *yet*, but he stopped any kind of exercise in the past few years, and he smoked like a chimney. The doctor doesn't know how much damage there is, but he can't be sure until later today. Then, if that isn't enough, they were giving him blood thinners to prevent clots, which are a real threat for someone so immobilized, but the thinners were making the internal bleeding worse, so they cut back on them, and now they found a clot in his groin. They want to do a procedure to go in and remove that before it moves to his lungs and kills him."

"Oh, my God. When are they going to do that?"

"They are waiting for me to sign the release on it. But they probably won't do it until they are sure his heart will be stable. I don't know…"

"You don't know what?"

"I don't know, I just mean that it's so hard to watch them poking and prodding him all day, every day—all the needles and tubes and bruises up and down his arms from the veins collapsing and them having to find new ones. They've got suction in one end of his lungs and the drain tubes out the other end, and none of it seems to be helping. He's deteriorating, not improving. Maybe they should just leave him alone, now. Just leave him alone." Tears rolled down her tired face and she did nothing to stop them.

"Mom, they can't just leave him alone. They are doing everything to try and keep him alive, right?"

"I guess so. I guess they are. But it just seems so barbaric in a way. Not at the beginning. At the beginning you think, 'this is going to save him' and you're all gung ho. But now, it just feels like he's some kind of guinea pig. Poke him here, and let's see what happens, then we'll react to that, and then see what happens and then we'll react to that...and it's like *he's* not there anymore. There's no, I don't know...dignity in it. I don't know if this is what he would have wanted."

"Mom, you need to go home and get some sleep. You are talking crazy. Daddy would want you to do everything, try everything to save his life. He'd never want you to give up on him. And you never have. Maybe you should have given up on him back when he had the idea to move to Crown Heights, but not now. Now is not the time to give up."

Lark watched her mother's face relax at the small joke. She was glad to be able to bolster her spirits but felt a little cheated. She knew she couldn't tell her mother anything right now that would add to her stress level. Lark wanted to be the child seeking her mother's comfort and guidance, but ended up having to be the adult after all. In fact, thought Lark, today was turning out to be one loud announcement that her childhood was pretty much over. A little blue circle on a plastic stick told her so.

CHAPTER THIRTY-NINE

L ark hadn't expected to find Jamal home when she walked down the alley she'd seen countless times on the news, crisscrossed with crime-scene tape, a raging mob, and police cruisers crowded around its entrance.

She had already put off coming here for two days, afraid of what his reaction might be, a little afraid of being alone with him in the apartment. They hadn't seen much of each other over the past couple of months, but what she'd seen made her worried that he was hardly functioning, let alone doing any planning of his future. What if he went berserk on her? Or worse, what if he turned on the charm and drew her in again, confused her about what she needed to do? Part of her hoped she wouldn't find him home, but then again, she needed to find him today. She had the appointment at the women's clinic already and she had to ask him for some money to pay for it. With her father in a crisis, it was clear she couldn't ask her mother. She thought of David, but already decided it would be better if he never knew about this chapter in her life.

Lark stood at the door to Jamal's apartment, and looked up and down the alley. She'd only been there before in the dark, during a time when Jamal was still her shining knight. The daylight and her frame of mind stripped the place of any romance it may have held. Today, the narrow passage was just a dirty alley that led nowhere. The apartment with its faded, paint-chipped door behind an iron gate, the low windows with bars on them seemed more a prison that the haven she once was sought. She waited and tried to hear a TV on inside or some sign that he was home. Maybe she could just leave a note and go? Just then the door behind the gate pulled open with a sucking sound.

"What do you want?" Pee Cee pushed open the gate and stuck his angry face out at her from the crack in the door, making her wish she hadn't come. But then, she found the chip she needed for her shoulder, and felt more convicted than ever about what she was there to do. The brutish cousin's unbridled hostility toward her was always unsettling, even frightening, but today she was on a mission and his disdain only fueled her.

"I'm selling Girl Scout cookies. What do you think I want?"

Stepping back and opening the door all the way, the burly protector yelled over his shoulder into the apartment. "Your Jew wants you to jump, so you better jump." He reached behind the door, snatched a jacket that was hanging there, then pushed his way out, knocking her aside as he passed her in the stairwell that led up to the alley.

"Have a nice day," she called to his back. He turned and flipped her the finger with both hands.

"You tell your daddy I said, 'have a nice day,' bitch."

Before she could answer, Jamal pulled her by the arm into the dark apartment. He tried to kiss her, but she pulled away. "Why does he have to bring my father into it? He's so twisted."

"Forget about him. C'mon, Bird, you didn't come here to talk about Pee Cee, I hope. I was just thinking I wanted to see you so bad, and here you show up, just like that." He snapped his fingers in the air with a flourish, but couldn't hide how his hand was trembling. She looked at him closer now as her eyes adjusted to the lack of light in the room. He was thinner, if that was possible. His eyes seemed to jump out of his head and they looked urine-yellow where they should have been white.

"If you wanted to see me so bad, how come I haven't seen you in a couple of weeks?"

"Well, you ain't so easy to find."

"I'm at the hospital or at home. What's so hard about that?" She didn't know why she was going down this track. She was relieved not to have seen him after their last emotional time together in her apartment. Lark had promised herself that it was going to be the last time she'd be with him that way, and kept that promise. Walking home from the hospital for the last few weeks, she'd avoided any route that might bring her in contact with him, and for the past couple of weeks the strategy had worked, or so she thought.

"The hospital and home and walking around with your college boys."

"Are you spying on me? My brother has been coming out to see my father. Remember, my father, is lying in the hospital in a coma? David brings a friend with him, his roommate. Anything else, James Bond?"

"Whoa, relax, Bird. I'm just saying I wanted to see you and I'm happy you are here, okay? Look, let's relax." He produced a joint from a drawer in the kitchen and lit it. The Formica table that took up most of the room was cluttered with cereal boxes, a milk carton, used bowls, dirty spoons, and a small mirror lined up with long dashes of white powder. He took a long pull from the joint, and then pushed it toward her, holding his breath. The smell of it, once sweet, now made her gag.

"No, thanks. I'm pregnant."

His breath exploded from him in a hacking cough, his eyes getting even wider as he took in her throwaway news. "You're what?" he managed between gasps.

"You heard me, or else you wouldn't be choking."

He tossed the joint in the sink, pulled out a chair, and sat down, putting his head between his knees until the coughing got under control. Finally done, he wiped his eyes and mouth with his sleeve. He looked at Lark and gave her a ridiculous smile. "I guess I wasn't packing raincoats with me that last time."

She wanted to slap him. Of all the responses she imagined from him, the look of downright pride in his work was not one she'd expected.

"I guess not. And I guess I'm an idiot for not thinking about it either, but it's too late for that."

He jumped up from his chair, excited. "Bird, this is perfect! I mean, I have been praying for guidance, you know. Praying for something. This is my answer."

"You've been praying? That's new. And what's all this shit? Is this your little altar to the gods?" She pushed the coke-striped mirror toward him, disrupting the neat, snowy piles. Lark picked up a pair of rolled up dollar bills lying on the table that he'd used for straws and stuck one in each ear. "Is this how you get your messages: 'Hello, God, it's me, Rain Man. Hel-looooo? I can't hear you because I am so fucked up!'"

Jamal bent down and swept his long, thin arm across the table, sending everything on it crashing to the floor. He kicked at the tumbling bowls and crunching colored loops of cereal underfoot.

"Shut up! I don't need this shit. This shit means nothing. This shit killed my mother, but it's not going to kill me. OK? Not now. 'Cause this is my sign, Bird, don't you understand? This is Jesus telling me to live, you know? He's saying, 'here is some life, here is something you can live for.'"

For all her bravado up until now, Lark was at a total loss as to how to react to Jamal's take on the situation. Not once, while thinking about telling him, did she consider that he would really want this baby. She thought he'd understand that she was too young and that he was in no position to become a father or support a family. To her, it was a mistake, an unfortunate stumbling block to her future; an obstacle to overcome—not without its costs, both monetary and emotional—but just something to get over with as quickly as possible.

And now, Jamal was building his salvation around it, making it his personal lifeline tossed out from God, as though it had nothing to do with her. The impact of having a child in her life was a minor detail in his little passion play. Whatever sympathy she may have felt for him was eaten up by her resentment for his self-centered, Jesus-justified scenario for her life. Nearly three years in Crown Heights had given her more of that kind of thinking than she needed in one lifetime. Different god, same shackles.

"I am not having this baby, Jamal. I came here to tell you so you could help me with the money for the abortion." After her mother left the hospital, Lark went to the OB/GYN clinic there and asked around. She got a hotline number for "family planning" and made some calls. Happy for the anonymity of the call she'd asked, *if someone was pregnant and they didn't want to have the baby, where could they go?* She had asked, happy for the anonymity the phone gave her. She wanted a clinic outside of Brooklyn and found one in the city that worked on a sliding scale, but it was still going to cost $280 she didn't have.

"Don't even say that. Don't say that Bird. This is our baby. This is a chance for us."

"A chance for what? To live in a dark, fucking cave with my drug-addict husband? Uncle Pee Cee could come by and call me The Jew and bounce our little chocolate-milk baby on his knee."

"This is all I need to pull myself out, baby. I been down, that's all. It's gonna be beautiful. I'm gonna clean up. I'm gonna make a life for us, for our kid."

Lark turned her back on him and walked toward the door of the apartment. He was scaring her. And she couldn't watch him beg her to save him. She felt him dragging her down to the depths of a murky sea where she would drown if she didn't act quickly to cut the line that connected them.

"I don't even know if it's yours. Could be the college boy," she shouted the lie over her shoulder and slipped out the door into the alley. As she ran past the ground level kitchen window, she heard a stream of anguished obscenities and the sound of more dishes crashing to the floor.

CHAPTER FORTY

H e'd seen him naked before. Almost daily, for all those years of early morning ritual baths, he knew Yakov had watched his body mature by way of sidelong glances and indirect peeks past the edge of a towel while pretending to be preoccupied with drying his face or behind him in the reflection of a mirror while combing his hair. These were quick, stolen impressions, since the atmosphere of a mikvah dressing room was hardly one of strutting masculinity.

So now, when Daniel came out of the bathroom stark naked and just stood there, his face a mixture of defiance and desire, he saw Yakov averting his eyes somewhere to the left of Daniel's ear.

"You can look at me. It's not the mikvah. No one is going to catch you. Wait, I'll give you a better look." Daniel reached over and switched on the lamp that was sitting on the dresser. As an afterthought, he took the framed wedding photo of Yakov and Rachel that stood there and laid it facedown.

"What are you doing?" Yakov had been slowly unbuttoning his shirt, but froze.

"What am I doing? I'm showing you my body. That should be a welcome sight, no?" He crossed the room to Yakov, who had backed up to the locked bedroom door without realizing it. Daniel wrenched the edg-

389

es of the shirt from Yakov's frozen fingers and continued unbuttoning it for him. Mounted on the door was a full-length mirror. It was partially blocked by Yakov, but Daniel could still see himself reflected there, and twisted his body so he could admire it while he spoke. "I've lost weight. Did you notice? Do you like it? Some people would say I have a nice body. A very nice body."

"What people?" Yakov was cornered by the big man, who continued to undress him.

"No one, just people in general. People who notice such things."

Daniel remembered Barry undressing him in the bright afternoon light that streamed into his little church room just a few days earlier. Barry had pulled a bottle of fine scotch out from under his bed and poured them both a stiff drink.

"This will loosen you up a bit." Then, he started by seducing Daniel into looking at himself, into examining his body. Barry slowly took off Daniel's clothes for him, not allowing him to help. "I want to do it for you. I'm going to do everything for you this afternoon. You just try and enjoy yourself for once in your life."

Daniel knew that something more than just the fading afternoon light had shifted in that tiny room at the top of a church. He saw that what he had with Yakov was just a trickle of pleasure, a meager flow that was damned up with pain, guilt, fear, and self-loathing. He knew it could take a lifetime to deconstruct the dam completely, but with Barry he had a taste of what it felt like to have the floodgates opened wide. He learned that his capacity for pleasure was enormous. He never wanted to have less than his fill of it again.

Now, Daniel kept a close watch on Yakov's face as he peeled off his limp shirt. He felt compassion for Yakov for the first time in weeks. Anger and frustration were being replaced by renewed love for his boyhood friend and made him feel expansive, generous, justified. He marveled at his boldness now behind the locked bedroom door in Yakov's apartment. Though Rachel was safely occupied by a shopping trip to Manhattan with her friend Lark, they were not far from where the Rebbe sat in his office, where Yakov's mother and Uncle lived, a few flights below them. At first, Daniel thought that being with Barry would mean the end of his relationship with Yakov. But when Yakov called to set up this meeting, Daniel wondered if the experience could enhance their intimacy. He indulged in a new "having-it-all" scenario that now included Barry. He hoped he could somehow give Yakov a taste of the incredible freedom he'd felt in the little room above the church.

Seeing the terror in Yakov's eyes as Daniel lifted his tzitses over his head, he realized something was missing. Scotch. "We need a drink." Daniel reached behind Yakov and unlocked the door. "Don't move. I'll be right back."

Daniel walked quickly through the tidy apartment to the polished hutch in the dining room. He pulled out the scotch from the cabinet below, and took two crystal tumblers out from behind the glass doors on the upper part of the hutch. His skin felt taut with goose flesh. Daniel had never walked naked through his own home, let alone someone else's. It felt dangerous, exhilarating. He poured out two generous portions of the gold liquid, and carefully replaced the bottle. He wanted to hurry back to Yakov before he locked himself in the bathroom, as he had the disastrous time they'd gotten a musty motel room in Queens. Daniel thought he heard a door close behind him and worried he might already be too late.

"Well, well, well." Yakov's uncle Yossi stood in the archway between the foyer and the living room, a ring of keys jangling in his fingers, a box of light bulbs stuffed under his arm. Daniel stopped abruptly and the scotch sloshed up from the glasses, spilling over his big hands, dripping down his wrists, splashing onto his feet.

"I came up to change some light bulbs for Rachel. I didn't know I'd be shedding light on so much." He looked straight at Daniel's quickly fading erection, a twisted smile spreading across his face.

From the bedroom they heard a desperate moan, "Oh, my God!" and then the bathroom door slamming.

Daniel wanted to run to the bedroom and join Yakov in his belief that a closed door could insulate him from what was happening, but something in Yossi's face, how he looked at Daniel now, made him stand his ground. He brought one of the scotches to his lips and drank it in one searing gulp. He offered the other to Yossi. "Drink?"

"You are filth." Yossi made no move to accept the glass from Daniel.

"Oh, really." Daniel threw back the other scotch. He turned and used every ounce of concentration he had to walk, without shaking, back toward the hutch where he calmly placed the empty glasses. He wanted Yossi to get a good look at him. He turned and faced him again. "Then why are you looking at me like that?"

"Like what? I'm looking at you like you disgust me—you and him, the Rebbe's little prince, the great 'artiste' and his filthy little drawings. Nothing but a cocksucker."

"Maybe not. Maybe you just feel disgusted that you like what you see. Hmm? I always wondered what happened to your little wife, what was her name? Zaporah? I wondered why she moved way back to her parents' house in Ontario, why she wanted a *get* from you after only a year of marriage. Maybe it's because you never looked at her the way you are looking at me now."

The uncle's twisted smile was replaced with a wide-eyed panic that told Daniel he'd touched on a raw truth the burly man was not prepared to bring to light.

"Faggot," Yossi spat out at him, backing out of the room toward the door. "*Toyevah.*" he nearly shrieked the Hebrew word for "abomination" at him, throwing it up like a shield against Daniel's insight into his darkest, most repulsive-to-him impulses.

"If you are thinking about telling anyone about this, think again, my friend." Daniel took a few steps toward Yossi, emboldened by the alcohol and his insight into the man's most protected weakness.

"Poor Yossi. Always overlooked. Never appreciated." Daniel pursed his lips to deliver his most condescending "tsk, tsk, tsk " while shaking his head in mock sympathy.

"First, your brother, Moishe, now his son, Yakov, always outshining you in the Rebbe's eyes. You try and tell anyone about this and see if they believe you. You'll look like a jealous fool. A jealous fool who, with a little secret of his own about his failed marriage, is hardly in a position to point any fingers."

"Shut up, you faggot!" Yossi screamed, throwing up his thick hands as against Daniel's indictment. The packet of light bulbs under his arm fell to the floor and Yossi kicked them into the room toward Daniel. He then turned and disappeared into the dark foyer.

Daniel's knees went soft with the sound of the slamming front door. He was trembling all over, cold despite the two scotches that had steeled his resolve and loosened his tongue enough to challenge Yossi. He padded quickly to the front door and locked it, even though he was fairly certain that the menacing uncle would not return. With the adrenaline seeping out of him, and feeling heavy, Daniel turned toward the bedroom where another locked door, one he feared he might never be able to open, awaited him.

*   *   *

Yakov stood on the toilet and looked out of the bathroom window and down onto the driveway below. The Rebbe's town car was parked there, next to the detached garage. A row of bulky black trashcans lined up like sentinels along the wall closest to the driveway. The window was small, but it occurred to Yakov that, if he really wanted to, he could snake his way out headfirst and simply dive to his death. He'd smash his aching, tormented head on the asphalt, releasing his mind from the never-ending struggle it was to be him—a sensitive boy with a cold, self-centered mother, who lost a loving father, who had a cruel uncle, and who loved his boyhood friend, body and soul, but had to be married to a woman he could never love that way. He was a pious, God-fearing scholar with consuming desires that flew in the face of all he was meant to worship and honor, an artist whose head danced with a catalog of images he would never be able to bring to life. He felt so compressed by the pain of his earthly existence that he thought he might just explode out of the window, as if from a circus cannon. The simple, direct act of falling the four stories to the ground would save him from it all and the degradation that would now come. His uncle Yossi's acquisition of this newest, most tangible evidence against him would take him from misery to misery, with no possible end in sight.

"He's gone." Daniel knocked loudly on the bathroom door. "I said he's gone. You can come out."

Yakov slowly closed the bathroom window, lingering on the view of the narrow river of pavement below, an escape route he knew he was not likely to take. The Torah and the Talmud were quite explicit in their prohibition of suicide. As tormented as he felt, he didn't feel capable of trading a finite lifetime of pain for what could amount to an eternity of struggle in the world to come.

"Yakov. Please, come out. We have to talk." Daniel had changed his tone. Yakov could tell he was trying hard to make his voice sound even, calm.

"Are you dressed?" Yakov knew as he asked it, it was the wrong thing to say, but he could not help his discomfort. And if Daniel had not been parading around naked, Yossi would have walked in on two old friends having a drink, and nothing more could have been proven. Their being together was enough of a sin. Why did Daniel have to push it, to flaunt it so much? Didn't this prove to Daniel that such arrogance was only going to lead to more suffering for them both?

"My clothes are in the bathroom, hanging on the hook behind the door." Daniel shouted, angrily. Yakov knew tonight would be the last straw for Daniel. He'd been desperate to find some acceptable measure of contact with Daniel, but couldn't. He had enough guilt about the forbidden sexual contact, but the idea of committing adultery on top of it, compounded this guilt beyond what he could rationalize.

The bathroom door cracked open and Yakov's arm poked out, holding Daniels clothes. "Here."

When Daniel grabbed at the clothes, Yakov pulled his arm quickly back into the bathroom and slammed the door. "I'll come out when you are dressed."

Daniel stabbed his arms into his crumpled shirt, nearly ripping the sleeve. "You know what, Yakov? You don't ever have to come out of the bathroom. How's that? You can live your whole life sitting on the *facockte* toilet, as far as I am concerned. I give up. You're right! Hashem must not want us together. He made you so afraid that you are totally useless. You are useless to me and you are useless to your wife. And if you don't start having children you are going to be useless to the Rebbe, too. What kind of successor are you going to be when everyone realizes you are as worthless a husband as Yossi was? His wife went running back to her family and she got a special *get* directly from the Rebbe. How soon before Rachel demands her divorce too, huh?"

Daniel sat on the edge of the bed and pulled his socks on.

"And while you are in there, my friend," Daniel pointed his voice sharply at the closed door, "look at yourself in the mirror. You see yourself? Is there anyone standing next to you? No. No, there isn't. You are totally alone. So holy, so untouchable—so unable to touch." He was yelling into the doorjamb now and rattled the locked door with a stiff kick. "I can't live like that. I need to be touched. I want to be loved. I believe Hashem gives us what we ask for, what we need, what we can handle. He's already given me someone who can be with me the way you can't, and more. I can't have you, but now I see it's for the best."

Daniel turned, picked up his jacket from the bed, and pulled it on. The door to the bathroom opened slowly and Yakov stepped tentatively into the doorframe. "What do you mean, Hashem has given you some-one? You mean Gavrielle?"

"No, I don't mean Gavrielle."

"You met another man who..."

"Yes."

"And..."

"And what?"

Yakov stepped into the room and sat primly on the edge of the bed. He studied his hands, as though the next right thing to say was printed there for him to simply read aloud.

"How did you get rid of my uncle?"

"Oh, are we changing the subject now? OK. Don't worry about Yossi. He's not going to say anything to anyone. Let's put it this way—you have more in common with your uncle than you ever imagined. And if you don't take care of your marriage, of your wife, you are going to end up just like him."

Yakov did not look up as Daniel walked to the door of the bedroom and pulled it open.

"I'm sorry," Yakov managed to say, lifting his eyes for a moment.

"I don't want your 'sorry.' Save it for Yom Kippur."

Daniel left the room, but came back holding the two crystal tumblers with an inch of scotch in each. He handed one to Yakov and clinked his own against it. "L'chaim, my friend." Daniel gulped his down. Yakov stared at his. "Live a little, Yakov. I hope you'll live a little. I intend to."

Daniel put his glass down on the dresser. He was about to turn and go, but first stopped to lift up the frame with Yakov's wedding picture and carefully put it back in place.

CHAPTER FORTY-ONE

L ark scanned the directory in the lobby. "There it is. Women's Services. Eighth floor."

Rachel followed Lark across the marbled lobby to the elevator bank. Lark charged into an opening elevator, bumping into a messenger leading a skinny bicycle out. Rachel stepped aside and let the remaining passengers leave, then got into the car with Lark, who began hitting "close door" button over and over.

"I guess I'm a little tense." Lark conceded.

"Are you sure you want to do this?"

"Rock, please. I don't want to get into it again. We went over it enough on the subway ride over here, and before that, too. I'm not changing my mind. I have to do what I have to do. If you are going to make me feel creepy about this, then I wish you hadn't come."

The doors opened and they stepped out into a large waiting area. At least twenty women of various ages sat in identical chairs with wooden armrests and knobby teal-colored upholstery, set up in rows across the room. Some women were filling out forms on clipboards, while others flipped through magazines. At the sliding-glass reception window, Lark got her own clipboard, which strained with forms and a pen. She and Rachel found two seats together at the far end of the room, under a poster in Spanish and English whose headline read "Perfect Partner Quiz" offering a series of yes and no questions below that. *Does your partner always tell you the truth? Is your partner attentive to your needs and pleasure? Does your partner treat you as an equal? Does your partner accept your decisions and feelings? Does your partner discuss problems about sexuality with you?* Rachel averted her eyes from the brightly colored checklist. She turned her back on the poster and sat down quickly, but had taken in enough to know that she couldn't answer yes to any of them. Her perfect Crown Heights match would not score well according to the criteria of this parallel reality. There was more than just a river and a few miles between her Brooklyn neighborhood and this Manhattan women's clinic. Lark got to work on the forms, hunching over them, moaning every time she completed one page and flipped it over to find yet another one below it.

"Hey, look, I'm sorry. I didn't mean to make you feel bad. I guess I'm nervous, too, nervous for you."

"Forget it, it's okay." Lark answered her without looking up from her forms.

Rachel picked up a magazine, a skinny girl with a lot of windblown hair on the cover. "Julia Speaks About Walking Away From Her Wedding Day," the caption across the girl's waist read in bold letters. Rachel had only a vague idea who most celebrities were. It hardly mattered, as she wasn't reading just now. She rolled and unrolled the thick periodical on her lap, trying to avoid reading the rest of the posters that hung around the waiting area: *Sexually Transmitted Diseases. Domestic Violence. Sexual Abuse. Birth Control. Family Planning.*

"You'd never see these posters anywhere in Crown Heights, that's for sure," Rachel said so only Lark could hear.

Lark looked up and glanced around, seeing the posters for the first time. "Yea, right. It's every 'do-not-ever discuss' topic for the Chasidic community." She pointed her pen at each one in turn. "Let me see…no STDs 'cause you shouldn't be with anyone else your whole life except

your husband. But what if your husband is screwing around with prosti-
tutes over on the west side, but you don't know it? And no need to discuss domestic violence 'cause we all know that Jews don't beat their
wives or molest their kids, right? At least no one admits it. Family planning? Plan to be constantly pregnant for the next fifteen years, 'cause
they set up the whole mikvah thing so you basically have sex every
month on the exact three days you are ovulating!"

"And birth control," Rachel chimed in quietly, holding the rolled-up
magazine in a death grip. "I guess you don't need birth control if you're
not even having sex with your husband at all."

"Exactly!"

Lark started back at the forms, then realized what Rachel had said.
"What? What do you mean, 'if you are not having sex with your husband at all'?"

Rachel kept up rolling the magazine and staring at her lap. When she
began biting her lower lip, a sure sign to Lark that her friend was going
to be in tears any second, she tossed her clipboard to the ground and
grabbed the now permanently tubular magazine away from Rachel.

"We met for lunch, remember? After all the riot stuff died down?
You were all blushing and stuttering and telling me everything was so
romantic and wonderful—that Yakov was so gentle and thoughtful, blah
blah blah."

Rachel looked straight ahead when she spoke. Her hands clasped together on her lap. "Well, there was all the stress and, you know, confusion after the wedding. He, um, we drank a lot of vodka that night and
fell asleep, isn't that funny? And then there was so much going on over
the next week or so...you know? With your dad and the riots and everything with the community and the press. I mean, he was exhausted; the
Rebbe was giving him more and more to do. We were all crazy with the
whole thing. Then I got my period, and that was almost two weeks before I could go to the mikvah, so it's, you know, "off limits" during that
time anyway. Then Yakov had that stomach flu, or we thought it was

the flu but the doctor said it was colitis, which he also said was stress-related, or something like that, so he wasn't feeling well and always in the bathroom. And then I got my period again. He has been very nice to me, and respectful…we're really becoming good friends…"

"Friends? Respectful? Rocky, are you trying to tell me that you have been married for almost three months and you haven't had sex with your husband yet? Nothing?"

"Well. No, I mean, yes. Yes. Nothing."

That's when no amount of lip biting worked anymore. The tears flowed.

"Rocky, why didn't you tell me?" Lark jerked her chair out of the row and pulled it around to face her friend. She grabbed her locked hands and pulled them apart and held them. They were ice cold.

"I just thought it would happen eventually, on its own, and I wasn't sure if I was doing something wrong, or what. I was trying to be like 'it's no big deal…'"

She snatched her hands away from Lark to cover her face. She was really crying now. Lark pulled a box of tissues off a nearby table, jerked six or seven out of the box, and pushed them into Rachel's hands. "Here."

Lark waited until Rachel was finished blowing her nose.

"Okay. First of all, I wish you told me, Rock. Second of all, you are not doing anything wrong and it *is* a big deal. Come on, you are gorgeous. What guy wouldn't want to jump your bones if given a chance, unless he's totally gay? I mean, are you talking to him about it, is anyone saying anything, or are you both just going around like, 'nothing's wrong'?"

"I don't know what to say. 'Oh, excuse me, Yakov. Aren't we supposed to be having sex now?'"

"Yes! Well, isn't it in the fucking *ketuba*? Didn't you guys sign a wedding contract that he's supposed to, you know, take care of your 'needs'? Isn't it grounds for divorce and all if he doesn't, or vice versa?"

"Well, what do you suggest? I get out the ketuba and mark that section with a yellow highlighter? Leave it on the bed for him to see? Believe me, I've thought of it! But the more time that goes by, the crazier I feel. Meanwhile everyone from my mother to the cleaning lady at the shul is looking at me funny, wondering why I'm not pregnant already."

"Oh, my God, Rocky. I had no idea. All you want to do is get pregnant and here I am dragging you along with me so I can get unpregnant. I am so sorry."

Rachel reached for the box of tissues as a new wave of sobs surfaced. When her breaths got less staccato, she drank in a deep one and blew out a long sigh. "I don't know if I'm dying to have a baby. I know it's expected of me now. It's the next thing for me to be doing. But the first thing for me was going to be *him*...you know? I was looking forward to being close to him."

"Well, that's normal."

"Yeah, it's normal, but it's not really happening. Nothing's happening in *that* way and I don't know what to do about it. We really do seem to have this great friendship going, so I'm so confused. Is it me? Is he just afraid, shy, too holy? Maybe a lot of women in Crown Heights never feel close to their husbands, but they still manage to get pregnant. And then they at least have the babies. They at least have the babies, don't they?"

"Look, um, maybe we should get out of here. This doesn't seem like a good time to..."

"No. No, I'm okay. I don't want to make you feel bad. I'm sorry if I was making you feel creepy about it before. I was just thinking about myself, and I was dying to tell you what was going on with Yakov. So now I have and I feel better just being able to admit it to someone."

"I feel so bad, Rock. All this time..."

"Finish your forms. We'll talk about it later. I'm glad I told you, finally."

"Are you sure?"

"I'm sure."

"We are not finished talking about this, OK?"

Rachel blew her nose and nodded.

Lark turned back to finish the long "family history" form, trying to remember who in her family tree suffered with what, died of what. She thought of her father, still lying in the ICU, her mother relentlessly by his side over the last three months. A cascade of complications kept him there. What would be his outcome? Certainly nothing on the list of diseases before her would account for his death *if* he did die now. On the bottom of the list was the word "Other" with a blank line next to it. There. There she could write it in. Hate. Hate killed my father.

Lark shook her head, as if to throw the thought off her before it could penetrate. *I can't think about that now.* She had to stay focused, do what she came to do, get on with her life, even as her father's life was suspended in an excruciating limbo. If she got through this day, she could start over. *I'm going to plan my life from now on, take control of it, instead of just having "shit happen" to me.* Lark finished the forms and handed them through the sliding-glass doors to a bored receptionist who flashed her a wooden smile in return.

"Have a seat. Someone will call you in soon."

Lark turned back to sit down in time to see Rachel coming back from the ladies' room, her face red from more crying and the cold water she had undoubtedly splashed over it. *Talk about shit happening!* She felt enraged for her friend's predicament. By this afternoon Lark would walk out of this building with her fresh start, but there would be no such easy "fix" for Rachel's problem with Yakov. Something was wrong, really wrong, and she didn't have a clue how to help her friend unravel it.

"You okay, Rock?"

"I guess."

"I don't know how you didn't explode from holding it all in these past weeks. I mean, I saw you at shul over the holidays, the little I was there, but you looked so normal. Better than normal. You looked happy. I even thought to myself, 'this is going to work out for her.' I even felt a little, you know, jealous. Not bad jealous, like I hated you for being happy, but more like, everything seemed so perfect and planned and working out for you, and my life was one mess after another lately. You know?"

Rachel nodded, fidgeting with a new magazine. "Yeah. Perfect."

"Lark Shulman?"

A nurse wearing puke-y green scrubs appeared in a doorway adjacent to the sliding-glass windows. She flipped through a file folder and waited.

Lark gathered her jacket and purse. "This is it. Try not to mutilate every magazine in here while I'm gone."

Rachel's face relaxed into a genuine smile. "I love you," she said and stood and hugged Lark tightly around her neck, all the while whispering something in Hebrew into her hair.

Lark thought she recognized the prayer. "A little protection? I guess I could use it."

"Yeah. You and me both."

Lark walked toward the waiting nurse. Just before Lark followed her through the door to the clinic, she turned to wave to Rachel with mock confidence, but her friend had already buried her head in her hands again and didn't see.

CHAPTER FORTY-TWO

"Ahhmein," they said in unison to punctuate the blessing, and Yakov drank from the overflowing cup of wine. He passed the gleaming, silver cup to Rachel. She took a deep drink, hoping the wine would take the edge off of her nervousness. They sat, just the two of them, at the perfectly laid table. Their wedding china and cut crystal, the bright silverware and polished napkin rings were cushioned on the creamy tablecloth and sparkled in the warm light of the Shabbes candles that Rachel had lit long before Yakov returned from shul.

They went to the kitchen together to wash their hands. Then, Yakov removed the ornately embroidered cover over the small challahs Rachel had spent a good portion of the morning making. He held the two of them bottom to bottom in the air in front of his face and recited the blessing over the bread, *ha motzeh lechem min ha-aretz,* thanking God Almighty for the bread of the earth. He tore off a corner of one of the golden, braided loaves, dipped it in the salt he'd spilled on his plate, and took a bite. He then quickly tore off a piece for her and, before he could put it down on her plate, Rachel took it directly from his fingertips. As she did, their eyes met and she knew he understood what she meant to convey with the gesture. *You can touch me today.* She wanted him to

405

know that tonight their period of separation, her time of *niddah*, was over.

* * *

That morning she'd made sure to catch him before he left for minion. She'd risen early, knowing she had an appointment to visit the mikvah later that day. It had to be tonight. She *had* to ask him.

"Yakov, I'd like to have Shabbes together with you tonight if that's all right."

"What do you mean? We always have Shabbes together."

"Yes, I know. But I meant together, alone. In our apartment."

He concentrated on placing his hat on his head. Yakov had his back to her, but Rachel saw his face in the hall mirror. Her husband looked as though he'd been up half the night, even though he was fast asleep when she returned from her "shopping trip" with Lark the night before. The mostly empty scotch bottle and the glasses she'd found on the dining room hutch explained both her husband's early, heavy sleep and the dark, puffy circles that hung from his eyes. She knew he'd had his weekly learning session with Daniel and it was likely they had more than a few friendly l'chaims.

Yakov finally had his hat in just the right place and turned to open the front door. "You don't like having Shabbes with the Rebbe and my mother? There are always interesting guests."

"Of course, I feel honored to share Shabbes with the Rebbe. I treasure every moment in his presence. And your mother is always so nice to me." Rachel stretched the truth a little here, as she found Rebetzin Rubinstein difficult to relax around. Yakov's mother looked as though she had a perpetual bitter taste in her mouth and her comments and observations reflected that bitterness. "There is no question that it's exciting to meet all those dignitaries and rabbis and everyone who comes to pay their respects to the Rebbe. It's just that I thought we could have one on our own, that's all. We haven't had one yet. I want to make a Shabbes for you." Rachel tried to sound matter-of-fact and cheery about it all. She didn't want to signal to him that she thought something was wrong, that she was tired of always being part of a crowd with him and putting on a pretense of being the happy newlywed. She didn't want to scare him with any hint of her plan to face him across the table and start a conversation about their "situation."

Yakov thought for a moment, looking at Rachel's eager expression, then nodded as if some internal argument had resolved itself. "Of course. We should have our own Shabbes. I've been thoughtless, assuming we would always have it downstairs. I'm sorry. But don't cook a whole meal. You shouldn't go to too much trouble. You can have most of the food sent up from downstairs."

"I will. But I'm going to make some things, too. I want to. Really. Will you tell them not to expect us tonight?"

A great sense of relief washed over Rachel as she closed the door behind Yakov and heard his light footsteps receding down the stairs. She was taking matters into her own hands as Lark had counseled her in her pep talk on the ride home from the city the day before. Lark had refused to talk about the procedure.

"I'm fine. It's over. I'm not going to make that mistake again," was all she wanted to say about it. A bit bent over from the cramping, Lark claimed riding the subway back to Brooklyn would be fine, but Rachel insisted on paying for a cab. Rachel's mother had set up a checking account for her daughter while she was engaged and had put five thousand dollars in it, proudly slapping the bank statement down on the table for Rachel to see. In her most conspiratorial tone she told Rachel, "You should always have a little money of your own. You don't want to have to ask for every penny you need for this and that. I'll make sure you always have some pocket change." Rachel was grateful she didn't need to explain the cash she'd lent Lark to pay for her "appointment" to anyone.

She was grateful to her mother, who wouldn't approve of this use of funds, but who had the wisdom to recognize a woman's need for a slush fund.

As soon as the cab had pulled away from the curb, Lark laid down on the seat with one hand over her belly and her head on Rachel's lap. Once comfortable, she launched into a planning session for Rachel's next move with Yakov.

"Okay, when are you going to sit down and talk to him? The sooner, the better. Tonight even, or tomorrow, the latest. He's your husband. If you can't talk to him about something as basic as this, then you do not want to be married to the guy."

Rachel was mostly silent during the ride home, listening to Lark's plan to set her marriage on track. Most of it was familiar ranting about everything that was wrong about the Chasidic way of life and marriage, but underneath it all she was rooting for Rachel's happiness and her conviction was contagious. Rachel began to have some hope.

"When's the next time you go to the mikvah?" No one but Lark would ask such a question.

"Tomorrow, actually." Rachel blushed.

"Well, that's perfect. And it's going to be Shabbes! Double-mitzvah time, baby!"

* * *

Rachel knew Lark was right—the timing *was* perfect. She'd gone to the mikvah that afternoon and felt for the first time the sense of renewal she thought she was supposed to feel covering herself in the ritual water and reciting the blessing.

Even more perfect, the Torah portion for the week was *Vayeitzei*, the story of the biblical Yakov and Rachel. It would give her something to talk about with him, to break the ice. She knew her husband was at his most comfortable when discussing some intricacy of Torah or Talmud, so she would start there.

She felt certain that God was bringing all the necessary elements together to make it possible for them to be intimate. Thinking of the Torah portion gave her confidence, too. Even the original Yakov and Rachel had a delay in being together, and their marriage ended up as the Torah's greatest love story, the basis for generations of kings. It proved that a slow start didn't necessarily mean the end of the world.

She understood from the time of her engagement that life with Yakov would be far from typical. In fact, the match's special quality, the privileged status his proposal promised to elevate her to, was, in large part, responsible for her abandoning all plans for escape she'd entertained in conversations with Lark. As exciting as a rebellious, secular life sounded on those sleepover nights when she and Lark would be up until nearly dawn playing out hypothetical scenarios for Rachel's life "on the outside," the possibility of being "first lady" of the community represented an honor that she could not, ultimately, refuse.

The pedestal, though heady at times, was proving to be lonely and, frankly, boring. She didn't really need to cook their meals, since the Rebbe's full-time kitchen staff prepared dinners for them, which they either ate in the big dining room with the Rebbe and his guests or had sent up to the apartment. Yakov was almost never home for breakfast or lunch, since he was out early for the mikvah and minion, and then spent the day studying or was with the Rebbe, assisting him in various ways.

She didn't clean the apartment herself either, aside from straightening out their clothes or doing dishes now and then. Monday and Thursday she put their laundry outside the door and Tuesday and Friday it was delivered back to her, clean, folded, pressed, and fragrant.

The only thing expected of Rachel now, her only job, was to provide progeny, to keep Yakov's rich bloodline of *tzaddikim* flowing into the future. The promise was that this "vocation" would not only be enough for her, but everything. She would, by raising as many children as

Hashem would provide, find all the joy, purpose, and stimulation her heart, mind, and soul could ever need. Rachel wanted this to be true. She'd staked everything on it. And she needed this part of her life to begin soon before she'd be forced to reconsider it all. Bearing and raising a dozen children over the next 20 years seemed a lot easier than facing what it would take to back out of her marriage now. Would this part of her life begin tonight?

*　*　*

Rachel stood alone in the kitchen arranging the homemade gefilte fish sent up from downstairs on the delicate china she and her mother had picked out months before. She placed a sprig of bright parsley on the right of the fish and layered deep red circles of silky cooked beets on the left. Bitter and sweet, side by side. Yakov sat in the dining room, quietly singing *shalom aleichem, malachay a melochim,* welcoming the angel of the Sabbath. He kept time with a loose fist on the tabletop. *He has a beautiful voice,* thought Rachel, and heard herself sigh. There was much that was beautiful about him—strange and beautiful. He was always soft-spoken and kind with her. He complimented her at every turn, addressing her as "my darling wife" in Yiddish. Some evenings he sat and studied with her, not condescending, but encouraging her to think as a man would and parry with him over passages, rather than just take his opinion as her own.

"You are a born thinker, Rachel," he'd said, "so think!" And she'd felt exhilarated when he applauded her logic for a particular argument. "Good. Good," he'd say and clap his hands.

During the days that she was *niddah,* he seemed more at ease with her and he'd spend more time in the apartment when the Rebbe didn't need him. One night they even played cards and he shared some of his favorite music tapes—some that surprised her. There was forbidden secular music: gritty rhythm and blues sung and played, according to him, by a blind black man, some rock and roll she'd heard before with Lark, and the cast albums of Broadway shows. She fell in love with *West Side Story*, as he explained the star-crossed story while the songs played; and they laughed at the familiarity of *Fiddler on the Roof*, finding themselves rooting for the rebellious daughters.

And now, here they were having their first Shabbes alone, the tumult of the wedding and the tragedy of the riots far enough behind them for a new beginning. They ate the lukewarm dinner and talked. There were gaps of silence, but she did not feel awkward. Rachel went in and out of the kitchen. Yakov offered to help bring dishes to the sink, bring food out, but she insisted he sit and let her serve. He touched her arm and left his hand there for a moment when he said, "This challah is perfect. You made it?"

Rachel gained more confidence as the evening wore on, certain that something essential had shifted in her husband, that the evening was moving toward the closeness they were meant to share. She touched his shoulder tenderly when she put his soup in front of him, and lightly brushed his hand while laughing at a story he told. Yakov seemed happy, presiding over his Shabbes table, and comfortable with her occasional touch. But Rachel wanted him to feel as she did, hoped that he too vibrated with the achy anticipation that intensified for her each time they touched. Rachel knew that he cared for her, their growing friendship proved that he even loved her in his way, but why didn't he want her? She was tired of reviewing the past few months, dissecting every nuance of her behavior, searching for definitive evidence of some indiscretion on her part that could have caused the physical distance between them. By the time she put dessert on the table and finished her second glass of wine, she didn't care about the reasons. She just wanted him more than anything she'd ever wanted before.

Finally, there was nothing left to do. Tea had been served. Pretty bakery cookies sat on delicate plates before them. Yakov poured each of them a sweet orange-flavored cordial in tiny glasses that picked up the candlelight and made the amber liquid glow.

"To my wife. A woman of valor." Yakov raised his glass.

Rachel bowed her head ceremoniously, accepting his toast to her. She took a big sip of the liquor, feeling it sear her throat on the way down, feeling as if it were igniting a wildfire out of the steady pilot light that had been burning inside her all night. *Flames are going to fly out of my mouth if I speak*, she thought. But she knew, too, that those same flames would eat her alive if she didn't.

She began. "Yakov?" Rachel covered his hand with hers. She waited to see if he stiffened or pulled away, even slightly. He did not.

"Yes?"

"I was wondering..."

"Yes?"

"Well, I was thinking about..."

"What is it, my darling?"

"I was thinking about us."

"Oh." She felt his hand twitch, just a little.

"I mean about us in relation to this week's *parsha*. It's our story, Yakov and Rachel's story."

"Oh, yes. Yes, it is."

"But you know what's funny, I really feel compassion for Rachel in the story. I know now how she must have felt."

"Oh?"

"Well, yes, I do, because she loved Yakov and, well, then she was forced to wait until she could be with him. That must have been so painful for her, you know?"

Yakov pulled his hand out from under hers to pour himself another inch of cordial, then kept it on his glass, away.

"Yes. I know. It must have been very painful."

Rachel could feel the panic rising in her throat. She was losing him, perhaps, but felt she couldn't turn back now. Lark's voice echoed in her head, "If you can't talk about this with the guy, then you shouldn't be married to him!" Rachel pressed on.

"I've been waiting too, you know."

She couldn't look at him. Whatever registered in his eyes as she spoke, she didn't want to see it. Rachel stared down at the tablecloth, counting crumbs and waited for him to speak, but he didn't. She heard his chair scrape the floor as he pushed it back. She wanted to sink into the floor, certain he was going to walk out, but then Yakov took hold of her arm and gently lifted her out of her seat. He looked solemn, determined.

Wordlessly, he led her by the hand to their bedroom.

*   *   *

When Yakov saw Rachel earlier that morning, waiting for him in the living room, his stomach churned with fear. She was sitting in her robe, holding her cup of tea in two hands, her brow knitted with thought. She had the air of someone waiting to make an announcement. After the debacle with Daniel the night before—the confrontation with Yossi—he had been especially anxious to get out early, to go to the mikvah and on to study before he ran into anyone. He needed time to think, to figure out how he felt about it all, how he would respond to it. Looking at his wife, the weak morning sun lighting up her hair, he wondered if she somehow already knew about the night before, and all the other nights with Daniel. Had Yossi already gotten to her? He could picture his self-satisfied uncle gleefully spilling the story, giving her not only the evidence she needed to divorce him and ruin him, but every reason to despise him.

When she simply asked him if they could have a Shabbes alone together, he was so relieved, he almost laughed out loud. *She doesn't know!* He was still safe. But was he? Yakov could see the pitiful longing in the poor girl's eyes even as she kept her voice light and cheerful. "I want to make Shabbes for you," she said. But Yakov read in her eyes, saw later in the perfectly laid table, in her careful dress for the evening that she was really saying, "I want to make love with you."

And so he knew it was time. The "jig" was up, whether Yossi told on him on not. The night before, after Daniel left, he was blind with humiliation, anger, and jealousy. Swallowing several scotches, he paced the apartment like a doomed man. Bitterly, he reflected on how the pain and punishment he knew all along would rain down on him was finally coming to pass. His Daniel, his sweet friend, had turned against him, was slipping away. *Hashem has already given me someone who can be with me the way you can't, and more.* Daniel's words screeched like a high-pitched whistle in his head, making him wince. *I can't have you, but I see now it's for the best.* Yakov didn't understand. How could their not being together be for the best? How could Yakov live his entire life without Daniel's touch, without his love as a constant, as a given in his life? He had wept scotch-fueled tears, as he went over the disastrous deterioration of their relationship in the last few months.

The wedding changed things in a way he hadn't anticipated.

It was as if the explosion that erupted minutes after his wedding ceremony was over blew apart every house-of-cards illusion he'd had about his plans with Daniel for the future. Huddled behind folding chairs on the chupah platform, his body thrown over the Rebbe's in an attempt to shield him, he understood with vivid clarity that God had other plans for him entirely. Yakov's whole body trembled that night as they waited under the chupah to be evacuated to the house—not because he was afraid of what was happening in the streets—but because he was certain that this unleashing of violence and rage and devastation at his wedding was a warning to him from God: *Don't fuck with me. I'll destroy you.* This was the message that screamed in Yakov's head that night.

Wasn't He the God that delivered plague upon plague on the Egyptians and finally sentenced their firstborn to death when the stubborn

Pharaoh didn't get the message to let his people go? Hadn't countless enemies of the Israelites been destroyed or miraculously held at bay when it pleased Him to do so? Hadn't He, in Biblical times, turned his back on the people of Israel themselves, when they wandered from the path of righteousness He demanded they walk? Hashem had sent armies to destroy everything the Jews held sacred, driving them from their homes, their homeland, and condemning them to live forever in exile. The Rebbe himself explained the Nazi Holocaust as God's wake-up call to the Jews of Europe who had gotten too assimilated to the secular world. Why wouldn't this same God, with the flick of a fingernail, rain devastation down on a sanctified celebration that Yakov and Daniel stood there intending to making a mockery of? Yakov was meant to someday stand in the shoes of his grandfather. He was to be the leader of a growing global community of Chasids whose reason for being was to hasten the coming of the Moshiach, thus allowing the dead to rise, peace to reign, and God to live amongst them once and for all. God was not about to let him screw with that plan.

The riots had made one thing clear to Yakov. God was watching closely. And He was willing to go to extremes to get Yakov's attention. And now, as if He was dotting His i's and crossing his t's, God had turned Daniel against him, turned his almost holy passion for Yakov into a mundane lust to be satisfied by some stranger, any stranger. If this alone was not enough to break Yakov, God threw Yossi into the mix. His uncle knowing, his having evidence now of Yakov's indiscretions with Daniel, was a humiliation that Yakov would have to live with for the rest of his life. The twisted, knowing face of his uncle would be a reminder that God was right there watching, and waiting to throw His head back and mock Yakov's best-laid plans should he try to stray from his divinely determined destiny.

"Of course we can have Shabbes alone together," he had answered Rachel, knowing what she wanted of him, knowing what God wanted of him, what He was saying through her. It was time.

So, when he took Rachel's arm and lifted her from her chair and led her to their bedroom, he felt as he imagined Moses may have felt when God commanded him to be the leader who would bring His word to the Jewish people, to lead them through the dessert to the Promised Land. Moses wasn't up for the job at first. A stutterer, he would have been content to live out his days herding sheep on a hill, ignorant of his destiny. Why did God choose a man with a speech impediment to pass on the words that would shape the faith of Jews and Christians alike, for thousands of years to come? *Why is God choosing me to lead,* he thought, *cursed as I am with passions that go against everything I am meant to stand for?*

Yakov felt exultant, heady with purpose, as he stood in his bedroom with his wife. In his mind he was sharing this moment with the most revered men of the Torah: Moses, who did what he had to do, facing his weakness to become the man to utter the words that would change the world forever; Abraham, who raised a knife to take the life of his own son when God commanded him to do so as a test of his faith; and the patriarch Yakov, whose own sacrifices in love were rewarded with being the father of the entire Jewish people. Suddenly, Yakov knew the struggles with his "unnatural" passions were just the *groundwork for his greatness.* It was in the overcoming of these passions that he would, like the angels in the patriarch Yakov's dream, ascend the ladder to heaven and help bring that heaven back down to earth.

The room was dark except for a band of light that slipped out from under the bathroom door. He still held her hand as they faced each other. Seconds before, his body had stirred with the excitement of taking his place at the end of a long line of heroic men, holy men, revered through the ages. Now, as Rachel dropped his hand and began unbuttoning his shirt and kissing his face, his neck, the top of his chest, he felt the thrill drain from him and panic rise.

Once she removed his shirt and his tzitzes, Rachel stepped back to look at him for a moment, then quickly undressed herself. Her neatly pressed skirt and blouse lay in a pile at her feet, her shoes and hose kicked off to one side. Her hair, once long and luxurious, Yakov remembered, was short now, but her soft curls caught the light, as did the soft curves of her young body. She smiled coyly, but unembarrassed. Her eyes were lit with triumph, and a little of the hunger he'd seen in Daniel the night before.

Her body stirred him only like the statues they'd seen together at the museum on one of their dates. She was beautiful, a study in symmetry, line, perspective. He wanted to draw her, his hands itching for a pencil, but not to touch her. As though reading his mind, Rachel took his hands and pressed them to her breasts. "Touch me. Please."

She led him now toward the bed and lay down close to him. "I want to touch you," she whispered into his ear. She kissed his mouth and he remembered Daniel's mouth; she moved her hand over him and a shiver passed through him as he pictured Daniel touching him there, holding him in his mouth, and he now felt himself responding.

"I love you." Her voice threatened to break the spell these memories were casting over him, so he quietly shushed her, and kissed her mouth to close it. He concentrated on mirroring her movements, running his hands over her back, sweeping over her buttocks, her breasts. He heard the rhythm of her breathing change, quicken. He was ready now, almost ready.

"Wait," he said. He reached over to the nightstand and pulled open the drawer. He grabbed the handkerchief that Daniel had given him on that afternoon before the wedding. Soiled with his sweat and smell, he had slapped it into Yakov's palm and said, "You are going to need this, my friend."

Now, Yakov clutched the handkerchief in his fist and leaned his face into its musky folds as he moved over his wife now, first slowly, then quick and hard, ignoring her tiny gasps. *I am Moshe, Hashem's messenger, I am Avram, Hashem's servant, I am Yakov, Hashem's instrument.* He repeated this to himself over and over—the images of these holy men passed like counted sheep before his tightly closed eyes. His breath now coming in moaning gulps, he saw that they all bore a striking resemblance to Daniel, and his body exploded into a thousand points of light.

CHAPTER FORTY-THREE

H appy Birthday."
Rachel stood framed in the doorway to the small ICU room where Lark sat, on a folding chair, near her father's bed. Lark smiled at the sight of her friend standing there with the two Mylar balloons she guessed Rachel had just bought at the hospital gift shop. One, pink and populated with shiny white unicorns, said, "It's a girl!" The other, the face of big fat cartoon cat proclaimed, "You're Purrrrfect!"

"Nice balloons. Are you sure in the right place? I think the psychiatric unit is on the 9th floor."

"It's not my fault the gift shop ran out of balloons that say 'Happy 18th Birthday To My Sarcastic Friend!'"

Lark's much-anticipated milestone had finally come on that gray, cusp-of-winter morning. Her long-planned declaration of independence and flight from Crown Heights was made temporarily pointless by her father's condition and the "on hold" status it imposed on her life. She was eighteen, finally, but the events of the past few months made her feel like she was old, much older than she wanted to feel.

"Thanks for remembering." Lark thought she had prepared herself for a non-event of a birthday, but seeing Rachel clutching those balloons in one hand and a beautifully wrapped present in the other made her realize how much she really wanted someone to make a fuss over her.

"How is he?" Rachel entered the small room.

"The same. Maybe a little worse. I don't know. It's kind of a roller coaster."

"I'm so sorry, Lark. I'm going to visit the Rebbes' graves tomorrow. I'll put a note in for your father."

"Sure, why not? Wake those dead Rebbes up and tell them they've been asleep on the job. The Heights have been a mess lately. Ask them to wake up my Dad and while they're at it they can give him total amnesia for about the last five years or so—let him pop up as his good old hippie-dippy self. Hey, why are you going to the graves anyway? I thought the whole thing creeped you out?"

Lark remembered a school field trip to the densely packed cemetery and Rachel's uneasiness there. It was when the Rebbe had his stroke. They had been instructed to add their wishes for his speedy recovery to the thousands of little folded up notes that had already been delivered to the graves of the old Rebbes and their wives. The hope was that these holy deceased would help expedite requests along heavenly channels on behalf of the earnest earthbound Jews.

"Well, Yakov goes often with the Rebbe to visit his grandmother's grave, and his father's. This time he wanted us to go to, well... put in a 'special request.'"

"You're blushing. Why are you blushing? What kind of special request? Oh my God! Don't tell me, I mean do tell me! You talked to him? And? Was it a 'good' Shabbes?" Lark winked broadly at Rachel. "Wait. Don't tell me here. The nurses come in and out constantly. And I'm starving. Let's go down to the cafeteria. I'll let you buy me some bad coffee. At least it'll be hot. It's freezing in here and my butt is killing me from this chair."

They got their coffees along with a slice of "birthday" cake for Lark and found a table near the floor to ceiling windows in the drafty cafeteria dining area. The glare of the sun on the tables made them squint but they wanted the warmth.

"OK. I'm ready. Well? Did you talk? Did you stop talking and you-know-what?"

Rachel suppressed a giggle, but couldn't stop another wave of color from staining her cheeks as she recounted the evening and its consummate conclusion.

Lark listened without interrupting to Rachel's account: her making sure she and Yakov were alone for Shabbes; the intimate dinner, his gentle, respectful manner with her, the coy discussion of the Torah portion and Rachel's pointed comparison of her own suffering to that of the biblical matriarch. Then off they went to the bedroom and Lark thought how Rachel's description of this part of the story reminded her of the old movies she watched for hours on the TV in her father's room—when the black and white lovers get down to "it", the camera always cuts to a curtain blowing in the breeze or waves crashing on the beach. No graphic details, just all swelling music and emotion. Not that she wanted a gritty blow-by-blow, but the whole story seemed a bit smoothed over for her tastes. Never one to tiptoe, she just came out with the million-dollar question.

"Did you ever get to talk about what was going on with him for the past couple of months? Why the long delay?"

"Well, I think it was a combination of things that might be embarrassing for him to discuss. It's like you once said— they keep us apart all our lives then toss us together on our wedding night expecting it all to just fall into place. Yakov may be just a lot more sensitive or insecure than most men his age and the more time that passed the more scared he got. Then there was all the stuff that was going on with the riots. I was so happy to get past it all that I didn't want to make him feel bad about the whole thing."

"In other words, you didn't really get into it. Weren't you curious? It would drive me crazy, I'd have to know."

"I just kept hearing my mother's voice in my head— 'Rachel, why do you have to analyze everything to death?'—and I decided do just leave it alone. The important thing is that, whatever it was, it seems to be over!"

"And you think everything is going to be fine now?"

"Well, it's only been a few days since...but yes, I think we just had to break the ice."

"So to speak..." Lark grinned.

"Shut up!" Rachel giggled like the schoolgirl Lark remembered, not the married lady she was becoming.

"So everything is all domestic bliss. Why the trip to the graves then?"

"Oh," Rachel fidgeted, embarrassed to say, but pleased too. "Yakov says it couldn't hurt to ask for a quick and healthy start to our family."

"One *schtup* and he wants you to be pregnant already?"

Now Rachel met Lark's eyes in mock defiance. "Who said it was only one?"

Lark laughed out loud and high-fived Rachel over the table with both hands.

"Well, I can see my work is done here." Lark made a show of patting herself on the back.

"Yes, oh wise one. I think the patient is cured! Seriously, I don't think I could have gone through with the whole plan if you hadn't been pushing me. So here, open your present. It's for your birthday, but also as a thank you for everything."

Rachel pushed the small, beautifully wrapped box across the cafeteria table toward Lark, who wasted no time in ripping through the ribbon and paper.

"Oh, Rocky! This is beautiful. Is this my birthstone?" Lark opened the tiny jewel box and saw a vintage-looking ring, with a large gold gemstone, sitting upright in the folds of satin. "This is too much."

"Read the card."

Lark tore open the little envelope that came with the gift and read: *"The Yellow Topaz is an alternate gemstone for those born in November. A gift of this gemstone is said to symbolize friendship and to strengthen one's capacity to give and receive love."*

"You are trying to make me cry, right?" Lark slipped the ring on her right hand and let the tears slip down her face. It fit perfectly.

"I'd say you helped me 'strengthen my capacity,' overall." Rachel tried to be serious.

Not having any of it, Lark shot back, "No, I was just trying to make sure you got laid."

Rachel's laughter echoed throughout the nearly empty cafeteria. Lark had made a job of making the quirky girl laugh since the day they met. She realized in a flash how much she loved the sound of it and had missed it in these past few months while they were both too busy growing up.

CHAPTER FORTY-FOUR

He woke up on the floor, and only because the pounding at the front door finally roused him. It took him ten seconds or so to remember why all the cabinets in the kitchen gaped open and broken dishes covered every surface. Another ten seconds passed, as he stumbled over more broken things, trying to get to the door, trying to figure out what day it was. His impossibly dry mouth, the alcohol stink that drifted up from his own sweat, the dried blood around his nose, and his pounding head brought back flashes of how he'd spent the past week or so. He knew he'd blown through many liquor store deliveries, along with a small mountain of coke, and God knows how many joints. A dozen cuts sprayed across palms, long crusted-over with clotted blood. He remembered the broken glass had flown in every direction when rage was all he could feel. Multiple dents in the wall, one near the front door, explained the bruised, scraped, and swollen knuckles on his right hand. He pictured Lark's face as she had walked out the door, discarding him like he was yesterday's trash. *I am not having this baby.* She wanted to discard that, too.

"I know you're in there, man. Open the fuck up!" The pounding, now alternating with the buzzing of the doorbell, punctuated Pee Cee's voice.

"What the fuck do you want, cousin? Stop all that shit. My head hurts." Jamal leaned on the door for support as he opened it.

"What the hell happened in here? Where you been man?" Pee Cee followed him through the apartment to the bathroom, where Jamal bent over the sink splashing water on his face, over his neck, washing the blood from his hands. There was dried vomit in the sink, on the floor.

"Nothing. Nothing happened."

"Uh huh, and you all fucked up and bleeding, and there's broken shit and puke all over and nothing happened?"

"Pee Cee, what do you want? Or did you just come over here so you could ask me those stupid questions? If I want to break every fucking dish in my house and punch every wall, it's none of your business. Just be happy I don't break your head right now for waking me up."

"That's very funny, cousin, cause you know I can kick your ass on a good day, let alone when you are this fucked up, but I'll just pretend you didn't say that. And you are going to thank me when I tell you why I came. I had to tell you, man."

Jamal covered his head with a towel and rubbed his face hard with it as though it could somehow absorb the pain in his head and make his cousin disappear at the same time. Pee Cee had more than tried his patience since the riots. For a week after "the incident" with Lark's father, his cousin had paced the apartment, glued to the TV to watch the reports of the man's struggle to stay alive. He was terrified that they had been seen, that they would all soon be arrested and charged with the Chasid's death. When the man didn't die and it was clear that there was no real evidence linking anyone in particular to the crime, he became cocky. He ranted on about how they had "taught those Jew-muthafuckas a lesson they won't forget," and how if he knew that it was Bird's Daddy he might have even stabbed him himself and finished the job.

"Go away, cousin," Jamal said from under the towel. "Just. Go. Away." He sat down on the toilet and draped himself over the edge of the sink. He felt like he was going to throw up. When was the last time he'd eaten something? He couldn't remember.

"Fine, you want me to leave? I'll leave. I thought you would be interested in knowing who cut your Mama's throat, but never mind, I'll just go. He can just go on about his business, killing women and children, since you don't want to do anything about it."

Jamal sat up and slowly pulled the towel off his head. "Keep talking."

"Oh, you're ready to listen to me now?"

"I said, keep talking." Jamal cradled his head in his hands and stared at the filthy squares of tile on the bathroom floor.

Pee Cee told him about the "word" he put out on the streets that any information leading to the dealer who killed his aunt would be worth good money to him.

"I got a lot of bullshit, but then I got some real leads, too, which I tracked down without you. I wanted to be sure when I told you that I had the right one. This one is the right one."

"How do you know?"

"The motherfucker brags on it. He's braggin' that if anybody tries to fuck with him, they gonna end up like 'the Crown Heights Mama and her baby boy, crying and begging me not to kill them.' I heard him with my own ears and wanted to take him out right then, but I knew you would want to do it yourself."

"I need coffee." Jamal pushed past Pee Cee and headed to the front door.

"I tell you I found the man who sliced up your Mama and strangled your little brother and all you can say is 'I need coffee'? What's the matter with you, cousin?"

Jamal left the dark basement apartment, leaving the door wide open, and headed down the alley toward the sunlit street. He squinted against the light and the pounding in his head. Pee Cee trailed behind, closing up the apartment, catching up to him at the entrance to the little family-owned bodega around the corner. The place smelled of fried plantains and burnt coffee. An impossibly small and old woman sat behind the counter, boxed in by the cash register, a wall of cigarettes, hanging bags of chips, and a little TV tuned into some game show.

Jamal moved to the back of the narrow store and helped himself to a coffee.

"Cousin, did you hear me? Did you hear what I said to you?"

"You want a coffee?"

"No, I don't want a coffee. What is wrong with you? Did you melt your brain with all that shit you been doing?"

Jamal took his time putting sugar and cream in his coffee. He wanted it light and sweet. He stirred it slowly, hands shaking, and found the right-sized lid for the cup. He pulled a napkin out of the chrome dispenser and wiped up what he had spilled on the counter. Pulling the little flap on the lid up, he folded it back and took a cautious sip of the hot liquid. He wanted to focus on nothing but how good the coffee felt going down his throat, not on what his cousin was saying. He wanted to put him off just a little longer. Even in his current binged-out state, with his stomach churning and head reeling, he understood that the next decision he made could alter his life forever.

The heat from the cup burned the little cuts on his hand, but felt good against the inside of his swollen knuckles. He took another sip, then let himself remember. The sick feeling in his gut deepened as he thought of Lark throwing back her "college boy" remark at him as she left the apartment. It occurred to him that he didn't believe her. The baby was his, he knew, but it didn't matter. He understood that it was over between them. She didn't belong to him and she was right to see that he had nothing to offer her. Why should she want to make a life with him? It didn't make him angry now to think of it. It was just the way it was.

He walked toward the front of the store to pay for his coffee, where Pee Cee stood stationed, waiting for him, temporarily absorbed in the final "$25,000 Jackpot Round" playing out on the old lady's TV.

"I'll take two of those," pointing to a hanging display of individual packs of aspirin, "and the coffee." He pulled some crumpled bills from his jeans and laid them out on the counter. The woman absently took the bills, her eyes fixed on the small flickering screen.

"Stay-tuned for breaking Eye Witness News at noon. A five-alarm fire in Queens leaves seven dead, including three children. Police suspect arson. The Crown Heights man who was brutally stabbed the night the riots there began loses his fight for life. There are still no suspects in the case. Last night's Pick 6 numbers..."

Without looking at each other, Jamal and Pee Cee turned and walked out of the door of the store to the sunny street. They walked quickly back down the alley toward the apartment and out of earshot of anyone before they spoke.

"Shit, man. He's dead." Pee Cee dug his hands deep into his coat pockets.

"Yeah. Shit." Jamal took a long sip of his coffee.

Punching the air, Pee Cee jumped in front of Jamal, blocking his way. For all his cousin's post-riot bravado, the man's death agitated him. "None of this would have happened if it wasn't for that muthafucka that iced your mother. That whole night would have never happened! We need to get that mother and make him pay." He slammed his fist into his palm. "Are you with me? Are you with me, Rain Man?"

"Don't call me that."

"Why not?"

Jamal shrugged his shoulders. "It's just a coat. It doesn't mean any-thing."

"Oh, so it don't mean nothin? So who are you now? Pain Man? Bird Man? What? Who are you?"

Jamal looked at his cousin chomping at the bit to do more damage even though they'd just found out that their actions on that night months ago had contributed to a man's death. He thought of Lark who just lost her daddy, whose heart would be broken by the loss, like his was over losing his mother, though neither parent had been perfect.

"Someone else, man. I'm gonna be someone else."

Jamal let himself in the apartment, turned and locked the door against his ranting cousin. He looked around the trashed apartment and wondered where he should begin picking up the pieces.

CHAPTER FORTY-FIVE

Sarah Shulman sat on the low stool and balanced a plate of food on her knees, brought to her by one of the many neighbors who had passed through the apartment during the week of shiva.

Even after the days of waiting for the body to be released from the coroner's office, and the funeral, which had been in New Jersey near Abby's parents' house, and the days of mourning, sitting in their apartment in Crown Heights, she still had the occasional panicked thought that she had to get back to the hospital to sit with her husband.

Then she would remember.

The attending physician had asked her to follow him down to the end of the ICU hallway. There was a small conference room where she'd seen doctors presiding over groups of interns, or nurses sitting and eating reheated food from home. She'd mostly talked to the interns assigned to the case over the past nine weeks, only occasionally getting the trauma department head to confer with her. The fact that he'd sought her out that day did not bode well. She'd been a nurse long enough to know she was about to get bad news or be asked to make a hard decision.

She was right. There was, he told her in practiced tones, extensive damage from the heart attack, more than they had expected at first. The infection that had stubbornly settled in his lungs was not responding to the antibiotics in a way they were accustomed to seeing. The fluid in the lungs and surrounding cavity, though they were suctioning it hourly, was putting even more strain on the heart to get oxygen to the bloodstream. From the numbers they'd gotten back on the last round of blood and urine tests, it looked like his kidneys were failing, a sign that his body was shutting down.

Sarah stared at the doctor as he spoke. He was good. He met her eyes and had an appropriately solemn cast to his face. She wanted to make it easier for him, to say that she understood what he was trying to tell her, that she knew what came next, but she found she needed him to say it.

"We are going to start dialysis this afternoon. There comes a point in some cases where we have to ask…"

"Yes, I know."

"…about the DNR." Do Not Resuscitate. If there were a DNR order on the file, if his heart stopped again, they wouldn't make a move to revive him. No "Code Blue" blaring over the PA, no crash cart flying down the hall, no big paddles juicing him back into this world—a world of tubes and drips and monitors and endless, dreamless sleep. And her endless waiting for him to come back to her would end.

Sarah knew that they didn't talk about the DNR unless it looked like the end of the road—a waste of time to keep bringing him back. She asked all the right questions. Would he survive another heart attack, even if revived? What would his quality of life be if they did? Was there a chance that his kidneys would ever come back now?

"Well, there are always those miracle cases," the doctor allowed.

He wouldn't be the one to take away her hope, or get caught inferring that one decision was better than the other—looming litigation and the threat of rising malpractice insurance premiums had boxed him into a noncommittal corner years ago. He wouldn't, like some TV doctor, put an arm around her crushed shoulders and help her cross the line.

"It's your call. Your husband left it up to you, according to the living will."

They would have never even had a will, let alone a living will, if Sarah's father hadn't insisted on one. One time, when Lark and David were young, she and Abby planned to leave the kids with her parents for two weeks in order to do one of their guru retreats out west. Her Dad, a CPA, "The Nutley Numbers Man" was his local newspaper column moniker, wasn't too sentimental to talk about death and "arrangements" and liked things to neatly add up. Sarah remembered him lecturing: "If anything happens, it just makes things easier if you put it down in writing what you want. I'm not going to end up in court with the in-laws over it."

He'd seen too many ugly battles with clients, and Abby's parents could be difficult. She and Abby went to see a lawyer and The Numbers Man picked up the bill. Since then, it was in writing who would be the guardian for the kids if she and Abby blew up in a plane on the way to enlightenment in the desert; who would handle their "estate," which was never much beyond life-insurance policies her parents also made them keep up; and who would be in charge of medical decisions should it come down to "it." Abby went along, even though he thought the whole thing was too morose. According to her husband, they were young and in charge of their destiny— "it" was not going to happen to them.

So much in her life, in her marriage, Sarah had been guided by someone else's hand. Her parents', her husband's, and the tight little grips of her children's hands on her heart. It seemed incredible to her that she was being forced to make this decision now, alone. "It's your call," the doctor said.

"I need to think about it," she told him.

"Of course. The forms are in his file, if you decide."

After that, Sarah went back to sit with her husband again. She busied herself the way she always did. Pressing "play" on the dusty boom box she'd brought from home weeks before, strains of Mozart filled up the small space, smoothing over the beeps and whirs of the monitors and pumps jammed in around the bed. David had given her the tape, saying the music could stimulate the brain, so she played it, even though Abby had never been a fan of classical. He'd preferred face-melting guitar licks or, in recent years, the manic rhythms of Klezmer music or talk radio. She ran hot water into a basin and dropped some scented oil in it. Soaking and wringing out a well-worn washcloth, Sarah wrapped part of it around her fingers, then ran it over his crusty eyes and mouth, over his forehead and around his sweaty neck, gently avoiding the area where they'd done the tracheotomy. Combing his hair, she saw how long it had gotten and it reminded her again of his world-changing hippie days.

Abby, Abby where are you? How could this have happened? Where is your God now?

The ache in her chest, building since she talked to the doctor, spread now, until it found its way out on a wave of air-sucking sobs. Still, she kept up the pumping of the body lotion into her palm and the daily massage she gave his bloated legs and feet, hoping he could feel her touch, could feel how much she wanted to revive him, to reach back ten years and retrieve him.

"I'm sorry. Um, I can come back." The technician in the doorway startled her. Sarah grabbed some tissues and tried to clean up her face.

"No, no. It's okay."

The tech had come to insert the additional shunt he needed for the dialysis machine, which now sat on a cart outside the room.

"I'll be out in a minute."

"Sure, no rush."

Sarah pulled a chair close to the bed. She released the side rail and eased it down, careful not to pull out or pinch off any of the tubes. She squirreled one hand under his, and put the other gently over the top. It was so cold—unrecognizable—blown up as it was by all the fluid, black and blue with punctures from moving the IV shunt around, searching for viable veins after others had collapsed. Leaning over, she tried to press her cheek to his hand and kissed his fingertips. "Oh, Abby. I love you," she whispered, then said it again, louder, more insistent. "I love you, Abby."

Sarah searched Abby's face for the slightest sign that he could hear, held her breath for a hint of a twitch in his fingers that she could assign meaning to, but got none.

At the nurses' station on the way out, she borrowed a pen and asked for Abby's file. She signed the DNR, and then went home to sleep. She was so terribly tired.

A few hours later he died, as though he had been waiting for that DNR all along. Perhaps he'd been terribly tired too. When the phone had jarred her from the first really heavy sleep she'd had in weeks, she knew what it was. It was over.

Sarah was grateful she'd encouraged Lark to take a break that day and sleep late instead of taking her "shift." She wouldn't have wanted her daughter to be there while her father's heart quietly stopped and no one moved to do anything about it. She was glad she hadn't been there either. She'd said goodbye to him and didn't think she could stand to watch him just slip away. Hadn't she seen enough of him die?

"Mom, you should eat something." Lark's voice snapped her back from what would have come next in her revisit of the whole thing—the *What if? What if I'd never signed the DNR? Would he still be alive? And if he were alive, would he ever wake up again? And if he woke up, would he be whole and healthy and happy and kind and love her like he once did?*

"I'm eating, look." She took a bite of the cold noodle kugel on her plate and chewed it slowly, without appetite.

It was time for the late evening prayer that concluded the day and the required week of sitting shiva. The ten men needed to complete a minion had assembled, including David, who'd been like a rock, never leaving her side since he heard the news and grabbed a cab over from the city. Now that he was back in her life, she wondered how she could have done without him all those years.

The community had been quite responsive with hundreds of well-wishers, bearers of baking dishes overflowing with food, and the simply curious passing through the apartment over the past week. At times—the apartment alive with conversation, women, young and old, pressing her hand, washing the dishes, the men arriving promptly to pray—Sarah felt more a part of Crown Heights than ever. Lark's friend Rachel had come and visited for hours each day. She could almost see herself staying, making a home here, allowing herself to be folded into the deep creases of family and faith that existed in the Heights. But it was too late. She'd been kept too long on the edges, held at arm's length. Now, Abby would be a part of this community in a way that was beyond his most ardent prayers—a martyr, a symbol, a catalyst, a beloved son.

When the prayers were over and the last of the neighbors left, Sarah walked slowly down the hallway to her bedroom, dragging her hand against the wall as if to steady herself, keeping her eyes from looking at the family pictures that hung there. *Not now. I can't look back right now.* There was something else she needed to see.

She heard Lark and David talking quietly in the kitchen as they cleaned up and put away the food that would last them for a week. Pushing the door open to the bedroom, she flicked on the overhead light. She walked directly to the dresser. The mirror that hung above it was draped with one of her good tablecloths, completely covered like all the other mirrors in the house, as the laws of shiva demanded. The cloth slid down when she pulled it, and the mirror showed her standing there. She met her own eyes for the first time in a week. *I'm old*, she thought, looking at the web of lines around them, fanning out toward her hairline. *I'm alone*, watching her frown deepen with the grooves that ran from her nose down the side of her mouth to her chin. Then the direction of her mouth changed, imperceptibly so, as she thought, *I am free.*

CHAPTER FORTY-SIX

The six of them stood around the faux-wood folding table that functioned as a coffee station for the meetings. There were Styrofoam cups stacked up, a box of sugar packets, one of Sweet & Low, and some wooden stirrers. A big chrome urn percolated loudly, chugging out coffee-infused steam, helping to mask the musty church-basement smell of the room. It was the last night of Chanukah and Barry brought down the cheap tin menorah he was using in his room and a box of multicolored candles. Gathered for the weekly religious/gay/lesbian support group that Barry was running, they stood near the table, coffees in hand, while Barry lit the head candle, the *shamas*, then passed it around for each of them to light one of the other eight. The group wasn't always the same six. Sometimes it was eight, sometimes four or ten—people came and went as their schedules and psyches allowed.

This was Daniel's second time—he'd finally given in to Barry's nudging to attend. Two months has passed since the "Yossi incident," which was the last time he'd seen Yakov other than from afar in shul or other public events. During that time, Daniel saw a great deal of Barry. The day after, Daniel had been frantic to talk about what had happened. Had he just ended it with Yakov? Did he really stand up to and threaten to "out" the menacing Yossi? He wasn't going to wait to run into Barry this

437

time. Daniel got to work early the next morning and called. They met at Barry's apartment for lunch.

"You just stood there, buck naked and offered him a scotch? Oh, if I could have only been a fly on the wall."

"If you were, you would have seen me shaking. I can't even believe I did it." In the recounting of it, and with Barry's apparent delight at the whole thing, Daniel began to feel as though he'd done something important and powerful for himself.

"And Yakov didn't come out of the bathroom and drool over you after that? Honey, it's making me crazy just thinking about it. Very John Wayne." Barry showed Daniel during that lunch hour just how "crazy" his standoff with Yossi made him feel, and for the next two months they met as often as they could for "lunch."

But they met for dinner sometimes, too, and these evenings were among the most eye opening for Daniel. He told Gavrielle he was studying with Yakov, when in truth those sessions never resumed after "the incident." On these nights, Barry took Daniel deeper into his world and farther out into the world in general. One night it was the ballet, where Daniel sat, stunned by the beauty and athleticism of the dancers, male and female, and swept away by the orchestral music. Another night it was a drag show, where the audience watched Daniel as much as the "girls" onstage, to gauge the Chasidic man's reaction to the racy show. Then there was the first of many dinner parties that Barry dragged Daniel to at a friend's downtown loft. Daniel didn't want to go.

"I'll stand out like a sore thumb."

"Nonsense. This isn't some backwoods where they might ask to see your horns. It's SoHo. You'll be a bit of a novelty, but everyone will love you and feel your pain, just like I do."

He was right. Barry's friends were, for the most part, welcoming, curious, and intelligent, drawing him into conversations, genuinely interested in his world and his struggle. There were other dinner parties after that, and they provided many firsts for Daniel. There was the first time he actually sat and talked with a woman who was not a relative or his wife; the first time Daniel exchanged more than a few perfunctory sentences with a Gentile man and a black man; and he didn't get struck down by lightning the way he'd imagined he would with his first taste of a bacon-cheeseburger.

At first, Barry trod lightly around the subject of Yakov or his situation at home. Daniel seemed content to have his focus diverted by all the shiny distractions Barry had to offer, and Barry was more than happy to be in denial for a while himself. Coming "out" had cost him a lot. His family had declared him dead. Even if he got the occasional letter from his sister, it was always in the "come to your senses" vein. The gay world in New York could provide unlimited opportunities for sex, but that didn't make a dent in his loneliness and longing for a partner in life. Baruch was raised to believe that there was a beshert out there for him, a soul mate. Just because Barry knew now that his partner wouldn't be a woman, it didn't mean he was giving up on that belief. Then there was the fact that he was falling in love with Daniel. Their stolen lunches and nights out, with Daniel having to go home to Crown Heights before the clock struck midnight, made him feel like he was the main character in a terribly romantic old movie.

But, between the two of them, Barry knew he had to be the voice of reason. He hadn't gone through the last ten years of soul-searching and found the courage to do what he did just to become someone's "mistress." That's when he started pushing Daniel to come to the support groups. In the group, Daniel could safely say out loud what he wasn't saying when he was alone with Barry, and Barry could start to figure out where he stood in the whole picture.

In tonight's group there were the two women Daniel had seen the last time. They were still religious, from Williamsburg. They left the community—one left a husband so they could be together. They brought a big Tupperware of latkes and another smaller one of applesauce. A modern orthodox rabbi from Riverdale, who was not "out" and still lived with a wife and high-school-age children, brought a bag of jelly donuts from the kosher-certified Dunkin' Donuts nearby. There was a Sephardic-looking guy in his late twenties with a middle-eastern accent, who wore a small knit yarmulke, tight leather pants, and carried a motorcycle helmet. He smoked one cigarette after another. Barry and Daniel made it six.

They finished with candles, refilled their coffees, and took their seats in the circle of beige metal folding chairs.

"Well," Barry began, "welcome, everybody. It's the Festival of Lights, and while Chanukah can never compete with Christmas for kitsch value, it's got its own magic. To me it's the idea that miracles do happen, whether it's a teaspoon of oil that ends up lasting eight days or six numbers that end up as the winning combo for the lotto—anything is possible. No matter how impossible happiness looks to some of us in this room, I thought we'd keep the idea of Chanukah and miracles as a theme for tonight's dialogue. And I don't have to remind you, but I'll say it anyway, this is a designated 'safe' space, so please respect the confidentiality of the participants and keep it a safe and welcoming environment for all of us."

Barry's enthusiasm was not quite catching on. The rabbi had his arms crossed tightly against his chest. The leather guy fidgeted with his helmet strap. Daniel sat with his eyes closed and his brow furrowed. One of the women impatiently waved her arm. Barry read her name from the peel-off nametag. "Dassie?"

"Well, for me, a miracle would be if my parents would let me come for Shabbes with Malkie, and they would accept us as a couple. We're happy. We love each other. Show me the halachah that says two women can't be together. We are still frum, we follow all the mitzvot to a tee. We can even provide grandchildren!"

Malkie put her arm around Dassie and told the group, "For me, a miracle would be if Dassie would stop expecting that miracle. Enough already, you might as well be waiting for Moshiach!"

"Well, I am waiting for Moshiach, too."

"Yes, you wait for Moshiach, but you live your life."

"I live my life. I'm with you, aren't I?"

"Yes, but you call your parents every Friday, expecting something different, expecting your father to pick up the phone, expecting them to let you come near your brothers or sisters again. You send packages of homemade cookies, expecting them to not come back unopened and I'm the one that has to deal with you going through the disappointment every time."

"That's an interesting point that Malkie makes," Barry stepped in before the whole meeting became about their relationship—again. "I know we are talking about miracles here, but there may be a point when expecting a miracle goes beyond a healthy optimism and gets into self-flagellation."

"Exactly!" The rabbi piped in. "This is why I can't do it. I can't face leaving what I have. So you go to all the trouble of leaving..." he unfolded his arms and directed both his hands toward the women, as though they were "Exhibit A" in his line of defense, "...and you are still suffering. It all haunts you—what you left behind. Sure, you have what you have— the freedom sexually, a relationship—maybe—with someone you really desire, but it's tainted because you have to sacrifice so much to have it."

"Well, I like to use the word 'trade-off' more than sacrifice." Barry got up and walked around the outside of the circle to a white board set up on an easel. "There is a definite trade-off in any decision you make." He picked up a marker and began writing on the board. "The word 'decide' breaks down to the Latin *cide*, which means to kill—like homocide, genocide—so, to decide something, whether it's who to marry or what to order off a menu, is to sort of divide the options. You kill off some and keep others. Think about it. Every decision you make is a mini fork-in-the-road. I'm taking this road and so I am giving up the scenery and the experiences on this other road."

"'Two roads diverged in a wood, and I—I took the one less traveled by. And that has made all the difference.'" They were surprised to hear anything from Ben, who had momentarily stopped playing with his helmet straps, let alone a broken-English recitation of poetry. "I like poetry. In a few words you get the picture, yes?"

"Thank you, Ben. That was from Frost, right? Look that one up, people. It's a good one to stick on the fridge. *The Road Not Taken*, I believe it's called."

Dassie was near tears. "So you start by saying, 'What's your miracle?' but then you're saying, 'There's no miracles, just these decisions and all these possibilities that get killed off.'"

"Look, Dassie, don't try to put what I am saying into some new version of the Talmud that you can live and die by. Part of why we want to escape from that world is because of all the things that are set in stone, all the rules, all the possibilities that are cut off, so don't come out here and build another tiny box for you to live in. What Malkie is saying and what I'm saying is that you have to take some responsibility for the choice you made and be on the road you are on. Don't choose one road and always be looking over your shoulder at what you might be missing on the other road. That's just going to make you miserable."

"What if," Dassie cast a sidelong glance at Malkie and hesitated, "what if you are not sure you made the right decision."

"Oh, FUCK YOU!" Malkie jumped up from her chair, sending it toppling backwards. It snapped shut, clanging to the floor.

"I walked away from a marriage for you. I was set. You were 22 and still living at home, practically an old maid by Williamsburg standards, and all you can do is whine about missing your daddy. I'm sick of it. You better make up your mind or you are going to be back in Williamsburg driving yourself crazy missing me." She lifted her skirt, took a long step over the fallen chair, and exited the circle and the room, slamming the door behind her.

"Why don't we take a five-minute break and get some more coffee and donuts," Barry directed the group. "Then we'll come back and give everyone else a chance to talk." He walked out of the room to try to retrieve Malkie. It wasn't the first time he would have to coax one of them out of the ladies' room and back into the meeting. Daniel followed him out. He looked visibly shaken by the whole exchange.

Barry worried he may have gone too far in pushing Daniel to attend, exposing him to everything in his world too quickly. He had his own miracle story he was trying to manifest, despite his warning to the group to stay grounded in reality. In it, Daniel would be madly in love with him and leave Crown Heights behind. They'd live together, two boychicks from the hood who managed to get away and find their happily-ever-after. Right now, looking at Daniel's face, that happy ending seemed very distant.

"Not pretty, is it? I guess 'gay' isn't always so, well, gay." Barry couldn't believe his own bad joke.

"That's not it." Daniel shrugged his shoulders. "My parents fought a lot, too. My mother was always saying, 'I could have married Moishe so and so from Monsey, but noooo!...' that kind of thing. That's not what's bothering me."

"Oh." It was worse than he thought. If he wasn't upset about the fight, Barry had a feeling what Daniel was being tormented by.

"What then?"

"It's Yakov." *I knew it!* Barry's stomach tightened around the latkes that lay there like so much lead. *So much for my miracle.*

"Barry," Daniel put his big paw of a hand on Barry's shoulder. *Here comes the kiss off*, Barry thought, and almost cringed under Daniel's touch. "I realized sitting there that my miracle is not what I thought it was. I always thought I wanted to have everything. Slowly...because of you," Daniel tightened his grip on Barry's shoulder, and the knot in his stomach relaxed a hopeful notch, "...I'm realizing that the 'everything' I wanted before is not the everything I want now. No matter what, I can't think of going on the way I'm going, from one lie to the next. I have to have honesty. I can deal with the compromises and the tradeoffs, I think, but I can't face a life of lying to myself and everyone else. So…"

"So," Barry interrupted Daniel, shrugging his heavy hand off his shoulder. He wanted to throw a tantrum and join Malkie in the bathroom. "You have to be honest and admit to me that you still want Yakov."

Daniel struggled to answer. It wasn't that simple. True, he didn't feel about Barry the way he felt about Yakov, but that wasn't a bad thing, as far as he was concerned. What he had with Barry was real. Barry had begun to show Daniel that there was a way out, not a perfect road, not a road without its potholes, but a road. There was life on the other side—good people, incredible experiences, meaningful work. Like Dassie and her father, Daniel realized that for him there was still Yakov. Was it love or guilt that made Daniel feel he couldn't take this road without inviting his lifelong friend along? In his world the two emotions were so cut from the same cloth, it was hard to tell.

"Well," he finally answered when he saw how hard Barry was trying to be neutral. "It's like you said about taking one road and then not spending the whole time looking over your shoulder. I just have to be sure."

Barry felt like the second choice and it hurt. "So you run back into the burning building and try to save Yakov. And if you can't, then you think I'll be waiting on the curb to tend to your wounds and take you in?"

"Well, we'll know then, won't we?"

"Know what?"

"That I *dee-cided.*"

If he was going to be honest with himself, Barry had to admit he'd take Daniel back, wounds and all, in a heartbeat. Second choice was better than nothing, and the man had a point. Daniel needed to make sure he was done with Yakov, had done all he could, in order to move on. In truth, all Barry's efforts with Daniel over the past two months had led to this moment: Daniel was trying to make an honest man of himself.

"I guess I'll be waiting with the bandages, Teddy Bear. Just do me a favor, don't come back unless that building is burnt down to the ground."

CHAPTER FORTY-SEVEN

Everyone warned Rachel that she would know when the time came. There would be no mistaking the nausea every morning and fatigue every afternoon. Close friends and relatives, practically taking bets on when it would happen, regaled her with a list of inconveniences she would experience as a result of being pregnant. She could expect to hate the smell and taste of foods she now loved, or crave things she normally despised. There would be colorful dreams ripe with good omens, and bad dreams she could be assured meant nothing. Her mood would be jovial if carrying a boy, tend toward depression if it was a girl. And though her hair would be thicker than ever, if she didn't take her vitamins, her teeth would rot. Veins would explode on her legs, and her feet would swell if she didn't keep them elevated.

Rachel knew she was disappointing everyone by reporting no other symptom than a sense of wonder at the possibility that a baby could be growing inside her. She had no evidence she was pregnant, in fact, in place of nausea or fatigue, she felt a surge of new energy that had her volunteering at the pre-school to help out with the youngest children, scrubbing already clean surfaces around the apartment, and endlessly planning the décor for the spare bedroom, which they'd referred to as the nursery from the day they decided to make the apartment their home. She'd taken more of an interest in cooking and started dropping by the Rebbe's kitchen to learn how to make Yakov's favorite dishes. If not quite a mother-to-be yet, she seemed to be enjoying getting ready for the role in a way that surprised her, and her mother.

"You look happy, what's wrong?" Miriam Fine teased when Rachel came by the store to visit.

"Can't I be happy?" Rachel took the bait.

"Give me time. I'm still getting used to seeing you smile for no reason." Rachel let her mother *kvell* over her. She'd had a reputation for being a moody, too-serious child, so she understood her mother's relief at seeing her youngest and most difficult daughter finally content. Rachel was relieved too. During the last few months, she believed she'd never find happiness. But now she seemed to have located it, mined like precious gems out of the time spent with Yakov, reading separately or studying together, having a meal, listening to music, talking, and planning their future.

The door to intimacy had barely been opened between them, yet Rachel was in awe of the pleasure that could be found there. Yakov was still awkward and shy, almost reluctant, but she was certain that they had only begun to scratch the surface of what was available in the dark privacy of their pushed-together beds. She had no idea what was "normal," (how often it was normal to be "doing it", how long it should last, what she should be feeling, doing, experiencing) having no frame of reference as far as sex was concerned, but she had faith now that they would find their way, find their "normal."

Rachel hadn't seen much of Lark since her father's shiva. She knew her friend was busy arranging a new life, the life she'd dreamed out loud about for years: moving to the city, college, freedom from all the restrictions of religious life. In a few short weeks Lark would leave Crown Heights for good. She'd only be a subway ride away but Rachel was afraid that the distance between them would grow in more ways than mere geography could account for. Rachel missed her already.

"I'll even make a lunch if you come over," Rachel offered over the phone.

"Is that a threat?" Lark teased her.

"Ha ha, very funny. I am actually learning to cook these days. It's fun, when someone other than my mother is trying to teach me."

"OK, I'll come, but only if you get some of those rugelach sent up from the Rebbe's kitchen. Talk about a religious experience! Those are amazing."

She was just setting the table for lunch when a heavy knock on the front door surprised Rachel. Lark was usually late, not early, and there had been no buzzer from the street signaling to let her in. Even more surprising was the sight of Yossi in the hallway carrying a big box he could barely see over.

"Oh. Hello Yossi." Rachel did not like the awkward man stopping by when she was alone. He stood just a little too close. His breath was stunningly sour. His big body blocked the light and cast a shadow. Strictly speaking, women were supposed to avoid being alone in a room with any man other than their husbands. But they were family now, and Yossi did so much of the maintenance around the big house. It was unavoidable. Just the same, she left the front door wide open when he came in.

"I thought I'd bring these to you." As he clumped toward her, Rachel wondered how this lumbering man could be related to her graceful Yakov. He was out of breath and struggling to recover from the stairs. "I've been cleaning out the attic study, the one Yakov used. The Rebbe needed some extra storage space." He dropped the box with a thud on the floor near the table, which made the plates and flatware laid out for lunch jump and a wine class tip over. Rachel caught it before it could break. Flipping open the folded-over flaps of the box, Yossi pulled a bulging, black leather portfolio out of the box and started unzipping it. "I know you're a big fan of Yakov's artwork, so I wanted to show you these."

"Well, that's nice of you, but I was just getting ready to..."

Yossi barreled on. "I'm sure Yakov would want to save these. I know they're very important to him. This box is full of them, but these are the best."

"Well, maybe we should wait until he comes home. They *are* his. I should make sure it's something he wants to show..."

Despite her hints to postpone, Yakov's uncle continued to zip open the portfolio, then laid it atop the place settings she just finished arranging, as if they weren't there.

"Why wouldn't he want you to see them? Do you think a new husband should have anything to hide from his bride? Come, look."

Rachel had been keeping her distance, but now she approached the table. He opened the big book of sketches with a flourish and flipped the pages for her as she looked at one exquisite, nearly photographic rendering of the naked male figure after another.

"Why are you showing me these?" Rachel felt uneasy, embarrassed. She walked around the table to the opposite side, feeling better with the solid piece of furniture between her and Yossi. She took a sudden interest in trimming dead leaves from a plant near the window.

"Aren't you interested in the truth about your husband, the brilliant grandson?" The big man shifted his considerable weight from foot to foot as he spoke, as if the floor beneath him were made of hot coals, jabbing his pointed finger at the air around him. "What was he doing for hours up in his hole in the ceiling? Studying? Davening? Meditating? No. He was doing this. Imagining his gallery of boyfriends."

"What are you talking about?" She was genuinely confused.

"Come on Rachel. You can't be that naïve, hanging around with that bali teshuva girl all these years. I'm sure she taught you a few things about the world. You never heard of a man who loves men instead of women—a gay, a faegella?" His mouth twisted into a challenging smirk. He turned the portfolio to face her and flipped through a few more images. "This is your husband's big passion. Not Torah, not Talmud. Certainly not you! What do you think?"

What he was saying was completely foreign to Rachel. Such people were not a part of her experience, her world. She didn't know any "gay" people, had never even met one as far as she knew. She'd first understood what it really meant when a rumor went through her school last year about someone's cousin who had moved to Atlanta and was living with another man there, "like husband and wife." Lark had to explain to her what they 'do' together and had delighted in shocking her incredulous friend with her limited knowledge of gay sexual practices. Was Yossi saying that her husband was one of these men?

Her instinct was to protect Yakov from his uncle, as she had the first night they met. "So what? He's an artist. He studies people, the human figure. It doesn't mean what you say," she countered, remembering their early dates, when Yakov had been her enthusiastic guide through the grand museums of Manhattan.

"What about these?" Yossi tore at the pages, stopping when he found what he was looking for. Most of the figures were headless, fading at the shoulder line, or sweeping down a back to strong legs, but Yossi made sure that Rachel did not miss those that bore the unmistakable face of Yakov's boyhood friend, Daniel. In her own portrait, she'd thought she'd seen Yakov's love for her reflected in the cast of her eyes. In these drawings, in Daniel's eyes she saw something she recognized too: desire.

Rachel couldn't help rewinding the past few months and playing them back through this new unthinkable filter: Yakov's spontaneous "proposal" at his friend's wedding, the months of waiting for her new husband to touch her, to want her; his many nights out with Daniel, nights that she, playing the magnanimous wife, encouraged him to spend; his respectful, yet mostly platonic handling of her that she had made into a patchwork version of domestic bliss. The truth of it descended on her like a sudden squall, stranding her in a downpour of emotions.

"Wake up little girl. I've seen them together. Here in this apartment, I caught them, like this." He pointed an accusing finger at the naked figures.

"When?" Rachel demanded weakly, already feeling defeated.

"Not too long ago, but I assure you it was only one of many meetings. You were out with your friend, shopping or something in the city. You asked me to change light bulbs for you, remember? I let myself in and Daniel was parading around here with no clothes on and your husband was in the bedroom. There was no studying going on."

Rachel knew exactly what night it was because of what she had really been doing with Lark in the city. And she knew that just two days later she and Yakov finally had their Shabbes together and began their marriage in earnest. It was about the time that Yakov said he wouldn't be studying with Daniel anymore. The evidence was stacking up neatly, blocking every turn away from the truth she tried to take. She felt nausea rising in her throat, but instead of a sign a life growing within her, it felt like something was dying.

"You deserve better, little girl. You should leave him now, before children get involved in this mess! You still have a chance to have a real man, a decent life! Why should he have everything he wants? No one else does." Yossi raised his voice to a near-hysterical pitch and brought his fist down on the polished dining table like a judge's gavel punctuating some irrevocable verdict.

"Hey Rock, I think your buzzer is broken." Lark stood in the doorway. "And that door down on the street is not latching right. Maybe someone should go and have a look. It's not safe. Any crazy man could wander in and bother the First Lady here." She threw a withering look at Yossi that told him his presence in the room had already proven her point.

Rachel could not have felt more delivered from evil if the Messiah himself had just appeared at her door.

Yossi backed away from Rachel and the table, muttering something in Yiddish. Lark stood with her hand on the front door ready to slam it behind him as he rushed out.

Rachel began to gather the scattered sketches and stuff them back into the portfolio.

"What's going on here, Rocky? I could hear him yelling from two flights down." Lark moved quickly through the room, reached across the table and grabbed Rachel's hands to interrupt her frenzied attempt at hiding the drawings. "Talk to me. Will you stop?"

Rachel dropped the sketches and gripped the chair in front of her for support. She waited for tears to come, but they did not. Too many had been shed already as she waited for Yakov to love her the way she loved him, waited for God to intervene and deliver her happy-ever-after. According to Yossi, the long-awaited shift that had taken place between her and Yakov had less to do with his devotion to her than it did to the fear generated by his getting caught that night with Daniel. Was their coming together just a part of some plan he was finally forced to follow, a resigning to a second choice in a realm of no choices?

What are my choices? Rachel tried to think if she had any.

Lark looked at the drawings, one by one, stopping longer at the likenesses of Daniel. They were beautiful and intimate. Too intimate.

"Alright, start from the beginning. What did that ape want?"

Rachel was sick of choosing her words carefully; measuring her sentences against what she knew everyone wanted to hear. Rachel waited too long to unburden herself to Lark the first time around. She wasn't going to make that mistake again.

"He says he's seen them together. Caught them together. Like this." She pushed the most startling of the nudes toward Lark

"Holy shit," Lark said, under her breath.

"Do you think it could be true, what he's saying about Yakov?" Rachel asked, hoping Lark would debunk this piece of news for her as she had done with so many Saturday morning sermons.

"Wow. Yakov and Daniel." Lark tested the idea of it out loud. "I don't know. I mean, he could be making the whole thing up. Isn't he like the evil step-uncle or something—always jealous of Yakov? This could be his way of slipping him the poison apple. Who else knows about this?"

"About what? The drawings, or his meetings with Daniel or the fact that my husband fantasizes about men?"

"Any of it."

"I don't know. No one, I think." An image of the Rebbe came to mind; a conversation about biblical matriarchs and patience and doing what's best for the Jewish people suddenly took on new meaning that took her breath away. She pulled a chair out from under the table and sank into it, her face gray and damp.

"Are you OK? You need some water. No, maybe you need a drink." Lark went to the hutch and poured Rachel a half tumbler full of vodka and rushed to the kitchen for ice. From there she shouted in to Rachel.

"Let's just calm down and think about this, OK? In any court of law, Yossi's story would be just hearsay—his word against anybody else's. Does he have any evidence? Photos, videos, hair samples, blood..."

"I don't know! It's not a crime scene, Lark. This is what he showed me and it's bad enough. Look at them!" Lark came in from the kitchen and looked again at the drawings spread out on the table.

"I see your point. These guys are practically panting."

Rachel took the glass that Lark plunked in front of her and nearly drained it. The liquid went down cold, but it was heat that rose up her throat and spread to her face. Color returned to her cheeks.

"But still, you can't jump to conclusions. You have to stick to the facts," Lark insisted, but didn't sound like she was convinced.

"Facts? What facts? I don't know what's true anymore. What do you think? Do you think it could be true?"

Lark took too long to answer and Rachel finished what was left of the vodka.

"I don't know, Rock. It's like someone flipping the light switch on and you can suddenly see what's in the room. I mean a few weeks ago I told you that anyone who wouldn't want to jump your bones would have to be gay. I was kidding, but it could explain a lot. What do *you* think? You've been living with him."

"How am I supposed to know? What do I know about men, gay or otherwise? I thought everything was perfect. We've been, you know...together." Even as she said it she saw the past few weeks in a new light. It was always her coming to him, reaching for him. There were times when he begged off for the same reasons he'd used before: too tired, too stressed, his stomach. He would hold her instead, and it was sweet, but now she saw that perhaps he was just holding her at a distance. When her period came he'd seemed genuinely disappointed that she wasn't yet pregnant, but she noticed that during those two weeks she was untouchable, his fatigue and digestive problems seemed to disappear.

"You need to find out if it's true. You are going to have to ask him. I know you're crazy about the guy, but trust me, you don't want to be married to someone who is fooling around on you, let alone fooling around with guys. It's dangerous and that big gorilla was right about one thing, you deserve better. You have to know now, before he gets you sick or pregnant."

Rachel's tears started then. Having a baby was going to be the big prize, something she'd been praying for and leaving notes to dead rebbes over. *This is how my prayers are being answered?*

Rachel bit her lips against the rising sob in her throat. Lark came around the table and gave Rachel a hug, then handed her one of the monogrammed cloth napkins that had been buried under the portfolio.

"Here, blow your nose on this. What do you care? You don't do laundry around here."

Rachel smiled weakly. "What am I going to do without you? You can't move away. I need you around here."

"If it turns out he's gay, I'm taking you with me when we move to Manhattan. That's final. We'll be like Charlie's Angels. You, me, my mother. Only there will no Charlie telling us what to do."

"What are you talking about? What angels?"

"Forget it, it's a TV show. Three gorgeous women fighting crime in bad 80's pantsuits, but never mind. I just mean, that you always have somewhere to go if you need to get away from here."

Rachel tried to picture it, another scenario for her escape from Crown Heights. She'd entertained so many of them in countless conversations with Lark. But what used to exist in her imagination as an enviable adventure, now sounded like a cold and lonely passage across an uncharted sea. Not only would she have to leave everything familiar behind—her parents, the community, and her well-worn paths in her neighborhood—but she'd have to let go of all that she'd imagined would be hers with Yakov too.

"Can't someone just decide not to be, you know, gay?" Rachel asked, hoping against hope.

"I don't know much about it, Rock, but I don't think it works that way. I think it's like the whole thing about being born Jewish. Doesn't it say in the Talmud or somewhere that all the souls gathered around Mount Sinai and a bunch decided to be Jews for all eternity, others opted out? Maybe being gay is like that...decided before you are even born."

"How can you compare the two things? Maybe it's not like that at all. Maybe it's just bad habit, something you think you need, but then you can do without. An addiction, like gambling or smoking."

"Oh sure, and you can just go to the drug store and buy "Gay Gum" or something like that for the cravings. I don't think so! Anyway, I'm not sure the gay people of the world would think of themselves as suffering from a bad habit, or like they had a disease that needed a cure."

"But the Torah says it's wrong. Maybe that's enough of a reason for Yakov to change if it turned out that he was..." Rachel knew this argument would not fly with Lark, but it was more than plausible in her world. Everyone she knew routinely denied themselves tons of things that the rest of the world partook of freely—food, clothing, and entertainment, even sex. Why should this be different?

"Please, don't get me started. That's why you're in this mess to begin with. If Crown Heights weren't in this time warp in the middle of the 21st century, a guy like Yakov—I'm not saying it's true—but if he was gay he could just go about his business and play house with his buddy Daniel without a second thought. Instead, they have to pretend they are something else, get married, have kids, and ruin the lives of two innocent women, not to mention the children that come along."

"Lark, I'm not trying to solve everything that's wrong with the Chasidic world right now, OK? I'll leave that up to you. I need to know what *I* should do, right now, to figure this out so that *I* can be happy."

Rachel thought about her parents, her sisters, the sea of wig-framed faces in the women's section at shul. Who would believe her if she declared that their precious Yakov was flawed, that he was an abomination? Who among them would stand by her if she walked away from being Yakov's wife and all that it meant?

Lark took a second look at the drawings and spoke slowly, without her usual ironic tone.

"Look, I'm the last person you'd want as a marriage counselor. I spent years thinking my mom would be so much better off without my dad. I used to pray they'd get divorced or that something would happen..." she shook off a chill that rose up her back. "Now I wonder if I ever really knew him or understood their relationship. I used to think that it was her biggest weakness—that she could put up with all his stuff and still love him. But I don't know what it's like to love someone like that. Maybe you do. Maybe I don't ever want to know."

Lark had given Rachel what she needed to hear, even if it came as an honest confession that she had no answers for her. She was saying that only Rachel could decide, only she could know if her marriage was worth saving, if her husband was worth loving.

Rachel moved the sketches around the table and held one up.

"They are beautiful in a way. Don't you think?"

"No doubt about it, Yakov has talent. I guess for a Chasidic guy, he's got a lot to offer," Lark's wry outlook returning. "Just be sure he's offering it only to you, OK?"

* * *

After Lark reluctantly left, Rachel tried to take her advice and review the facts. Like the Lady Justice her friend had once shown her in a book, she wanted to blindfold herself to everything but what she knew to be true: Yes, Daniel and Yakov had spent many hours together alone, supposedly studying. They were the closest of friends, had the kind of bond that was not unusual between men in their community. But, over the last few months they hadn't met or spoken at all, as far as she knew, so whatever they had between them had changed. She remembered a quick conversation she'd had with Daniel's wife, Gavrielle, in shul a few weeks ago. The hugely pregnant girl joked about how Yakov probably saw her husband more than she did these days. Rachel thought nothing of it then, but realized now that it could be an important clue. If Daniel was out a few nights a week and he wasn't with Yakov, where was he? And what did it have to do with all of this? It was too complicated to think about, especially with a glass full of vodka now working its way into her already muddled brain. Keep it simple, she thought. *I love him, I think. He loves me, I think. He's been a good friend...*

...Or has he? *Do friends lie about the most basic things to each other?* True, Lark had hidden her relationship with Jamal from her for months, but this was entirely different—her whole life was at stake. And Rachel began to see that she could only comfort herself with the idea of Yakov as a good friend for so long. He was her husband. Nights of studying and listening to music were all well and good, but they had to be lovers to make it a marriage.

His deception, if it were true, had led her to fall in love with him, to alter her life, discard her dreams, as unrealistic as they might have been. She could feel her bitterness rising from a place where she had pushed it, sealed it away all these months while trying to be a good wife, a good girl, the perfect daughter. If what Yossi said was real, Yakov had been *cheating on her from the very beginning,* maybe even just using her to make Daniel jealous, or prove to himself he could be the model, pious grandson the Rebbe needed him to be. If so, then it all had nothing to do with her!

In a horrible instant Rachel saw that her marriage to Yakov could possibly be nothing but a monumental mirage—desirable, enticing, and quenching from afar, but once you stood inside it, it was dry, disappointing and deadly. The fact that Yakov's lover might be his best friend—a man—was too surreal, too outside of her perception of what was possible to focus on. But cheating was basic. Cheating she understood and could anchor her fury on.

Yakov was just downstairs, working in the Rebbe's office. In a few minutes she could have him standing in their living room and confront him with Yossi's "evidence," reveal what she now knew, and demand he tell her the truth. And then what?

Rachel walked slowly around the apartment, dragging her hand over surfaces–the back of the sofa, the gleaming hutch, the deep, plant-lined windowsills. She traveled from one solid thing to another. In the bedroom she opened Yakov's closet and let his starchy shirts brush against her cheek, and stooped to wipe non-existent dust from a pair of his shoes.

Suddenly, Rachel felt unbearably tired and sat on the edge of Yakov's bed. She pulled back the heavy bedspread, uncovering his pillow. Dragging it onto her lap, she buried her face and inhaled. It smelled of a laundry soap version of "spring rain". There was no trace of him on it; as if while sleeping there these past few months he had managed to hover a few inches above the bed instead of inhabit it. She reached over to her "side," the other twin bed that for this week was rolled up against his, and grabbed her own pillow to find a trace of her smell there, but couldn't. Then she remembered it was the day the housekeepers changed the sheets. This morning, while she was out buying a few things for her lunch with Lark, they had quickly and quietly done their job, like so much else about her life that was orchestrated by others. The room was pristine as a hotel's and felt just as blankly accommodating. Rachel lay down, wanting nothing more at that moment than to slip into unconsciousness. She reached over to take the phone on Yakov's bedside table off the hook, but it rang before she could. The thought that it might be Yakov calling made the tears, that had not yet come, spring to her eyes.

When she heard Daniel's deep voice on the other end of the phone instead, her first instinct was to scream, *why don't you leave us alone?* Instead she heard her own measured, if slightly slurred words, her lilting tone—what Lark mocked as her "married lady" voice—answer his small talk inquiries. There was nothing in his manner to suggest that anything was amiss, and there never had been. He was always polite and jovial to her and she with him, aware they shared Yakov between them but gracious in doing so. It was only now that she knew to what extent they may really have shared him. Rachel observed with a detached awe her ability to mask her rage so easily and pretend that all was well.

Daniel lamented about not seeing Yakov for so long—he had been busy with work and other obligations. He wanted Yakov to meet him at 7:30 tonight, downstairs. He'd pick him up in a cab. Yes, she'd let him know it was very urgent, that he had to speak with Yakov this evening. Rachel promised again that she'd relay the message, her hand shaking as she replaced the receiver.

CHAPTER FORTY-EIGHT

"Where are we going?" Yakov got in the cab's backseat, where Daniel was waiting.

"I thought we'd meet on neutral ground, just drive around. Talk in private." Daniel slid the bulletproof partition between the backseat and front seat shut. He knocked hard on the thick Plexiglas for the driver to start moving.

Yakov was wary. After the debacle with Yossi, he had missed Daniel with an intensity he didn't think he could bear—everything reminded him of the loss. But after a while, it was a relief not to have to be alone with him. Aside from a few pointed looks at shul, they'd had no contact since that catalytic night. When Rachel told him earlier that Daniel had called, he was caught off guard.

"He wants you to meet him outside after dinner...7:30. He's picking you up in a cab."

"For what?"

"I didn't ask, but it sounded important."

"Well, I can't just meet him like that without warning. I planned to spend the evening with you, my love. I've been so busy lately."

Rachel gave him a look that dismissed the excuse and continued setting the table for dinner.

461

"Yakov, I would have to be blind not to notice that something's wrong—friends since childhood and suddenly you are not speaking for months? What's going on? Whatever it is, you should talk to him."

"What could be so urgent?"

"I didn't want to bother you with it, Yakov, but since you are going to see Daniel tonight I thought you should know. I talked to Gavrielle last week at shul. She thinks Daniel is still meeting you a couple of nights a week to study. What could I say? If he's not meeting you, then he's meeting someone or doing something that's not kosher. It's none of my business, but maybe your old friend is in trouble. Maybe you should help him."

"Help him?"

"Well, maybe," Rachel spoke tentatively, her eyes cast downward, "he's a little lost, you know. You could lead him back."

Yakov was surprised by the way his heart leapt at the thought. *What if I could lead him back?*

He quickly calculated all that had changed since that night Daniel told him he had someone else. He'd been able to finally consummate his marriage with Rachel, even if what they had now could hardly be called a regular sex life. Even so, it was only a matter of time before she would be pregnant. As soon as that happened, Yossi would be neutralized as a threat. Yakov imagined sharing the good news with his family and savoring the confused and crushed look that would appear on his uncle's face. It would change everything.

But one thing hadn't changed. Even as he strove to take his place among the great tzaddikim of the Torah, he missed Daniel. Now that he was giving Rachel, the Rebbe, the community, and God what they wanted of him, perhaps he could take that one thing, that one small detour from piousness for himself. Could he dare to believe he could still have Daniel, too?

"If you are going to meet him by 7:30, we should eat," Rachel interrupted his reverie.

"I didn't say I was going." But he knew he would. He had to find out what Daniel wanted with him. Besides, if he didn't go, he would seem petty to Rachel. He enjoyed being her hero over these months and seeing himself reflected in his wife's eyes as the man she thought he was.

The cab was waiting when he got to the street. Daniel waved him over from the back seat. The car eased into ongoing traffic on Eastern Parkway.

"I'm glad you decided to meet me," Daniel started after a few awkward moments.

The big man shifted his body in the seat so he could face his old friend, pulling his knee up and almost touching Yakov's leg. Yakov pressed himself closer to the door, and opened the window a few inches. He felt suddenly too warm.

"It's a nice night," Yakov said loudly into the cool air that rushed through the open window.

Daniel felt himself already losing heart. "You don't have to hang out the window and freeze your ears off," he said. "I'm not going to do anything to you. I just want to talk."

Yakov whirred the window back up, but kept staring out through the glass.

"Where are we going?" he asked again.

"Can you forget about that for a minute? We haven't said a word to each other in nearly two months. What does it matter where we are going?"

Yakov turned to him, his face stony. He'd acted out this scenario in his head a hundred times, going over and over how, if he had the chance, he'd give back the pain Daniel left him with that night. He wanted to control his anger, to speak of reconciliation, but found he couldn't.

"What do you expect? You told me you had someone new! Someone better! Hashem sent him to you. So what do you want me to say? Mazel Tov? You want me to invite you and your new boyfriend over for Shabbes? And if your wife asks where you are, you can say you're having a study session with me."

"I'm sorry." Daniel said after a moment, and meant it.

The compression in Yakov's chest began to release with Daniel's apology. *He's sorry!* It was a beginning.

"I drove you away." Yakov answered after a while.

Passing headlights suddenly illuminated their faces as they merged onto the highway. Yakov could see Daniel's eyes shine with tears as he tried to begin again. "What's done is done. I was hoping we could talk about the future."

Yakov noticed that they were heading into Queens. Was Daniel taking him back to that motel they went to that one time? He cringed, remembering how he had locked himself in the bathroom, how Daniel sat on the floor on the other side of the door, begging him to come out. *If that's where we're going*, Yakov thought with growing excitement, *I'll make it up to Daniel tonight. I'll make it up to God tomorrow.*

"Yes, I was thinking about the future, too."

"Really?"

"Yes. When you called...I started thinking. So much has changed..."

"I know. A lot has changed for me, too. I have so much to tell you."

"Me too!" Yakov allowed himself a smile.

For a moment, it was as though no time had passed since they were eager boys sitting across an old wooden study table excitedly talking over each other.

Daniel continued. "Remember the afternoon before my wedding? You came to talk me out of it. I should have listened to you, but what you were saying was too... I don't know...big, maybe."

"I was crazy. I didn't know what I was saying."

"No, you weren't crazy. It was a dream, a vision really—about us—about having a life together. A life without lies. That's what I want now. No wives, no lying, no pretending. Just you and me."

Yakov's eyes narrowed, puzzled. "But, that's impossible. It was impossible then and it's even more complicated now. All this time, you were the one who was right. I finally realize that. Your plan was the only way we could have everything. But I couldn't see it. That wasn't your fault."

"Look, if it was anyone's fault, it was mine. I tried to force you to go against everything good inside of you. If only I knew then what I know now. The life you had in mind, our escaping...it *is* possible to be happy out there. I've seen it."

The cab had taken them to a neighborhood Yakov didn't recognize. The streets were lit only by the occasional streetlamp, intermittently pulling their faces out of the shadows.

"What have you seen?" Yakov asked. But he didn't want to hear what Daniel had been learning on his "study" nights out.

"I've had so many experiences. You can't imagine how beautiful a ballet is! Or what it's like to sit around a table and listen to all different kinds of people—*good people*—and to understand who they really are. Not just, '*Oh, that's a goy, so he can't be of importance to me. Or that's a schvartze, I know what he's all about already. Or I can't talk to that person because she's a woman.*' And to have people accept me, a man, with another man as a partner and be totally OK with it. It's all happening out there." Daniel smacked his open palm against the window, as if the thick pane of glass was all that stood between Yakov and this new world. "That kind of freedom is possible. Back when you first spoke of this, I'd thought about everything I'd have to lose, but I don't think I realized all there was to gain."

"It sounds like you and your new 'partner' have been having a wonderful time—learning *so much* during these 'study sessions' you're lying to your wife about."

"Exactly what I mean, my friend," Daniel rushed ahead. "I *hate* the lies. I *hate* the compromises. It's *you* I want to share this world with.

That's why I needed to talk to you tonight, to tell you that I still want to be with you, I want to share this all with you."

Yakov could barely breathe. The monstrous jealousy he felt wrapping itself around him and squeezing through his flesh, was threatening to cut him in half. He felt utterly betrayed. Daniel did not belong to him anymore. He belonged to this other world, this world created for him by all these people he'd met. Yakov had to pull him back in. He had to think of something.

"Oh, you don't know, yet! Oh, I wish you could have been there, to see his face—to see Yossi's face—when I told him. You would have loved it. Everyone drinking l'chaims and happy, and Yossi with his sour, bitter face."

Yakov saw that Daniel was confused, but he pressed on. "Rachel. She's pregnant!" he lied. A pregnancy would show Daniel how their original plan was working out, that Yakov was functioning now as a husband, and *the plan* was back on track. All they had to do now was to resume their relationship and all would be well. "And you were right about being with her. It was fine, no big deal. I don't know what I was so afraid of. I saw finally that it was all part of the plan that Hashem has for me. I get it! I am meant to have everything, as long as I give Hashem everything he wants from me."

Daniel's heart sank. "But what about the riots, all the personal omens and punishments you were convinced Hashem was throwing down at you?"

"I misinterpreted, I was wrong...but now that I'm able to be with Rachel I feel blessed. She's happy. I'm happy because I know I can satisfy her and everyone else, too. Your call today was the last piece of the puzzle for my happiness."

"I see." Daniel wanted to cry. "Mazel Tov."

"We can make it work. We can be 'twice-blessed' now." Yakov grabbed at Daniel's sleeve.

Daniel sat upright as the cab stopped under the elevated train tracks that ran from Queens into the city.

"I'm leaving." Daniel said it flatly, taking his arm back.

Yakov looked around at the darkened street, all the shops closed except for the "XXX Adult Video" across the street, its neon sign blinking behind iron bars.

"You're getting out here? What is this place?"

"No, I'm not getting out here." Daniel's voice turned impatient. "I'm leaving, don't you understand? I'm leaving the community—everything. I'm not going to try and be 'twice-blessed' anymore. I'm going to live an honest life. I'm inviting you to do that with me."

Yakov felt the words like a slap in the face. "Oh, that sounds so noble, Daniel. What about your wife? And the baby? You can just walk away from that and feel honest?"

"I'm not proud of the mess I've made of Gabrielle's life. I can't undo it, but I can at least put a stop to any further messes. Anyway, I can't go on living this way, lying to her, being with her when I don't want to. People get divorced—it happens. I'll pay child support, alimony. Whatever I can do, I'll do, to try and make it up to her. She's very young, she comes from a good family. If I leave, she'll have a chance to find someone who'll really love her. Don't you ever feel bad about what you are doing to Rachel, Mr. Holy?"

Yakov's voice became derisive, panicked. "You won't be able to come back! Your parents will never speak to you again and your sisters and brothers will be disgraced. Who'll want to marry them? You don't care about all that? You just want your ballet and your *goyishe* friends and your new experiences?"

Daniel closed his eyes against Yakov's words.

"I can't help the way it is with them. You know, my parents *could* love me no matter what; people *could* realize my siblings have nothing to do with who I am or what I do. The community *could* open up its arms to me and embrace me as a child of God, created by Him to be the way I am. But they won't. They're so sure I am worth throwing away—defective. They'll write me off as dead, and they'll think how much better it would be for them if I really was dead, instead of just different. Whatever I do, I have to give up something. If I live the life they want for me, I die a little every day. If I do what I want to do, I'm dead to them. But at least I'll feel alive."

"So, you think it's better to live as a *faggot* than as a Chasid?" Yakov crossed his arms against his chest, challenging Daniel. He would build the wall between them back up again, each insult a brick, the mortar, his certainty that he was right.

Daniel grabbed Yakov by the lapels of his jacket. He pulled the gasping man toward him until their faces were inches apart.

"Let me tell you something, little man. I was born a Chasid *and* a faggot." Daniel spat the slur back at him and turned it into a badge of honor. "And so were you. But only one of us has the balls to face the facts and leave." Daniel released Yakov with a thrust that slammed him back against the door.

Yakov sank back, then retrieved his hat from the floor of the cab, where it had slipped when Daniel grabbed him. He took his time brushing it off and smoothing the brim, all without looking up.

"I'm asking you, Yakov. For the last time. Come with me."

Yakov did not hesitate. Whatever door had opened to allow him to hope, to feel his love for Daniel again, had slammed shut. "No. I won't. I guess I'll be the one with the balls to stay."

Yakov felt his panic recede and replaced by a sense of power that was new, but familiar. This feeling been there the first night he managed to be with Rachel. It was there more and more as he delivered his sermons to a rapt congregation in a shul packed to the rafters with people who believed what he had to say could alter their lives, elevate their souls.

Daniel pointed to something outside the cab. Then he tapped on the window with the tip of his finger.

"Look."

A long black limousine had pulled up in front of the XXX Adult Video shop, giving a short blast from its horn. The door to the shop opened and three slim men—boys, really—came out and crowded around the dark back window of the car. The window slid down and the boys stood back a foot or so from the car, preening, as though on display.

"What am I supposed to be looking at?" Yakov asked impatiently.

Two of the boys stepped away from the car and walked back toward the shop. The limo's back passenger door opened. In the dim halo of the cabin light, just before the wiry, dark boy climb in and shut the door, Daniel and Yakov could see the unmistakable silhouette of the wide black hat, the long beard, the small triangle of white shirt under the familiar black coat.

"Your future, my friend. We're looking at your future."

Yakov was by turns enraged and frightened by the bitter prediction. He shook his head to empty it of the image, and he wondered: *How does a Chasid find his way onto this dark street, into this pitiful scenario?* But he had only to look into in his own obsession with Daniel to understand how a man could try to justify his actions, to negotiate with God, to pretend that he could strike a deal that satisfies all parties. Daniel had been convinced that he could love Gavrielle, that he could have a *haimish*, Chasidic life and put his "other" desires to rest. Yet, not even two months of married life had gone by before he gave in to them.

What makes me think I can do it? Yakov posed the question both to himself and his God. Instantly, the answer came to him in the form of faces—one by one, across his consciousness—Rachel, her eyes bright with love for him; his grandfather, who'd given him so much, and his father, who, through the filter of his faith and optimism, found only the best in his son.

Yakov understood for the first time that there would be no negotiating for him. There was only one way he could take. Like Daniel, he would choose the path he needed most. There would be a price and he would pay for it. He had to do it for himself and for those faces. The revelation didn't make him any less angry with Daniel, but perhaps that would come in time.

"No, Daniel, that's not my future. Maybe it's your future if you stay— why you have to go. You can't resist this other world, filled with all your precious experiences. I can. I will."

"Oh, really? Five minutes ago I was the missing piece to your happiness." Daniel opened the window halfway, and gulped at the cool, damp air as if he were suffocating.

Yakov pulled at his sleeves and straightened out his jacket. "I was wrong."

Daniel reached up and knocked on the cab's partition signaling to the driver that it was time to leave. They drove back to the Rebbe's residence in silence. The small physical space between them, a matter of inches, had expanded into an emotional universe.

"Good luck, my friend." The two men said simultaneously as Yakov opened the door to step out. In some other time and place this coincidence of speech would have been proof of their closeness, now it only mocked it.

Yakov climbed the stairs to the apartment. It was over. He'd made a choice and it wasn't Daniel. He was surprised by how relieved he was. He would no longer be trying to straddle two worlds. He would surrender to the life that was always planned for him, not because it was the right thing to do, but because he could see, finally, that it was right for him. He was going to make it enough.

*   *   *

When she heard footsteps on the stairs, Rachel checked the clock for the hundredth time since Yakov left to meet Daniel. He'd been gone less than two hours. She'd made the decision to marry Yakov in an instant, the night of Daniel's wedding, but the entire afternoon of grappling with the information Yossi had dumped on her that morning, had not yielded a clear decision about whether she should stay married. The only thing she could be certain of now was that she would have to hear the truth from Yakov first. His truth. Then she would know. She began to murmur a prayer for strength, and for certainty, then stopped mid-sentence, her feelings of betrayal suddenly extending out beyond Yakov to God Himself.

She'd made a bargain with Hashem—given up all her secular longings to do what everyone, from her parents to the Rebbe, assured her would certainly please Him, and certainly secure for her a lifetime of blessings and happiness. Instead, her marriage began with an explosive public riot and sputtered along with private heartaches and humiliations. There could be no point in asking God to intervene now, she reasoned, skipping the prayer and steeling herself for Yakov's entrance without God's help.

"How did it go?" She took his coat and hung it up for him, then before he could answer she offered, "I was just making some tea, I get you some too and we can talk."

Rachel brought a tray with two steaming mugs and a plate of cookies to the table, then sat across from her husband. She pulled her robe tightly around her, retying the belt. She felt chilled even as the radiators in the apartments hissed and clanged with a new burst of heat.

"Yesterday I had a craving for *Mandelbrot.* I found a recipe, but I think I messed them up. They're supposed to be crunchy, but these I think, I could use as door stoppers." *If I talk about cookies and tea, if I can hold on to this moment of normalcy, everything will be fine.*

"Perfect for dunking." Yakov took one of the almond-studded biscuits and dipped it into his steaming cup. His hand, she saw, was trembling.

"So? How was Daniel?" Rachel persisted, her chest tight. She imagined Lark whispering in her ear: *Enough with the small talk, Rocky, get to the point!*

"He was, well..."

"You don't have to tell me if it's private."

"No, I can tell you. It's just..." The words died on his tongue.

"He's in trouble, isn't he?"

"Yes, I'm afraid he is."

"Is he...does he have someone else? You know, the study sessions...the lies to Gavrielle?" Rachel tried to keep her tone neutral.

"Yes. He met this person," his jaw tightened, "no one we know—someone from outside the community—not religious. He says he's going to leave Crown Heights—leave Gavrielle, everything."

Rachel was stunned by this revelation. *And she felt betrayed?* Poor Gavrielle. If what Yossi said about Daniel and Yakov were true, then Rachel understood for the first time that this was not just a personal catastrophe—its devastation was exponential. It extended beyond her and Gavrielle. The damage would affect all of their families and ultimately the entire community.

"What did you say to him? Doesn't he care about anyone? About losing everything? About losing...you?

"He cares, I think. But he cares more about what's out there for him. I couldn't talk him out of it. Believe me, I tried."

I bet you did, she thought, but said, "He should go see the Rebbe," knowing as she said it that the situation was beyond that. Way beyond that.

Yakov shook his head. "No, he's made up his mind."

"I feel so bad for Gavrielle—to think your husband is one person, and then to find out he's a complete stranger." Rachel trained her eyes on her husband but he looked down into his cup. *When is he going to realize I'm talking about us?*

"How do you feel about it, Yakov? How do you feel about Daniel leaving *you?*"

This head snapped to attention and the blood drained from his face. Rachel saw the panic and question in his eyes. *Does she know?*

He reached a tremulous hand for another biscuit, but dropped it back on the plate. He forced himself to meet her gaze.

"How do I feel? I feel sorry for him. He'll lose everything that I know is important. But I'm relieved too."

"Relieved? In what way?"

Rachel waited for her own relief wash over her as Yakov's choice became clear. He was choosing her.

"Well, the lies will stop." He proceeded carefully, walking a fine line between the truth and what he was still willing to hide from her. "I've known Daniel was betraying Gavrielle for some time now. I won't have to go on living with the lies."

Rachel reached across the table and patted his hand. "Won't it be difficult for you to lose such a close friend?"

He caught her hand and brought it to his lips and said, "That's why I'm so lucky to have you. You're the only friend I need now. My best friend."

It sounded as if he meant it. It was the answer she thought she had been waiting for, but instead she felt only impatience. And anger. It was clear he wasn't going to tell her anything, that he was willing to extend the masquerade indefinitely.

"Well, then…" Rachel proceeded with what she knew she had to do. "You need to tell me what I should do with these." This was the stroke on the canvas. After this she would see the whole picture and decide if what she was looking at was a marriage.

She reached under the table where she'd stowed the portfolio and lifted it to the table.

"Where did you get that?" Yakov jumped out of his chair. She didn't answer him. She took her time and unzipped it slowly and, opened it up on the table in front of him. She began flipping through the sketches that Yakov had drawn—his "book of Daniel."

"Your uncle Yossi dropped these off this morning. He made a point of showing them to me. He wanted me to understand just exactly how close you and Daniel were."

Yakov sunk back into his chair. He let his head drop to the table and pulled his arms over his head. The quiet moan he let out told her more than anything he could say. Incredibily, was not denying it. The blow to the belly she felt now made her realize that a part of her had been waiting for his complete rejection of Yossi's story, a vehement and appalled protest that would assure her he was man she hoped she'd married. When she caught her breath, something had irrevocably changed. Her instinct was to run to him and protect him from what he must be feeling—fear, shame, humiliation—was easy to resist. She waited for him to speak. But he didn't. The longer he stayed silent, the angrier she became. Rachel felt like hurting him, paying him back for all the moments of her own suffering over the course of their short marriage.

"And Yossi was kind enough—yes, I think it was an act of kindness now—to tell me what he saw when he dropped in on your last 'study session' with Daniel. Right here in our home, in our bedroom!"

Finally, Yakov raised his head slowly to look at his wife. "Why did you insist I see Daniel tonight, if you knew about this? Why didn't you tell me before I went?"

"I don't know! I listened to what Yossi had to say, but I still needed to know if it was true. Maybe I thought I if you saw Daniel one more time, I would see something in your face when you came back...I'd just know from looking at you that everything Yossi said was a lie, and we could just go on living our lives. I knew there was a possibility you'd come back and tell me that you love Daniel in the way Yossi said, had always loved him, and you were going to leave everything behind to be with him. Either way...I had to know..."

Rachel zipped up the portfolio and laid it back on the table. She watched him search for words, and wished she could prompt him with just what she needed to hear, the exact speech that would make everything right again, erase the events of the day and return her to her fairy tale existence.

"You didn't think of one possibility," he offered.

He stood up and began walking back and forth as he spoke, his image reflected in the darkened windows behind him. She watched the two Yakovs as they paced.

"The other option is that I tell you the truth about everything—because I know you deserve that—but that I choose you, choose our marriage, our beautiful life together, our bright future instead. Rachel, whatever I had with Daniel, you must forgive me and believe that I understand now what an *aveira*, what a horrible sin and mistake that was. It's a terrible sickness, it *was* a sickness, but I'm well now. I'm well now. And you have so much wisdom, for such a young girl, such wisdom to know that for me to see Daniel again tonight *was* important! Because I did see, and I do know once and for all that that part of my life is over forever. Daniel will be gone—that part is true too. He's leaving for someone else, but it's a man, not a woman. He asked me to go with him, to live a so-called "honest" life with him but I refused. I rejected him and everything that goes along with it because I belong here with you, and with the Rebbe, living the life that Hashem wants me to live. Rachel, I understand now that this has all just been a test! For both of us. Don't you see that I am destined to be a great, holy man like my grandfather, and you are destined to be a great, holy man's wife?"

Rachel slid the portfolio across the table toward him.

"I see. And what do you want me to do with these?"

"I don't care, you can throw them away, or burn them. Or better yet, we will shred them into a thousand pieces and take the ferry out into the harbor and toss them over the side. It will be our own private *tashlich* ceremony, we will cast it like bread crumbs on the water and have a fresh start."

Yakov's pacing had picked up speed, his slumping frame straightening as he painted this picture of their future together, as vivid as any of his drawings.

He kept going. "We'll build our life together and wipe these pictures from our minds. We'll be even happier because we'll know everything about each other with nothing hidden. And we will know that we've already passed the most difficult test of our marriage. It will make us strong. And it will make us love each other more deeply knowing that we have this strength."

"Strength." Rachel repeated without conviction.

She folded her hands in front of her on the table, clamping them together tightly as if they might fly up and slap him if she didn't. She spoke staring at her white knuckles.

"But you forgot one detail, Yakov. You didn't come in here intending to tell me the truth. You were going to be perfectly happy telling me another lie—completely fine with giving me only part of the story about Daniel, letting me believe he was simply leaving his wife for some woman he met. If Yossi had never shown me the pictures, if I hadn't known about it all, you would have continued this lie forever."

Yakov turned his arms and face upward as if addressing the heavens as much as answering her accusations.

"Well, what good does all this honesty, all this knowing the truth do? It poisons everything. Daniel's honesty will ruin a dozen lives. Yossi's honesty—this is what Yossi wanted! He wanted to destroy us, to destroy you. Do you blame me for trying to protect you from that?" He sat down and faced her, but she found she couldn't look at him or be near him and jumped up from her chair. It was her turn to pace.

"You know Yakov, the Rebbe sat me down before the wedding and gave me this whole sermon about how I was going to have to make sacrifices being with you, that I was going to have to be strong and you were this 'complicated, special man'. And like Rachel in the Torah, I would have to share my husband. He said I might have to wait for my happiness. He made it sound like the more I gave up, the more I would have...the more holy I would be. I had no idea what he meant at the time. But now I do."

"My grandfather said that?"

"Yeah, he knew what was going on. You knew what was going on... Daniel... everyone knew that I was being used, except me. I'm supposed to be this sacrificial lamb, give up my life so you and the Rebbe can have what you need. But you know what Yakov? I'm no holy person. *And neither are you.* I don't know how much strength I have, but if I have any I don't know if I want to use it to keep this going."

"I understand how I've disappointed you, Rachel. Believe me, I know it will take time for you to totally forgive..."

"And how long will it take for you to totally love me like a real husband? How long, Yakov, before you really, really want to touch me, can be with me without thinking about Daniel?" She pulled the crumpled handkerchief out of her robe pocket, the one she'd found in Yakov's bedside table after her nap. It was embroidered with Daniel's initials. She tossed it on the table.

He ignored it and came toward her.

"I already feel that way, Rachel, please, you must..."

"Stop!" Rachel found herself backing away from him, her arms extended, her palms pushing at the air between them.

The clarity and peace that Rachel had hoped would come from this evening eluded her. Hot anger and a crushing headache overwhelmed her instead.

"I will figure out what I 'must' do, but I can't right now. I'm tired. I feel sick. I don't want to talk to you anymore."

Yakov gathered their cups from the table.

"You're right. Maybe we should clear our heads and talk about it tomorrow when we are not so emotional. I'll clean up. You get some rest. I'll be in soon."

"No. I think it would be best if you spent the night downstairs in your old room."

"But what will I tell the Rebbe?"

"You'll think of something."

He brought the dishes into the kitchen and heard Rachel gently close the bedroom door. After putting them in the dishwasher, he went around the apartment turning off the lights, all the while, mouthing a furtive prayer to Hashem to bless him with a long and happy marriage.

CHAPTER FORTY-NINE

Her mother had gone ahead to meet the truck, emblazoned with *"Nice Jewish Boy Moving and Storage"* at their new apartment in the city. David had done some legwork and found them a prewar, two-bedroom with high ceilings on West End and 108th. Sarah and Lark would now be near Columbia and David, not to mention Sarah's new job at Columbia-Presbyterian. The apartment had big rooms, big windows, and wide molding, thick with layers of paint. Her new bedroom provided a sliver of a view of the Hudson, and Lark would be able to watch the sun paint the water with streaks of gold and fiery red each evening. It wasn't quite her fantasy of being able to hear the crashing of waves from her window as she drifted off to sleep, but it was a lot closer to it than the view of the asphalt playground she was leaving.

She did one last walk-through of the empty Brooklyn apartment, making sure the cupboards were empty and clean. The walls were stripped of all their photos and personal effects, but that wasn't why she felt oddly disconnected, as though the time spent inside these walls was an unfortunate detour from her real life. Even the memories she clung to of her father had nothing to do with this place. Her boot heels echoed against the bare wood floor. The radiators hissed and banged as the heat rose through the cold pipes. She hoped the next occupants would find more warmth here, more happiness than her family had.

It was time to go.

She put on her heavy coat and wrapped her scarf over and around her head. Winter was in full force. They'd had a big snowstorm the week before, delivering two feet and a white Christmas, which most residents of Crown Height felt less than sentimental about. More snow was forecast for that night, New Year's Eve. She had to make one more stop in the Heights, to say goodbye to Rachel. Then she'd hop the subway into the city where she, her mother, and David would usher in the New Year, sitting amongst their boxes eating Chinese.

Just before she dropped the keys off with the building super, Lark remembered to check the mailbox one last time. Her mother had filled out a change of address form the day before, but told her to check, just in case the order took a day or two to go into effect. Pulling out a tubular wad of mostly junk mail, she locked up the little cubby and positioned herself over the trashcan near the front door to thin out the pile. Grocery store circular: trash. Nursing uniform catalog: keep. Bill. Bill. Bank statement. All keep. Credit card offer, some local fundraiser thing—trash. A recruitment mailer from the Marines: trash. As she flipped this last one into the can, she saw a familiar scrawl on the back-side. She snatched it back. It wasn't junk mail, but a postcard. The front of the card showed the mud-caked face of a soldier with the bold caption above his eyes, "IF YOU ARE GOING THROUGH HELL, KEEP GOING." Then in smaller letters below the soldier's chin. "The Few. The Proud. The Marines."

The note was for her. *"Bird, you're not the only one who gets to fly away. I'm in N.C. doing my basic training. Have a sweet life. You deserve it. Jamal."*

"Wow." Lark said out loud.

She read the card again. The Rain Man in the Marines! She tried to picture it and found to her surprise that she could. She thought about the night she went to his apartment and saw his brother and mother, and who he was for them. Remembering his father's medals and the posters and the jacket hanging from the ceiling, Lark finally understood. Jamal had always had a dream he'd wanted to live up to, but, like her, was held back by people who needed him to be someone else. It was a great piece of news and she quietly thanked him for realizing that she needed to hear from him and needed to be forgiven for walking away the way she had. She tucked the card into her purse, promising herself she'd write back.

Lark started automatically walking toward Eastern Parkway and the Rebbe's residence with her head tucked down against the wind. Halfway there she remembered she was supposed to meet Rachel at her parents' house and changed direction.

When Lark walked up the steps to the front door of the imposing house, with its bay windows that looked like overfed jowls, she remembered the last time she'd been there. Rachel had modeled her wedding gown for her. Twirling around the upstairs landing, holding the gown close to her body, she'd had all the optimism of a Cinderella preparing for the ball. Today, when Rachel answered the door dressed in an old skirt and blouse that Lark recognized from school, her shorn, but growing-in hair uncovered, her eyes sunken from a week of crying and arguing, it looked like the trip to the castle had stripped her friend of more than just a glass slipper.

"Hey, you should have told me your parents were hiding the old Rock here. I'd have come over much sooner."

"Very funny. I give you credit though. Not many people around here are seeing the bright side of what's going on."

"Are you kidding? A daughter gets married to the Rebbe's grandson, then leaves him because he's secretly gay and they can't have a good laugh over it? What's wrong with these people?"

Rachel directed her to the kitchen. It was one room in which they were least likely to be interrupted by her mother.

Rachel sat down at the kitchen table smiling up at her old friend but her eyes were droopy with emotion.

"Sorry Rock. I'm an idiot for cracking jokes. This is like your worst nightmare..."

"Yeah, I guess. But it also feels like I woke up, too, you know? Like this whole time, since the day I met Yakov, has been a dream and now I've opened my eyes and it's over."

"Yeah, I get it."

"Well, you seem to be the only person in the universe who thinks I made the right decision. Though my parents are coming around now since they met with the Rebbe."

"Whoa. You finally met with him? And he convinced your parents you did the right thing?"

"Well, I couldn't face him at first. I was afraid he'd talk me out of leaving. So the morning after I confronted Yakov, I just left. I came home and told my parents and let them deal with it. I told them I didn't want to talk to anyone for a few days, except you, of course. Eventually, the Rebbe insisted on seeing me, but at least I had time to think it all through...a million times."

"Was Yakov in on this meeting?"

"They sent Yakov to Israel. Two days after I left. To 'study', and 'purge himself of his weaknesses'"

"Oy. For how long?

"A few months...a year...whatever it takes, for everyone to forget, I guess."

"But what now?"

"Well, of course, the Rebbe had been thinking about it too. He gave me options. He wanted to know if I was willing to either join Yakov in Israel, or wait until he came back, but continue living at the residence, pretending everything was fine."

"What? I thought you said he was on your side?"

"He also said that he understood if I wasn't willing to do that. He said something about my fundamental rights as a bride have been violated."

"Wow. What are your parents telling you to do? Does anyone else know?

"No, it's not like the Rebbe's office is putting out a newsletter on this, but it won't be long before everyone realizes that I'm living here again, that Yakov is gone and something is wrong. My parents couldn't believe me at first. But I told them everything—by the way, do you know how embarrassing it is to discuss your sex life, or lack of it, with your parents? And I showed them the sketches, which for some reason I had the good sense to take with me."

"Oh that was good, Rock. I could just see them getting rid of those in hurry and leaving you with no real proof of anything."

"Yeah, well, I knew that evidence was going to come in handy. In fact, when I left, I took nothing but that portfolio. I'm glad I did, because that's what finally got my parents to come half way around. And the meeting with the Rebbe yesterday took them the rest of way. He was talking about 'Yakov's demons' and confirmed what I told them. I guess Yakov finally told the truth about it to his grandfather, because he knew everything too. This morning, my father practically started crying at breakfast. He said he wanted to strangle Yakov and that it was a good thing he was in Israel and not down the block, because his skinny neck would be broken! Then my mother started crying about how bad she felt that I didn't come to her during the first few months that Yakov wasn't...you know..."

"Yeah, well I know how she feels." Lark gave Rachel a mock punch in the arm. "No more monumental secrets, OK?"

"OK." Rachel punched her back.

"So...now what? Are you going to take the Rebbe up on his offer? Go live in the tower and throw down your hair when Yakov gets back all 'healed?'"

"Like I said, the alarm went off and I'm wide awake. Did you ever try to get back to sleep and keep a dream going? It doesn't work. I may take a couple of weeks and go visit my sisters. Get away from Crown Heights for a while and then decide what I want to do after that."

"Is that a good idea? Hanging out with them, all cozy and secure in their arranged marriages? Won't it make you feel bad?"

"I don't know. Maybe it will be good for me to see what a normal marriage looks like. See if my sisters are happy. See if that's what I want...someday."

"Well, I don't know if I can agree that what your sisters have is 'normal,' but don't get me started. Don't forget about the Charlie's Angel's option too. You, me, my mom. Superwomen on the loose in N-Y-C! You know you are always welcome in my world, which no one is claiming is normal. Which reminds me, I brought you something."

Lark fished around in her bag and brought up a thick brochure, a half bottle of champagne and a small gift, wrapped in tissue paper.

"This," handing her the booklet, "is a course catalog for Stern College that I picked up for you. Hey, it's a Jewish school in the city and it's all girls, so maybe your parents would go for it. If you're going to visit your sisters and all that, fine, but when you get back and start making decisions about your life, I hope you'll think about it. And this is something else to remind you." Lark pushed the little wrapped package toward Rachel and she tore it open. It was a tiny bronze Lady Justice, holding two scales in balance at her sides.

"Just to remind you to keep following your own truth, my friend. Promise?"

"I promise." Rachel caught a tear travelling down her cheek, but it was her first in days that wasn't prompted by sadness or anger.

"Now let's celebrate." Lark began opening the little split of champagne.

"There's only enough here for two glasses, but I thought that we needed to have a toast. It's New Year's Eve and there's all these new beginnings...my classes are starting up at Hunter in a couple of weeks, the new apartment in the city, my mom's new job. And your life, well, it's..."

"To be continued..." Rachel finished as she jumped up to get two flutes from the dining room.

Lark popped the cork and quickly poured the foaming wine.

"Look at us, Rock, we're having a glass of wine, and we don't have to do it hiding in the girls' bathroom." Lark lifted her glass.

Rachel laughed at the memory. It seemed lifetimes ago.

"I think we should say a *bracha*, don't you?" Rachel said with mock innocence. She raised her glass toward Lark, who smiled at what she already knew was coming.

Rachel announced, "I am so incredibly grateful for wine...what a cool world!"

"AMEN!" They shouted, and drank deeply.

ACKNOWLEGEMENTS

This book would never have been started were it not for the weekly writing group that Hope Harris ran in her living room and was gracious enough to allow me to join back in 2001, when I was living down a winding wooded road from her in East Hampton, NY. I will be eternally grateful to this core group, talented writers in their own right, for their unwavering support, encouragement, constructive feedback and friendship. From the first pages I read aloud in that safe space, I was told "this is a novel" and their continued delight in the story and belief in me as a writer kept me going. They are Bobbi Cohen, who gave me a place to stay in on the East End so I could continue to meet with the group even after I moved 100 miles away, Laurraine Freethy, Bill Cowley and Leah Sklar.

I was lucky to have found Madeleine Beckman, a talented poet, writer and teacher (Stern College For Women, Yeshiva University, Writer in Residence NYU, Advisory Board NYU Gallatin Review. (www.writedowntown.com) at a time when I had reached a wall and my writing slammed to a halt. With her expert guidance, patience and encouragement I was able to finish the book, while learning so much about the craft.

When I was in 7th grade I wrote my first novel. It was 150 handwritten pages and based on my mother's experiences as a young girl in

Nazi Germany, her internment in two concentration camps, her escape and subsequent life in hiding until WWII ended, and her good-natured triumph over these dire circumstances. The title of the book was *Where Did They Go?* and it was my mother's suggestion. This, she explained, was the question that repeated itself over and over in her head after the war, when she faced the reality of losing so many, including her mother and beloved brother. *Where were they? How could it be that they were no longer there to share life with her?* They had disappeared from the physical plane, but never left her thoughts or her heart. I don't know if I "got it" back in seventh grade, but today, eleven years after my mother's passing, I too am asking that question, and wishing she were here to *kvell* in the completion and publication of this book. Mom, you taught me, by example to be enthralled with books, and you always believed in me as a writer. I miss you every day of my life. Wherever you are, Mom, I hope you are reading.

Rachel Reuben is a writer and classically-trained chef and the founder of FOOD FIX KITCHEN. (www.foodfixkitchen.com). *The Faithful* is Reuben's first novel. She lives in New York City.

Made in the USA
Middletown, DE
30 September 2017